Be very afraid of what
waits in the dark...

THE SEVENTH VICTIM

"Burton's crisp storytelling, solid pacing and well-developed plot will draw you in and the strong suspense will keep you hooked and make this story hard to put down."
—*RT Book Reviews*

"A nail-biter that you will not want to miss. Terrifying . . . it keeps you on the edge of your chair."
—*The Free Lance-Star* (Fredericksburg, Virginia)

BEFORE SHE DIES

"Will have readers sleeping with the lights on."
—*Publishers Weekly* (starred review)

MERCILESS

"Convincing detective lingo and an appropriately shivery murder venue go a long way."
—*Publishers Weekly*

"Burton just keeps getting better!"
—*RT Book Reviews*

"Terrifying . . . this chilling thriller is an engrossing story."
—*Library Journal*

"Mary Burton's latest romantic suspense has it all—terrific plot, complex and engaging protagonists, a twisted villain, and enough crime scene detail to satisfy the most savvy suspense reader."
—Erica Spindler, *New York Times* bestselling author

SENSELESS

"Stieg Larsson fans will find a lot to like in Burton's taut, well-paced novel of romantic suspense."
—*Publishers Weekly*

"This is a page turner of a story, one that will keep you up all night, with every twist in the plot and with all of the doors locked."
—*The Parkersburg News & Sentinel*

"With hard-edged, imperfect but memorable characters, a complex plot and no-nonsense dialog, this excellent novel will appeal to fans of Lisa Gardner and Lisa Jackson."
—*Library Journal*

"Absolutely chilling! Don't miss this well-crafted, spine-tingling read."
—Brenda Novak, *New York Times* bestselling author

"A terrifying novel of suspense."
—*Mysterious Reviews*

"This is a story to read with the lights on."
—*BookPage*

DYING SCREAM

"Burton's taut, fast-paced thriller will have you guessing until the last blood-soaked page. Keep the lights on for this one."
—*RT Book Reviews*

"A twisted tale . . . I couldn't put it down!"
—Lisa Jackson, *New York Times* bestselling author

DEAD RINGER

"Dangerous secrets, deadly truths, and a diabolical killer combine to make Mary Burton's *Dead Ringer* a chilling thriller."
—Beverly Barton, *New York Times* bestselling author

"With a gift for artful obfuscation, Burton juggles a budding romance and two very plausible might-be perpetrators right up to the tense conclusion."
—*Publishers Weekly*

I'M WATCHING YOU

"Taut . . . compelling . . . Mary Burton delivers a page-turner."
—Carla Neggers, *New York Times* bestselling author

"Creepy and terrifying, it will give you chills."
—*Romantic Times*

Books by Mary Burton

I'M WATCHING YOU

DEAD RINGER

DYING SCREAM

SENSELESS

MERCILESS

BEFORE SHE DIES

THE SEVENTH VICTIM

NO ESCAPE

YOU'RE NOT SAFE

COVER YOUR EYES

BE AFRAID

Published by Kensington Publishing Corporation

BE AFRAID

MARY BURTON

ZEBRA BOOKS
KENSINGTON PUBLISHING CORP.
http://www.kensingtonbooks.com

Prologue

Monday, August 14, 4:30 A.M.
Nashville, Tennessee

Reason and Madness, like Jekyll and Hyde, were two sides of the same coin. One worshipped peace, the other devastation. One told the truth. The other, rule breaker and thief, always lied. Once again, a war raged between the two.

The cell phone on the granite kitchen counter buzzed with an incoming call. A glance at the display revealed Sister was calling again. This was her sixth call in the last two hours. Sister could see past the smiles and the assurances. She sensed when meds had been skipped and Madness regained control.

Ignoring the call, Madness reached for a half-full tumbler of whiskey and held it up, letting moonlight illuminate the honey-brown liquid depths. A quick toss of the glass, and the whiskey slid down a parched throat, soothing tense muscles and pushing aside all thoughts of Sister's call. It wouldn't do for Sister to know about tonight's endeavor. Tomorrow Sister would get a visit. There'd be lots of wide smiles and a box of her favorite chocolates gift-wrapped in a bright blue bow. Blue was her favorite color. They'd play the question-and-answer game for a time. She'd be satisfied and then shift talk to regrets and the what-should-have-beens.

Madness washed the glass in the sink, careful to dry it with a paper towel before replacing it in the cabinet. A few wipes of the cabinet knobs, the faucet, the whiskey bottle, and the surrounding area erased all fingerprints. Some might consider the action overkill but attention to detail was key to a successful performance. Madness had learned well from Reason.

Down the dimly lit hallway carpeted in neutral beige, Madness admired the new coat of antique white paint. Fresh paint was a wonder. One swipe of the roller eradicated dirt, grime, and shadows of framed memories that no longer mattered.

A few more steps toward the master bedroom and the scent of paint gave way to the aroma of diesel fuel. This room—center stage for tonight's performance—was painted a pale yellow with white trim. A tasteful landscape of the Smokey Mountains hung on the wall by the door, a gilded mirror topped an oak dresser displaying strategically placed crystal perfume bottles, a new hairbrush and a tiny camera displaying a bright red RECORD light.

In the center of the room was a four-poster bed. On the bed lay a woman, the actress in this play. Her near-naked body nested in twisted sheets damp with sweat and flecks of blood. Ropes lashed hands, manicured nails painted a soft pink, to the headboard and feet to the baseboard. A river of mascara-stained tears trailed down pale cheeks and a duct-tape-covered mouth.

Carved in the headboard above her was the word FAITHLESS. Madness thought it a fitting tribute to another woman, Sara, who'd plagued them during their youth.

As Madness approached the bed, green bloodshot eyes alert with panic darted from the man standing in the shadows back to Madness, the night's true master. Her wide, pleading gaze reflected panic and desperation. Good. She understood who was in charge.

The man in the shadows, Jonas Tuttle, stepped forward, his large, calloused hands wrapped tightly around the grip of a .45-caliber handgun. Tall and broad-shouldered, he stood over six feet. A man's man, some might say. But fear all but vibrated off every inch of his muscled body. "We've been waiting for you. I need you to tell me what to do next."

The warmth of the whiskey kept anxiety at bay. "Patience, Jonas. Patience."

Jonas, the bloodthirsty and angry hero tonight, had nurtured a murder fantasy since he was a young boy. Careful observation of Jonas over the last six months told a lot about the man. His likes. Dislikes. Fears. Wants. Needs. Stalking the stalker.

Jonas's murder obsession had chased him most of his life, his fantasies playing over and over like a worn record. As much as he craved killing, he also feared the cops and prison. And so, he'd bottled up his wants and needs for years. Madness had found this want-to-be killer ripe for guidance in a bar six months ago drowning frustrations away with whiskey.

"I can show you how to kill," Madness had whispered.

Jonas's gaze had danced first with hesitation, then interest, and finally excitement.

Madness had taught Jonas how to stalk, to watch and to plan. Madness worked with Jonas for months, priming him for this kill.

Now at the brink of the grand finale, Jonas oozed desperation and need. Nervous energy buzzed around him as if live wires zapped his nerve endings. This was the moment he'd dreamed about a long, long time.

One nod and he would fire.

Instead of giving permission, Madness shifted attention to the woman. Pretty and slim enough, the woman, Diane Smith, until hours ago had been dressed well and had walked with confidence. She, no doubt, had caught the eye of many men. She liked rich, buttery chardonnays paired with a creamy Brie or goat cheese. She liked good conversation and old movies. Reason might have befriended her if not for Madness.

In this macabre scene, Madness, not Reason, was the ultimate authority. Madness chose the staging, the casting, and, of course, the final execution. Moments like this thrilled because it gave Madness the one thing he could never sustain: control.

"Can I do it now?" Jonas's timid voice had a familiar, annoying ring.

"Savor the moment," Madness rasped.

Jonas's hunger was razor sharp and, of course, the woman's senses had never been so acute. Being this close to death made everyone in the room feel alive.

Diane's watery gaze was a mixture of terror and confusion. *How could this have happened to me? I'm careful. I play by the rules.*

Madness saw the question flash. A soft chuckle rumbled. "But you didn't play by all the rules, did you, Diane? In fact, you like to break them every so often. Not too much. But once in a while, you enjoy the walk on the wild side."

Diane shook her head as tears streamed down her cheeks.

Gently, Madness approached the bed and sat. The mattress sagged. Diane's black hair was plastered to her forehead by sweat. "Didn't you ever hear that cocaine is a bad habit? If not for that little quirk in your personality, you'd have been fine." Jonas had lured her out of her car with the promise of coke. "You'd be on the other side of that door right now sitting in your living room watching that cooking show you enjoy so much. But you couldn't control it and now you must pay your toll."

She closed her eyes and shook her head, a soft moaning rumbling in her throat.

"Maybe it's not a crippling compulsion, but it's there nonetheless." Madness continued to stroke her hair, so soft and dark. "You're no different from me. Once in a while, I get the cravings. I can ignore them for a time. But the more I deny them, the more they grow until one day I just must have one little bite." A snap of even white teeth close to her ear made her flinch. "You're my bite."

She closed her eyes and wept.

Madness drew in a deep breath, and the scent of her fear smelled sweet. Deliciously intoxicating.

"Now?" Jonas asked.

The world and the people in it were in such a rush. "In a moment."

"I can't wait! Why do I have to wait?" He pressed the handle of the gun to his head as if trying to soothe the pounding behind his eyes. *Bang. Bang. Bang.* The tantalizing promise of release was painful.

"Anticipation is the sweetest part of dessert." Madness patted Diane on the arm, rose, and moved to the back corner of the room by the dresser.

Madness double-checked the camera's angle and then hefted a red can of diesel fuel and jerked off the cap. A tip of the canister splashed the fuel on the gray carpet, over the blue bedspread and up sheer white curtains that blocked the light of the full moon.

Jonas shifted from foot to foot. "Haven't you spread enough of that stuff?"

"Never can be too careful." Diesel burned longer but didn't have the initial combustive power of gasoline, which could spread too fast or burn out.

The woman twisted at her bindings. She rolled her head from side to side as if willing this nightmare to end.

They were all suffering with anticipation.

Backing up to the room's threshold, Madness stood silent, savoring the scene one last time. Finally, Madness retrieved a box of matches from the deep pockets of a blue Windbreaker and dug out a single match and struck it. The flame danced and swayed as if begging to be sent out on-stage.

Diane closed her eyes, as tears streamed down her cheek.

A breeze caught the flame and blew it out.

"What're you waiting for?" Jonas asked.

One. Two. Three. Savor. Savor. Savor.

"Okay, Jonas."

"I can shoot now?" Excitement and fear rumbled under the words.

"Yes."

Diane's eyes shot open and a muffled scream rumbled in her throat as Jonas raised the gun. She jerked at her bindings until her wrists bled.

Jonas pulled on the trigger and, as the gun fired, he closed his eyes on reflex. The bullet hit the woman directly between the eyes. Her body jerked as blood splattered and her eyes rolled back in her head. In one second she was gone, dead.

Jonas opened his eyes and looked at his gun in shock, as if the entire moment had been lived by another. He pressed the gun to his chest, cradling it close. "I killed her! I finally did it."

Madness pocketed the camera. "Yes, you did. You did it just right."

Jonas studied her. "She's so still."

"Yes."

Seconds passed as Jonas stared at the carnage. Slowly the brightness in his gaze dimmed. The near-bursting bubble of anticipation had popped with one sharp prick of a bullet.

"You're feeling let down," Madness soothed.

Jonas looked at the gun and the woman. "How did you know?"

"Because I feel it too. All the planning, thinking, and dreaming. All gone in an instant."

"Yes."

"And just like that, it's over." The snap of two fingers echoed in the room.

Jonas flinched. "I thought it would last longer."

"It never does. It's always over in a blink."

Jonas shook his head. "I thought there'd be more."

"I told you, anticipation trumps the moment." Breathe in. Breathe out. "That's why I made us wait."

"I can't believe it's over."

A clap of hands made Jonas start and look up. "Time to go. Time to destroy the evidence."

Jonas sat on the bed and took the woman's cooling, still hand in his. "I won't see her again."

"No."

"Can't we just stay a little longer? I don't want to leave her."

Madness moved toward Jonas and gently pulled the gun from his hands. "We have to go. We need to destroy this evidence and leave."

Tears welled in Jonas's eyes. "I don't want it to be over."

"No one ever does." Madness took Jonas by the hand, and with little effort guided him toward the door. One last glance back at the room, the strike of another match, a quick toss, and the room immediately was ablaze. Quickly, the flames generated white, then gray billowing smoke that thickened and blackened to a dense inky shade. Smoke and flame moved up the walls, over the ceiling and back down to the floor again in a deadly whirlpool.

If they stayed, they'd see the flames devour the floor, walls, ceiling and, of course, the woman. It all would be reduced to cinders in fifteen minutes. There'd be some forensic data to retrieve, but not much else. The body, perhaps, and the bullet. But not their DNA.

Out the front door, they moved into the darkness toward Jonas's car, a station wagon. The actors always drove to the scene, never the master, in case a witness happened to look.

Jonas fired up the engine, revving the accelerator.

"Remember, drive slowly. We don't want to be noticed."

"Right." Jonas gripped the wheel and drove.

The rearview mirror gave a perfect view of the flames consuming the house. In the distance, fire engines wailed. Someone had already called 9-1-1.

"Is that the cops?" Jonas asked.

"No. The fire department." They rounded a corner and the fire faded from view.

In silence, they drove for several minutes before Jonas gripped the steering wheel tighter. "Can we do it again? I want to do it again!"

"Not right away. We have to wait." Anticipation burned under the yoke of Reason's screams to be freed.

But like Jonas, Madness didn't want to wait. Madness had been starved for too long and would not allow Reason to dictate terms.

Lights from Broadway in Nashville's music district flashed across Jonas's face as they made their way toward an open bar. "I don't want to wait."

"Let's get a drink."

Jonas frowned.

"You've trusted me this far. Have I ever let you down?"

"No."

"Then trust me."

Chapter One

Detective Rick Morgan's nickname was Boy Scout. He didn't like the moniker, given to him by his partner Detective Jake Bishop, but in the four weeks they'd been partnered, it had stuck.

"Why?" he'd once asked Bishop.

The answer came with a shrug. "You couldn't lie if you tried, you keep your hair buzzed, walk like you've a stick up your ass and, Christ, what's with the Johnny Cash black suits?"

If Rick had cared, he'd have explained that a natural bluntness limited conversations to the facts; the haircut and suits were convenient, and, well, better a rigid gait than reveal the limp, a reminder of the two bullets that had sliced into his upper leg and spilled his blood on I-40.

Memories of lying on hard asphalt heated by the July sun as he bled out remained vivid. Broad daylight. Not a cloud in the sky. It had been a routine traffic stop. A blue Ford truck with a busted tail light. He'd flashed his lights. The truck had pulled to the side. No signs of trouble. Plates called in, he'd approached the car, careful to touch the back trunk and leave fingerprints, a precaution in case of trouble. Before he cleared the trunk, the gun muzzle flashed. He'd drawn his gun. Gunfire. Pain. His thumb had jammed against the release button on his vest, opening the back door of his vehicle to free his canine Tracker. The shepherd had leapt into action. Snarls and barking mingled with more gunfire. Tracker had gone down in a heap, the whimper of his pain echoing in Rick's ears as he'd fired again and mortally wounded the shooter.

It had all gone down in less than thirty seconds. Thirty fucking seconds.

A horn honked.

Rick straightened and glanced up at the green light. He pushed the accelerator and drove the remaining blocks to the Nashville Police Department's offices located on Union and Third Avenue North. He parked, shoved out a breath hoping it would take some of the tension with it. He'd been in the homicide department four weeks now and still hadn't fallen in step with his new partner.

Out of the car, he was grateful the persistent throb in his hip was manageable today as he opened the back door. Tracker looked up at him and barked, his signal that he was ready to work.

Rick pulled a ramp from the floorboard and rested it against the seat and the ground, allowing Tracker an easy exit from the vehicle. Tracker had lost a good portion of his back right leg and, though he walked well enough, he was no longer certified for duty. The department had allowed Rick to adopt the dog as a personal pet.

But Tracker was no more built for the civilian life than Rick. During his medical leave, Rick had tried returning to school but found the day-to-day classes underwhelming. No buzz. No excitement. Just boring.

And so he'd put in his papers to be reinstated and, as luck would have it, he'd been tossed the new spot on the homicide team. Rick wasn't foolish enough to believe he'd gotten the job strictly on merit. He was a good cop, maybe a great one, but it had been his father's forty-plus years of service to the department, as well as his brother's current spot on the homicide team, that had tipped the scales. Family connections had opened the door to this opportunity and he sure as hell wasn't going to squander it.

"Beggars can't be choosers, right, T?" He and Tracker made their way to the front doors.

The two, both stiff from the car ride, moved slowly to the elevators. So far, Rick and Tracker had held their own. Not setting it on fire but closed a few slam-dunk cases. He punched the second-floor button.

When the door opened, the hum of the fluorescent lights and chatter offered a half-hearted welcome. A few detectives glanced up in their direction. One or two tossed an appreciative glance toward Tracker, none toward Rick. No one had an issue with the dog.

Tracker settled on a thick army blanket next to a metal, five-drawer desk as Rick glanced at the stack of homicide files he'd been reviewing yesterday. A teen knifed behind Broadway in an alley. A floater in the Cumberland River. A hit-and-run near Fourth Street.

He shrugged off his coat and moved to the break room to pour a cup of coffee. He'd not slept well last night or any other night since the shooting. A year should have loosened the hold of that night but time apparently didn't heal all wounds. Nightmares still jerked him out of sleep, leaving his heart pounding like a jackhammer and his body doused in sweat.

He eased into his chair and sipped coffee as he reached for a file.

"Don't get too comfortable, Boy Scout." The brusque request wrapped in a Boston accent came from his partner, Jake Bishop. In his late thirties, Bishop wore his jet-black hair slicked back and a dark beard trimmed close to his angled features. He favored dark shirts, ties that popped, and suits cut especially to his lean frame. He could have just been plucked out of South Boston if not for the polished black cowboy boots, his only concession to Middle Tennessee.

In the month they'd been partnered, Bishop had barely spoken to Rick, who by virtue of his birth had the inside track Bishop had worked a decade to reach.

Rick reached for his jacket and coffee and he and Tracker moved toward the elevators. Bishop punched the button and when the doors slid open the trio rode the elevator down. They generally used Rick's car, a dark SUV, which was Bishop's unvoiced concession to Tracker.

Bishop buckled his seat belt without comment and glanced toward the backseat at the alert dog. "Dog looks good. You're moving kind of slow though, aren't you, Boy Scout?" His tone was light, friendly almost. "Feeling okay?"

"Feel great."

Rick could hear the wheels turning in his partner's head. The transplant had worked hard to fit in, earned every bit of ground he'd made in homicide, and his reward had been a crippled legacy and his dog. Bishop had not said he was waiting for Rick, the favored son, to screw up, but that was exactly what he was doing.

"Where're we going?"

"Centennial Park. Skeletonized remains have been found," Bishop said. "The maintenance crews were tearing out an old fountain and found a bag. Inside the bag was a pink blanket and bones. It appears to be a child. Not more than three or four."

Rick rubbed the back of his neck and started the car. Hell of a way to start the week. "How long has the body been in the ground?"

A gold signet ring winked from Bishop's left pinky as he

placed hands on his thighs. "Forensics just arrived on scene. They seem to think it's been in the ground at least a decade." Ten years in Nashville and Bishop still dragged out his *A*s and dropped his *R*s; still got called Yank and Carpetbagger.

Rick pulled out onto Union Street and drove toward Broadway. No one liked these cases, but everyone would work overtime until it was solved. "Has Missing Persons been called?"

An index finger tapped against a black belt next to his Beretta. "Ten minutes ago. They're going to start digging back into old files. I asked for all similar cases reported in the last twenty years."

Rick shifted his weight, swallowing a wince when the nerves in his hip burned suddenly. Nerves were a funny thing. You could pound on them and not feel any pain. Brush of a jacket and it was wildfire shooting down his leg.

Bishop flicked imaginary lint off sharp creases in his pants. "Seems there's always pain after your kind of shooting."

"You've been shot?"

"No."

"Ah."

Bishop eyed him closely, searching for any sign of weakness but Rick would have swallowed nails before saying a word. Say anything you want about him but he was no quitter.

"I know injuries." The signet ring winked in the sunlight. "Our pace has been slow, but it always heats up sooner or later. It could get rough."

Deadpan, Rick said, "When it does, stick with me and I'll see you through."

Bishop laughed. "Yeah, right."

Nashville morning traffic was congested with the early commuters scrambling to work. As the crow flies, the drive to the park was mere miles but it took a good twenty minutes to make the trek.

When they arrived at the 132-acre park they were greeted by a collection of squad cars with lights flashing, and a dozen officers standing by a string of yellow crime-scene tape that roped off a pond that had been recently drained.

In the center of the taped area stood Rick's sister, Georgia Morgan, a senior member of the Nashville Police Department's forensics team. She'd fastened her red hair into a topknot and wore a hazmat suit that swallowed up her small frame. Her knee-high boots were submerged in the pond's ankle-deep mud; she snapped pictures of the old fountain and the hole beside it.

Rick and Bishop got out of the car. Rick opened the back door and helped Tracker out. The dog barked and wagged his tail and Rick couldn't help but smile. He rubbed the Belgian Shepherd between the ears as if to say, "Yeah, I like the work too."

Bishop eyed the dog.

"Don't underestimate either one of us."

Bishop shrugged, touched his gun, a habit he had before they entered a crime scene. As the trio approached the yellow crime-scene tape, Georgia glanced up, nodded, and then dropped her gaze back behind the viewfinder of her camera. She leaned forward and aimed it at a faded, muddy splash of pink peeking out from a tattered plastic bag. She snapped and the camera flashed.

"Who found the body?" Rick asked.

Bishop removed a notebook from his breast pocket and flipped it open. "Maintenance crews were draining a lily pond to fix the plumbing when they spotted the garbage bag. They opened the bag and found the pink blanket and the body, which is only bones now."

"Any identifying information on the body or blanket?"

"Not at first glance but from what the responding officer said, once Georgia arrived she wouldn't let anyone near the site until she'd documented every detail. Your sister is a real ballbuster."

"She wants to get it right." He bit back a more heated defense of his sister, knowing Georgia would not want big brother fighting her battles. Bishop's jabs at him rolled off his back like water off a duck, but if it went too far with Georgia, well, he'd learn a lesson about pain.

"We all do, pal," Bishop said.

"Does my baby sister scare you?"

"Fuck, no."

"Sure about that?"

"Very. And let me say now," he said, his voice low. "If you got any physical issues that come up during this case that you think might make you drop the ball, let me know, so I can catch it. I don't want this case fucked up."

"Don't worry about me, Yank." The reference, a reminder of Bishop's outlier status, had the other cop shoving a hand in his pocket and rattling change.

Georgia, like many officers, took extra care and caution when she had a murder case involving a child. Rick noted the flat set of her lips and the stiffness of her back. She was pissed and not a woman to be bothered.

Rick glanced toward the maintenance crew. "I want to talk to the guys that found the body."

"Me too."

The detectives moved toward two men wearing green coveralls and mud boots. One leaned on a shovel while the other stood back, cigarette dangling from a large sun-weathered calloused hand.

Rick pulled his badge from his pocket and held it up for the two men who straightened when they approached. The smoker dropped his cigarette to the ground and doused it with the twist of a booted foot.

Bishop flicked his badge quickly. "I'm Detective Bishop, Nashville Police Department. Got questions for you about your find."

The men looked at Bishop. Neither said a word but a subtle narrowing of their eyes said the Boston accent pegged him as an outsider.

The smoker, a tall, lean man with stooped shoulders and graying temples, spoke. "I'm Tate Greene and this is Neville Jones. That dog going to bite me?"

Rick glanced at Tracker who watched the men carefully. The canine hadn't gotten the memo that he'd been retired and though he didn't move like he once did, his eyes and brain remained sharper than ever. "No."

Greene eyed the dog. "You two are the ones shot last year?"

"That's right," Rick said. Their story had been all over the news for weeks. The media scrutiny had been stifling and left a distaste for reporters in Rick's mouth. "I'm Detective Rick Morgan."

"And that's Tracker," Tate said. "I saw you two on the television."

"Correct."

Tate studied the canine's dark gaze. "Reporter said you screwed up."

"I didn't."

"But you got shot."

"The other guy's dead."

Tate nodded. "Right."

Bishop shifted, never happy with a slow-paced conversation. He fired questions like bullets and though that worked sometimes, often it was better, Rick thought, to toss the questions out easy and slow so when the curveball came no one expected it.

"I don't like dogs," said Neville, the younger of the two men. In his late twenties, his build was plumper and his hair darker and thicker. Both men shared the same square-faced bone structure and flat noses.

"He's my nephew," Tate said. "Got bitten bad when he was six and hasn't liked dogs since."

Tracker eyed both men with keen interest.

"How long you two been working for the parks department?" Rick asked.

"Going on ten years." Tate shifted his attention from the dog to the detective. "And Neville started last month. Used to work at the hospital but he got laid off."

Neville glanced at his uncle, seemingly annoyed by the added explanation but he made no comment. He jerked a bandanna out of his pocket and wiped sweat from his brow.

"Why were you draining the lake?"

"Maintenance. One of the fountains hasn't been working for a while and we have an order to replace the head," Tate said.

"Walk us through what happened, if you don't mind." Rick said.

Tate met Rick's gaze. "Took a good day to pump the water out of the lake. Neither one of us noticed the bag right off. It was covered in mud."

Neville nodded agreement. "I was making my way through the mud when my boot got caught. I stumbled and damned near fell forward. Just as I righted myself, I saw the edge of the bag. A bit of plastic sticking up. I tugged and realized pretty quick it was a garbage bag."

Tate shook his head. "I've found all kinds of crap in places like this when we drain away water. A bike. Car tires. Hell, even a shotgun. But never a body. When I saw the pink blanket, I peeled it back and saw the skull. Shit. Shit. Shit."

Rick's gaze flickered to the bit of pink in the muck. Anger banded around his heart, digging in cold talons. "What'd you do after you realized you'd found bones?"

"We got the hell out of there," Neville said. "Can't be

good luck to find bones. Never know when the spirits are lingering around."

Bishop arched a brow but didn't comment.

Rick nodded as if he understood. "Never can be too careful. What'd you do next?"

"I called the cops," Tate added.

Bishop's sunglasses hid his eyes, but his lips flattened into a grim line. "You have any information about the maintenance of this pond?"

Tate glanced toward Bishop and frowned. "Like I said I been here ten years and I haven't worked on it before."

"Where can I get maintenance records?" Rick asked.

"Front office," Tate said. "Marvin Beard runs maintenance. Call him and he can tell you what's been done in the area."

Rick pulled a notebook from his pants pocket and jotted down the name. He also took down contact information for Tate and Neville. "Thanks. Do me a favor and stick around a bit longer." He tossed a smile that had the two men nodding and retreating back to the shade of a tree.

Rick and Bishop moved back to the pond in time to see Georgia struggling to get out of the muck without dropping her camera.

Georgia shook her head. "Don't even try. The mud will suck you in and ruin your pants." Two more steps and then a hard pull on her right foot and she stepped up onto the grassy bank.

"What did you find?" Rick asked.

She huffed out a breath and brushed a curl off her forehead with the back of a gloved hand. "As I told the uniforms, it's a child. I can't say for certain about the sex or cause of death. I can tell you the child was very young. Judging by the size of the skull I'd say five years old but in cases like this . . ." Realizing her tone grew increasingly bitter, she paused. "Children who've suffered a history of abuse often can be small for their age. Malnutrition." Again a heavy silence. "I'd say female judging by the pink blanket but that's just a guess at this point."

"A pink blanket," Bishop said more to himself. "Fuck me."

"It could be a sign of remorse," Rick theorized, his voice even. "The killer didn't intend to kill the child and when it came time to dispose of the body, guilt kicked in hard. The pink blanket may've been a favorite of the child's."

"I'm going to enjoy catching this son of a bitch." Bishop, for all his jabs and digs, was a good cop with a stellar close rate.

Rick shared his partner's sentiments but kept his emotions buried well below the surface. "When can you remove the body?" Rick had already made a mental shift. He couldn't think of the victim as a living, breathing child. Cases like this required a step back. Distance from the victim kept emotions in check and heads clear.

Georgia, like Bishop, wasn't adept at separating from cases like this. "Any minute. The medical examiner should be here any moment. I've all the photos and sketches I need so I'll wade in now and pull the body free."

"Can I help?" Rick asked.

"You got boots?"

"Boy Scout's got enough equipment in those storage bins to supply a small army," Bishop quipped.

At this point, Rick actually welcomed a verbal jab. It helped put distance between him and what he and Georgia needed to do. "I've got waders."

She looked as if she'd argue against the walk into the pond, which wouldn't be easy for him. But instead of speaking her mind, she swallowed the comments. "Suit up, Bro. You can get a good view of the scene and I could use your muscle."

Bishop rested his hands on his hips, tapping his index

finger against his belt. "I'll do it. Better to get the extraction right."

"No," Rick cut in. "I got this. I'll be right back."

"It's more important we do this right. You falling isn't going to help solve this case."

"I'm not going to fall." He left Bishop by the pond and he and Tracker made their way back to his car. He put Tracker in the backseat, switched on the car engine and A/C, and promised to return soon.

Rick, like most cops, kept his vehicle stocked with a variety of items. Change of clothes, extra ammo, MREs, and, in his case, boots. No one ever really knew what the day would deliver, so most were ready for all scenarios. And Rick could admit that Bishop was right. Rick had over-stocked his supplies.

He removed his tie and folded it carefully before placing it to the side. He removed his shoes and placed them next to the tie. From his trunk he fished out waders, which he slid over his feet and pants. In the growing heat of the day the nasty, smelly muck gained strength as the wind shifted in his direction. He cursed, remembering his trip to the dry cleaners yesterday. He stripped off his dress shirt and put on a faded Titans T-shirt.

When he returned, Georgia greeted him at the edge of the pond and handed him a shovel. She dropped her voice so that only he could hear. "You going to be able to do this? It's a short walk but a tough one."

He kept his gaze on the pond, refusing to consider failure. "I'll be fine."

"Detective High-and-Mighty can't hear. I could make up an excuse . . ."

Annoyance snapped like a rubber band against naked skin. "Georgia, even if we were here alone, I'd still do this. Let's retrieve the body."

She studied him a beat. "Bishop's an ass. He wants you to fail."

He grinned. "Good thing I'm not going to. Let's go."

With a shrug of her narrow shoulders, she moved into the mire. She staggered in mud that quickly reached her calf but kept moving. Rick followed. Immediately, he realized this was going to be tougher than he'd imagined. What was that line in the movie about his ego writing a check his body couldn't cash?

Swallowing an oath as his hip burned, he kept walking, his gaze nailed to the center of the pond and the splash of pink that made him forget all his pain and frustration. Several times he used the shovel to steady himself. When he arrived at the center of the pond his breath was faster. The sun had burned away the morning mists and heat beat down directly onto the site.

He glanced beyond the threads of pink to the small skull cradled inside. "Have you examined the skull?"

"No, I'm afraid to handle the bones too much. They could be very fragile. I want to pull it all out as one unit and let the medical examiner do her thing."

"Fair enough."

"Let's see if we can dig her out. Start at least a foot away from the remains. If we can loosen the bag we might be able to get her out easily."

"Stop saying *her,* Georgia. It's only going to make this harder." Mental distance had saved him more times than he could count. "We're retrieving evidence, not a child."

With the back of her hand, she pushed aside a tendril of damp hair. "I don't have your ability to detach, which you've elevated to a superpower, Bro."

He offered no sympathy. "You aren't doing yourself a favor. Work now. Feel later."

Blue eyes snapped. "Oh, like you're going to feel that hip pain later. You know you're not doing yourself a favor by mucking through the mud. And yet, here you are. What does that say about you?"

Sweat dampened his T-shirt between his shoulder blades. "We're both dumbasses. Let's dig."

That coaxed a smile. "What kinds of people do this work for a living?"

"Insane people."

The two began digging a couple of feet out from the body. With the first shovelful of dirt, the muck and mire sunk in on itself, filling the hole quickly. Cursing, Rick dug faster, determined that the mud would not win. As he shoveled dirt, Georgia's breathing grew more labored.

"What's wrong, Sis?" Aggravation had always coaxed her out of a mood. "Haven't been hitting the gym lately."

She hissed out a breath. "I work out."

Laughter rumbled in his chest. "You've never worked out a day in your life."

"I joined a gym last year."

"How many times did you go?" He worked out regularly. Running wasn't an easy option anymore, but he found weight training very effective. Biking also worked well and he'd learned to love swimming. Surrounded by the cool water and cut off from sound, he discovered each stroke calmed his mind.

"Twice."

He laughed.

Again she brushed the unruly curl from her forehead with the back of her hand. "I'm not a fan of sweating."

"Really? How do you like it now? I bet you're doing a hell of a lot."

"Now's different. It's work. Gym sweat is boring. Mindless." Her voice faded, her body demanding she hold on to her oxygen.

"Right."

Finally, they got ahead of the mud. It took them another

twenty minutes to dig deep enough so that the plastic bag could be lifted out of the mire.

The medical examiner technician arrived with a body bag. While Georgia cradled the plastic bag, cocooning the pink blanket and bones, Rick went to shore and took the bag. When he returned, she laid the body into the bag and he zipped it up. Georgia and Rick carried the body out together. Walking in muck while balancing the bag took more effort and by the time they handed the bag to the technicians, both were hot and winded.

Rick watched the techs put the bag on a stretcher in the back of the van and then slam the doors shut. The humid morning air seemed to thicken with each passing second. He'd sweat through his T-shirt and pants and smelled of the foul mud.

Georgia unzipped her jumpsuit, revealing a sweat-stained shirt. A swipe of mud brushed across her pale forehead.

Bishop approached but stopped short as the wind shifted and he got a good whiff of them both. He stepped back. "Nice work."

"You should've joined us for the fun," Georgia quipped. "That fancy suit of yours is perfect for this kind of work."

"I tried. Boy Scout wanted this gig." Bishop's leveled, calm gaze stoked her short temper.

Rick knew from experience she'd fire back but he didn't want to watch the verbal sparring. Too sore and hot to get involved in their skirmish, he headed back to his car.

His car engine still hummed and a glance in the backseat revealed Tracker, lying with his eyes closed, ears perked. From a storage bin, Rick grabbed a bottle of water and drank. The morning heat had warmed the bottle but he savored the liquid as it washed away the stale taste in his mouth. He stripped off the waders and then pulled off the T-shirt, wiped off with a towel, and put his shirt and shoes back on. At the station, his first stop would be the showers and the lockers where he kept a spare suit.

At the SUV's driver's-side door, Rick was anxious to sit down and get the weight off his leg when Bishop appeared. Without comment, he got in the car and Rick followed.

Bishop wrinkled his nose. "You stink."

Rick put the car in drive. "No shit."

Bishop shrugged. "See anything of note around the body?"

"No. But Georgia and her crew will check."

"She's driven," he said more to himself.

Rick didn't comment.

"The pond must've been drained when the body was buried. While you were in the muck, I talked to the maintenance office." He flipped pages in his notebook. "Pond was drained seven years ago, twelve years ago, nineteen years ago, and it was built twenty-five years ago. That gives us four windows of opportunity."

The air conditioner's cool air seemed to sizzle as it hit his hot skin. "Will help narrow the missing persons files."

"Yeah."

Rick drove to the station, put Tracker at his desk with orders to stay, and found his way to the showers. He moved quickly to the locker room, stripping off the morning's clothes and stepping under the hot spray of the shower. As the water beat down on his sore left side, he breathed a sigh of relief before turning his face to the spray. He soaped liberally and washed his hair, wondering if he'd ever get the smell of the muck from his body.

Out of the shower, he toweled, glancing only briefly at the scar that ran over his hip and down his thigh. He dressed and found Bishop at his desk on the phone. Tracker stared at Bishop, who looked at the dog and held up a hand as if to say, "What?"

Don't let him off the hook, T. Suppressing a smile, Rick poured a coffee.

Bishop raised a brow at the dog and then turned back toward his desk as Rick approached. "The medical examiner says it will be a day at least before she has an evaluation but she's making it top priority."

"Great. What about Missing Persons?"

"They've sent some folders and are digging out the rest." Bishop nodded toward Rick's desk to a stack of manila folders that had to be forty deep. "Files of missing children who fit our rough description and our most recent time parameters. Basically the last thirty years."

Rick sat and flipped open the first file and read. Tanya Logan, age four, missing for eleven years. He glanced at the image of the child's smiling face. "Going to be a long day."

"Give me half. Let's see if we can narrow it down to at least a short list."

"There's no telling if our victim is in these files. No telling if a report was filed."

Bishop unfastened his cuffs and carefully rolled them up, revealing muscled forearms sprinkled with dark hair. "Agreed. But we still got to do the work."

He handed over half the stack. "I'll do whatever it takes to catch this bastard."

Detective Deke Morgan, Rick's brother, arrived as he opened the first file. The frown lines in Deke's forehead and around his eyes were deeper than normal and the graying at his temples had thickened. He wore his customary dark suit and white shirt and simple black cowboy boots polished to a high sheen.

A perpetual frown deepened as Deke studied the stack of files. "Good, you're on the case. Let me know when you have something." Deke had given Rick the nod to join homicide, but if he'd shown any favoritism in that moment he'd not shown any more. He'd chew Rick's ass as quickly as Bishop's or any other member of the team. He was all about equal opportunity when it came to doling out crap.

"I thought you were on vacation."

Deke's frown softened for a split second. "I was. I'm back. What's going on with the case?"

Rick shifted as the tension snaked up his back. "We'll let you know if we've any kind of hit."

Deke rubbed Tracker's head. "I've had that reporter, Susan Martinez, calling. She got wind of the story and wants in."

Memories of the reporter hounding him after the shooting set Rick's teeth on edge.

"I know you don't like Martinez."

"I can deal if she can help. I just don't trust her."

Martinez and her crews had been on the scene as rescuers were loading him in the ambulance. Later, after surgery, she'd found him in his hospital room and asked for an interview. He'd been pissed at himself and worried for Tracker and he'd said a few choice words. She'd not scared easily but in the end had left him. She'd covered the shooting extensively, showing the dash-cam footage and interviewing other officers. *What was his critical mistake?* All agreed he'd made no mistake. The job came with hazards. Few of those quotes had made it on air.

"If you don't give her some information, she'll find some," Deke said. He glanced toward the coffeemaker as if he needed a jolt.

The line between cop and brother was thin, but there nonetheless, and Rick had avoided being too familiar with Deke while on the job. Still, he couldn't resist a tiny jab.

"You're looking a little rough," Rick teased. "Rachel and city life wearing on you?"

His brother had initially inherited the family home, called the Big House by the Morgan family, when their father had died. However, Deke had no taste for country living and had deeded the house to Rick. Deke had moved into his new girlfriend's city place six months ago.

Deke's frown darkened even as his gaze softened. "She never misses an opportunity to bark at me about the handling of an arrest."

"Shouldn't have moved in with a defense attorney."

A slight smile tugged at Bishop's lips. He had no qualms about a jab or two. "Not just any attorney. Rachel Wainwright. The meanest in the state."

Deke shrugged as he poured himself a cup of coffee. "I like her mean. Keeps it interesting."

"Like living with a python?" Bishop asked.

Deke sipped his coffee. "What's life without a little danger?"

Danger. They all lived with it every day. It was waiting for them the minute they strapped on a badge and stepped out the front door of their home. Even when they were off duty it was impossible to shut off the defense mechanisms or worries. When Rick ate in a restaurant he always kept his back to the wall and his eyes on the door. He always carried his off-duty weapon and he always knew a room's entrances and exits.

"Yeah, can't get enough of it myself," Rick said.

Rick and Bishop had been reading for three hours when Georgia reappeared. She'd showered and changed into a clean pair of khakis and a blue collared shirt worn by the forensics team. Her pale skin glowed pink as she tried to scrub the mud, as well as the memory, away.

Rick leaned back in his chair. "What brings you here?"

Bishop had loosened his tie but when Georgia spoke he straightened it. His gaze roamed over Georgia, taking in her slim figure.

She scratched Tracker between the ears. Few touched the

canine but his baby sister had never hesitated to pet him. "Any luck on the missing persons cases?"

He stretched out his leg and rubbed the stiffness banding his thigh. "Some leads but nothing solid."

If she noticed he was in pain she gave no sign of it. "What do you think the chances are that we'll find out who this kid was?"

"I don't know."

"If you had to bet?" she asked.

It was Bishop who leaned back in his chair. "Slim."

She frowned at Bishop. "Why do you say that?"

"Too many variables. We can pour through all the old files we like, but if we can't ID the kid, we won't get anywhere."

Georgia rested her hand on her hip and Rick could almost hear the wheels grinding and turning. "What if you could make an identification?"

"The medical examiner pushed up her schedule and will have a preliminary report in less than an hour. She'll have basic physical stats for us. And we might get lucky and find a match in the file."

"And if you don't?"

"Then we're SOL," Bishop said. "A needle in a haystack. We don't even know if the victim is from Nashville."

"I can't believe this," she challenged. "All the science and we can't ID the child?"

Bishop held up his hands in surrender. "Sometimes the truth sucks."

Her frown deepened and her eyes blazed.

Softening the news with a platitude would only stoke her frustration. "Bishop's right. If we don't have a file match," Rick said, "our chances diminish."

Georgia shook her head, just as she'd done as a child

when she received an answer she didn't like. "This isn't acceptable."

"You think this is what I want?" Bishop asked.

"Sounds like you're giving up."

"No, I'm not." Bishop's eyes blazed with fury. If Georgia had been a man, he just might have slugged her.

Georgia noticed his annoyance but didn't seem to care. "I hate this."

"No one likes this, Georgia." Rick reached for his coffee and raised it to his lips until he discovered it had turned to black sludge.

"We're doing all we can," Bishop said.

She waved away his comment and to Rick asked, "What if I could get you a face?"

"A face?"

"Of the child. What if we had her face?"

Bishop shook his head. "You're talking about forensic reconstruction. Hell of a cost that isn't likely to get approved in the near future. We could be waiting for months. Years."

Georgia shifted her gaze to Bishop. "What if I knew someone who would do it for free?"

"Free." Bishop looked amused now. "We're talking about thousands of dollars of work."

She held up her hand. "If I got the help, would you take it?"

"You aren't going to get that kind of help just like that for free."

"What if I can, smart-ass?"

Bishop interlocked his hands behind his head, leaned back, and smiled. "So you got connections we don't know about?"

"Yeah."

"I know all the artists in the state," Rick said. "Whom are you talking about?"

"This gal I met at KC's bar."

"In KC's bar? The place where you sing once in a while?" Bishop laughed. "I can't wait to explain this one to the judge if we ever get this case to court."

Georgia had a great singing voice and when she wasn't working she sang at KC's bar, a place called Rudy's. KC, a former cop, had bought the bar last year. No one thought he'd make it work, but he'd surprised everyone by not only keeping the business afloat, but also growing it. He packed them in nightly with singing acts.

"Does she sing too?" Rick asked.

"No, she doesn't sing. She draws. Portraits. Six nights a week. She's really good."

"Georgia, what're you smoking?" Rick asked. "Just because you can draw a face doesn't mean you can reconstruct one."

"She's a cop, jerk. Baltimore Police Department. And she's a trained forensic artist. She's taken some kind of leave."

"On leave? Working in a bar in Nashville drawing portraits?" Bishop asked. "So what the hell kind of issues does she have?"

"I don't know," Georgia said. "She's nice. She's talented, and she would do this if I asked."

"I don't know, Georgia," Rick said.

"I got her a lead on a house that she rented a couple of weeks ago so she kind of owes me."

"Is she the one you got to rent the Murder House?" Rick asked.

Georgia shrugged. "She said that kind of thing doesn't bother her."

Bishop laughed. "Hell, if anything, I got to meet this woman for a laugh."

Rick rolled his head from side to side. "Georgia."

"Rick," Georgia said. "She's really good. I've seen enough of these artists in action. She's good."

He shoved out a sigh.

"You aren't considering this, are you?" Bishop asked.

"If the medical examiner's preliminary write-up doesn't match our records, then we'll be at a loss. You got a better lead?"

"Not now."

Rick rose. "Give her a call, Georgia. If we end up needing her, I'll pay her a visit."

She clapped her hands in victory. "You won't be sorry."

Rick wasn't so sure.

Chapter Two

Monday, August 14, 3 P.M.

Eyes were the mirrors to the soul, weren't they?

Jenna Thompson studied the eyes in the sketch. Lately, when she sat down to draw, she was never satisfied with the subject's eyes. Often she'd draw, erase, and redraw them. She'd developed an issue with eyes that had started as a quirk but was getting worse.

When she drew at KC's, the portraits were quick and dirty. Twenty bucks for a ten-minute drawing and forty bucks for a twenty-minute drawing. She always saved the eyes for last and when she drew them, she sketched quickly and refused to study them too closely. It often pained her to hand over a drawing when all she wanted to do was refashion the eyes. A bit more light. Wider. Narrower. Brighter. Sadder. They were never right. But she didn't have the time to worry.

But when she was at home in her studio, and time wasn't an issue, she found herself trapped in endless drawing cycles.

She studied the portrait of the young bride. She'd met the woman at KC's when she'd done a quick drawing. The woman had been so thrilled she'd asked Jenna if she could do her wedding portrait. It had been years since she'd done any commission work but the added cash was too hard to resist.

She studied the preliminary attempt. Why couldn't she capture the eyes of the young woman? She leaned to the left and studied the dozens of photographs she'd taken of the young blond woman with the bright smile and dancing eyes. The photos had captured her image perfectly. But it was her job as the portrait artist to capture her soul. Her essence. In the eyes.

As Jenna reached for her eraser, someone knocked on her door. Quick, hard raps that spoke of impatience, annoyance, and anger. Frustrated, she glanced at the cottage's front door and then back at the portrait. The eyes reflected happiness but somehow fell short. What were they missing?

Another knock.

Irritated, she turned the easel away so that whoever was barging into her quiet time would not see the work. She grabbed a rag from the back pocket of her jeans and wiped the paint from her hands as she padded in bare feet across the cabin's pine floors, which smelled faintly of pine cleaner.

Jenna had rented the cabin a couple of weeks ago. The price had been too good but Georgia Morgan had been upfront about the place's history. A woman, a private detective, had been killed on the property. Locals knew the story well and had no interest in a sale or a rental. They called it the Murder House. But Jenna had agreed to see the house and, the moment she'd seen it, had fallen for the rustic exterior, large windows overlooking expansive woods ringing the open field, and stream behind the house.

A day after she'd signed the one-month lease she'd been at the local grocery store. When the clerk had read her handwritten new address on her check, he'd raised a brow.

"The house is haunted," the clerk had said.

"Everyone's got to live somewhere, even ghosts," Jenna had joked. She could have explained that she wasn't afraid of death or ghosts and she had an affinity for the damaged and lost. All had stalked her most of her life. But she'd only smiled. Sharing too much about her past never won her points.

Knock, knock, knock.

Jenna glanced out the door's peephole and saw the two men. One had his back to the door and the other faced it. A tension rippled through their bodies; each was braced ready to fight. The body posture might have been clue enough but then she also noticed the one in front had a mid-grade suit, sensible shoes, and a short haircut. The one facing away from the house dressed with more style, but she also had him pegged.

They were cops.

Jenna could spot a cop because she was a cop in Baltimore, Maryland. She'd entered the academy when she was nineteen after two years of college had eaten what savings her aunt had squirreled away. She'd been faced with taking on more debt or getting a job. Becoming a police officer had never been on her life list, but when she'd read the recruiting ad and seen the salary and benefits, the decision to apply made sense. She'd never imagined a life of service when she'd made the commitment but she'd taken to structure and regime like a duck to water.

She'd been raised by a woman who craved organization like a junkie craved drugs. No dirty dishes in the sink. No clothes on the floor and the ones that landed in the hamper didn't stay there long. Jenna still associated liquid pine cleaner with her aunt Lois.

Aunt Lois had been in her mid fifties when she'd made the decision to take Jenna away from Nashville. Many of Lois's friends had questioned her decision to take on a troubled five-year-old. But Lois had been determined to take the child who was her last living blood relative. The two had made the seven-hundred-mile trip from Nashville to Baltimore alone. Jenna didn't remember much conversation on that long-ago trip, only growing relief as they'd driven farther and father away from Nashville. There was never a lot of money to go around, but Lois saw to it that they got by. Turned out living together had been good for both. Lois and Jenna had come out of their shells, at least partway, together.

Pine cleaner. The scent lingered in Jenna's new home, a holdover from the big scrubbing she'd given the home when she'd moved in her few belongings. Jenna inhaled and opened the door.

Her gaze landed first on the cop who faced her. He had dark eyes reflecting disbelief and curiosity. Those eyes would be hard to capture on paper. Too elusive and she'd always wonder if what he chose to reflect was indeed true.

Dark Eyes reached in his pocket and removed a slim black wallet and with the flick of his fingers revealed a shiny, new police shield. "Jenna Thompson?"

She studied the badge an extra beat and then nodded. "That's correct."

"I'm Rick Morgan. I'm a detective with Nashville Metro Homicide. This is my partner, Detective Jake Bishop. My sister, Georgia, said you'd be expecting us."

At the sound of his name, Bishop turned. His eyes, a vivid gray, flickered over her, cataloging her loose peasant top, faded jeans, short nails dirtied by paint and charcoal, and a long, black braid that looped over her square shoulder. "Ma'am."

"You're Georgia's brother?" She studied him for a family resemblance but didn't find one.

"Yes. She said you might be interested in working with us on a case."

Those eyes studied her and she suspected he was trying to peel back the layers. No doubt he'd asked around about her. He knew about Baltimore, knew she'd taken leave abruptly to visit Nashville. Dark Eyes wouldn't be satisfied with the facts in her employee file. He'd keep looking and searching until all the stones had been flipped over and examined.

A fist of tension clenched in her chest. She'd said yes because she'd liked Georgia but now questioned the decision. "She said you had a tough case."

Rick drew in a breath. "You'll help?"

"Yes." When Georgia had called her an hour ago, Jenna had said no. She needed a break from police work. It had been police work that had triggered this need to come to Nashville. But Georgia had not heard her first or her second no. She'd pressed and pointed out the victim was a child.

Hearing that, Jenna's opposition had melted. She'd agreed to this one favor.

Detective Morgan raised a manila folder she'd not noticed before. "I've pictures I can show you. Can we come in?"

"Sure." She stepped aside and allowed them into the cabin. As they moved toward the large A-framed living room, she slid her feet into a pair of flip-flops and followed behind.

As if he'd entered a crime scene, Detective Morgan's gaze wantonly roamed the room. He absorbed the scene: two small sofas that faced each other, the coffee table between and the stack of art books arranged neatly in the center, a kitchen counter sporting only a bowl of apples, and then the easel that faced away. The furniture had come with the house, but the books and small touches were hers.

"I hear you do portraits at KC's now," Detective Morgan said.

"Yes."

He moved toward the picture and for a moment she was

distracted by the very small hitch in his step. He was doing his best to hide it but she catalogued the detail as if she'd never left the job.

"She said a few weeks."

"That's about right." An image of half-erased eyes crossed her mind. "And I don't allow anyone to view my work before it's finished. So if you don't mind."

Detective Morgan hesitated just inches from the canvas but to his credit didn't overstep. He faced her, a measure of curiosity now humming behind those eyes. "Sure."

Extending a hand toward the couches, she looked at the other detective, taking comfort in his lack of interest. "Have a seat."

Both officers took a seat on one sofa and she chose the one across.

"It appears to be the skeletonized remains of a child," Morgan said. "We believe the child's age would've been between four to six years old at the time of death."

Sadness pressed against her chest. She mourned for the child who had died far too young. "How intact is the skull?"

"We have it all."

"Including the mandible?" The mandible was the lower jaw, which after decomposition became detached from the top of the skull. Animals often scavenged the remains spreading them far afield.

"Yes," Morgan said. "The body was wrapped in a blanket and then encased in a plastic bag."

She opened the manila folder and laid out the crime-scene pictures. In the center of the shallow hole was a black muddied plastic bag that had been sliced open like a large pod. Lining the bag was the blanket. Pink. Detective Bishop had not said pink. Seeing the pink added an element of humanity that jostled her concentration. Pink. A little girl. A chill crackled through the woman even as the cop celebrated a clean sample. It would make the work easier. "Was there any other identifying information in the bag?"

"No," Morgan said. "Just the blanket."

The pink blanket. "What about remnants of clothing?"

"No signs of clothes." If the blanket had remained so should have the clothes. She'd been naked when she'd been buried.

"Okay."

"Georgia said you used to be a forensic artist," Morgan said. "You worked for Baltimore Police Department but you quit."

She noted the extra emphasis on *quit*. "I haven't quit. I've taken a six-week leave of absence." She'd told herself the day she'd left that the break was temporary. But each day away from Baltimore took her another step away from the job. One day she might cross the thin blue line and find herself on the outside, unable to get back. She suspected this detective had already branded her as lacking. A failure.

"You drew for them," Detective Morgan said.

"Correct." There were still some cops who didn't put much stock in her work, leaving her always at the ready to recite the facts about cases closed by a forensic artist. Whereas fingerprints caught criminals ten percent of the time, forensic artists had a success rate closer to thirty percent. She'd encountered skepticism in Baltimore at first, and then she'd started to work with victims, many traumatized, and painstakingly re-created the faces of their attackers. Many faces would later prove to be dead-on matches to mug shots.

"I've heard the stats on your kind of work," Morgan said. "Impressive."

His tone, bordering on boredom, stoked her temper. Who was this guy to get an attitude with her when she was doing him the favor? If not for the child, she'd have called it quits. Told him to get the hell out. "Wait until you see the sketch

I draw for you. You'll be impressed." Yeah, she was letting her annoyance get the better of her. But she'd be damned if she'd let this guy judge her or her work.

"You can give this victim a face?" Detective Bishop asked.

"Yes." She sat back, confident in her skills. "You aren't from around here?"

Bishop shrugged. "Boston. But I been here ten years."

A challenge underscored the last two words. Still an outsider. "What brought you to Nashville?"

Bishop's brow arched. "I could ask you the same."

A smile tweaked the edge of her lips at the dodge. "I heard good things."

"Me too." Bishop leaned back on the couch and folded his arms. "We don't have a budget."

"That's what Georgia said. I told her I'd donate my time." She dropped her gaze to the photos and zeroed in on the empty eye sockets that glared up at her. *Who are you?*

"Why?" Rick asked.

"Why what?" Jenna asked, raising her gaze.

"Why're you donating your services?"

Her shoulders lifted in a small shrug. "I've a skill." She tapped her index finger, calloused from holding a drawing pencil for countless hours, on the photo. "I can give this child a face. Isn't that enough?"

He studied her, shaking his head. "Just seems odd a sworn cop ends up in a bar drawing faces. Who takes that kind of path?"

She closed the file but fell short of pushing it back toward him. "I didn't realize volunteering would come with so many questions."

"Wouldn't you be asking the same questions?"

"Sure. I'm on leave but I'm still a cop. Hard not to help." And now she had the last kind of case she'd ever wanted. A lost little girl. In a pink blanket.

Detective Bishop put his hands on his thighs and pushed to his feet. "I've seen your work. Checked it out before we came. You're good. Real good. And frankly I'm not worried about the whys driving you. I want this case solved."

Jenna rose, meeting his gaze. "Me too."

"When can you get started?" Detective Morgan stood and shifted his stance as if he was working out a painful kink in his hip.

She searched for a grain of pity but couldn't find one. "I've a freelance project but I can work around it. When do you want me to start?"

"The medical examiner will have a clean sample for you by tomorrow afternoon. She said you could start any time." Clean sample. That meant that the skull would be stripped of any remaining flesh and ready to accept the clay she'd use to create muscle and flesh.

"Tomorrow then at two at the medical examiner's office?"

"I'll be there."

"You know where it is?" Detective Morgan asked.

"I can find it." She'd have to do some figuring, but she'd not ask Detective Morgan for help. His *you quit* rattled in her head, making it impossible to ask him for help.

You quit.

She'd not quit. She'd taken a break so that she could get her head together. She'd not walked away from Baltimore forever. Just for now.

Jenna walked Detectives Morgan and Bishop outside and without a backward glance, left her to consider the task she'd accepted. As they got into a dark SUV, she withdrew back into her home. She closed the door to the sound of the car engine rumbling and gravel crunching under tires.

Nervous tension simmered in her belly as she thought about re-creating the face for Morgan's Lost Girl. It was a job. A favor. Nothing she hadn't done a thousand times before in Baltimore. But this time the idea of drawing the child's face unsettled her enough to make her reconsider.

You quit.

Though tempted to back out of the job, she wouldn't, if only to prove to herself and to Detective Morgan she was no quitter.

Facing her easel, she turned the image around and studied the half-erased eyes. Automatically, she reached for her pencil and began to sketch. Eyes. Why was it always the eyes that haunted her?

Her chest tightened and the more she stared at the portrait's unfinished eyes the more anxious she grew. The cabin's walls shrunk. Finally, unable to draw, she crossed the room and stepped out onto the back deck. Tilting her face toward the sun, she inhaled the sweet scent of wildflowers, pollen, and hay. Breathe in. Breathe out. She glanced down at her trembling hands. Never in her life could she remember being scared. Her aunt had always said Jenna attacked life. And yet here she stood unable to finish a damn portrait.

"What the hell is wrong with me?" she whispered.

Frayed edges of a pink blanket coiled through her thoughts.

A similar blanket, soft and smelling of milk, had been a treasured item of hers when she was a child. She'd held it close when she'd laughed and played with her mother and father. Sometimes, she'd imagined it had been a princess cape or a magic carpet. Other days, it kept her warm and soothed her to sleep at night.

Days after her fifth birthday, when the bad man took her from her home, her pink blanket had become her lifeline. She clung to it when he'd taped her mouth closed and tossed her in the trunk of his car. Later, when he'd thrown her into a closet and locked the door, she wept into that blanket.

He eventually took the tape off so she could eat the fast-food burgers he brought her. He spoke sweetly to her, tried to coax her to eat but all she could do was cower in the corner, clinging to the blanket. Finally, he'd slammed the door closed and left her in the dark.

Ragged pink threads brushed more memories to the front of her mind.

Later she would learn that he had killed her family and he had held her for nine days in that closet. But then, when she'd been alone and afraid, time had stopped as she'd cried for her mother. She'd been the lost child and could easily have been killed and found later wrapped in pink. Dead and tossed in the cold ground.

But her captor had been a drug user and on the ninth day of her containment, he'd overdosed on heroin. It had been hours before cops had broken down the door and found her in the closet, half starved.

"You're one lucky girl," the officer had said as he'd carried her from the small apartment. Clinging to her blanket, she'd blinked as the sun had hit her eyes and she'd tucked her head in the officer's broad shoulders.

One lucky girl. How could she respond to that?

Jenna folded her arms over her chest and savored the open space and the warm breeze flittering through the trees. No amount of pine cleaner could wash away the memory of the tiny, putrid closet with walls that left her with a lasting fear of confined spaces. That fear had found renewed life in the last few weeks until finally it had driven her out of Baltimore.

You quit.

"No, I didn't quit, Detective Morgan." She glanced back at her house. It would be hours before she could return inside.

"She's an interesting piece of work. Attractive but different," Bishop said.

Different didn't come close to describing Jenna Thompson. There was a solemn look in her gaze that reached far beyond her thirty years. The eyes of a woman who'd seen bad things. She'd been a cop so that stood to reason. However, he suspected, what she'd seen went beyond the Force. He'd watched how her hands had trembled very slightly when she'd tapped her index finger on the picture. The image had struck a nerve. Was it because the victim had been a child? Lots of cops took emotional hits when the victim was young and innocent. The case certainly had touched Georgia deeply.

Rick glanced in the rearview mirror at a sleeping Tracker and then pulled out onto the main road. As the lush green trees lining the backcountry road whooshed past, he pictured the petite, trim, controlled woman with the long, dark braid that draped over her shoulder like a seaman's rope.

"What did her captain say about her when you called?" Bishop asked.

"She was decorated and served with honor. Her boss, Mike Ferrara, was sorry to see her go and said the door was always open if she wanted to return. He said she can create a face from just about any witness, no matter how rattled. She's one of the best. He has hopes she'll return soon."

He'd tried to walk away after the shooting, but in the end, he couldn't walk away from the job. The Force was in his blood, just as it was in Tracker's. Some canines couldn't make the transition to civilian life. They lost the will to live and died soon after retirement. Tracker would have been like that. And he wasn't much different. Civilian life had made his skin itch and crawl with impatience.

He was no damn quitter.

As they grew closer to the city, trees gave way to more and more concrete. "What else did you find out about her?"

"She's been in Nashville several weeks, rented the house of a murdered woman, and draws pictures. That's it."

"The dots don't connect."

Bishop yawned. "I really don't care if the dots connect or not. We've got a talented forensic artist who's going to create a sketch for us. We'll have a better chance of figuring out who killed that child if we've a face."

Rick tightened his hand on the wheel. "You're right. I shouldn't look a gift horse in the mouth."

Even as he spoke the words, he knew he'd stop by KC's bar tonight and find out more about Jenna Thompson.

Just before four, Rick and Bishop were minutes from the station when they received the call from dispatch. There'd been a fire in a small West End home and crews had found a body in the midst of the rubble. Likely the victim had died in the fire but a dead body was a dead body and homicide had to be called.

Rick shifted in his seat, stifling a groan. His leg was stiff and he needed to stretch and work out the cramps. But with another call on the heels of their meeting with Jenna Thompson there'd be no time for PT stretches. He did what he had to do. He sucked it up. He did not quit.

He parked behind a fire truck at the end of a cul-de-sac. Water hoses sprayed on the black smoldering embers cordoned off by yellow crime-scene tape. The house's brick foundation remained, as did blackened wooden struts that had once been the east wall. The heavy scent of burned wood clung to the air as heat hissed a dying breath from the embers.

Judging by the other houses on the block, the charred timbers had been a small bungalow with a brick front porch and a low-pitched roof. A few firemen stood in puddles of water while neighbors gathered to watch the scene as if it were a live-action crime drama playing out in their own front yards. The drama of the flames might've passed but Rick guessed this had been a hell of a fire.

A Channel Five news van had angled on the street behind and Susan Martinez gripped her mike as she spoke into the camera. The dark-haired reporter wore a red dress that hugged her trim frame and waterproof boots that kept her feet dry.

"Look, it's your buddy, Ms. Martinez," Bishop said.

"My lucky day."

Rick let Tracker out of the car so that he could move and stretch. The dog sniffed the air and his ears perked as he took in the scene. A uniformed officer moved toward the detectives, a small notebook in hand.

The officer's name badge read PRINCE. He was a tall, lean kid with short, black hair. Fresh-faced and a spring in his step, Rick guessed he'd not been working the streets for more than a year.

Prince extended his hand and introduced himself.

Rick accepted the hand. "So what do you have for us?"

Prince glanced back at the scene. "Firemen responded to the call early this morning. The flames ate through the house in a matter of minutes. Crews didn't even attempt to enter the building, which was completely engulfed when they arrived."

Bishop pulled off his sunglasses and studied the carnage. "What time did the fire start?"

"Just before sunrise. They put the fire out hours ago but the rubble has only just cooled enough so the arson investigator could examine the scene more closely."

Rick sniffed. "Do I smell diesel?"

Prince's eyes widened with surprise. "Good nose. The fire crews suspected arson from the moment they pulled up. The flames were hot and spread fast."

"Who owns the house?" Rick asked.

He glanced at his notes. "A couple by the name of Nesbit. They recently moved out into a home in Franklin. He got a big promotion and they could afford a bigger house."

Rick rested his hands on his hips. "They've been accounted for?"

"They have. I spoke to them a half hour ago and they're on their way here." They turned toward the house and pointed to a trampled white sign in the center of the yard. "That's a FOR SALE sign. They put the house on the market six months ago but no sale yet. Just had it staged to attract buyers."

"A fire would solve a lot of problems," Rick said.

Bishop nodded. "Clean and simple."

"Except that there's a body in the house," Rick added. "Any clue who it might be?"

"Not yet," Prince said. "Waiting on the medical examiner's van."

"Who's in charge of the arson investigation?"

Prince pointed to a broad-shouldered man wearing a fireman's jacket and pants, heavy boots, and a helmet. "Inspector Dean Murphy. He's the one that found the body."

"Okay. Thanks."

Rick and Bishop made their way across the water-soaked yard, up a cement sidewalk to a set of brick stairs that now led really to nowhere. In the center of the blackened remains stood Dean Murphy.

"Inspector Murphy," Rick said.

The man held up a hand, asking Rick to wait, as if he were engrossed in midthought. He scribbled notes on a page and then slowly faced them. In his early sixties he sported a large stock of white hair, full eyebrows, and a ruddy complexion.

Rick made introductions. "The uniformed officer tells me it was arson."

Inspector Murphy shoved out a breath. "No doubt about it." He pointed to several sections of the ruins that had all but disintegrated. "Those spots are ignition points where our arsonist poured lots of accelerant, likely diesel or kerosene. As you can see, we've got multiple ignition points, but if you look over here where the body was found, there's quite a bit of damage. That area was the bedroom."

Rick studied what had been the bedroom and could make out the faint impression of a body. High heat not only seared flesh but it melted the body's fat and ate into bone turning it to ash and dust.

"At this point, I can't tell you how the person died," Murphy said. "Witnesses tell me the house was vacant except for the staged furniture. A neighbor was keeping an eye on the house. I don't know if this is a suicide or a murder. Can't even tell you at this point if the victim was a male or female. The fire was deliberate and intended to obliterate the house."

Removing a body from a scene damaged by fire was tricky. Often the body had fused or dissolved into the surrounding area so crews scooped up all they could from around the body and took it, knowing it could be sorted at the medical examiner's office. However, lots of photos would be taken and the scene carefully mapped before the body could be removed.

Flashing lights reflected off the windows of the house in the yard adjoining this one. Rick turned to see the Nashville Police Department's forensic van arrive.

"Can you take me closer to the spot where the body was found?"

"Spot is still too hot. But there's something I can show you," Murphy said. He pulled a digital camera from his pocket, clicked on the camera, and scrolled through several pictures. "Have a look at this."

Rick and Bishop stared at the image. At first, it only

appeared to be blackened wood, but closer inspection revealed the faint impression of letters. "A word."

"Appears to have been carved into what I think was the headboard of the bed. "I missed it the first time through."

Rick removed his sunglasses and, squinting, studied the image. "I see an *F* and an *A*." The remaining letters were faint, but a careful study of the letters' curves nudged the puzzle pieces into place. *"Faithless."*

Murphy rubbed his hand over the side of his square jaw. "That's exactly what I saw. I also think, judging by the remains, that the body was tied spread-eagle. Likely to the bed."

"Why do you say that?"

"Most people die in the fetal position. They're trying to protect their face and airways. This person is facing up with hands out."

Fire ate through the outer extremities first: fingers and hands, toes and feet. The limbs of this victim were gone but shoulders remained in place.

"Hell of a way to destroy evidence," Bishop said.

Murphy shrugged as he shut off the image. "Fire obliterates a lot but not everything."

Rick stretched his neck from side to side. "Faithless."

It was after ten by the time Rick reached KC's bar. The former cop had retired last year after thirty-five years in the Nashville Police Department. KC and Rick's father, Buddy, had been partners for twenty-nine years. KC and his late wife had never had children, but they had been honorary members of the Morgan clan and had broken bread with them many times.

Short, with a thick chest and a large, hard belly, KC wore a Hawaiian shirt that hung loosely over jeans. He'd let his regulation short hair grow since he'd retired and now secured it back in a small ponytail at the base of his neck. KC, badass cop, had gone native.

The walls were decorated with hundreds of black-and-white photos of country-western singers. Some had shot to stardom while most faced obscurity. Tradition dictated that when a singer hit the big-time they returned to Rudy's and had their picture taken with Rudy. His image taken over decades covered the walls. No signs yet of KC with a big star but he'd said it was only a matter of time.

No band onstage tonight. Piped-in music blared overhead as Rick moved toward KC who filled a couple of beer mugs from a tap. When he set the mugs in front of a couple of women dressed in sparkling denim, he glanced up and caught Rick's gaze. He grinned and, grabbing a towel, wiped his hands before motioning to a second bartender and ducking out from behind the bar.

He extended a large hand to Rick. "Well, look what the damn cat dragged in."

Rick shook KC's hand and smiled. "Looks like you're staying out of trouble."

"Can't complain. We seem to pack them in night after night."

"There's life after the department?"

"Who knew? Where's Tracker?"

"Home. He was ready to call it a day. Georgia's staying at the Big House most nights."

"How's she doing?"

Rick shrugged. "Putting one foot in front of the other."

KC's smile faded to a troubled frown before he caught himself and straightened. "So what brings you down here?"

"I've come about Jenna Thompson."

"The artist?" A thin veil dropped over his expression and

Rick sensed he'd mentally shifted to attention. Was he expecting trouble or ready to defend Jenna? "What's up?"

"You know she's on leave from the Baltimore Police Department?"

He puffed his chest, a proud peacock. "She didn't say she was a cop but I knew right off she'd worn a badge. Something about the vibe."

"How'd you two meet?"

"She just showed up and ordered lunch. While she ate she started drawing me. Hard not to look." He jabbed his thumb toward a sketch tacked to the wall behind the bar. The pencil sketch had captured KC laughing.

"Hell of a picture."

"That's what I said." He cast another glance at the picture and then faced Rick. "She said if I let her draw pictures outside the bar, people would stop. Would really help with the families—the before-seven-P.M. crowd. Said she'd done it a good bit back East and always had a crowd. The overflow would come in here."

"Just like that."

He leaned in a fraction. "She didn't blink once and gave me the sense she was doing me the favor. I like confidence in a woman."

Rick could see KC had a slight crush on Jenna. Thirty-plus years separated them in age, but hell, a man could dream. "So you said yes?"

"I refilled her coffee and we chatted. Never can be too careful."

The bitterness humming below the surface hinted to KC's last girlfriend who'd done a number on him. He was cautious these days when it came to women.

"But you said yes."

"I thought it couldn't hurt. No skin off my nose to give it a few nights. Hell, I really expected her not to show."

"But she did."

"Right on time. And she was correct. She brings in business."

"How long she been here?"

"Two weeks. Her one night off is Monday. Come back tomorrow and you'll see her."

KC folded his arms over his chest, shoving a sigh free. "So what's the deal? She in some kind of trouble?"

"Does that surprise you?"

KC grinned. "My ex taught me never to judge a book by its cover. What did she do?"

"She's a forensic artist back East. She volunteered to help with a case."

"She came in and volunteered just like that?"

"Georgia asked for her help and Jenna agreed. I met her today."

"And you're trying to figure out why a young healthy cop would walk away from the job and end up drawing pictures in a honky-tonk."

Rick rested his hands on his hips. "That's about right."

"She has always been nice to me and does a good job. She gives me a ten-percent cut of her take and I put that in the tip jar for the waitresses. She's never caused trouble and people seem to like her."

"No red flags?"

He scratched the stubble on his thick jaw. "The best ones never wave the red flag."

"Right."

KC shook his head and his shoulders slumped a fraction as if he lumbered under a great weight. "Look, Georgia knows people. If she likes her then she must be okay. Be nice to think not everyone has an agenda."

Rick rubbed the back of his neck with his hand. "I hear

ya. I just like to know who's volunteering their services to me."

"We're not a very trustful pair."

Rick laughed. "You ever met a cop who didn't question an unsolicited gift or a kind gesture?"

"Not many. But I got to say, you're one of the worst. You're one hell of an untrusting soul."

"Guilty as charged."

"That broad Melissa did a number on you."

He could hear her name now and not wince. "Takes one to know one."

KC chuckled. "We're a sorry couple of sacks."

"Maybe." He scooped up a handful of nuts from the bowl on the bar. "If you hear anything about Jenna that I should be worried about, tell me."

KC considered the request before nodding. "Least I can do."

Chapter Three

As the sun rose, Rick and Tracker moved through the woods near his house. They enjoyed this time of day, when the only noise was the chirp of birds and the rustle of leaves. Morning starts were slow-going for both as they worked the kinks out of their joints. Neither relished that first roll out of the hay, but neither would have passed on the morning routine. They could out-tough anybody.

This early, the heat of the day had not taken hold of the city, the phone had generally not started ringing, and each could move at their own, sometimes uneven, pace. There'd been a time when they'd climbed the rocks into the mountains and enjoyed the stress and strain of the uphill climb. There was a time when they would have been gone for half the day.

These days, Rick stuck to the even path that ringed the woods surrounding the Morgan family house. The Big House was a hundred years old and located on thirty acres twenty miles south of Nashville near Franklin. Prime real estate. The home had been a wedding gift to his parents from his mother's parents. His father, Buddy Morgan, had been a legend in Nashville homicide and he'd had the good fortune to fall in love with a woman from money. They'd moved into the house days after their honeymoon and raised their three boys and daughter here. When his mother had died thirteen years ago, his dad had remained on the property mostly, he'd said, because he was close to his wife. Eighteen months ago, when Buddy had died of a heart attack after a steak dinner in his favorite diner, the house had gone to Rick's older brother, Deke. Deke wasn't a country boy and had taken the house out of family obligation, but he'd never loved the place. When Deke had finally opted to move into downtown Nashville, he had happily deeded the property to Rick.

A day after he'd moved in, he'd gutted the kitchen and knocked through the dining-room wall to make one large eat-in kitchen. As he'd pondered the next step in his life and he and Tracker had healed, he'd sanded floors, installed new cabinets, painted, and laid granite countertops.

Rick paused at the door to the screened porch and reached for a rag he kept on hand. Quickly, he wiped down Tracker's damp paws and underbelly before the two walked the ramp into the house. Ramps for Tracker had been another part of his renovation.

In the kitchen, he filled the water and food bowl for Tracker and then made himself a cup of coffee. As he sipped from a favorite UT mug, he grabbed a piece of left-over fried chicken from the fridge.

He had plans to renovate the bathrooms but when Deke had offered him the slot on homicide, he'd taken it without a second thought. The bathrooms were functional but in need of an upgrade that would have to wait for his next vacation.

After his own breakfast, he showered and shaved with careful precision. Dark eyes stared back at him from the mirror. Hooded and a bit flat, they reflected the trademark stubbornness that had dogged him since he was a kid. That stubbornness had bred arrogance and prompted him to walk up worriless to that vehicle last year. That stubbornness had gotten his canine partner and him shot. And that stubbornness would not allow him to give quarter, no matter how much his bones ached.

He dressed and a half hour later, he and Tracker were headed north into the city. This morning, he drove across the Victory Memorial Bridge toward the medical examiner's office. As he turned onto Rs Gass Boulevard, he passed the sleek offices of the Tennessee Bureau of Investigation where his brother Alex worked as an agent. A little farther down the road past an old building there was an old brick building that had once been an orphanage run by the Masons. He pulled into a parking spot in front of the office of the medical examiner.

He brought Tracker inside and after they were admitted beyond the lobby, the dog was able to follow him as far as the hallway outside the exam room. Rick ordered Tracker to sit in the hallway while he pushed through metal doors. There he found the medical examiner standing at the head of a stainless-steel table sporting a sheet-draped body.

In her mid thirties, Dr. Heller had moved to Nashville two years ago. She'd quickly won the respect of the officers who admired her work. A tall woman, with the long, lean body of a runner, she rarely wore makeup on her smooth olive complexion and always twisted her long, dark hair in a tight knot. Her blue eyes had an almond tilt that gave her an exotic beauty.

"Where's wolf dog?" Her lab coat covered a silk blouse and skinny jeans.

"In the hallway hanging out."

"How long will he just sit there?"

"Until I return." A handler and his canine operated as a

single unit and much was communicated with a look or a sound.

"How's his leg?"

"Not bad. No more running for him but he gets by."

"And how're you doing?"

"Me? I'm just fine." And that had been the party line since he'd woken up from his first surgery after the shooting. He'd never considered himself permanently injured or disabled. Never. "I hear you have the house fire victim."

"Finished the autopsy last night."

The doors to the room opened and Jake Bishop appeared. As always, he wore a crisp dark suit, dark shirt, and those damn polished cowboy boots. He moved with swagger.

"Good," Dr. Heller said. "The whole gang's here. I won't have to repeat myself."

Detective Bishop nodded. "Dr. Heller. How goes it? Looking lovely as always."

An amused brow arched as she removed rubber gloves from her white physician's jacket and moved to a wall of refrigerated body-storage cabinets. She donned the gloves and opened the second from the left. Inside lay a draped figure. A sheet covered the body's shriveled flesh and sinew eaten by the fire. She pulled back the sheet and revealed a blackened skull attached to a torso, singed black. Hands and feet had been burned away as had the arms to the elbow and the legs to the knees.

"Your victim was a female. I was able to take X-rays and as luck would have it, she had a hip implant that had a serial number on it. I've sent off a request to the manufacturer for a name of the doctor who implanted it."

"She was older?"

"No. Mid thirties. My guess is the implant came after an accident."

"Good work," Rick said.

"Your victim also didn't die as a result of the fire. She

was shot in the head. Judging by the hole made by the bullet at her right temple, I'd say she was shot at close range." Dr. Heller reached for an evidence bag, which contained a single slug. "She would've died instantly."

Rick took the bag and held it up. He guessed the gun had been a .45 caliber. "The fire was set to hide the forensic evidence."

Bishop shrugged. "Or because the killer likes fires."

A legitimate theory. Arsonists set fires for a variety of reasons. Some did it for profit, others to hide evidence, and others set their blazes because they liked to watch the flames dance and destroy.

"I X-rayed her bones and there're no signs of older breaks or traumas other than the hip. I've run some tests on what flesh I do have and am testing for drugs but I won't have toxicology test results for a few weeks on that."

Rick stared at the bullet hole in the side of the skull and tried to imagine how the murder had played out. Murphy had said the fire had frozen her extremities outstretched, leading him to believe that when she'd been shot, she'd likely been tied to the bed. Had the killer planned the murder and fire all along or had the fire been an afterthought? If he had to guess, he'd say very planned considering the amount of diesel found at the scene.

"As soon as we've a name, we can start putting the pieces together," Bishop said.

"Anything else you can tell me about her?"

"I estimate her height to be about five-seven. She was Caucasian."

Rick pulled his notebook from his breast pocket and scribbled down the details.

Dr. Heller pulled the sheet back over the body. "Keep me posted. I want to know who would work so hard to destroy all traces of another human being."

Rick nodded. "Sure. We'll make sure you get updates. How about the little Jane Doe's skull?"

"The child." A bitter edge had crept into her tone.

"Yes."

"I can't tell you much. At a young age, bones aren't fully formed so many of the markers that would tell me more aren't there."

"We spoke to the forensic artist yesterday," Rick said. "She's agreed to help."

Dr. Heller's solemn expression grew more severe. "Whom did you line up?"

"Her name's Jenna Thompson," Rick said. "She's a sworn officer in the Baltimore Police Department. She's taking leave and will be here a few more weeks."

"I've heard of Jenna Thompson," Dr. Heller said. "She has a good reputation."

"You've heard of her?"

"It's a small world. She's done some excellent work. I look forward to meeting her."

"I told her to be here by two this afternoon."

"Excellent." Dr. Heller moved to another cabinet and opened the drawer. Lying on the large slab was a collection of tiny bones.

Rick's chest tightened and, with some effort, he mentally took a step back to study the bones with a critical eye. "Georgia has the blanket and the bag and is going over both. Doubtful there'll be much but she's going over it with a fine-tooth comb. Missing Persons sent us files yesterday. We set aside files of all possible matches, but they need more information from you before we can narrow the search."

Dr. Heller folded her arms. "Jenna Thompson will give you a good likeness. And when she does, consider the media. They work with us on missing persons cases, especially when we're dealing with a child."

"The press." Rick kept the bulk of his frustration out of his voice. "Got to love 'em."

Dr. Heller grinned. "They aren't all bad, Detective."

He thought about the dash-cam video of his shooting that had played over and over again on the news stations. "I'll keep telling myself that."

Dr. Heller's phone buzzed and she checked the display. She answered the call and listened. When she hung up, she looked pleased. "We've a call back on the hip implant. The company was able to match the serial number of the implant with a name. Your victim is Diane Smith, age thirty-six."

Rick wrote down the name. "Damn, that was fast."

"The implant was installed ten years ago. I don't know if the address is still good."

"Hell, this is more of a break than I was expecting."

"Better to be lucky than smart," Detective Bishop said.

Rick heard the meaning simmering under Bishop's words but let it pass. Sooner or later they'd have a show-down about whatever was chewing on his ass, but not today. "Now that we've a name, we can get moving on this."

With Diane Smith's name in hand, it hadn't taken long to find her home address and employer's name. They opted to start with her employer, Temperance Real Estate. Rick dropped Tracker off with Georgia as she ended her shift and then he and Bishop drove to Temperance Real Estate, located in an historic stone building resting in the shadow of several sleek office buildings in downtown Nashville.

Temperance Real Estate offices were on the third floor of the building. After speaking with the company's reception-ist, who seemed a little rattled by the arrival of detectives, they were escorted to a corner office.

As they entered, a man moved out from behind a tall desk, buttoning his suit jacket as he moved. He shrugged broad shoulders and extended his hand first to Rick. "I'm Trent Lockwood. I own Temperance Real Estate. My secretary tells me you're homicide detectives."

"That's right," Rick said. "Rick Morgan."

Bishop held up his badge. "Jake Bishop. We're here to ask you a few questions about Diane Smith."

Lockwood's unnaturally dark hair was slicked back, sharpening the angles of a tanned, long face. He appeared to be in his early fifties, but preliminary recon before the interview put him in his sixties. His expensive, hand-tailored suit and gold cuff links spoke to the success his firm had enjoyed the last few years. Temperance and Lockwood had influenced three of the top ten Nashville development deals in the last two years.

A frown furrowed Lockwood's brow as he absently tugged on his cuffs. "She's one of our most productive real estate attorneys. Been with us about ten years. Why? Has something happened?"

Bishop studied the office, silent and content to let Rick handle the interview. Bishop had been giving Rick lots of opportunities on the cases and he suspected it had more to do with giving him enough rope so that he could hang himself.

"Does your company own a property in the West End? It's on Dover Street," Rick said.

Gray eyes narrowed as if Trent didn't appreciate the dodge to his question. "I've no idea. I'd have to look it up. Again, why?"

"Has anyone questioned why Diane didn't come in to work yesterday or today?"

"She's on vacation. She's been planning a trip to her cabin in the Smokey Mountains for months and finally texted in Saturday night that she was taking a break. She's closed big deals lately and deserved the time off."

He wondered if Diane had sent the texts. "Diane Smith's

body was found in the burned-out ruins of the Dover Street house yesterday."

The lines rimming Lockwood's eyes and mouth deepened. "Are you sure you've the right person?"

"We identified her from a hip implant. The serial number matched up to her name."

His face paled. "She wasn't recognizable?"

Rick studied his face closely. He'd developed a nose for liars since he'd joined the Force. Amazing how shocked and sad a really good liar could look when the spotlight shone on them. "No, sir. Not after the fire."

"My God." Lockwood's eyes held the right blend of surprise and shock, but no one earned this kind of money without a good poker face. "Did she have any trouble with coworkers or clients?"

Lockwood's buffed fingernails caught the light as he drummed his fingers. "No. She's a talented real estate attorney slated to be partner in this firm by the spring."

Bishop stared out the tall window behind Lockwood's desk. He took his time shifting his gaze back to Lockwood. "Did she have any business deals that went sour? Make anyone mad?"

"Not everyone wins in every deal. That's par for the course. Of course she bested other agents. That's why she was slated to be partner."

"What deals was she working on?" Rick asked.

"A new strip mall out on I-40. Several condo developments and a proposed housing project. All her work was high dollar with large profit margins."

"Anyone express anger over a deal recently?"

"Bob Boone wasn't happy with her."

"Bob Boone?"

"He works for a competitor. He lost out on a development bid last winter. He was angry and called Diane a few choice words. Didn't like losing to a woman. She's stepped on toes, but you've got to break a few shells to cook the eggs."

Diane had been most likely tied to a bed and shot at close range, both indicators that the killer had enjoyed controlling her last minutes. "Where can we find Bob Boone?"

Lockwood looked through contacts on his cell and rattled off a number and address. "He's got a reputation for his temper but he's well respected in the community. Active in his church."

Neither Rick nor Bishop commented, both knowing they'd arrested their share of respected, churchgoing men.

"Where did Diane Smith live?" Bishop asked.

"She just bought a new home near Franklin. It's an older home and she's restoring it. I do know she was having trouble with her landscape architect over a bill. I don't remember the name but if you visit her home you'll get the number from a neighbor. Also speak to her neighbors. I'm not sure it's the one to her left or right, but one of them wasn't happy with a tree she'd cut down a few weeks ago."

A real estate deal. A tree. A landscape job. People killed for far less.

"You said Diane worked here ten years?" Rick asked.

"That's right." The lines deepened with sadness. "She was one hell of an employee. She'll be missed."

After collecting Lockwood's alibi contacts, Rick and Bishop left Lockwood's office and climbed into Rick's car. "Why do I get the vibe that guy's not telling us all he knows?"

Bishop slid on his sunglasses. "Because he's not."

Rick fired up the engine. "We still have time before Jenna's scheduled to be at the medical examiner's office. Want to have a chat with the neighbor and Bob Boone?"

He scowled. "Would love to."

A half hour later, they arrived at the 1920s home that Diane had just purchased. Its color was a faded white that peeled and bubbled in several spots. Three stories high, it sported a wide front porch, faded blue gingerbread trim, tall gabled windows and a high-pitched tin roof that had dimmed from red to a muddy brown. Overgrown bushes blocked the view of the large bay window. An oak with a trunk at least three feet thick hovered close to the house. The roots were thick, reached into the foundation, and likely threatened the house's sewage system.

Rick had firsthand knowledge of old houses. He had learned a few valuable renovation lessons working on the Big House and just a glance told him that this place, though it had been a showpiece at one time, was going to cost a fortune to restore. "She must like a project."

Bishop shook his head in disbelief. "Must like to spend money. It's one hell of a money pit if you ask me."

To the right of the house were three large, freshly cut tree stumps as well as a large, empty construction dumpster. Judging by the size those trees had been at least eighty to one hundred years old.

"Computer search says that the neighbor, Toby Stewart, is the president of the local historic association. He's big on keeping the property as is."

"She made changes and it looks like she was going to make a whole lot more."

They walked around the side of the property into the backyard. Large stakes with orange flags marked a large square area that looked as if it was going to be a deck and maybe even a pool.

A glance at the back of the house showed five test strips of new paint color: white, gray, sapphire blue, fire engine red, and green. Rick couldn't imagine the red or blue was a viable choice. Maybe she'd done it to stoke the neighbors who'd given her a hard time for the trees.

Boxwoods warmed by the sun had released an acrid smell in the air that you either loved or hated. Several were marked with red flags that made him wonder if they would also go the way of the trees.

They walked back around to the front of the property in time to see a white van pull up in front of the house. A magnetic sign on the side of the front doors read STEWART RENOVATIONS.

A long, lanky man unfolded himself from the car, pausing long enough to adjust wire-rimmed glasses and straighten a thin, black tie. His gaze slid over Rick's car and to the detectives as they crossed the yard to him.

"I'm Toby Stewart." He spoke with the authority of a man in charge. "I'm president of the historic preservation association. And you are?"

"Detective Rick Morgan and this is my partner, Jake Bishop."

"Did someone finally call the cops on that woman?"

"That woman?"

"Diane Smith. What she's done to this property is a crime."

"What's she done?"

Eyes widened with surprise. "See the tree stumps? See the tree out front marked for destruction. See the outline of the addition and the pool. She's totally destroying the historic beauty of this house." A sneer curled his lip. "She's an attorney. A real estate attorney. Got it written into her mortgage that she could bypass the historic codes."

"She wasn't breaking any laws."

His eyes widened with outrage. "Not technically. But she shouldn't be changing so much."

"You two argue about this?"

"Several times. Over dinner last week, I told her the landscape architect she hired was a butcher."

"Dinner?" Bishop asked, as if he were bored.

"We've been out a few times. I like her. I thought we had

an understanding but then she cut down the trees and told me about the addition."

Rick looked at the house and shook his head as if he disapproved. "Sounds like you're mighty steamed."

He puffed out his chest as he rested a hand on his hip. "Steamed doesn't come close. Like I said, what she's doing is a crime."

Is. Not was. "When's the last time you saw her?"

"Three days ago, we talked about paint colors."

"That was Saturday?"

"Yes. Early in the morning. I saw the swatches. She threatened to paint the house red." He shook his head. "Money doesn't buy history or taste."

Rick kicked a rock with his boot. "A woman like that must get a lot of grief from neighbors?"

"Grief? I gave her plenty. And her landscape architect, Linwood Carter, I told her where to go."

"Looks like that tree is biting into the foundation," Rick said as he scribbled down the name of the landscape architect.

"Tree comes with lots of history that dates back to the Civil War. To lose it would be losing history." He cocked his head. "Why're you asking so many questions about Diane. She in some kind of trouble?"

"She's dead," Bishop said. "Murdered."

Stewart's mouth dropped open and he shook his head as if his brain wrestled with the words. "How? When?"

"Found her charred remains in a house in Nashville yesterday."

"What?" The thin face paled, whitening to ashen.

Delivering news of death was always a wild card. He'd witnessed the full range. Tears, screams, laughter, stunned stupors, shock, outrage. He wasn't interested in the reaction as the intent humming beneath the surface. He studied Stewart, paying close attention to the twitch tweaking the fingers of his right hand, the bead of sweat on his brow, and the flare of his nostrils as he breathed.

"Burned beyond recognition. Had to ID her with a hip implant."

Stewart dragged a trembling hand through his hair. "Shit."

"Yeah." He left out the detail of the gunshot wound to Diane's head. That tidbit he'd share only with a few cops and the killer. "Flesh and blood melted."

"God."

"When's the last time you saw her?" Bishop's even tone disarmed the repeated question designed to test Stewart. Whereas the truth came naturally, lying took work. Easier to trip up on stories hastily made up in panic. *Can you keep your stories straight?*

"Three days ago."

"You argued at dinner last week?" Rick countered.

He shook his head slowly. "Over the trees. She cut them down."

"Pissed you off." An edge sharpened Rick's words.

His gaze grew vacant as if he'd gotten lost for a moment and then he shook his head. "Yeah. But I didn't kill her. I didn't. Couldn't."

He could. Anyone could. Rick believed everyone had a magic combination that when dialed drove them to do just about anything, including tying a neighbor to a bed, shooting her in the head, and setting the house on fire. Stewart wasn't the kind of guy who had it in him to destroy a tree or an old house, but Rick suspected a difficult neighbor or a one-story house in the West End was fair game. "Where were you two nights ago, Mr. Stewart?"

"Two nights ago?" he echoed. "Sunday night. I was at the gym until seven and then went to an Italian restaurant for dinner. I had a taste for pasta."

"Where'd you sleep?" Rick asked.

"In my own bed."

"Got a name of the restaurant?" Bishop pressed the tip of his pen to his notebook. Diane had been killed in the middle of the night so where Stewart ate didn't really matter. But the more details they gathered the more lies Stewart would have to remember.

Outrage flashed in Stewart's gaze. "Why do I have to give you a name? I told you I didn't do it."

A smile tugged the edges of Rick's lips. "Believe it or not, I've heard that line before."

"But I'm innocent!"

"Names," Bishop said.

Stewart huffed out a ragged sigh and then rattled off the name of his gym and the restaurant, even giving them the name of the waitress who'd served him. Bishop wrote it all down.

Rick shifted his stance and cursed the uneven ground bearing on his left leg. "Anyone else you think might have wanted to hurt Diane?"

"She wasn't a nice woman," he rushed to say. "She did what she wanted, when she wanted and she irritated a lot of people."

"No one specific?"

He seemed to think as if he groped and scraped for another name to feed the cops so they would leave with a fresh suspect. "None that come to mind."

"None?" Rick taunted.

"No, but there're others." The sentence crested in a high tone.

"You'll call when you've a list."

"Yeah."

Rick nodded, not willing to let him off the hook. "We'll keep in touch, Mr. Stewart."

Stewart shook his head like a child caught with his hand in the cookie jar. "It was just a few trees."

Rick's thoughts strayed to the aspirin in his glove box. He could use a few now. "I know. Just a few trees." He turned to Bishop. "Let's see if Boone or Carter had bigger issues with Diane Smith."

Susan Martinez sat at her computer screen typing out the story she'd read on the six o'clock news. She'd spent a frustrating day calling her contacts in the Nashville Police Department, trying to find out if the cops had identified the body pulled from the house fire. She'd covered her share of fires and murders in the last thirty years and she'd developed a sixth sense that alerted her to a high-profile murder. Right now, her senses buzzed.

At the fire, when she'd seen homicide detectives Morgan and Bishop inspect the carnage, she'd known by their grim expression the victim had not died by accident.

She'd put in a few calls to Morgan but he'd ignored her, as had Bishop. Eventually, Morgan would include her but he'd stretch it out as long as he could. She'd questioned his judgment on air. When she'd cornered Rick after his release from the hospital and asked him about the shooting, she'd seen the muscle in his jaw tighten and the fingers on his left hand curl into a fist. He'd not spoken to her but she'd known that day she'd burned a bridge.

If she had a nickel for all the people she'd upset over the years, she'd be worth millions. She wasn't paid to play nice. People liked to turn their televisions on in the evening and get the scoop. They didn't care how she got the details, only that she did.

"Susan, how's the copy coming?"

She turned toward the voice of the new general manager, Andy Bolen. He was a young guy, not more than thirty. With his tall stature, muscles, and thick blond hair, she

could have invited him into a few of her dreams if not for
the fact she was old enough to be his mother and he considered her ancient. He was also trying to force her out in favor
of younger reporters willing to do her job for half the pay.

If not for her coverage of the Jeb Jones retrial last year
and the national exposure her reporting had garnered, she'd
have been gone by now. But the glow of that story had all
but faded and no amount of Botox or decades' worth of experience was going to save her career. She needed another
big story soon.

However, when she smiled up at him, none of that worry
reflected in her green eyes as she sat a little straighter. "Will
be ready in a half hour."

"Cops talk to you?"

"Not yet, but I'm working on them."

"We could send in Brandy."

Ah, Brandy, the cub reporter who looked as if she still
had one foot in college or maybe even high school. She
couldn't tell anymore. They got younger and younger every
year.

"What would she be able to do that I haven't?" Susan
asked. "The cops aren't talking."

"She can sweet-talk just about anyone," Andy countered.

Cops barely respected her and she'd been covering them
for three decades. They sure as hell weren't going to talk to
a baby. "I've got a couple of leads, but they'll only talk
to me."

Andy studied her and she sensed that no matter what she
said, Brandy would be covering this story soon. "Let me see
the copy when you have it."

"I'm reporting this story."

"I didn't say you weren't." He folded his arms, a sign
he'd soon be real trouble.

Cat and mouse. They could dance all afternoon if she had the patience. "I'm not stupid, Andy."

A brow arched. "No, you're not. Look, Susan, you know the drill. Brandy has tested well with viewers. Your tests have not been as positive in the last few months."

She picked up a pencil and held it so tight in her hands she could feel the wood bending, bowing to the point of snapping. "Smart but bitchy . . . I remember that from one of the focus groups."

He slid a hand into his pocket. "That's about it."

"Andy, I thought we were better than cotton-candy news."

"We are. We've got the awards to prove it."

"Many of which, I earned."

"Susan." Her name traveled over a long sigh. "If I don't keep the ratings high, we're all going to be out of a job."

So you throw me under the bus to buy you another year on the job before you move on to greener pastures. As much as she wanted to argue, any argument wouldn't save her. She considered the pills in her purse. They'd bring emotions into focus, but they'd also take the edge off and right now she needed every edge she could sharpen.

Only a great story would buy her more time.

And she'd walk over hot coals to get one.

Chapter Four

Jenna glanced up at the concrete building that housed the Nashville Police Department and tightened her fingers around the strap of her satchel purse. As she'd dressed for the appointment, she'd had a moment of panic, wishing she'd had her uniform to wear. In her uniform, with the Baltimore Police Department badge pinned to her chest, she'd felt armored, buffered from worries.

But in Nashville, she was on her own. There was no Force, no friends, and no distractions to keep her nerves calmed. An hour ago, when her nerves had rattled and jangled, she'd considered canceling. This was not her town. She wasn't here to stay or put down roots. There were many reasons not to help, but in the end she realized she'd keep the appointment. Not for Morgan, Bishop, Georgia, or even her own pride. But for the Lost Girl.

So as a compromise, she'd opted to wear a makeshift uniform: dark slacks, a white blouse, and flats. She'd chosen simple gold-hoop earrings and a small cross, which nestled in the hollow of her neck. Instead of twisting her hair into a regulation bun secured at the base of her head, she'd worn her hair loose as a reminder to herself that here, she was not a cop but a volunteer.

She came into the city six nights a week to draw street portraits, but she was discovering she didn't enjoy the noisy fast pace. Too many people. Too much buzzing of needless activity. But she kept returning to joke with KC and to study the endless stream of faces that passed by her easel. And KC was one of the few fragile links to her past that she wouldn't let go. She'd researched this town when she'd arrived, pulling old newspaper articles at the library on those nine days she'd been lost. KC Kelly had been one of the cops on her case. One day, she'd screw up the courage to ask what he remembered.

As she approached the medical examiner's office, Morgan's Lost Girl triggered one memory after another, each jostling the next like falling dominoes until she was remembering her last call in Baltimore.

Though she was a trained forensic artist, she worked the streets several shifts a month to keep her skills sharp. She and her backup had responded to a domestic call. Man and woman fighting. Neighbors reported sounds of shattering glass and one thought they'd heard a gunshot. That night there had been the roar of cars racing on side streets, honking horns, and people shouting in back alleys.

Jenna and Officer Gus Bradford had guns drawn as they approached the crumbling row house, tattooed in spray-painted gang signs, and ringed with broken glass and trash. A cat had howled as they'd climbed the stairs. Though the streets were alive with people and chaos, there'd been no noise from inside the house; in fact, the house had been as quiet as a tomb.

But the hair on the back of her neck had been standing up and her stomach had been churning. Quiet did not mean safe. Gus had stood to the side of the door and rapped hard while she'd remained at the bottom of the front stairs, the flesh of her hand pressing into the cold metal of her Glock.

When there'd been no answer, he'd banged harder. Shouted, "Police!" And then there'd been the twin gunshots. *Bam! Bam!*

Gus had kicked in the door and they'd found the man and woman dead on the avocado-green kitchen floor, blood pooling around her chest and his head. The male had been clutching the gun. The female had been shot in the head, a terrified expression frozen on her face. Murder-suicide.

She'd called it in and the two had begun a room-to-room search. She'd climbed the darkened stairs to the second floor and moved slowly down the long hallway, carefully, her heart pounding as it always did when she had a room-to-room search. All clear so far. And then she'd reached the back room.

Seeing the closed closet door had ignited a fear that had flashed and burned hotter and hotter as she moved closer. Little had really rattled her during her nine years on the job, but moving toward that closet had triggered her heart to race and pound against her chest and Kevlar vest. Her shirt and undershirt had been soaked in sweat.

She'd laid trembling fingers on the door handle and opened it slowly. At first she found no signs of life. The closet was large and dark but it smelled of urine, fouled clothes, and rotted food. And then, she'd heard a faint rustle and she'd shone her flashlight into the dark recesses of the closet. When her light landed on the face of a young girl, Jenna had started and nearly dropped the flashlight. The child had long, matted, black hair and a large, stained, white T-shirt engulfed her thin frame. She had stared at Jenna with a gaze hovering closer to feral than human. A loud mew had escaped the child as she shielded startled eyes that winced under the light's glare.

In that moment, Jenna was the child. This little girl

hadn't been rescued in nine days, but had languished in that closet for years.

You are the lucky one.

Lucky.

Yes, she had been lucky but the luck had exacted a price. She'd been rescued from the closet but a dark fear had remained lurking silently for nearly twenty-five years. And now it was free.

She'd called for her partner, heard the hiss of his breath when he'd seen the child. She'd kept it together until rescue crews had arrived. The next day she'd filed her report and requested leave. Baltimore, like a skin that had grown far too tight, was squeezing the life out of her.

"Lady, are you going inside or not?"

She turned to find the assessing gaze of a woman with red hair and dark-rimmed glasses.

Jenna mumbled an apology and then reached for the cold metal handle of the door and entered the building. She crossed to the information desk, gave her name, showed her driver's license. She accepted a visitor's badge and as she pinned it to the collar of her shirt, she faced the window that overlooked the parking lot and rolling fields. The receptionist announced her name over the telephone.

Five minutes later, a side door opened and a tall woman with dark hair and almond eyes appeared. She crossed to Jenna, her strides smooth and exuding an enviable confidence.

The woman extended a long hand with nails that had been cut short and buffed. "I'm Dr. Miriam Heller. You're Jenna Thompson?"

Jenna accepted the outstretched hand. "Yes."

"I understand you're going to help us with an identification."

"That's correct."

"Do you have your supplies?"

"They're in the car. I wanted to see where I'd be working before I started unpacking. They can be bulky and unwieldy." In Baltimore, she'd had a small office that had been her base of operations. People came to her so it wasn't necessary for her to pack her equipment unless she was visiting a victim in the hospital.

"I've the specimen and as soon as Detectives Morgan and Bishop arrive, we can decide where you can do your work."

She would have liked to work in her studio at home. There she had the sunlight and the space to create. But the cops, worried about the chain of custody, would never release the skull to her. When she came up with a face, cops would have to defend her work in court and that meant keeping a strict eye on the evidence.

"Of course."

Dr. Heller glanced at a simple black watch on her wrist and checked the time. "Detective Morgan called me minutes ago and said they were on their way. Another case pulled them away."

"No need to explain. I understand."

Dr. Heller slid her hands into the pockets of her white lab coat. "You worked for Baltimore Police Department, didn't you?"

"I've been with them for nine years. I'm currently on leave."

Questions sparked in the doctor's gaze but she didn't voice them. "I've seen some of your work. Very impressive."

"Thanks."

"The detectives can meet us in the exam room."

"Sure."

"Mind if we take the stairs? About all the exercise I get when I'm working long days are the stairs."

"Love the stairs."

As they moved toward the locked door, Dr. Heller swiped her key card and the door opened. Jenna stepped through with the doctor on her heels. As the doctor turned to close the door a deep masculine voice called out, "Dr. Heller!"

They turned to see Rick Morgan and Jake Bishop entering the building. Detective Morgan moved with a controlled, steady gait, his gaze resting squarely on Jenna. She sensed the detective did not like her. Whereas Detective Bishop didn't seem to care one way or the other about her, Morgan acted as if he had a burr under his saddle when it came to her.

You quit.

He wouldn't be the first cop to criticize her. She refused to justify her choices.

Morgan flashed his badge to the receptionist behind the glass and he and his partner joined Jenna and the doctor. As Dr. Heller headed to the stairwell, Morgan hesitated and Jenna sensed him brace before nodding to Dr. Heller to lead the way. He kept pace with them and the four made their way down to the exam room. The doctor escorted them to a stainless-steel table where a box sat.

Dr. Heller donned rubber gloves and then lifted the lid off the box. Gently, she removed the small skull as the others gathered around. "The skull belongs to a female, who would've been about five when she died. I determined age based on the presence of baby teeth still in place. If the child had been six or older, there's a good chance some of the front teeth would've been missing." She turned the skull sideways. "Also note the delicate ridge of bone above the eye sockets is slight, suggesting female. And based on the width of her nasal cavity, I'd say she was Caucasian."

"Do the bones tell you anything else about the victim?" Morgan asked.

Dr. Heller's face grew more solemn. "Malnutrition. Her bones are brittle, which suggests to me she didn't eat well."

Jenna thought about the confines of the closet that had been her prison for nine days. Many nights, she'd been hungry and her belly had ached. "Did she starve to death?"

"No," Dr. Heller said as she turned the skull revealing spiderweb-like cracks. "Blunt force trauma to the head. A single blow. It would've killed her almost instantly."

"Suggestions on the object?" Morgan asked.

"Maybe a fist. A wall. A hammer would've left a small indentation. It also could have been a fall. One hard push back and, if she hit a hard surface, that would have done it."

The four stood silent for a moment as the doctor carefully set the skull down.

"May I hold the skull?" Jenna asked.

Dr. Heller handed her gloves. "Sure."

Carefully, Jenna donned the gloves and then gently lifted the skull. Light, fragile, so delicate. She turned the skull over, staring into the empty eye sockets. Already, she imagined the muscles that banded across a human face and gave it shape and depth. She imagined skin, hair and, of course, the eyes.

"How long will it take you to give her a face?" Detective Morgan asked.

"A week." That was a conservative estimate. Already she knew she'd put aside her portrait work and make this job her priority. This child deserved a face. An identity. She studied the nasal cavity. "Any other thoughts about her appearance that would be helpful?" Jenna already knew when she created the face it would be smiling. The child deserved to be remembered as happy.

"She was found only with the pink blanket," Detective Morgan said. "We don't know anything else about her."

Jenna set the skull down, her body already humming with a need to work. It had been like this in Baltimore. Her need to create a face, a likeness, of a killer, rapist, or lost soul was always powerful. The Baltimore cops had called her the Mistress of Lost Souls, a moniker she'd always thought fitting.

The walls of the exam room tightened and the craving to be in her brightly lit studio tugged hard. "My supplies are in my car. I can bring them in and get started as soon as possible."

Dr. Heller glanced at the clock. "You want to start today?"

"I can work for a few hours this afternoon." She'd be late getting to KC's tonight but decided the tourists could wait.

"I don't see how you can create a face," Detective Morgan said.

"Just know that I can," Jenna said.

Dr. Heller's gaze sparked with approval. "I've set aside an office space that's all yours for as long as you need it."

"I'll help you bring in your supplies," Officer Morgan said.

Her skin prickled at what sounded more like an order than an offer. What was he expecting? Her to go to her car and not return? For her to quit?

As much as she'd have liked to refuse his help, she wasn't foolish. Many hands made light the work as her aunt used to say. Let him lug the easel.

"I'm parked out front."

Detective Morgan held out his hand, telling her to lead the way. As she moved into the hallway, the elevator doors dinged opened and Georgia appeared. She wore jeans, a blue blouse, and red cowboy boots, and had twisted her red hair into a topknot that left a sprinkle of curls free to frame her face. Despite her choice of soft colors, it only took a glance to see that intensity all but radiated around her. Her movements were crisp and her steps short, clipped, and hard as if she were annoyed. She was like that onstage, a trait many of the men seemed to like.

Georgia, Tracker at her side, appeared to check an invisible box in her head. "Good, you're here. Have you started work?"

"What're you and Tracker doing here?" Detective Morgan challenged. "I thought you were done for the day?"

"I was and then after I took Tracker for a walk I got to thinking about this meeting. I thought I'd touch base. And you know how Tracker likes to ride in the car."

No good-evenings or how's-it-goings for Georgia or her brother. This clan cut to the chase.

When Jenna had met her at KC's that first night, she wasn't sure if she'd liked Georgia. No doubt, the woman had real singing talent, but she could be cutting and direct. After they'd crossed paths the third night, she'd found the forensic tech's brutal directness had its own charm. She'd not been able to say the same for Rick Morgan.

"Good afternoon," Jenna said.

Georgia blinked, nodded, as if computing the words. And then she seemed to realize she'd skipped a pleasantry. "Yeah, hey. Have you started yet?"

"She's known for her lack of tact," Detective Bishop said. "A real steamroller."

Detective Morgan glanced at his partner and then looked tempted to tease Georgia as well. But something in his sister's glare stopped him short. He knew when not to poke the bear.

Teasing was what siblings did. She'd had a sister once but remembered little about her older sister, Sara, who had been eleven years older than Jenna. Blond, pretty, and popular, Sara, in Jenna's last memories of her, had been a girl with sights set on becoming captain of the high school cheer squad and president of the student government. Sara had been nice to Jenna from what she could remember but other than the occasional family dinner, their paths didn't cross much toward the end.

"Georgia, this is your afternoon off. I've got this," Detective Morgan said.

"I know. I know." Georgia shifted her gaze to Jenna. "Where're you headed? You aren't leaving, are you?"

Jenna bristled at Georgia's tone, which silently asked *Are you quitting?* "No."

Bishop reached past Georgia and pressed the elevator's DOWN button. "Bright and happy as usual, Georgia."

Georgia glared at the detective. "What's that mean, Bishop?"

Bishop looked bored. "Don't you ever get tired of running the show?"

Georgia seemed to consider the question for a split second. "No."

Bishop shrugged. "Not surprising."

Georgia's lips flattened. "I've words I could sling like knives, Yank, but I won't."

"Have at it, princess."

Tracker yawned, as if he'd heard similar squabbles before. Jenna's mood eased. Clearly, Georgia chewed on everyone's ass. "We're going to my car to get my supplies. I start work now."

The elevator doors opened, and Detective Bishop stepped inside. He held the door open with his hand.

Georgia stepped inside and pushed the OPEN button. "Let's get this party started."

Jenna, Detective Morgan, and Tracker joined the two in the elevator while Dr. Heller remained behind. "I'll see you in a few minutes."

"I'll be waiting."

The doors closed. Jenna stood in the back next to Georgia and Tracker. The two detectives stood in the front of the elevator, feet braced as if ready for trouble. This close she could smell the scent of Morgan's soap. His shoulders were wide and his stance rigid, radiating a bullish stubbornness that she wasn't sure was an asset or liability. This guy never quit.

She glanced down at the dog, and on reflex scratched him between the ears. He didn't seem to mind her touch and she felt an odd kinship with him. Both were cops relegated to the outside.

On the first floor, the doors dinged open and the four walked down the hallway and into the lobby.

"Guys," Georgia said. "I'll help Jenna with the supplies. You head out. I heard you've got a lead on the murder and house fire."

Jenna's ears perked. Once a cop always a cop. What house fire? What murder? But she didn't ask for details, knowing she wasn't enough of an insider to hear. "It will take Georgia and me one trip. No reason to hold you two up."

Bishop shrugged. "Will do."

Detective Morgan hesitated, as if he had more to add but, in the end, nodded and he and Tracker followed his partner.

Jenna was sorry to see the dog go. An offer to hang on to the dog for the afternoon rose in her throat but she swallowed it. She did not need attachments.

Georgia watched him walk away, her gaze narrowing as she studied his gait before turning to Jenna. "I'm here to help."

With Detective Morgan gone, the tension banding her muscles eased a fraction. "This is your afternoon off. I've got this. I've hauled supplies more times than I can count."

"Nope. I'm here to help. I want you working as soon as possible."

As Jenna unlocked the door on her Jeep, she glanced at Georgia. "Thanks for the help, but why're you here?"

"As Detective Bishop mentioned, I've control issues. I brought you into the loop."

"And you want to make sure I deliver."

"Basically."

Jenna shrugged. "Fair enough. I'd have done the same if you were in my backyard in Baltimore."

"This is personal for you."

"I could say the same for you."

Georgia's gaze sharpened as if she were searching for the smallest forensic crime-scene detail. "I'm giving up a few hours. You're giving up a few days. Why?"

She opened the back tailgate of the Jeep. "A child was killed. I guess we're all feeling it."

Georgia shook her head. "No. It's more for you. I can sense it."

"Really?" She kept her tone light as she reached for a box filled with clays, paints, and sculpting tools. "How can you tell?"

"It's a gift," she said.

Jenna's laugh had a nervous edge. "What're you, some kind of psychic?"

Georgia folded her arms. "I can read people like books."

Jenna didn't doubt she could read most people, but she wasn't most people. She was good at hiding her thoughts, emotions, and plans. "Really?"

"Since the day you came into KC's you snapped like a live electrical cord."

"I'm a cop. We can leave the job but it doesn't quite leave us. KC's no different, nor were the half-dozen off-duty cops sitting in the bar on any given night."

"Yeah. We're not good at turning it off." She held out her arms. "I'm a prime example of not being able to leave it at the office. But you're different."

"I'm not sure what you're digging for, Georgia. But you aren't going to find anything interesting." That wasn't true. If Georgia did some digging she'd find a long, sordid story about Jenna in the archives of the Nashville Police Department.

"My instincts are never wrong."

"That so?" Jenna lifted a box and dumped it into Georgia's outstretched arms.

"Yeah."

Jenna hefted the second box containing an easel and a few other necessities, closed the back tailgate, and locked the Jeep. "Most of us have a personal gripe they're working through. Cops don't like not being in the know. Part of what brings us to the job."

"All true."

They walked back to the building and took the elevator down to a small, windowless room. The boxed skull remained in the center of the table, waiting for the identity that Jenna had promised.

"Is there anything else I can do for you?" Georgia asked as she set down the box.

Jenna placed her box next to the other. "No. It's all me now. If your brother ends up with a missing persons report that fits let me know. Otherwise, I'll catch up with you when I finish."

Georgia slid her hands in her back pockets and had the look of someone who didn't want to leave. Almost seemed to dread it.

As much as Jenna wanted to include Georgia this process was a personal, solitary job. "I don't work with an audience."

"Even one that's quiet and sits in the corner."

"Even one of those." She smiled to soften the rejection. "I promise to keep you posted."

Georgia moved toward the door. "Well, I'll leave you to it."

"Georgia." She hesitated, reaching for a word she rarely

used. "Thanks for bringing up my name. This is a good deed I can do and I'm glad for the opportunity."

She hesitated, her hand on the doorknob. "I really want to catch this killer."

Jenna nodded as she slowly pulled out a sketchpad. "I know. So do I."

Rick dropped Bishop off at headquarters and after a quick walk with Tracker the two were back in his vehicle. "Ready to catch a bad guy, boy?"

The dog barked.

Soon the two were headed to the home of a woman named Lorrie Trent, Diane Smith's sister, who had filed a missing persons report just hours before the fire. Lorrie Trent owned a small bakery in East Nashville.

With evening traffic building, the drive over the Cumberland River to the bakery took him about thirty minutes. When he arrived, he left Tracker in the backseat, the car still running and the air-conditioning blowing out cool air.

He crossed the parking lot and pushed through the front door of the bakery. Jangling bells above his head and the scents of cookies and cakes greeted him.

Two females stood behind the counter—one a teen and the other a woman who appeared to be in her thirties. The duo waited on several customers. Rick opted to stride toward the older one. She had dark hair, skimmed back into a tight ponytail, and wore a white shirt, faded jeans, and an apron that crisscrossed around her full waist and tied in the front.

As Rick reached for his badge, the woman's gaze rose as if she'd been expecting him. She reached for a white towel, wiped her hands, and after speaking to the teen moved around the counter toward him.

He noticed a resemblance to Diane Smith. Though their

coloring was different, their eyes shared the same watery blue and each had full lips that tilted at the corners.

He showed her his badge. "Ms. Lorrie Trent?"

She nodded. "Yes. You're here about Diane?"

"Is there somewhere we can talk in private?"

She flexed her fingers. "Why don't we go into my office? We can talk there."

Behind the counter and through a kitchen, they moved into a small, cramped office stocked with shelves crammed full of cookbooks and file holders. "You've come about Diane?"

"I have."

She drew in a steadying breath as if reading his expression as a harbinger of bad news. "Have you found her?" She twisted the apron strings around her hands. "I tried to file a missing persons report. She missed our Monday dinner appointment. The officer said she'd only been gone a few hours and he couldn't activate the report until today."

Lorrie had a Monday dinner appointment with Diane. So why had Diane sent a text to her boss about an impromptu vacation and not her sister? Siblings fought. He had his own cold war going on with his brother Alex. "Ma'am, Diane was murdered."

Blue eyes widened and filled with tears. "What?"

"We found her body in a burned-out building yesterday. We only made the identification today."

Pressing fingertips to her temples she sat down in the lone chair in front of the desk. "She was burned alive?"

"No, ma'am." He studied her pale face wondering how he'd react if he'd received similar news about Alex. A stabbing feeling cut, leaving him vacant and sad. Alex might be a dick but he'd never wish him ill. "We believe she was dead before the fire was set."

Tears welled and spilled easily down her cheeks. She

didn't bother to swipe away her tears. Her hands trembled as she fingered the apron strings.

This kind of news rocked foundations. Devastated lives. Murder happened in other places, bad neighborhoods, to people who'd crossed some kind of line that divided good from bad.

Finally, Lorrie cleared her throat. "How did Diane die?"

"We aren't releasing that information yet." He shoved his pity aside for her. As sad as Lorrie appeared he took a mental step back. She could get comfort from a friend. What she needed from him was an objective mind. Diane deserved justice.

"I don't understand why anyone would want to kill her? She was well liked and the sister that everyone respected. She had a super job and was making money hand over fist. She was the one that my parents had always pinned their hopes on before they died. I'm the fuck-up dreamer."

Thoughts strayed to his brother Alex. Their dad had called him the Golden Boy. "Was she dating anyone? Was there anyone in her life that made you worry or think twice?"

"A guy in her neighborhood. And a guy at another real estate firm. I don't remember names, but neither one liked the fact that she was smarter and wouldn't allow them to be in charge. Diane's a woman who knows her own mind." She frowned. "Knew her own mind."

He shifted his stance. "And you two got on well enough."

"We fought sometimes. We're sisters." A sigh shuddered through her. "Stupid fights."

"What did you fight about?"

She pulled at a white towel tucked in her apron string and wiped her eyes. "Lately, we argued about money." She muttered an oath. "I asked her for a loan and she said she'd have to do a cost analysis on the bakery. I was pissed but I needed the money so I went along."

"What happened?"

"Diane said the bakery was a losing investment. I tried to tell her it was my dream but she'd said numbers were numbers. I hadn't spoken to her in a month. Monday's dinner was supposed to be my chance to apologize. She was right. The bakery is losing money."

"Why did you try to file a report? Why didn't you just assume she just didn't want dinner with you?"

"When I had a chance to think I realized she's never missed an appointment in her life. She just doesn't blow people off, even sisters who're too emotional."

"When was the last time you two spoke?"

"Like I said, nearly a month ago." She swiped tears with the back of her hand. "We communicated about dinner via text."

"What did you do after she didn't show for dinner?"

"I called her cell. No answer. Then I called her office. They said she was taking a day off. That didn't sound like Diane. I've seen her work through a raging case of the flu and another time after hip replacement surgery. Vacation days are spent working on her house. She never rests. And if she did take a day off, she'd have told me."

Would he know if something had happened to Alex? Rick could fix just about anything but he'd been unable to push past his own anger to fix his broken relationship with his younger brother. "So you sensed trouble."

"I went to her house. No lights. No sign of her. This isn't Diane. We've our differences but I know trouble, so I went to the cops. And like I said, they weren't convinced she was missing." She rubbed her eyes. "Shit. To think she might've needed my help and I couldn't do anything."

Family, friends, or acquaintances committed most murders. A year ago, he'd been mad enough to strike out hard against Alex. He would've regretted the act later but in that hot moment his combination had been dialed. "She was last seen at her office on midday Saturday. The fire was set late Sunday night."

Lorrie's eyes widened as she considered the statement. "That's a thirty-six-hour gap. What happened to her during that time?"

"We don't know. Her ATM card wasn't used, nor were her credit cards. Somewhere between her office and her home, she went off the grid."

She sobbed. "You mean she was taken to a house that burned to the ground."

"Yes, ma'am."

Fresh tears filled her eyes and spilled down her cheeks. "Who would do this to her? It doesn't make sense."

"That's what we're trying to figure out."

The recording tape played on a small computer screen, glowing bright in the darkened room. On screen, the woman, Diane, was tied to the bed, spread-eagle. She stared past the man holding the gun toward the camera and the one she knew really directed this dark scene.

Reason sat back, disgusted at the display. Such unnecessary damage. "That should satisfy you. That should fill your belly so you can take a long slumber."

Madness growled. *"I'm still hungry and restless for more."*

Trembling fingertips reached out to the computer monitor and circled the image of the woman's terrified face. "That moment required months of planning."

"Yes, and it paid off with a rush so delicious, didn't it." Madness had howled in satisfaction.

"We need to lie low for a while. Take a break. Let the cops move onto a new murder."

Madness stared at the computer screen. In the next picture frame, pawn looked at master, waited for permission, and when it was finally given, shot the woman. And like the snap of fingers, the moment was over. The energy deflated from the room as if they'd burst a balloon.

Pop.

Gone.

Madness had shivered in the wake of the orgasmic rush. It closed its eyes and lay back, searching for satisfaction. *"I'm still hungry. I need more."*

"That's why we made the recording. So you could watch whenever you wanted. Be content with that."

This little scene had stirred Madness's cravings, much like bread stimulated the taste buds of a starving man. The taste was just enough to remind it of what it had been missing.

"It's not enough. I want another taste." Raising a frustrated gaze from the computer, Madness, no longer willing to be a silent partner, studied a Peg-Board with neatly arranged images of several women. The shots were candid. One woman was leaving a gym, another was waiting for a cab, and the third was in a bar.

Extending from each woman's image was a red string and that string extended across the board to the images of different men.

Three women. Three men. The two sets were puppets in plays yet to be staged. The players in these productions had been chosen months ago. They had been the understudies in case the Diane performance had failed.

"I want to do it again."

"No. I won't allow it. Sister is already worried about us."

Sister. Worried. Allow. Madness smiled. *"Do you really think Sister or you can stop me?"*

"We stopped you before."

"It had suited me to be stopped. I saw the danger around us."

"It's around us again!"

"We're older. More clever. We can get away with more."

Madness zeroed in on the image of a woman with pale white skin and long, dark hair. It had been watching her for weeks and planned to wait several months before it put her into play. Usually, just the planning, the knowing a kill was within reach, was enough. But not now. The restless energy burned with a roaring vengeance.

"Sit back and study the board. Give the game time to settle. Give the cops time to forget about the last play. Let the drama die down."

"No."

Reason could feel control slipping away and Madness's desires grew stronger. "Please, wait!"

Pulsing energy tapped inside their skull. *"No, I want to play again. All the loose ends on this production have been handled, so why not set up another play?"*

"Not now, please!"

"Shh. It will be all right. No one will catch us," Madness whispered. *"Just one more. One more. And I will return to the shadows and leave you alone."*

"You swear?"

"I swear."

Chapter Five

Wednesday, August 16, 12:21 A.M.

The phone rang fifteen minutes after Rick closed his eyes. The hope of three or four hours of shut-eye dashed, he groaned, rolled on his side, and flipped open his phone. "Morgan."

"This is Officer McDonald. We've a body in an alley off Fourth Street. An overdose."

He lay back on the pillow and closed his eyes. "Why're you calling me?"

"We found Diane Smith's photo in his pants pocket. Written across the image was the word *faithless*."

Rick sat up, energy surging through his body. "You're sure it's Diane Smith."

"Saw her picture at the briefing before the shift."

He swung his legs over the side of the bed and stretched his neck from side to side. Skimming his hand over his short, dark hair, he rose. "I'll be there in sixty minutes. Have you contacted Bishop?"

"Not yet."

"I'll do it."

"Sure."

He padded toward his bathroom, past a waking Tracker, and switched on the shower. He called Bishop and relayed the information. As Bishop asked Rick to repeat details, a woman's voice sounded in the background. The voice sounded pouty, tired. "I'll be there in forty-five minutes."

"Right."

As coffee brewed, he took a quick shower and within fifteen minutes he and Tracker were headed toward Nashville. This time of night, there was no traffic so the drive was quick. When they arrived at the alley, two squad cars blocked either end, their blue lights flashing against the building's brick walls.

Spotting Bishop by the yellow crime-scene tape, he got out of his car, stifled a groan, and moved toward the body. The smell of death was heavy and putrid. Whoever they'd found had been here a while.

Bishop glanced up at him, nodded, and reached in his pocket for a set of black rubber gloves. Both officers donned gloves and, with the forensic tech's approval, ducked under the tape and moved toward a dumpster. Behind the green, dented trash bin was the body, now covered with a yellow tarp.

Rick squatted, grateful his hip cooperated, and pulled back the cover. Lying facedown on the damp asphalt was a man who appeared to be in his late thirties. He had long, dark hair, a thick, muscled body, and wore tattered jeans and a black shirt. Tattoos of skulls and twisting vines snaked up each bloated arm under his shirt to his neck. Rick turned the man's arm over and counted five needle marks. He lifted the dead man's curled fingers. The skin had receded making the dirt-encrusted nails appear long. The skin on his face and neck were a dark blue. When the heart stopped pumping, gravity took over and drew the blood to the lowest points in the body. Called lividity, it suggesting he'd died facedown. "Where's the photo?"

Bishop handed him a picture now sealed in a plastic bag. "Found in his right back jeans pocket."

Rick studied the image of Diane Smith. It was a candid shot of Diane sitting in a café. The wind was blowing through her long hair and she glanced up with a wide grin that made her eyes sparkle. Scrawled in blood-red ink across the pale skin of her face was the word FAITHLESS.

He reached in the dead man's back right pocket and pulled out a thin, worn leather wallet embossed with a skull. Inside the wallet was an expired driver's license featuring the dead man's frowning face. Pale and droopy-eyed, he looked half dead in the image. "His name was Jonas Tuttle, age thirty-four."

"I'll run the name in my computer." Bishop raised the back of his hand to his nose. "Jesus, I can't believe no one smelled him."

Rick handed him the license. As Bishop returned to check the name, Rick searched more pockets. In the other back pocket he found a smashed pack of cigarettes, a handful of candy swiped from a restaurant, and a pay stub from a grocery store.

He plugged the name of the store into his phone and came up with an address that was not far from Diane's home. A connection. Tuttle didn't look like the kind of guy a woman like Diane would have given a second glance, but he would have noticed her. If the grocery was close to her house, she could have passed through his line, never really looking up at his face or past his clerk's smock. He would have been invisible to her.

Bishop returned with pen in hand and his notebook open to a fresh page. "I've an address for Jonas Tuttle." He rattled off the address of a motel that rented on a daily and weekly basis. When Rick had worn a uniform he'd worked a prostitution sting. While a female officer had lured johns into a room rented by the cops, he and two other officers had hid in the bathroom waiting to make an arrest.

"Let's go have a look at his room."

After a quick drive, they pulled up at the motel, got a key from the clerk, and opened Tuttle's room. The heavy scent of cigarettes and mold assailed them the instant they opened the door.

"This place has always reeked." Bishop pulled rubber gloves from his pocket and put them on.

"We've all run a sting at this motel at one point." He donned gloves.

Bishop shook his head as he flipped on the light. "Good times."

The thin, reedy overhead light cast a pale gray glow over a bed of rumpled stained sheets and a dark comforter. Empty pizza boxes and beer cans littered the floor next to a pile of soiled laundry.

Rick moved toward the bathroom and paused to open the folding doors of a closet. The instant he glanced inside he froze. The walls of the closet were papered with pictures of Diane. Diane at the grocery store. At work. Coming from the gym. Laughing with girlfriends in a café. "Have a look."

Bishop turned from a dresser drawer and crossed to the closet. He shook his head. "Well, if that isn't an open-and-shut case."

Good fortune rarely was so generous. "I don't usually get so lucky."

Bishop rolled his head from side to side as if working out the tightness brought on by fatigue. "I suppose it happens once every so often."

Rick studied the images so carefully cut into neat squares and so carefully glued to the wall. All the images were straight. "Guy's a pig and he takes the time to create a neat collage of Diane?"

"This little space gave him a sense of control over Diane.

He knew so much about her and she knew nothing about him. Control like that must've given him one hell of a thrill."

"Judging by the images, he's been taking pictures of her for months. Planning to kill her all along?"

Rick studied the images, which seemed to be arranged seasonally. On the far left, backgrounds featured snow and barren trees; then came trees with green buds, and then full leaves. "He started taking pictures in the winter and he's followed her all the way through spring and half of summer. The winter pictures are distant. He didn't have the nerve to get too close. It's almost as if he was afraid to take the first pictures."

Bishop nodded. "But he got progressively closer and closer. By spring he's within feet of her."

Rick moved to the dresser drawers and dug through them until he found several very small cameras. He held them up. "You don't find these at the local store."

Bishop took one of the small cameras in his hands. "They're also expensive."

"Say he crosses paths with Diane at the grocery store where he worked. She passed through his line. Or smiled or glanced his way while he was unloading a truck or ringing a register. He decided she's really into him. He starts paying more and more attention to her when she comes into the store. Can't stop thinking about her. He begins stalking. Realizes he doesn't have the means to get a woman like her, and he gets angry over his lack of control."

Bishop looked at the pictures, his gaze burning. "He gets closer and closer to her, gets bolder and bolder and then decides to take ultimate control when he kills her."

"Finds a house that's for sale, lures her there or takes her there and kills her. Sets the house on fire."

"That's a lot of planning."

Rick glanced around the chaotic, stinking mess of his

room. "Jonas Tuttle doesn't strike me as a guy who could plan. Judging by his room it looks like he can barely take care of himself."

"This might've been the only place in his life he was organized." Bishop checked his watch. "It's two A.M. The grocery opens at six."

"Let's have a chat with the motel clerk. He might have information about Jonas."

They found the clerk, a very large man with a bulging belly and thick stubble over wagging jowls. He sat in a worn and tattered plaid recliner in front of a television tucked behind the counter and was watching a rerun of *Gunsmoke.*

Rick let the front door close hard and when the man didn't turn as they approached, he smacked his hand on the rusted silver bell on the counter.

Ding. Ding. Ding.

The clerk hunched closer to the television. "Leave your money on the table."

"This isn't about money," Rick said.

Shoving out a breath, the clerk groaned. "Then I don't care."

"You can care right now or you can care when I've a half-dozen cop cars here in ten minutes searching your rooms."

The clerk turned, his narrowed gaze reflecting mild interest. "Cops. Just what I need. Which room fucked up?"

Clearly this was not his first conversation with the cops. "What can you tell me about Jonas Tuttle? Room Seven."

He glanced back at the television, cursing when he realized the show had gone to commercial break. He didn't bother to look back at them. "Nothing."

Rick drummed his fingers on the counter, fatigue and stiffness in his leg straining his patience to breaking. "Turn around. Now." His sharp, crisp tone cracked like the snap of a whip.

The clerk, cursing more, turned and faced the detectives, his brow arched. "I don't know shit about the guy in that room or any other damn room. All I care about him is that I get paid on time."

"Dig deep. Think real hard. Jonas Tuttle," Rick said. "What do you know about him?"

The guy swiveled his easy chair until he faced them. He leaned back in his chair and scratched his belly through a stained T-shirt. "Room Number Seven? Always late on the rent and when he paid it was short. Money's due tomorrow as a matter of fact. Never had money to pay me but plenty of money for beer, pizza, and whores."

Rick shifted his stance, glancing at the cubbies behind the clerk. Number Seven was filled with envelopes.

"How long has he been here?"

"Two months. Maybe nine weeks."

Many of the photos Jonas had taken of Diane had been taken months and months ago, suggesting he'd brought at least half the images with him. "Where'd he come from?"

He plucked at a loose thread on the arm of the recliner that had been patched once with duct tape. "How the hell would I know? I put up a sign saying I got a room and within a day he was here with the first week's rent in cash."

"Did he have any visitors?" Bishop asked.

"No idea."

Rick flexed his fingers as he turned to look out the office's front window. The view was a straight shot to Room Seven. There was no way he couldn't have seen some odd behavior in the last two months. As he stared out the window, Rick said, "Detective Bishop, call dispatch. We need uniforms down here to search all the rooms."

Bishop reached for his phone and punched in a few numbers. "How many cars you want?"

"Seven or eight."

"Consider it done."

"You really going to pull that shit?" the clerk growled.

"I am," Rick said, facing him. Catching a hint of distress on the man's face gave him a measure of satisfaction. "And we're going to drag every one of your residents into the street. And then we're coming back tomorrow night and the next. No one will want to stay here after I'm finished."

The clerk tightened his jaw, accentuating sagging jowls. "Why you being such a dick?"

"Been a long day and I'm looking for a pound of flesh, I guess," Rick said. "I'll have ripped you a new one by the time we're done here, if you don't start offering me more information."

Large, fatty cheeks paled. He sniffed. "Can't tell you what I don't know."

"Better dig deep, pal. I don't like getting jerked around even on a good day." Bishop's accent had grown thicker with fatigue. He sounded as if he'd just arrived from Boston.

The clerk sniffed and his face wrinkled as if he inhaled a foul odor. "Like I said, Tuttle moved in about two months ago. A couple of weeks ago, he brought in a hooker. I know because she has this loud laugh. She was cackling like a hen when they went into his room. But she didn't stay long. Less than five minutes later and she slammed out of his room. She told him to fuck off. Looked pissed."

"She got a name?" Rick asked.

The clerk moistened his lips. "I'm supposed to know a whore's name?"

Rick cocked a brow. "You know every girl that works this block. Half have given you kickbacks or blow jobs."

The clerk cursed. "Terry. Her first name is Terry. Don't know her last name. Works down the street on the corner."

"Why was she mad?"

"Hell if I know. Ask her yourself. You can find her pretty easy. She's here several times a night. Wait an hour and you'll see her. Tall, dark hair, and likes to wear lime green."

"Call her."

"What?"

"Call her. Tell her she's got a client."

"I don't have her number."

Rick smacked his hand on the counter. "Don't fuck with me."

The clerk looked as if he'd argue, but then imagining a dozen cops swarming in and out of the rooms, he reached for a flip phone. He dialed the number easily and told Terry that she had work waiting for her in Room Two.

The officers waited less than ten minutes before a woman pushed through the front door of the motel's office. She wore a red wig, a lime-green tank top and skirt, and white cowboy boots. Thick blue makeup lined dull brown eyes and a wide swath of rouge added garish color to pale sunken cheeks.

When she spotted Rick and Bishop, she clearly smelled cops right off and turned to leave. "Shit."

"We aren't here to arrest you." Rick reached the door before her. "Have a question about a john."

Close up he smelled the blend of cheap perfume and booze. "Fuck me. I'm going to get the shit beat out of me if my pimp sees I'm talking to the cops."

Rick didn't move. "Answer quick and your pimp will never know. What can you tell me about Jonas Tuttle?"

"Who?"

"Room Seven," the clerk said. "Smells like pizza."

She thought for a second and then held up her hands, palms out. "That fucker's crazy."

"We hear you didn't stay long," Bishop said. "Why?"

She chewed gum, snapping it a few times. "Look, I don't want him coming back and finding me. I don't need that kind of trouble. Like I said, that fucker's crazy."

Rick rested his hands on his hips. "The guy overdosed in

an alley a few days ago. He's not going to bother you. Why was he a freak?"

"He's dead?"

"That's right. Dead."

"Oh, well, when you put it that way." She sniffed. "He paid me and I was on the bed ready to get down to business. Then he started calling me by another woman's name, which ain't that unusual. Shit, some guys call me Mommy."

"Stick to it," Rick said.

She hooked her finger in a beaded necklace and pulled it back and forth. "Well, he pulls out a set of handcuffs. Not the worst that's ever happened. I tell him it costs extra and he says fine."

"But . . ."

She glanced over her shoulder out the office window as if half-expecting to see him or her pimp. She lowered her voice a notch. "I'm reaching for the cuffs and he puts a gun to my head and asks me to beg for my life."

Rick tapped a calloused index finger against the smooth leather of his belt, inches in front of his gun holster. Diane had been shot in the head. "That's all he said?"

"He said, 'Beg me, bitch, for your life.'" She hesitated. "'Beg for your life.' I won't forget that too soon."

"How'd you get away?"

"Fucker was nervous. Sweating like a pig. I could tell he hadn't done anything like that before." With a trembling hand she fished inside a pack of cigarettes tucked in the waistband of her skirt.

Rick watched as she raised a cigarette to her lips and lit it. "He was scared."

She inhaled and blew out a lungful of smoke. "He was real scared. I was scared but I was also mad. He was gonna be my last score for the night and I thought, 'Great, I'm gonna die here,' when I was thinking I'd be home in thirty minutes and standing in a hot shower. I love hot showers.

Shit. I fought back and he just about pissed in his pants. Big guy but no balls."

"How did you get away?"

"I popped him in the nose with the heel of my hand." She drew in another lungful of smoke and released it slowly.

"And he let you go, just like that?" Bishop's gaze shifted from the shadows rimming the parking lot to her face.

"I think the bloody nose freaked him out. I didn't stop to ask or think, but just ran."

"Did he mention the other woman's name?"

She stared at the glowing tip of her cigarette. "Deidra. No. Diane. He said her name was Diane." She met Rick's gaze. "Johns call me all kinds of names. As long as the money's green I don't care. And I don't usually remember."

"But he put a gun to your head," Rick said.

"That has a way of making words stick." Again trembling hands raised the cigarette to her lips. "Something happened to Diane, didn't it?"

"What makes you say that?"

A seasoned gaze danced with bitter humor. "Because you're here. You ain't the kind of cops that care about pimps and whores. Bigger fish to fry."

Rick released a sigh. "Any other girls talk about this guy?"

She arched a brow. "I made a point to ask around. A couple knew him. No one likes him. We all deal with crazy but he's crazier than most."

"He's a user?"

"I don't know. Last I heard, you don't need blow to act crazy. Crazy is crazy." She scratched the blotchy skin of her forearm. "I got to get back to work or I'm going to get beat."

"You got a name?"

"Jane. Jane Fuller. But on the street ask for Terry."

"If I need to talk to you again?"

She dropped the cigarette on the floor and ground it out with the pointed toe of her scuffed cowboy boot. "Terry's here every night. Just ask. I'm easy to find."

Hollow, eyeless sockets stared at Jenna, emanating a desperate energy that pulsed from the inky depths. She turned, covered her own eyes, but the phantom eyes glimmered back at her, reached out, and beckoned.

I see you. I see you. I dare you to find me.

The words, or rather, the feeling, radiated as she started awake. Her gaze darted around her bedroom, lighted by several night-lights she always kept burning. She dragged a shaking hand through her hair. Breathe. Breathe. She'd had nightmares before and used the breathing techniques the psychologist in Baltimore had prescribed.

I see you. I see you. I dare you to find me.

Breathe. In. Out. Seconds passed, and the whispering voice faded as her vision sharpened on the blue dresser with a half-open top drawer dripping with clothes she'd not bothered to quite put away.

Jenna swung her legs over the side of the bed, her toes curling as they touched the cold tile. She always kept the AC low and huddled under thick blankets . . . another trick from the psychologist when her insomnia had been at its worst.

She moved toward the window near her bed, which looked out over the thick woods that circled the cabin. The air-conditioning had left condensation dripping down the window. Through the mist, she stared at the stand of darkened trees that ringed the property.

Jenna had spent nearly an hour today cradling the tiny skull in her hands, staring, trying to picture the face. She wanted to imagine smiling lips and light brown hair that framed full pink cheeks. But as hard as she tried to conjure the face of a healthy child, she knew this child had not been healthy. The eyes would have reflected stress, the hair would have been thin and the lips flat in a grim line of worry.

She'd left the skull and gone to KC's to draw for a few hours. She'd made a hundred bucks, grabbed food at a grocery store, and returned home.

Under the glare of the fluorescent lights at the medical examiner's office, she could distance herself from the reality of that child's life. But during the quiet hours of the night, alone, the emotion ruled. Faces of this dead child haunted her and she wanted to weep for the Lost Girl.

She traced her finger through the condensation on the window and knew she would not cry now. She was too much of a cop to give in before the job was done. For now, emotion wouldn't run the show. Instead of decrying this sad loss to the world, she'd focus on bone structure and the sinew that stretched and wound around this small face. She'd think about hair and eye color.

Later, much later, once the job was done and the case closed, she would give emotion a small nod. A tear or two would make sense and certainly would be healthy but she'd not allow them. Nor would she succumb to the shallow promises of booze or sex. Sex. Sex with Rick Morgan would be a very tempting diversion but sex with him promised too many complications.

After this case was solved, she would get in her car and drive for hours; perhaps she'd volunteer at an animal hospital or stroll around an amusement park and savor that joy. And perhaps she'd finally come to terms with the lost child who had brought her to Nashville.

She glanced at the clock. Three thirty. It would be an hour later on the East Coast and she knew he would be awake. Like her, Mike didn't sleep well. His own unsolved cases and demons would not allow him more than a few hours of sleep at night.

She reached for her cell and dialed.

He answered on the first ring, his voice clear and bright. "You said you'd sleep better if you left Baltimore."

A wan smile tweaked the edges of her lips as she cradled the phone closer to her cheek. "I did, too."

The low hum of his television filtered through the phone. "The ghosts have found you again."

No sense lying to him. He'd hear the false words in her voice. "Yes."

A silence emanated worry. "Old or new ghosts?"

She stared into the darkened line of the trees wondering what lurked in the shadows. "Both, I think. But you know me. I'm good friends with ghosts."

Ice clinked against a glass as he sipped his favorite scotch. "You never told me about the old ghosts."

Tension radiated up her spine. "I never thought about them much."

"Until that case. It was that case that drove you out of Baltimore."

The Lost Girl. The child locked in the closet. "I didn't realize the ghosts had such power until I found that little girl."

She imagined Mike sitting in his recliner, his large hand tracing the outline of the television remote buttons. They'd been friends for nearly five years and three weeks ago as he helped her pack her belongings into her Jeep, he'd leaned in to kiss her. The kiss had started as benign, but the skin-to-skin touch overwhelmed her senses. Desperation and fear had welled and before she'd stopped to think they'd been half-naked and moving toward her bedroom. A coherent thought shouted, *Don't screw up the best friendship you've ever had!* A tidal wave of lust had obliterated the warnings.

She'd not pulled her lips from his or tugged away from his embrace. She'd allowed him to tug off her shirt, unsnap her jeans, and push inside of her with a desperation that had surprised them both.

"Stay," he'd whispered in her ear, as their hearts had hammered in wild unison. "We'll figure this out together."

"I can't," she'd whispered back.

He'd risen up on his elbows and stared into her eyes. "Stay."

A shake of her head and he'd drawn in a breath and pulled away. No anger. No begging. In Mike's mind, no was no. End of story. She'd moved from the bedroom, fearing that if she didn't get away from the bed, she'd toss reason to the curb and ignore Nashville.

Mike had left immediately, as if he warred with his own angels and demons, but he'd returned early the next day as she'd closed up her Jeep. She'd hugged him and told him she loved him. He'd kissed her on the cheek and told her to be careful. Call whenever.

"I'll be back soon," she'd said. "Only six weeks."

His smile had been sad as if she'd already left forever.

She'd not called him in the last couple of weeks. She'd been tempted many times but she'd held back. Now, she hoped the distance between them would make it easy to fall back into the roles of friends. No more danger of being lovers tonight.

"What does the little girl have to do with you?" Mike asked.

"I think she's why I'm back in Nashville. She made me realize there's something lurking in the shadows I've got to find."

"Back in Nashville. When were you ever in Nashville?"

She rubbed a stiff muscle on the left side of her neck. "I was born here. Lived here until I was five."

"I didn't know you were from Nashville." His frown radiated through the line.

"I didn't talk about it much because I didn't remember much. All I really remembered was Baltimore."

More silence, a signal of a deepening frown. "What happened in Nashville?"

Scant memories of Nashville remained: echoes of laughter, a mother's embrace, a father's tender kiss, and a sister's good-natured jab. And then, of course, there was the closet. The nine days in the darkened, stinking box where she'd been deprived of light, decent food, and her family.

"I'm not exactly sure," she hedged.

His voice dropped as if he questioned a suspect. "Aren't sure or aren't saying?"

Her lips curled into a smile. Mike was one of the best cops she'd ever known. Could piece together the fragments of a murder faster than anyone. So intuitive, it was as if he could read minds. "Don't do your suspect voodoo on me."

He chuckled. "I just asked a question."

"You never just ask a question. You're always searching for the extra layer that lurks beneath the words."

"What's the extra layer, Jenna?"

She didn't know. All she knew was that she'd chosen to work outside of KC's bar because he'd not only been a cop, but a cop old enough to have worked her case. She'd said yes to Rick Morgan not only because of the child but because he was a step closer to the case files that held the details of her past. "When I've a few more answers, I'll call, okay?"

"Not ready to say?"

"Not yet. But I'll call."

"Promise?"

She tucked the phone close to her lips. "I promise."

A heavy silence hummed and she dreaded a reference to her last night with him. Finally, he said, "Get some sleep."

Relief washed over her. "I will, if you will."

They both laughed. Neither would get any more sleep tonight. Soon, he'd give up on his late-night movies and go into the office. And as soon as she could get into the medical examiner's office she'd be drawing again.

After she hung up, she rose and moved into the kitchen to make a fresh pot of coffee. Steaming coffee in hand, she moved into her studio and flipped on the lights. She had several hours to work on the commissioned portrait she now had and, knowing mornings were her best time, she opted to see what she could finish.

She turned the picture of the young bride around and studied the image. She'd captured the gown with long, sweeping strokes of white and ivory. She'd drawn lovely elegant hands grasping irises of vibrant purples. She was even pleased with the sweep of hair the color of wheat and gold. This project was coming together nicely and no doubt would earn her more commissions.

However, her gaze was drawn away from the bridal job. Instead, her gaze was drawn to the board where she'd pinned pictures she'd snapped at the medical examiner's office and printed off on her laser printer at home. They were the pictures of the Lost Girl's skull.

The skull was no longer naked. It was now covered in small plastic markers. She'd spent most of yesterday cutting and gluing twenty-one rubber markers onto the skull's forehead, cheekbones, and chin. The depth of the markers mirrored a standard table of measurements created by forensic anthropologists. Based on sex and race, the markers served as landmarks that indicated the skin's thickness at various points on the face.

She set down her cup and reached for a piece of transparent paper, which she placed over the demarcated skull. Carefully, she taped the paper to her drawing board so that it would not shift.

Moving her head from side to side she reached for a drawing pencil. Her work was part science and part guesswork. She had scientific formulas that determined the sides of the eyes and bone markers to help shape the nose and lips but as with any artist she made judgment calls throughout the process. Her judgments would add the spark of life that made the sketch all the more real.

Pencil point at the midpoint of the eye, she began to draw the ligaments that controlled eye movement. She worked for nearly an hour just on the basic underlying structure of the eyes. And then she moved to the lids. The upper lids curved slightly more than the lower and dipped partially over the iris of the eye. Soon, a set of colorless eyes stared back at her and she found herself setting down the pencil and reaching for her coffee.

She winced when the cold liquid touched her tongue and she gratefully moved away from the image to heat the cup in the microwave.

Punching in a minute, she watched the microwave's interior light up and the cup rotate in slow steady circles. Her thoughts strayed to Tracker. The animal's gaze burned with his desire to work, to be relevant, and to be needed. Rick had included Tracker and her in his work, giving them both a sense of purpose. But was she, like Tracker, too damaged to ever be a real cop again?

The microwave dinged and she shoved aside the thought. She grabbed her mug, shifting her thoughts back to work.

Next she'd work on the nose. Another formula dictated how wide the nose should be based on the nasal opening. There was one width for a Caucasian and a slightly wider one for an African American. A bony spine at the base of the nose would tell her how far the nose projected and whether it should be tipped up or down. She'd base the shape of the lips off the canine teeth's position and then she'd work out from there.

The process took time. But it was important that she capture the essence of the child. No doubt the cops would work with the media and broadcast the image on local stations.

Someone out there knew this little girl and wondered and worried about her. Someone had not forgotten her.

Soon, she would no longer be a lost girl.

She lost track of the time until fatigue crept up her arms and through her shoulders. She'd reached the edge of her stamina and if she continued to work, the drawing would suffer.

Jenna took one last look at the eyes staring back. "It's just the two of us now, lost girl to lost girl. We'll figure this out."

Eyes filled with a mixture of longing and fear stared back. She shut off the light and returned to her bed, curling on her side. "We'll find out who did this to you and bring you home. I promise."

Chapter Six

Rick, with Tracker at his side, arrived at the medical examiner's office and took the elevator to the second floor where he knew he'd find Jenna working. His eyes itched from lack of sleep and as much as he'd like to have a solid eight hours, with two homicides on his desk and a hip that always throbbed, he knew he'd get precious little sleep in the days to come.

He found Jenna sitting cross-legged in a chair, bare feet tucked under her as she leaned over a sketchpad on her desk. Her long, dark hair hung in a silky mass, curtaining half of her face.

Beside her, the small skull set staring at her as if waiting. The skull was now covered with rubber plugs, which he knew indicated skin depths. Her row of pencils and erasers arranged in a neat line on the table reminded him of the workspace at her house. It too had been well organized. Order was so important to her.

"Good morning," Rick said.

The sound of his voice drew her gaze up, but it took

several seconds for the trancelike haze glazing her eyes to clear.

"Detective Morgan."

Her gaze skittered to the canine, hesitated, and then met his again. No warm welcomes. No smiles. "I thought you were going to do a clay bust," he said.

"I considered that. But it will take a lot more time and I thought sooner rather than later would be best for an image."

She unfolded her legs, slipped on flats, and rose. Pencil still in hand, she stretched her head from side to side and he found his gaze drawn to the slender lines of her neck.

He leaned around to look at the picture but she shook her head no. "Can't I have a look?"

Almost flinching, she turned the easel away from him an inch or two more. "Not until it's finished."

Her reticence amused and annoyed him. "Why not? What's the big deal?"

She'd pulled her hair up into a topknot and secured it with a pencil. She missed a few long stands, which dangled to frame her face. A nice effect. "No one sees my work until it's done. That's always been my policy."

Tracker yawned, lowered to the floor, and closed his eyes. Clearly, none of this interested him.

However, Rick was very interested. The word *no* had stoked his interest. He didn't like hearing it or when an answer eluded him. He liked having answers whether the question concerned a picture, a killer's identity, or a woman's backstory. He always figured that, given time, he could crack any code.

But like it or not, the Jenna Thompson code wasn't so easily solved. "Sure, I'll wait."

A subtle tension around the edges of her lips eased. "It should be done by tomorrow. I'm close to the end. Sometimes the finishing touches just take me a while."

He noticed how her gaze darted around the office once or twice as if the space was too small. "You don't like this space."

"No. I don't."

She didn't mince words, as he'd expected, but her dislike of the space surprised him. "Why not? It's one of the better rooms in the building."

She sat a little straighter. "No windows. Too much like a closet. I like natural light."

"Yeah, I'm not a fan of being inside. I'll take any task that gets me moving outside."

Jenna allowed her gaze to travel over the length of his body. "So what happened to your leg?"

He folded his arms, not sure why he'd shifted to defense. "You've been talking to Georgia."

A half smile tugged at the corners of her mouth. "Sure. But not about you. I noticed the way you shift your weight. And I noticed your expression when you tackled the stairs yesterday."

An artist who re-created human figures would notice inconsistencies, anomalies. However, he didn't like being the subject of her scrutiny, especially when it zeroed in on his weakness. "I thought I did a good job of covering it up. Worked pretty damned hard with my physical therapist to make sure that I have an even gait."

A shrug of her shoulders softened some of the intensity in her eyes. "There's no limp when you walk but there's a subtle stiffness. I draw people. And, I'm a cop. Part of what makes someone who they are is how they move."

"You were just summing me up."

"You. Bishop. Georgia."

"Bishop? What did you figure about him?"

"He has a keen eye for Georgia."

Morgan laughed. "The two fight all the time."

"I think, for those two, arguing might be flirting."

"He's not fond of the Morgans."

"Don't be so sure." This was not the conversation he'd intended. He shifted to offense. "I was comparing your space here to your home."

A brow arched as hesitancy flashed in her gaze. "And what do you see?"

Good, they were now both uncomfortable. "Can you say *control issues?*"

That made her laugh. "Did you miss the part where I said I'm a cop?"

"The trait comes with the job. The question is where did it come from? We all had it before the first day on the job."

"Where did it come from in you?"

Nice deflection. "Genetics, I guess. A legendary homicide detective raised the Morgan kids. We all have our share of issues."

"Ah."

"Now, your turn. What's your excuse?"

A slight tension tugged at the edges of her lips. "Who knows?"

"No, I'm not letting you dodge this so easily."

"Really."

"Want my theory?"

She turned back to her sketchpad and opened it. She began to draw. "Sounds like I'm going to get it."

"It was definitely from your past. Something that instilled a need to control."

Her pencil stilled for a beat before moving again. "Maybe it was genetics in my case as well."

"I don't think so." He dropped the line in the water wondering if she'd take the bait.

She swam right past it as if it would take more to get her to open up. Fine. He'd drop it for now. "Sorry, Detective, I didn't sign on for analysis."

And with that, the door slammed shut. However, he

wasn't worried. He'd find a way to open that door again soon. "So the picture will be ready tomorrow?"

"Likely. The day after at the latest. Like I said, the final details always take more time than I figured."

"What kind of details?"

"Subtleties. The quirk of a mouth, the spark in the eyes. There's always something I miss until the very end."

What was he missing about her? A lot. In time he'd figure her out. He figured everyone out eventually. The only worry with her was time. Would she be around long enough to decipher. That shouldn't matter, but it did. "You'll call me when you're finished."

"You'll be the first."

"Great."

"What's your dog's name?"

"Tracker."

"So Tracker's a retired canine. Belgian shepherd?"

"Yeah. Good eye."

She rose, like yesterday, but made no move to pet the dog. She knew, though Tracker was retired, he considered himself a working dog. She seemed to understand that not petting Tracker was a sign of respect. "How old is he?"

"Five."

"You two were shot at the same time."

Her certainty made him wonder again if she'd talked to Georgia. "Yeah."

"It's a hell of a business, being a cop."

"I've often questioned my sanity." *But I didn't quit.*

She glanced back at her drawing as if reading his thoughts. "So it's just you and Georgia?"

"No. Older brother, Deke Morgan, heads up homicide. He's just back from vacation with his girlfriend and is digging out. And there's another Morgan, Alex. He works for the Tennessee Bureau of Investigation." No need to mention he and Alex hadn't spoken in months or that nothing had been right between them since Melissa.

Nodding, she kept her gaze on the drawing. "A regular family dynasty."

A fact he took pride in, even when someone like Bishop mumbled complaints about connections and good ol' boy networks. "That we are."

"Nice."

Curiosity jabbed him in the back. "What brought you to Nashville? We're off the beaten track for folks hailing from the East Coast."

Her gaze darkened a fraction and he'd have missed it if he hadn't been watching closely. "I was born here. Lived there a few years before my aunt and I moved east. Tapping into my family roots, I guess."

"The Morgans know a lot of folks. Your family name is Thompson?"

"It is. Though there're none of us left in Nashville. Both my parents were only children." As if suddenly uncomfortable, she retreated back to her chair. "I've a good bit of work to do here so if you don't mind?"

He read her discomfort as if he'd opened the pages of a book. "Tossing me out?"

Her grin was broad and bright. "Throwing you both out."

The turn in conversation to her family had made her nervous. She tried to cover but failed. So what had happened to her family? "Call me when you have the sketch."

"Consider it done."

She tore the paper free from her notepad and handed it to him. "There's a drawing for you."

The image was of Tracker, wide eyed and staring. "This is good."

"I know my stuff, Detective."

Careful not to crease the image, he nodded. "Thanks."

He and Tracker made their way to the elevator and as he

pushed the button, he glanced back toward the small office. Jenna was again seated, kicked off her shoes, and bent over her sketch, her gaze totally focused on the work as if they'd never spoken. Curiosity jabbed him in the ribs. She didn't want to talk about the past. It wasn't a huge leap to assume it couldn't have been great if she'd left the area at age five to live with an aunt nearly one thousand miles away.

As he glanced at the sketch, the whys buzzed around Jenna Thompson like flies. Professionally, she was one of the best. She was offering her skills for free. So he figured the rest just wasn't any of his damn business.

The door dinged open and they stepped inside. As the elevator descended, he reminded himself that poking into someone else's private business wasn't so nice or politically correct. Clearly, Jenna wouldn't want anyone digging too deep.

"Shit."

Tracker glanced up at him, hearing the anger in his voice. He smiled, telling the canine that everything was fine.

He wasn't so worried about being nice or PC. He cared about the truth. Whatever was buried in Jenna's past . . . well, he just might dig it up.

Rick's first stop after leaving Jenna was the local news station. Frankly, he'd rather eat dirt before he had to cozy up with the media, but sometimes it took a deal with the devil to get the job done.

The department had worked with several reporters on missing children cases and they'd found the local anchor, Susan Martinez, helpful. She could be a pain in the ass when it came to the hard news stories—she did whatever it took to get her story—including hounding his ass after he'd been shot. He still had memories of her camped out in front of his hospital giving her evening news report. Vultures picking off his bones even before the docs could tell him if he would walk properly again.

But like him, when it came to cases involving a child, she played nice. Both knew the gloves would come off in the next round, but for now, it would be all smiles.

He and Tracker moved through the glass doors of the news building and after a brief chat with the receptionist, waited for Susan.

She appeared minutes later with a bright smile. Dressed in a sleek red suit that accentuated ink-black hair, she moved with a grace he had to admire. In her mid fifties, she'd worked the Nashville market for almost thirty years and had broken several major cases.

She held out a manicured hand as she approached him. "It's the junior Detective Morgan."

He accepted her hand, shook and released it quickly. He'd heard his share of "junior" references since he was a kid and he'd heard a belly full since returning to the Force. Hard to compete with his old man, Buddy the legend, and an older brother like Deke. And so he hadn't tried to compete. In fact, he'd stopped worrying about which Morgan had the biggest set a long time ago. He let the "junior" crack roll off his back like water down a storm drain. "Ms. Martinez, how're you doing?"

The scent of an expensive, spicy perfume wafted around him. "I'm hungry for a great story. Tell me you have a great story. Maybe a tidbit about the fire and fatality on Monday night. The victim was identified as Diane Smith and a little bird tells me you caught her killer."

"I might have something for you on that case later today, but I'm here about a favor."

"What happened to you scratch my back and I scratch yours?"

As if she'd not spoken, he said, "We found the skeletonized remains of a child in Centennial Park a few days ago."

The spark in her gaze eased and her smile faded. "I'd heard a little buzz about that. No one seems to be saying much."

"Because we don't have much to say at this point. Very little forensic data. No match to existing missing persons files."

She brushed a strand of hair from her green eyes. She'd not totally dismissed him yet, but it was coming if he didn't ante up more. "Not sure what I can do to help you."

"We've a forensic artist who is willing to do a facial reconstruction. She's working on it now." He didn't feel the need to get into Jenna's past in Baltimore, feeling a little protective of her. "She should have a likeness ready to go in a day or two. We're hoping you could air it on the news."

Her nod was easy and natural. "Of course. I can do a whole segment. Though, without many details, it will be a quick segment. Nothing else you can tell me? Was there anything found with the body? What was the child's approximate age? Signs of trauma?"

Instead of feeling annoyed, he grinned. "You should have been a cop. You don't know the meaning of 'no' or 'you will get more details later.'"

She folded her arms. "Hon, if I'm not pushing and prodding, I'm not doing my job. When you get your sketch, I'm going to want as many details as you can dig up. Age, sex, possible time the child went missing, manner of death. I'd also like to interview the forensic artist."

"Why?"

"Will add flavor to the story. And, it'll extend a sixty-second mention into a four- or five-minute piece. More air time."

"I'll have all details for you and I'll ask the artist."

Her head cocked a fraction. "I know the forensic artists in the area. Most are mighty backed up. How'd you get one so quickly?"

"Connections. And I'm persuasive."

A laugh rumbled in her chest. "Oh, all I've heard about you, Detective, is that you're one tough stubborn son of a bitch." She glanced at Tracker. "How's the hero dog? He's getting along?"

"Doing just fine. We're not as fast as we used to be, but we're smarter and meaner."

"Good to know." She held up her finger. "Now, back to that house fire in the West End. I hear the victim was shot in the head."

Working with the press was give-and-take. "You got yourself some good sources."

"So you really think you found the killer?"

"We're still doing some double-checking." The case could easily be pronounced closed but, for reasons he couldn't explain, something about it was too neat and easy. Lucky breaks did happen but not so much when he was around.

"And when you confirm, you're going to call me, aren't you?" She tossed him a wide grin with a conspirator's gaze.

"You'll be the first I'll talk to." Give-and-take.

"Darling, perhaps this could be the beginning of a beautiful relationship."

"Right."

When pigs fly.

Rick arrived at his home, the Big House, at five minutes to five for a family meeting. Since their mother and father died, the four siblings rarely met anymore. Georgia had tried to cobble together the fraying family ties but with each passing day and month, they grew thinner. After today's bit of business, he wouldn't be surprised if they snapped entirely.

The business was the final matter in Buddy Morgan's estate. The house now belonged to Rick, and according to Buddy's will, the owner of the Big House could not own more than ten acres of land. Deke had made it clear he did not want the land in exchange for the house so, as stipulated in the will, Rick's land had to be offered to the remaining siblings, Georgia or Alex.

Georgia had declined the land but the remaining Morgan brother, Alex, had agreed to take it. No one had been more surprised than Rick. He'd assumed Alex's job with the Tennessee Bureau of Investigation kept him on the move so much he didn't want to be saddled with land. And so the two brothers, via Georgia, had agreed to meet at the Big House to sign the legal papers transferring the land from Rick to Alex.

Deke and Georgia did not need to be present at the signing but, given the tension between Rick and Alex, both had offered to attend. So, by default, the Morgan siblings were having a reunion.

Rick helped Tracker out of the backseat and let him free so he could roam and take care of business. As Rick loosened his tie, he climbed the front steps and reached for the front door. As he fished in his pocket for keys, his gaze dropped to the lock and he froze. The door was slightly ajar.

Without thought, he reached for the gun holstered in his waistband. His nerves jingling, he eased open the front door. Memories of approaching the car on the dark stretch of road, gunfire, and searing pain flashed in his mind. The shrinks said he'd likely never forget that night, but perhaps the heart-pounding adrenaline would ease, given time.

The rattle of pots and pans had him hesitating even as he pointed his gun down the long hallway.

"Rick!" Georgia's voice echoed out from the kitchen. "If that's you, I'll put my gun away."

Relief flooding like a spring storm, he slid the gun back into its holster and shut the door. "I'm putting mine away too."

Laughter drifted on the heels of more pots and pans clanging. "Sorry, my hands were full when I came in and I forgot to close the door."

Down the hallway, he entered the dimly lit kitchen. "Where's your car?"

"In the shop. Caught a ride with a friend. I figured I could hitch a ride back to town with you in the morning."

His nerves danced as residual electricity jolted through sinew. "That works for me."

Georgia had had a rough year and found staying at the Big House gave her the security she needed. Rick was glad for the company and had told her the door was always open. "I'm meeting a few friends in Franklin tonight so I'll be back late. So don't shoot."

"Sounds good." He moved to a high-tech console on the wall and pressed a button. Overhead lights blinked on, chasing away the gray light and the dark shadows.

Georgia set a serving platter on the new granite island he'd installed. "You've really done a great job. When you were tearing stuff up, I was a little freaked out."

Rick arched a brow. "You hid it so well."

She shrugged, knowing she'd been difficult and second-guessed him at every turn. "I must admit, you've dragged the old homestead into this century."

He moved to the refrigerator and pulled out a beer. "Hell of a project." But the sweat and frustration had been deeply satisfying. He'd taken what had been his parents' home and put his mark on it.

"I like that you saved Mom's pots and pans and her china. It's your space, but she's still here."

"That was the idea." He twisted the top off the beer and took a long sip. "Do I smell food?"

"I stopped at the Mexican restaurant in Franklin and grabbed food for us."

He picked up a tortilla chip and bit. "You figure we can't fight if we're eating."

That jostled a laugh. "Then clearly you don't remember our family dinners. Remember when you and Deke came to blows at Thanksgiving? You were fourteen and I guess he was sixteen."

The fight had been over whose football team was the best. Banter had escalated into punches. Buddy had yanked the two apart and ordered them to eat the damn meal. The old man had also made the two clean up after every meal for a week.

"I think Alex and I can be civil. We're just signing papers." There'd been a time in the last year when he'd imagined pummeling Alex, but he wouldn't tonight. He hoped.

Georgia blew out a breath as if she'd read his thoughts. "Food won't stop you two from fighting but, maybe, it'll slow you down."

Rick sipped his beer, not wanting to recount any more family dramas. "Jenna said she's almost finished with the picture of the Lost Girl."

"Lost Girl?"

"Jenna's expression for the little girl from the park."

Georgia smiled. "I'd heard she was one of the best. I've watched her in action in front of KC's and she's so good."

"Amazes me she just sauntered into KC's and offered to draw pictures." Seemed a bit too neat for him.

"Girl's gotta eat, I guess."

He took a pull on the beer. "Seems a waste of talent."

"I was thinking the same, but she's on leave and no doubt will be back on the job in Baltimore before long. Unless we can get her to fall in love with Nashville."

"Meaning?"

Georgia always thought three steps ahead of the Morgan men. "If you solve this case because of her drawing, it makes me wonder what other cold cases out there could be solved with her help. And she might find that living and working here is a better fit. She's said she likes the open spaces."

His tone remained neutral. "I got the impression Jenna was doing a one-time favor and she wasn't staying."

"It's only because I've not asked for another favor or really started to sell her on Nashville. Give me time." She grinned. "You know how persuasive I can be."

"I do."

"KC and I were talking yesterday about cases that weren't solved because of time, money, or the science."

Rick shifted his stance. "We've a cold case squad."

"Doesn't mean they couldn't use a fresh set of eyes on their cases. And if we were our own group, we wouldn't be limited to Nashville." Her eyes danced as she nodded.

"Before you take this idea and start running, let's see if we can solve this case."

"Yeah, sure."

He could almost hear the grinding of the wheels in her head. "What else do you know about Jenna Thompson?"

"Professionally?"

"Personally?"

Her grin turned wicked. "Rick, are you interested?"

"No. I just sense there're pieces missing to that puzzle."

Nodding, she didn't discount his statement. "I did a little digging with Baltimore. She's had a distinguished run with them. Went to high school there. Some college. All good. No trouble."

Absently, he scratched at the beer label with his thumb. "Why'd she take leave?"

"From what I've been able to piece together, she and her partner took a call to a run-down part of the city. They found a little girl locked in a closet. She was alive but she was in rough shape. Seems she'd been in the closet for months. Jenna quit two days later."

A case like that couldn't have been easy. "When was that?"

"Almost four weeks ago."

"And she moved to Nashville three weeks ago. She pulled up stakes pretty quickly after the call."

"The ones with kids are always hard."

He'd been tempted to chuck it all after the shooting. A few times he'd been seconds away from packing up Tracker in his car and just driving. But his roots in Nashville ran too deep. "I couldn't imagine leaving Nashville."

Nodding, she picked up a tortilla chip from a bag on the counter. "A couple of the guys on her team were shocked when she quit."

"How do you know?"

"I called in a favor."

"I didn't think you just skimmed the surface. What did you learn?"

"My buddy learned when he called her commander that she handled all kinds of nasty cases and never blinked. A lot of the guys thought she was bulletproof. And then this case, and she splits."

"Hit a nerve."

"Seems so."

Unanswered questions swirling around Jenna shouldn't have mattered, but they did. Fact, they bugged the hell out of him. "She said she was born in Nashville. Spent the first five years of her life here."

"Really?" She gobbled the chip and opened the stove and with oven mitts pulled out a pan filled with enchiladas.

The smell filled the kitchen, his stomach grumbled, and he realized he'd not eaten since breakfast.

She set the dish on hot pads on the counter. "I guess it would be pretty rude to dig into her past and find out what happened when she was five."

He sipped his beer. "What makes you think anything happened?"

Georgia arched a brow. "Something happened."

Great minds think alike. "How do you know?"

She held up her index finger. "A five-year-old leaves Nashville." Her next finger rose. "Raised by an aunt in Baltimore." Another finger. "Has a tough call involving a child and returns to a place she's not seen in almost twenty-five years." A fourth finger. "And then she's busting a gut to help solve the case of a murdered five-year-old."

"Wouldn't be too hard to search cases from twenty-five years ago involving a young girl."

"Bet you a dollar you find something connected to her."

"It's really none of our business."

She laughed. "And you believe that line?"

"No." Smiling, he drained his beer.

"Dig a little. It's no skin off anybody's nose and if you don't find anything, then no one's the wiser."

"I will."

Her head cocked. "You like her?"

"Like? That's a strong word. I appreciate her work and she's a good-looking woman. But I'm more curious than anything."

She shrugged as she opened another tin of food. "I could not care less about the pasts of people I don't like."

He snagged another chip. "I don't care about her."

She leaned forward. "It would be okay if you did. Really. Nice to see you move on after Melissa."

The mention of Melissa's name soured his good humor. "Don't go there. Not tonight. I want to be civil to Alex."

"Understood. No sense in poking the hornets' nests." She pulled a serving spoon from a utensil drawer. "How long has it been since you and Alex really talked?"

"Right after Buddy died."

"That's too long, Bro. I met Melissa a few times. Hot, but not worth this kind of strife. You two are brothers."

Which had made the sting of betrayal all the more painful. The sound of two cars pulling in the driveway was followed by the slam of car doors. Rick straightened. "Speak of the devil."

"Be nice. If you don't want to fight, eat."

The front doorbell chimed. "Why ring the bell?"

"Respect. It's your *casa,* Bro."

Frowning, Rick moved to the door and snapped it open. He found Deke and Alex inspecting the rehab work he'd done on the front porch.

Deke turned first. The oldest of the Morgan children, he was tall, broad-shouldered, with a perpetual grim expression, a carbon copy of their father. Many of the old-timers on the Force still called him Buddy as if caught off guard when they saw him. Twice divorced, Deke had moved into the house while Rick was recuperating. He'd blamed the move on decimated finances after his second divorce but he'd basically been keeping the place afloat until Rick could stake his claim. He'd happily moved back to the city last fall and was seriously dating a local attorney, Rachel Wainwright.

Alex shared his brother's olive complexion and dark hair but he had a long, lean build that stretched to six foot three inches. He wore his thick hair short, his shirts starched, and his suits were handmade. Since he was a kid, all the Morgans had assumed Alex would not only run for public office but would land in the governor's mansion before he turned forty.

Deke grinned when he made eye contact with Rick. "You've done a hell of a job with this place. How do you like living in the sticks?"

Rick's stomach knotting, he accepted Deke's hand and shook heartily. "Seems to suit Tracker and me. Never asked, but how was vacation?"

"Nice to get away with Rachel for a few days. No phones. No work."

Rick barely heard the answer as he faced Alex and wrestled a surge of annoyance and anger. "Alex."

Alex gave no hint to what was happening behind eyes as black as coal. He possessed an icy demeanor that had always made him very hard to read. "Rick. Place looks great."

"Thanks."

"I hear you closed the Diane Smith case," Deke said.

Word was getting around about Jonas Tuttle, but Rick still had too many missing pieces to close the case in his mind. "Looks that way. We'll see."

"Any idea why the guy killed her?" Alex asked. He extended his hand to Rick.

Homicide had always served as neutral territory for the Morgans. No better way to dodge emotions than to dig into the latest murder. He accepted his brother's hand and this momentary truce. Each squeezed hard, giving as good as the other before releasing the grasp. "He was stalking her for months. Acted out killing fantasies with a hooker. But why he chose Diane, I don't know. And he had expensive camera equipment that would have been beyond his means."

"Sounds like you don't want to mark it closed," Deke said.

Alex stood silent. He'd done his due diligence by breaking the first chunk of ice.

"In a day or two," Rick said. He stepped aside so his brothers could enter. As they moved down the hallway, he added, "I want to dig just a little deeper. Something doesn't seem quite right."

"Is that Mexican I smell?" Deke asked.

"Georgia brought food."

"Did she cook it?" Alex asked.

"No," Rick said.

The relief on his brothers' faces almost made him smile. This moment was the most normal the three Morgan brothers had had in so long. Homicide and jokes about Georgia's cooking . . . didn't get better than that. "She figured we'd behave with food on the table."

"She has a short memory," Alex said.

Rick let the comment slide and to Deke asked, "How is Rachel?"

Deke's expression softened in a way it had never done before. "Working on another case and determined to save all the downtrodden in the world."

Rachel's intensity reminded him of Jenna. The women were different in many ways but both carried with them a drive that set them apart from most people. "She should've come."

"She's in court tomorrow. Will be hard to get her to focus on much until she's got a resolution."

As the three Morgan men entered the kitchen Georgia grinned up at them. She, more than any of the four siblings, missed the family gatherings. For that reason, and that alone, he was sorry for the rift with Alex.

Georgia moved to the sink to fill Tracker's water bowl. The dog knew he was most likely to be heard if he came to the kitchen, the place where Rick had all but lived the last few months during the renovation.

"Wolf-dog was at the back door," Georgia said. "Should I feed him?"

Rick checked his watch. "Sure. His food is in the pantry. He gets exactly one scoop."

Georgia frowned. "That sounds kinda mean? Can't I give him a chew or a bone?"

"If I keep his weight in check, he feels and moves better. Extra weight equals pain. So no more sneaking him chips."

Looking innocent, she vanished into the pantry and appeared with a bowl of food that looked to be exactly one scoop. "Seems kinda sad never to be able to have a fun snack again."

Rick shrugged off his jacket, the shoulders suddenly feeling tight. "We'll play with his chew toy tonight and he can bark at squirrels later. He'll be fine."

She dumped the food into the bowl. She winked at the dog and rubbed him between the ears. "Whatever you say, boss."

Deke set a file folder on the counter. "Don't look so sad, Georgia. He loves the chew toy."

She shrugged and snapped up a chip, which she ate in one bite. "Whatever."

Rick nodded toward the folder. "Those the papers?"

Deke lifted the case slightly. "Rachel drew them up just as we asked. They're ready to sign. I brought copies for everyone to read after we eat."

"I don't have time to eat," Alex said, checking his watch. "Deke, do you mind if we sign the papers now? I've got to get back to town."

"You can't eat?" Georgia asked. "Alex, I did takeout and didn't cook just for you!"

Alex's gaze softened a fraction. "Sorry, Georgia. Got a dinner date in town."

The word *date* reverberated through the house and no

one spoke for a moment. They all knew Melissa had been dating Rick and after his shooting had taken up with Alex.

Deke spread the papers on the counter. "Copies for everyone to read."

Alex reached in his coat pocket and pulled out an expensive-looking pen. "It's as we discussed?"

"Land transfers from Rick to you, in accordance with Dad's will."

Without reading it, Alex reached for the top copy and flipped to the last page. He scrawled his name in the spot indicated for him.

"Don't you want to read it?" Deke asked.

"I don't need to read it. I trust Rachel got it right." He handed the pen to Rick.

Rick accepted the pen. "You brought the money?"

"I did." Rick signed and handed the pen to Georgia and then Deke who signed as witnesses.

Alex reached in his pocket, pulled out a dollar bill, and laid it on the counter.

Rick pocketed the money and signed. "Land's all yours."

Alex carefully tucked his pen back in his breast pocket along with his copy of the deed. "Excellent. Sorry I can't stay." Relief, not remorse, hummed below the surface. They'd avoided World War III but had also not signed a peace treaty. In fact, it might not take much to make the fireworks fly again.

"Alex, want a plate for the road?" Georgia offered.

For her, Alex's smile was genuine. He gave her a kiss on the cheek and she hugged him fiercely. "Thanks, but no."

Georgia smiled as she stepped back, but Rick knew their brother's early departure had dashed whatever hopes she'd had of a family gathering. That sparked irritation, which peeled away whatever good intentions Rick had brought with him to the meeting. Dinner date. Melissa. Shit. "Don't want to keep her waiting."

The sarcasm-laced words melted the ice and for a moment, Alex's eyes burned with fury. Instead of commenting, he turned. The steady clipped strike of his shoes echoed through the house and seconds later the front door slammed so hard that the windows rattled.

For a moment, no one said anything. Then Georgia pulled a beer from the refrigerator and popped it. "No blood was shed. I'd say we've made some progress."

Progress. All-out war had cooled to bitter resentment. "Who're you kidding, Georgia? We're a fucked-up fractured excuse for a family."

A small shrug lifted her shoulder. "So you admit we're a family? Good. That's progress."

To Jenna fear tasted like fast-food hamburgers and fries.

Since Jenna had been held prisoner in that closet for nine days, she'd not been able to eat hamburgers in any way, shape, or form. And the smell of fries turned her stomach. Her aunt had taken her to a local fast-food place when she'd first moved to Baltimore as a treat but Jenna took one look at the meal and had cried.

She stopped at the traffic light and her stomach grumbled. She had a chicken and a salad in her fridge at home but as she glanced over at the hamburger chain restaurant, she wondered if she could finally walk into the place and order a meal like a normal person.

Her stomach curdled just imagining the smell but stubbornness had her turning into the parking lot. Before she had a chance to overthink, she grabbed her purse and pushed through the doors, soon finding herself standing in front of the light-up display menu. The choices seemed overwhelming.

When it was her turn, a teenage girl behind the counter

barely looked her way when she asked, "May I take your order?"

Jenna had no idea what she wanted so she opted for the food that churned the worst memories. "Hamburger."

"What kind?"

"Kind?"

"We serve it a dozen different ways."

A dozen ways? All she remembered was the small, round disk of meat floating in a bun of white bread that her jailor gave her each day. "What do you recommend?"

The girl shrugged. "Number one is our best seller."

Jenna glanced at the board overhead but found the choices staggering. "I'll take a number one."

The girl dropped her gaze to her register as if her thoughts had already moved to the next order. "You want me to supersize that?"

"What?" God, she wasn't sure if she could eat a small. "No. Small is fine."

The girl drummed her fingers and attempted a smile. "For here or to go?"

The place wasn't too busy or crowded and if she waited until she got home, the meal would be cold. "I'll eat here."

"Kind of drink?"

"Drink?" So many choices. "Water is fine."

"You get a soda."

She watched as the cooking crew prepared the burgers behind the counter. Such efficiency. "No, thanks. Just water."

The girl rang up the order, took Jenna's money, and handed her the red tray filled with a neatly wrapped burger, a sleeve of fries, and a small iced water.

Jenna moved to a seat by the window and carefully unwrapped the burger. She smoothed out the paper. She hesitated and then reached for the burger and held the soft warm bread in her hands.

"Little Jennifer?"

The man's voice drifted through the cracks of the door. Even as she remained huddled in the corner, exhausted from weeping for her mother, a part of her was grateful to hear his voice. It had been too silent for so long and she'd lost track of time.

Now he was talking to her.

"Little Jennifer?"

She clung to her pink blanket. "Yes."

"I have food for you. Are you hungry?"

Her stomach grumbled. "Yes."

The sound of locks turned and clicked and the closet door slowly opened. Dim light from the other room drifted into the closet, which smelled of her urine.

She looked up into the vivid blue eyes that danced with an unnerving excitement. He set down a fast-food bag and a cup of soda with a straw. The scents of the food made her mouth water and chased away some of her fear.

"Go on. Take it."

She reached out with a trembling hand and then snatched the bag.

"Just a little longer, Sugar Pie," he said. "Just a little longer and then you and me is gonna move to California and be a family. You're gonna be my girl and I'm gonna be your man."

Jenna sat straighter in her chair. With a trembling hand, she set the burger down and reached for the water. She sipped the cool liquid, which soothed her dry throat.

Seconds passed as she looked at the food. She picked up the burger again, closed her eyes, and bit into it without thinking. She chewed once, twice before she heard his voice again.

"Little Jennifer?" Her jailor's voice rattled in her memory.

Her stomach rolled as nausea rose. She quickly pulled

several napkins from the holder and spit the uneaten burger into the paper before balling it up into a wad.

"Little Jennifer?"

She tipped her head back, feeling her rapid heartbeat in her throat. Unable to touch the burger again, she scooped it all back in the bag and quickly dumped the entire meal into the trash. She hurried outside to her car where she stood for several minutes. She pulled in a deep breath, filling her lungs, hoping for fresh air but getting a lungful of the thick burgers-and-fries scent. She coughed and got into her car.

Behind the wheel, she closed her eyes and tried to calm her racing heartbeat. "It's just a damn burger. Just a damn burger."

But a glance back at the fast-food place told her she'd never go back inside there or anywhere like it again.

With a trembling hand, she reached for her sketchpad and started to draw the outline of a face. She quickly drew the face of Ronnie Dupree, the man who'd locked her in the closet. Memories of his image had faded over time and for years she'd not thought about him. Now, however, his face came into sharp focus as if it had only been seconds since she'd last seen him.

Her fingers moved quickly, drawing his deep-set eyes, flat nose, and wide, full lips. She traced a large forehead and thinning hair that brushed narrow shoulders. When she was finished, her breathing had grown rapid and shallow and a headache had formed over her left eye. "Why did you do it? Why did you kill my family? Destroy my life?" she whispered.

As she stared at the sketch, the eyes of another came to mind. In the margin, she began to draw a darker set of eyes. She couldn't say if they belonged to a man or a woman, but their deep, piercing glare unsettled her. She'd been drawing these eyes for three weeks but never once before with Ronnie's face.

"Who are you?"

The faceless shadowed figure refused to step into the light so she could draw it.

As a forensic artist, she'd been able to coax vivid memories from the most traumatized of victims. She could sit with them for hours and gently draw out details that she used to create a face. What song was on the radio? What did the air feel like? Did the breeze blow against your skin? Think about his chin? What did the room smell like?

She flipped the page in her sketchbook and stared at the blank page for a long time. *What did the room smell like?* Hamburgers and fries? *Was it hot or cold?* Hot. Stifling hot. The pink blanket scratched against her sweaty skin. *Did the Shadow person ever speak to you?* Not to me. Only to Ronnie. *What was said?* Precise words escaped her, but she remembered a tone of voice. The person was mad at Ronnie. Furious. And then the shadow was quiet.

An answer danced at the edges of her mind, just out of sight. She closed her eyes, summoning it out of the darkness. *Show yourself.* She waited. But nothing came forth.

Drawing in a deep breath, she set her sketchpad aside and turned on her car and the radio. She chose a station with classical music, and allowed the music to drift over her.

"Keep real quiet now, Jennifer. We don't want anyone finding you. There're bad, bad people in this world who can hurt you," Ronnie had said.

She absently stared into the parking lot of the fast-food restaurant. "Who's the bad person, Ronnie?" she whispered.

Ronnie remained silent and the whispered words in her memory faded as if they'd never been spoken.

When she was little, her aunt had taken her to the zoo in Washington, D.C., and they'd gone to the lion exhibit. Another little girl had cried in fear but Jenna had not been afraid. The fence, she'd reasoned, would keep her safe. However, that night, as she'd dreamed of watching the lions, she'd touched the fence and it had fallen. All her protection had vanished and the lion had charged. She'd awoken, screaming.

Her aunt had held her close and told her over and over to keep the fences in place. They will protect you. And so she'd stayed behind the fence where she was safe and no one could really reach her. No pain. No love. No intimacy. But life had gone on as normally as possible.

Until she'd found that little girl weeks ago and the fence had collapsed into rubble around her feet. No amount of mental effort could rebuild it and she was left bare, vulnerable, and waiting for a lion to charge.

She knew, now, the fence could never be put back in place. It was gone forever. Obliterated.

"You're here to get to the bottom of it all," she said.

Time to remember the closet and understand why Ronnie had been so worried that last day that he'd tied Jennifer up and put tape on her mouth. Who had argued with him and then vanished?

Jenna glanced over at her sketchpad. The eyes she'd just drawn floated on the empty page and glared at her. Breathe in, breathe out.

With the tip of her finger she traced the eyes. Her hand didn't tremble nor did her heart race. "I'm gonna find you."

Chapter Seven

Wednesday, August 16, 7:20 P.M.

Unable to return to a dark and silent home, Jenna ducked into a grocery store and grabbed a fresh loaf of bread and a wedge of cheese. Not super-fancy fare, but it would fill her belly. She ate in her car in the grocery's parking lot, her thoughts returning to Morgan's Lost Girl. She could keep tweaking her sketch of the Lost Girl for days. A bit more shade here. A softening of the nose or chin. More curls or less curls in the hair.

But as she drained the last of her coffee, she realized it was time to let her go. She knew herself well enough now to know if she kept playing with the sketch, she'd overthink it and ruin the image. Better to put it on Rick Morgan's desk and be done with the assignment.

She dropped her head back against the headrest. It wasn't like her to overthink or be indecisive. It wasn't like her to sit alone in grocery store parking lots too afraid to go home.

"What the hell is happening to me?"

She'd come to Nashville to answer a question that might not ever have a real answer. Why did Ronnie kill her family? *Because he was troubled, insane.* Not fair, but the truth.

Who was Shadow Eyes? *Maybe in Ronnie's drug-addled mind, he'd imagined the second person and was talking to thin air.*

Whether her questions had clear answers or not she had to dig into both and be sure. "I don't quit, Detective Morgan."

She checked her watch. There was still time to draw a few faces in front of KC's. She couldn't say no to the money.

Thirty minutes later, she'd parked behind Rudy's and set up her easel and stool. Broadway hummed with a mixture of tourists this time of night. The family crowds were looking for a place to eat, knowing many excluded the under twenty-one set after seven. The later customers were ready to rock and party. While one set looked bedraggled and ready to ease up for the day, the other group was freshly coiffed, smelling of perfumes and aftershaves in anticipation of a fun night on the strip.

Jenna set up her easel right outside of Rudy's because it was a prime location. It was impossible to pass her by and not see the older drawings she'd done, which she'd matted and leaned against the brick wall.

Jenna wrestled the three wobbly legs of her easel into place and made sure it stood steady. She opened her box of colored chalks and clipped a clean white sheet of paper to the easel. The afternoon sun had eased and the air cooled. The night promised to be lucrative.

As she unfolded and adjusted her small stool, KC spotted her through the window and nodded. He filled a large glass with water and made his way through the tables outside.

"Wasn't sure if you were going to make it tonight."

"Been a crazy week. I almost bailed but decided the weather was too nice to pass up."

He handed her the water, her standard drink when she worked. "I hear you're helping on an old case."

She shrugged. "I am."

He pursed his lips as if a swell of emotion threatened to break his voice. "That's good of you."

She opened her bag and pulled out a rag to wipe her hands clean. "Let's hope we catch the bad guy."

"I worked a fair number of missing persons cases back in the day. When I heard about the kid found in the park I tried to remember her but I couldn't."

Do you remember me?

"No one seems to remember her."

A frown furrowed deep creases between his eyes. "I would have remembered a kid reported missing. I always remembered the child cases."

She straightened her shoulders, knowing she'd been one of those child cases. *Just ask him!*

"Yeah. They're the worst."

Folding his arms, he cocked his head. "Georgia told me you were born in Nashville?"

So Rick and Georgia must've talked about her. "That's right."

"Why come back?"

She wasn't fooled by the easy questions. She'd bet he'd played good cop back in the day. "Asked myself that question a lot."

"I was a cop long enough to know when someone is searching. What're you searching for?"

A breeze caught the music from the honky-tonk's open door and sent the sounds swirling around her. Her heart thudded faster and faster in her chest. "Can't say."

"Can't or won't."

"Both, I suppose."

He rubbed his hand over the line of his jaw. "You can talk to me, Jenna. I've got no dog in the fight."

She reached for a chalk and started to draw the outline of a face. "I bet there're places in your past you don't want to look."

A frown furrowed his brow. "You've been asking around about me?"

"No." She'd not asked but had read up on him shortly after she started drawing here. He'd appeared in quite a few newspaper clippings. There'd also been articles about Georgia, Deke, and Rick. And if she dug deeper, she knew there'd be articles about her. She'd been unable to muster the courage to read those accounts.

His breath rushed, carrying with it words he rarely spoke. "There was some crap last year in my life. A person I trusted turned on me. Tried to hurt people I love."

His story had been covered in the paper. "I'm sorry."

"I don't like talking about it. Do my best to pretend it never happened. As much as I deny the memories, they find me when I least expect it."

Shadow Eyes. Never in her wildest dreams had she expected that specter to haunt her. Her voice dropped to a whisper. "So what do you do?"

He shoved out a breath as if expelling poison. "Come here to work. Sometimes I drink." His gaze narrowed. "What do you do?"

That teased a bitter smile. She almost denied she had troubling memories and then heard herself say, "I draw."

"What do you draw?" She focused on the sketch, quickly drawing KC's nose, lips, and finally his eyes.

"You draw me?"

Smiling, she handed him the picture. "No, I draw this." She flipped through several pages in a sketchbook until she reached a page filled with dark, penetrating eyes.

He grabbed reading glasses from the breast pocket of his shirt and adjusted them on his nose. "Eyes. Who's that supposed to be?"

She traced the bottom edge of the page. "I have no idea. But the image won't leave my mind."

"Is it attached to one of your cases?"

"I'm not sure where it comes from."

He arched a brow as he studied the picture. "Is that why you're in Nashville?"

Yes. "Maybe. I think so."

"Jenna, you aren't giving me the whole story."

A grin tipped the edge of her lips. "I'll work up to it eventually."

Before he could respond, a family with two blond girls stepped out of a barbecue restaurant and caught her eye. The girls were about five and six and wore matching pink shirts decorated with rhinestone guitars. The mother studied the easel and Jenna spotted her first customer of the night.

"Much as I want to chat, KC, I got a customer."

He looked past her to the family. "They aren't Rudy's customers."

"Ah, you know how it works. A couple of cute kids get their sketch done and folks stop and watch me draw. Before you know it, you got guys promising girlfriends they can have a picture. I always send the ones willing to wait into your place."

A sly grin tugged the edge of his mouth. "It's worked out pretty well."

"Darn right. Now get back to work." The order came with a smile, which had him rolling his gaze and calling her sassy before he vanished back into the bar.

The father of the family approached. "You open for business?"

He was a pleasant looking guy. Midsize, dark hair, glasses, and a round belly. A very dad kind of guy. "You would be my first customer of the night." She smiled at the mom, knowing she'd cinch the deal, not the dad. "I could draw them together."

The mom brushed back long bangs hanging over deep-set eyes. "I doubt they'd sit together right now. They've been fighting for the last couple of hours."

She studied the girls. Red cheeks and a couple of yawns told her she'd not have more than fifteen minutes to capture them on paper. "I'll make it appear they're together. You can even walk one around while I work with the other."

The mom considered Jenna's suggestion and then nodded. "Fair enough." They negotiated a price and Jenna was soon sketching the younger of the two. Millie. She had large green eyes, a pug nose, and lips that curled up a little even when she wasn't smiling. She was cute, but clearly not up for sitting still. Her mother sat on the stool set up for customers and held Millie on her lap.

Jenna talked about cowboy hats and guitars and songs as she quickly drew the girl's face and outlined her eyes. She hesitated only briefly and then quickly finished the last details. No time to fret or worry. Just draw.

When Jenna had been in high school, she'd set up an easel in the Inner Harbor of Baltimore. With the waters of the Chesapeake lapping gently, she'd refined her portrait skills. She'd charged only a few bucks for the first drawings, but as that first summer had gone on, she'd gotten better and better. She'd even caught the eye of a guy representing an amusement park in Virginia. The park was two hours south of Baltimore, but the offer was too good to resist. She'd found someone to bunk with the following summer and had spent ten hours a day drawing. Drawing-crazed families at a park had honed skills that would later serve her well on the Force.

Jenna glanced at the picture of Millie and smiled. She could have spent longer, shading and refining, but forty bucks only bought so much detail. Next on Mom's lap was the older sister who looked like a slightly older carbon copy of Millie.

"What's your name?" Jenna asked.

"Sara."

Jenna's heart stilled for an instant. Memories of another Sara flashed in her mind. Her Sara wasn't smiling but arguing with her father. *"Leave me alone! You don't understand!"*

The memory fluttered away as quickly as it had come. "My sister's name was Sara."

The mother gazed at Jenna over her daughter's head, clearly catching Jenna's use of the past tense. "Did you two look alike?"

Jenna nodded. "Mom said we could've been twins if not for the decade separating our birthdays."

"How long has she been gone?"

"A very long time. I was only five when it happened." Emotion clogged her throat. She could never remember a time when she'd talked about Sara and here she was with a stranger opening up.

The mom hugged her Sara a little closer. "I'm sorry."

"Thanks."

Sara nestled closer to her mother. Jenna ignored the tightening in her chest and focused on face, hair, and eyes and when it came time to draw the girl's mouth she laughed. "You don't want me to draw that thumb in your mouth, do you?"

The girl nodded. Mom pulled her thumb free and talked about eating an ice cream if she could smile. She smiled.

A crowd had gathered around Jenna as it did most nights here. Any other night and she'd have welcomed the scrutiny.

Jenna rolled up Millie and Sara's portrait, put a rubber band around it, and handed it to Mom while Dad paid her with two crisp twenties. Soon, she had a young girl sitting in her subject's chair. The next couple of hours went quickly and she drew a half-dozen people. She'd earned nearly three hundred bucks. A nice haul.

It was nearing ten and her hands and back ached. She

rose, ready to pack up and call it a night as a man approached. "Still open for business?"

She looked up into a lean, rawboned face with blue eyes that cut and pierced. Her heart skipped a beat as she thought about Shadow Eyes in her sketchbook. "Sure."

She searched around for a girlfriend. Most men didn't sit for a picture but were happy to treat their lady. "For you?"

"Yeah. Mom will love it."

This guy had to be in his early forties so she didn't picture him as the type worried about Mom but if life had taught her anything, sometimes a book didn't match its cover. "Forty dollars for twenty minutes."

He dug two rumpled twenties from his jeans pocket. "Sure, why not?"

She sat back down and he took his place across from her. She loaded a clean piece of paper on the easel, fastening it with binder clips. She reached for the charcoal and started to sketch the outline of his long, lean face. "So what brings you to Nashville?"

"I lived here all my life. I normally don't get down to Broadway. Too many tourists but figured what the hell tonight. What about you?"

"New to the area."

"From where?"

She didn't mind asking the questions but didn't like answering them. "Back East."

He nodded. "You sound like an Easterner."

"That so?"

"Yeah. Where?"

"D.C. area." Give or take thirty miles.

"So what're you doing tonight after you finish up here?"

She sat a little straighter. "I've got an appointment."

"Too bad."

She didn't comment as she rose and began to pack up her supplies. "Thanks for the business."

He hesitated and then with a quick nod, turned and left. She watched him move down the sidewalk crowded with laughing tourists and then vanish around the corner. Her fingers trembled. "What the hell is wrong with me?"

She thought about the Lost Girl's picture in her case and suddenly had a real need to give it to Rick and be done with the case.

Jenna packed up her supplies, loaded them in her car, and drove to the Nashville Police Department. She parked in the nearby lot and shut off the engine. Large humming lamps cast an eerie glow on her pale skin as she grabbed her sketchpad and headed across the lot to the front doors. She moved to the main desk where a uniformed officer sat.

"I need to leave a sketch for Detective Rick Morgan."

The female officer had red hair twisted into a tight bun at the base of her head. The sprinkle of freckles across the bridge of her nose did little to soften her demeanor. "And you are?"

"Jenna Thompson." Explaining herself had not been as easy as she'd hoped. Carrying a sketchpad and saying she knew Rick Morgan didn't mean squat to the officer on duty, who would not let her inside without a badge.

"I need identification."

She'd left her badge in Baltimore. "Best I can do is a driver's license."

"That'll do."

She dug it out of her purse and handed it over.

A glance at the license prompted a frown before she handed it back to Jenna. "Detective Morgan should be back in the next fifteen minutes. You can wait or give whatever it is you need to give him to me. I'll see that he gets it."

Instinctively, she hugged the sketchpad closer to her chest. "Thanks. I'll wait."

"Suit yourself."

She moved to an empty bank of chairs and sat. Seconds

later, two uniformed officers moved past the front desk, flashing badges and exchanging smiles with the redhead before vanishing behind the locked double doors.

How many times had she breezed through the lobby of the Baltimore Police Department, barely tossing a glance toward the people in the waiting room? She'd never given a thought or questioned her total access.

And now here she sat. She was on the other side of the desk. An outsider. She'd chosen to take leave from the Force. She'd needed the break. But until this moment she had never felt like an outsider looking over the thin blue line. She missed belonging to a fraternity that was more family than job.

Ten minutes passed. She drummed her fingers on her thigh as she sat and watched people come and go. Whether they were laughing, frowning, or stoic, they moved beyond the double doors with ease.

Rick Morgan pushed through the front door. His jaw was set, his gaze hard and focused. Not a happy camper by her estimation.

Good. Join the club. She stood. "Morgan."

At the sound of her voice, he turned, assessing her with a quick sweep of his gaze. "Jenna."

With her sketchpad tucked under her arm, she moved toward him. "I have your sketch."

Surprise widened his eyes a fraction as he met her halfway. "It's finished?"

"Yes." She nearly explained that, as always, she'd struggled with the eyes but caught herself and remained silent.

"Come on upstairs. I'd like to have a look at it."

She could have handed it off to him and been done with it. In fact, that's exactly what she wanted to do. But she couldn't do that to the Lost Girl. Somewhere along the way she'd become invested in this case. She might have crossed

the blue line, but this case was as much hers as it was his.
"Sure."

They took the elevator and wound through a series of
cubicles and desks until they reached a windowless conference room. He flipped on a light and reached for his cell.
"I'll text Bishop. He'll want to see this."

"Okay." On a credenza, a coffeepot filled with stale
coffee that resembled sludge reminded her of the Baltimore
Police Department. The furniture looked overused and tired.
The walls had faded from white to a dullish gray. Some
things were universal. She set her sketchpad on the table.

Rick's phone vibrated and he checked the text. "He'll
be here in twenty."

More waiting. She'd not have done it for anyone other
than the little girl whom she'd captured in her sketch.
"Sure."

"Can I get you coffee?"

She laid her sketchpad on the table. "Was it made in the
last decade?"

A smile quirked the edge of his lips. "Within the last few
weeks. I'll make a fresh pot."

"Don't bother."

"I could use one."

"Then, sure." The coffee would mean she wouldn't sleep
but her racing mind had already signaled this was going to
be a long night.

"Be right back." He vanished and reappeared minutes
later with two steaming cups. "I'm fairly good at making
coffee."

It smelled fresh, rich. "A man of hidden talents."

He nodded, and a smile curled his lips as he raised the
cup to his lips. "Sugar or milk?"

"No, thanks."

He motioned for her to sit and if she'd been left alone,

she'd have stood. Too much energy buzzed in her body. But if she stood, so would he.

She sat in the chair and watched as he sat and angled his seat away from the table so that it faced her. "Can I have a look at the sketch?"

"You don't want to wait for your partner?"

"No."

She hadn't been away from the Force so long that she'd forgotten how to read a tense vibe. "There a turf war between you two?"

His fingers tensed a fraction as he sipped from his cup. "No. I just don't feel like waiting."

"You ooze tension, Morgan."

The next smile didn't reach his eyes. "Don't know what you're seeing."

She opted not to press. "Long as it doesn't interfere with this case, then I don't care."

"You talk about it as if it were your case."

"It is. Not officially, of course, but I'm invested. I want her killer caught." She opened her sketchbook and flipped past several pages filled with sketches of half-drawn faces.

He studied her a beat. "You miss the job, don't you?"

"Sure. I miss it."

"Why'd you quit?"

Ah, there was the question. The elephant that danced in the room each time they were together. "I didn't quit. I took leave." He'd turned the tables on her. "Does it really matter?"

"Not in the big scheme but I'm curious."

"Just needed a break."

He shook his head. "That's a lame answer, Thompson."

Just because he asked, didn't mean he deserved an answer to the question. "Didn't you take a break after you were shot?"

"A bullet to the hip forced the time off so I gave school a try while my body healed. Matter of time before I returned."

"We should all be so lucky to have your clear vision."

Jenna shifted, her discomfort growing like a flame fed with dry kindling. "Let's look at the sketch." She opened her sketchpad, more than ready to be finished with this conversation.

As she flipped through the pages his attention was drawn away from her to the page filled with eyes. "What're those?"

"I'm always drawing. Often, I'm intrigued and work on a face and then I lose interest and don't finish it."

"You got a thing for eyes."

"They're the mirrors to the soul."

"You believe that?"

"I do."

"Seems odd that you wouldn't finish the sketches. Or maybe that's kinda your thing. Not finishing a job."

"Damn, Morgan, does your brain only entertain one thought at a time?" Irritation burned under her tone.

"I'm like a dog with a bone."

Did he just want her gone from Nashville? "I didn't come here to talk about me. These partial drawings are a part of the drawing process."

"Whom are you trying to draw?" he said, pointing to the eyes.

"I don't know exactly."

"You don't know?"

This close, his energy radiated. She offered another shrug of her shoulders to soften another incomplete explanation. "Artists and their quirks."

She quickly flipped more pages; aware he watched each page and sketch as they passed. When she found the page featuring the little girl, she carefully folded the sketchpad so that this was the only image he saw. She turned it to him, nerves biting at her. There was always a rush of worry when she showed any work for the first time. And for reasons she couldn't explain she wanted Detective Rick Morgan to approve of this job.

A deep frown furrowed his brow as he reached for the sketchpad and then hesitated. "May I?"

"Yes."

He lifted the sketch and studied the image. The little girl smiled back revealing an uneven crooked tooth. Her eyes were hazel green, her face round, and angel-soft hair haloed dimpled cheeks. She wore a soft pink collared shirt that enhanced her glow.

"She's beautiful." He spoke softly, his voice thick with emotion. "I can almost imagine hearing the sound of her laughter."

The knot in her chest unfurled just a little. "I wanted her to be pretty because I think she must have been very sweet."

"Why the smile?"

What he didn't say was that he feared, as she did, that the little girl had had little to smile about in her short life. "She deserved to be seen by the world smiling. I've also another sketch of her. In that sketch I drew her with a closed-mouth expression. I realize she might not have been a happy child."

He didn't bother to flip the page but continued to stare at the smiling image. "This is excellent, Jenna. Really some of the best forensic art I've ever seen."

"I'm one of the best."

He lifted his gaze to her. "I believe it now."

"You didn't before?"

"If you were so good, why'd you end up in a bar seven hundred miles from home, drawing pictures on the street?"

She didn't answer because she didn't have a credible answer for him or for herself.

"I can't believe you walked away from this." When she

opened her mouth to correct him, he held up a hand. "Took leave."

A shrug.

He sat back in his chair and stared at her with a keenness he had to reserve for suspects. She realized he knew why she left Baltimore. Not surprising. Made sense that someone would check up on her. She'd have checked up on her. "Who did you talk to in Baltimore?"

His hand rested on the conference table, his thumb tapping. "Not me. Georgia. She's a suspicious sort."

That jostled a laugh. "Smart gal."

Any humor evaporated like ice on a hot Nashville day. "Why the leave?"

She held his gaze, refusing to look away. She'd done nothing wrong. "Job just got to be too much. I couldn't handle the pain anymore." She sat back in her chair. "I needed to take a break and get my head together."

He studied her, jaw clenched. "The Baltimore case of the little girl, that hit a huge nerve with you. Why?"

The door opened to Bishop and Deke who entered the room, shattering the tentative connection Jenna and Rick had forged. They rose.

Relief flooded her body. A moment ago, she'd been ready to drop her guard and talk to Rick. Openness was not a trait she enjoyed and she was glad now for the disturbance. She armored herself in as many professional layers as she could scramble around her.

Rick's ease had also vanished. His was the expression of a man with much to prove to his brother, his partner, and himself. "Detective Deke Morgan, Jenna Thompson. She's our forensic artist. As you may have guessed by the name, Deke is my brother."

As Deke reached out a hand to her, she found herself cataloguing the similarities between Rick and Deke. "You two look alike. Is Georgia the outlier?"

The brothers exchanged a glance and then Rick said, "She's adopted."

Bishop's expression held no hint of emotion but she sensed a keen interest in him.

"Like me," Jenna said. "Explains the connection when we met."

Deke studied her a beat but, without commenting, picked up the image and held it out so all could see. "Hell of a job."

"Thanks."

"Flip the sheet and you'll see her with a closed-mouth expression," Jenna said.

Deke turned the page and showed it to Bishop.

"I like the first better," Detective Bishop said.

"Me too," Deke said.

"We need to get the image out to the media," Bishop said. "The sooner, the better."

"Susan Martinez is on board," Rick added. "We just need to get a copy to her and she'll put it on air."

"She said yes, just like that?" Deke asked.

Rick shook his head. "She'd like to interview Jenna. I didn't commit."

Jenna had assumed she'd be behind the scenes. It had never occurred to her she'd take center stage. "That really necessary?"

"No. But she said it would get the story more air time."

Jenna had arrived in Nashville with little purpose other than to understand where she came from and why Ronnie had taken it all away. She had researched the town and her family through old news clippings, but she'd stayed under the radar, basically hiding behind her sketchpad. So stupid to come this far and hide. She was no coward.

Maybe now it was time to let Nashville know she was here. "Okay."

"Okay what?" Rick asked.

"She can interview me. Shouldn't be that hard to explain what I do?" She looked like her mother and her sister. If Shadow Eyes was watching, he'd recognize her.

Rick shook his head. "I don't fully trust this reporter."

A smile tipped the edges of her lips. "I can handle her."

Rick frowned. "It's not necessary."

"I know."

Deke's gaze lingered on the sketch. "Would you be open to doing another sketch? Budget's going to be smaller than this one."

"This one was for free," Jenna said. "Can't beat that price."

Deke studied her. "Right."

"Who am I drawing?" She tossed out the question, more interested in shifting Rick's attention away from her.

"There's an attorney, a public defender, in town. Rachel Wainwright. She has a new client who's been accused of drunk driving. Rachel thinks there're mitigating circumstances. Long story short her client says she was raped two months ago and has been suffering from PTSD."

With the Lost Girl, she'd felt volatile. With this new witness, she held on to a healthy dose of skepticism. "Sounds like a ploy."

"I would agree," Deke said. "But Wainwright says the woman is telling the truth and Wainwright has a good nose for this kind of thing."

She folded her arms and cocked her head. "Homicide detective working with a public defender?"

Deke's craggy face lifted into a smile that almost looked friendly. "Yeah."

Rick chuckled. "Give her the whole story."

Deke shoved his hands in his pockets. "Rachel and I are dating." The admission softened the detective's features. Rachel had breached his armor.

"Ah."

"Rachel is a tad driven when she thinks she's defending the innocent," Deke offered.

"Not easy to be around, right, Bro?" Rick offered.

"Just a bit."

Jenna looked at Rick. "You don't like her?"

Rick shook his head. "On the contrary. I respect the hell out of her. She stepped up for Georgia last year. Saved her life. So I'll always be in her corner."

Jenna waited for more explanation. She'd read the articles but knew there was more. When he didn't explain, she didn't push.

She'd never planned to stay here long, and then she'd signed the monthlong lease, accepted one assignment and now another. A simple no would have severed her growing connections to the town and this family. And still, she only shrugged and said, "Sure."

"When are you available?"

"When is the witness available?"

"She's at Rachel's office now. Rachel just got her out on bail."

"Has Rachel got that look in her eye?" Rick asked.

Deke nodded. "She believes her client, no matter what the preliminary evidence says. She's on a mission."

Jenna didn't want to go home and this was a good excuse to delay it. "I've got my kit in my Jeep. If Ms. Wainwright is open to a visit now, I'll do it now."

"I'll call Rachel," Deke said. "Her office is only blocks from here."

"I'll walk you over," Rick said.

"Sure." With care, she tore the images of the girl off the sketchpad and handed them to Rick. "She's in your hands now."

"I'll get those to Martinez," Bishop said. No hint of bravado or challenge.

Rick handed over the pictures. Whatever turf war these two were having, well, they'd called a truce during this case.

They moved down the hallway, down to the first floor and out to the parking lot. The sun had set and a gentle breeze blew cooler air. She fished her keys from her purse and opened the back door. She grabbed her art box.

Rick took the box from her. "Her office is three blocks that way."

"Handy location."

"She'll tell you she picked the place because it's cheap. Her place used to be a restaurant. She works on the first floor and lives on the second."

As they walked down Union, she inhaled a deep breath, savoring the open space. "Where's Tracker?"

"Home. We had to swing by the house for a few minutes and this late in the day he's better off resting."

"I bet he wasn't happy."

"No. Not thrilled. But I gave him a chew stick and that seemed to buy some forgiveness."

A smile played on the edges of her lips. "I took leave from the Force willingly and I realized today how much I miss it. I can't imagine having it snatched away."

"It's not fun."

The walk to Rachel's office took ten minutes and just as they reached it, Rick's cell buzzed.

"Deke," he said as he raised the phone to his ear. He listened and nodded. "Great. I'll let her know."

As he hung up, Jenna said, "Ms. Wainwright has agreed to the sketch."

"She did. She's getting her client ready now."

"She doesn't waste time."

"She's a dynamo. Not the kind of attorney I'd want to deal with in court."

Deke, who'd driven, had beaten them to the office, a

brick building with a large plate-glass window that read
WAINWRIGHT AND ASSOCIATES.

Deke and a slender woman with short, black hair greeted
them. Intensity radiated from the woman who wore a black
sleeveless dress that showed off fit arms and the lean legs
of a runner.

"Jenna Thompson," Rick said. "Meet Rachel Wainwright. Attorney-at-law and champion of the downtrodden."

Rachel arched a brow. She was tall, lean, and possessed
a severity that might have made her unapproachable if not
for her eyes. They radiated a softness that weakened some
of Jenna's defenses.

The attorney extended her hand to Jenna. "I hear you're
a forensic artist."

Jenna accepted her hand, noting Rachel's firm handshake. "I am."

"She's very talented," Rick said.

Jenna shrugged. "I am."

Rachel's gaze sharpened. "I like a woman who knows
her worth."

"Where's your client?" Jenna asked.

"And you don't like to waste time. We might become
friends," Rachel said. "My client is inside. She's taking a
quick shower but will be downstairs in a minute."

They entered the building to find a large, open floor
plan. There were two desks, one piled high with papers and
the other stripped clean as if it had been vacated. Looked
like "and Associates" was for show.

"Is there a private place she and I can meet?" Witnesses
often relaxed in more private conditions.

"No formal conference room but there is the kitchen. It's
become an impromptu conference room at times. My client
will join us there soon."

She glanced toward double swinging doors that looked
as if they led to the kitchen. "Great."

"I'll be sitting in, of course."

"No," Jenna said.

"Excuse me?" Rachel's tone took a hard right from easy-going to challenging.

"I always meet with my 'clients' alone. In the early years, I'd allow friends and, once, an attorney, to stay. But having the other person in the process affected the outcome. The witness will always relax more if it's just the two of us."

Rachel looked as if she'd bitten into something sour. "I'm looking out for Belinda's best interests. I wouldn't hamper her description."

Rick, to his credit, did not offer a comment. *Points for him,* she thought. She fought her own battles.

"You wouldn't mean to, but you would. We always alter what we say based on our audience, even if we don't realize we're doing it." She knew her job, but these folks didn't fully believe that. One sketch had earned her some points but cops, and clearly Rachel Wainwright, were a hard sell. "I promise it will be best. You'll end up with a better image."

Hands planted on narrow hips, Rachel considered Jenna. "I'm going to hold you to that."

Rick shook his head. "On that note, I'll leave you two."

Rachel looked at Rick as if she'd forgotten he was there. "Thanks."

Smiling as if accustomed to Rachel's tunnel vision, Rick saluted and with a nod to Jenna said, "Good luck."

The Morgans didn't smile much as a general rule but when they did, it was hard to be indifferent. "It's getting late and this is going to take a few hours."

"Sure."

As Rachel led the way, Jenna followed. The two entered the industrial kitchen equipped with well-used stainless-steel appliances and a large counter surrounded by a half-dozen stools.

Rachel reached in a bulky briefcase and pulled out a thin file. "I was just assigned her case this morning. Her name is Belinda Horton. She's twenty years old and she's a waitress at a local pub in East Nashville."

"What happened?"

"She was attacked. Raped. The man held a knife to her throat and told her if she moved, he'd cut her throat. She was terrified and complied."

Jenna had felt helpless and terrified when she'd been five, but as an adult, she'd learned self-defense as well as how to handle a gun. She'd never, ever wanted to feel that kind of fear again.

As if reading her thoughts, Rachel added, "She's a small woman and her attacker was well over six feet. She'd never encountered any violence before."

"Why was she in jail?"

"According to Belinda, the attack happened two months ago. She never told anyone and she never sought out help after the attack. She's been drinking heavily. Last night, she was drunk when she slammed her car into a park bench. She walked away unscathed but totaled her car as well as the bench. The judge wasn't happy and wanted to send a message to drunk drivers."

"Understandable."

"He's ready to throw the book at her. When I got the case, she started weeping almost immediately and told me about the rape. No one else knows."

"Could be a convenient lie." Jenna traced her finger over the smooth edge of the visitor's table.

"I know. Believe me, I know. That's why I'd like a picture of her attacker. If we can somehow identify him then maybe we can prove the attack happened and she can receive counseling instead of jail time."

"Fair enough."

Seconds later, they heard footsteps in the back hallway and the back staircase doorway swung open to a petite woman whose short, blond hair hung damp around her round face. Mascara had smudged below her eyes and the jeans and gray shirt she wore made her skin look sallow. She wore chipped red-tipped nail polish and had a small butterfly tattoo on her wrist.

Belinda's eyes were bloodshot as she looked at Rachel with a measure of relief. "Ms. Wainwright."

Rachel smiled. "Belinda. How're you doing?"

"Hanging in there. I'm so tired and want to sleep but my brain won't shut off."

"It will later tonight and then you can get some sleep." Rachel placed a steady hand on Jenna's forearm. "This is Jenna Thompson. She's a forensic artist and she's here to help you remember the face of the man that attacked you. We've pulled a few strings to have her here."

Belinda shook her head as she sat at the counter. "I don't want to remember. I've been spending the last few months doing my best to forget."

Rachel slipped behind the counter where a pot of coffee brewed. She poured her client and Jenna a cup. "You have to remember. You have to or you're going to jail for as long as that judge can send you away. I have to prove that you've been suffering post-traumatic stress from the rape."

Tears welled in her blue eyes. "I can't."

Jenna cleared her throat. "Rachel, why don't you give us a few minutes. We're just going to talk and I'm going to draw. Nothing serious. No pressure." She'd get the image but getting the details would be slow-going.

Rachel smiled at Belinda. "I'll leave you with Jenna. She's a nice lady and she's here to help." Rising, she took a step back, hesitating when Belinda swiped a tear from her face.

Jenna sat at the counter and opened her sketchpad to a face she'd drawn earlier. She showed it to Belinda. "This is one of my drawings."

"Is that a bad guy?"

Jenna glanced at the image of a man she'd drawn just a couple of days ago. "No, he's a cop. Detective Rick Morgan. I draw pictures when I get bored. I just wanted you to see what I can do."

Belinda sniffed. "It's good."

"I think so. Though I'm not sure of the eyes." She studied the image with a critical eye and as with most artists thought about a dozen things she'd do differently if given another chance.

"How'd you get started drawing faces?"

"When I was fifteen I talked my aunt into letting me draw portraits in Inner Harbor in Baltimore. I set up an easel and she watched as I waited for people to stop. That first day was warm for so early in the summer and I was soaked in sweat when my first customers stopped, a woman and her boyfriend. I drew her and she loved it so much he gave me a twenty-dollar tip. I spent several summers on that corner and made money for school."

A swinging door whooshed behind them and she realized Rachel had left. Now the work could begin.

"I know you don't want to remember."

"I don't."

"If we can get him on paper, then maybe we can get him out of your brain and nightmares."

Her eyes widened with surprise. "How'd you know he's there?"

"Men like him thrive in the shadows. They feed on our fear and they return over and over again if we don't find a way to lock them behind bars."

She dropped her face to her hands. "Will he really go away?"

Jenna felt herself moving to this woman's corner. "We won't know unless we try."

A ragged sigh shuddered from her small body. "Okay."

And so the two of them began the process of questions and answers. If Jenna had been back in Baltimore she'd have had access to facial identification catalogues or even a computer. But she only had her sketchpad and charcoal. Not as easy as she'd have liked it but also not impossible.

At first Belinda sat straight, her hands fisted on the table. But as Jenna began to draw, the woman relaxed and with each swipe of the charcoal she became more drawn into the process.

By the time they'd finished the sketch, it was nearly midnight and both were exhausted. Jenna's back ached and a dull headache pounded behind her left eye, but she considered both a small price to pay for the image that now radiated from the page.

Jenna turned the sketch around so that Belinda could get a clear view. "Is this the guy?"

She stared at it for long, tense seconds before she finally nodded. "That's him."

He was a man in his late thirties with a long, narrow face and sloping, wide-set eyes. Based on her description he was Caucasian with rough skin pockmarked by old acne scars.

"I'll give this to Rachel and see what she can do with it?"

Her gaze sparked with hope and fear. "Do you think they'll be able to find him?"

She pulled a rag from her back pocket and wiped the black charcoal from her fingers. "I don't know, but having a face will certainly help."

Belinda stared at the face. "I hate that face. I dream about it."

"Maybe not so much anymore." Jenna rose. "You did a good job here tonight, Belinda. Try and get some sleep."

"Thanks."

Jenna moved to the door and pushed it open. Rachel sat at her desk, reading a brief. There was no sign of Deke or Rick.

"We're finished."

Rachel rose and moved toward the kitchen door. She followed Jenna back to the counter where Belinda sat. "How'd it go?"

"Well." Jenna tore the picture from her sketchpad and handed it to Rachel. "You have a face now."

Rachel studied the picture. "This image just might get us in the game for a sound defense."

Belinda nodded, too tired to smile. "I hope so."

"You need to sleep," Rachel said. "I'll run you home."

Belinda nodded and as she started to follow stopped and turned to Jenna. "Are you going to come back?"

"Why would I?"

"So I can tell you about the other man."

"What other man?" Rachel asked.

"The one that stood in the shadows and watched while the other man raped me."

Rachel's narrowing eyes suggested this was all new territory to her. "You never told me about the second man."

Frowning, Belinda shook her head. "I only just remembered him when I was talking to Jenna."

"Did you see him?" Jenna asked. Drawings could trigger memories.

"No. Not really. I just heard his voice. He was telling that guy what to do to me."

"He was directing the rape?" Rachel asked.

"Yes. I think so."

"But you never saw him?" Jenna asked.

Belinda seemed to consider the question. "Once very

briefly. I got away from the first man and as I ran through the house, the other man was at the front door. He was locking the door and closing the drapes." She pressed fingertips to her temples as if the memories pounded her brain. "When the rapist grabbed me and took me back to the bedroom, the second man turned and I saw him for a second or two."

"I could work with her," Jenna offered.

"That would be great." Rachel glanced at the clock on the wall. "But it's late. And Belinda, you're exhausted. We'll talk in the morning about this other man."

Belinda looked relieved and disappointed. "Okay. But Jenna will come back?"

"Yes. I'll come back," Jenna said, offering the young girl a smile. "You did a good job."

As Belinda gathered her purse, Rachel studied the sketch. "This is very good, Jenna."

"Thanks. Hope it helps. Now if you don't mind I'm heading home. I'm exhausted."

"Sure. You remember where you're parked?"

"I can manage."

Outside, Jenna glanced up at the clear night sky, savoring the twinkle of so many stars. Clear nights in the summer were rare. Humidity and heat usually wiped a thick haze over the sky, blurring and hiding the stars. But not tonight. Tonight, even with the lights from the city, the stars shone brightly.

Energy buzzed in her system. She rolled her head from side to side. The Lost Girl had a face. A nameless attacker had a face. She'd made a difference, as she had in Baltimore. And it felt good.

"So how'd it go?"

Startled, she turned to see Rick push off a wall and move toward her with a steady, deliberate gait. He'd loosened his tie. A slight breeze caught the folds of his jacket brushing them back enough to offer a glimpse of his revolver. He radiated an energy that drew her. Damn. No. She would not even let her mind go in that direction. Hormones coupled with a crash of emotions had driven her into Mike's arms weeks ago and that had been a mistake. She was not going to repeat the error.

She cleared her throat. "It went well. We've the face of the first attacker."

A dark brow arched. "First?"

She kept walking, fearing if she stopped she might be tempted to touch him. She really just needed to get some distance and clear her head. Jenna and Rick. Out of the blue, she pictured their names carved on a tree and nearly laughed at the image. "At the very end of the session she said there was a man directing the attack."

Rick's gaze sharpened. "She get a good look at him?"

"I don't know. We'll have to meet again. Maybe in a day or two when she's rested. She's so tired now and it'll take her time to process what she remembered tonight."

He shook his head. "So Rachel really has a case and it's not a bogus defense attorney move?"

"Maybe. Belinda strikes me as genuine. I've been fooled before, but I don't think so this time."

They moved down the sidewalk and cut down between the buildings, coming out into the lit parking lot where she'd parked her Jeep. He followed her all the way to her car and waited as she unlocked it and put her sketchpad and purse on the front seat.

"Thanks for the escort, but I could've managed," she said.

"No extra trouble."

She lingered, the hormones tugging at her. "I guess you can get back to the paying work now?" She ran a hand through her hair. "I've a portrait I have to finish by Friday. The subject is coming to see the final product. She's a very high-strung bride who wants to display the portrait at her reception."

"Killers to brides. That's a jump."

His deadpan tone made her laugh. "Both dangerous in their own ways."

For an instant, the hard lines of his face softened into a very appealing face. Those hormones hopped and jumped. *Touch him. Just for tonight. This isn't for keeps.* Like buzzing flies, she swatted away the desire. "Thanks again for all your help, Jenna."

"Glad I could be of service." She offered her hand. "Keep me posted on the case. I'd really like to know what happens."

He wrapped a calloused hand around hers, squeezing and then holding her hand an extra beat. "Will do."

She pulled her hand free and slid behind the wheel of her car. Firing up the engine, she shifted into reverse and backed out of the space. With a final wave to him, she drove off, glancing once in the rearview mirror to see him standing and staring at her as she drove off.

She didn't play for keeps. It was safer that way. Easier. Rick did play for keeps, which put him in a league with the likes of Mike. Dangerous.

Chapter Eight

Rick and Tracker arrived early at work. Tracker was well rested. Rick had barely three hours under his belt and was feeling the fatigue in his stiff muscles. Last night after he'd dropped off Jenna at her car he'd doubled back to the office and read over Jonas Tuttle's file again. What the hell about this open-and-shut case bugged him? Maybe it was because a guy like Tuttle, with a string of arrests, didn't have the brains or temperament to pull off such a detailed operation. Had he been working with someone? And then something Jenna had told him about Rachel's case stuck in his gut. *She says another guy watched.* He'd texted Rachel the picture, with the words: *I will find him.* It was after one in the morning but she'd responded almost immediately.

Her text had read: *If you can find him, I'll buy you dinner.*

He'd studied the face Jenna had drawn of Belinda's attacker and Tuttle. They weren't a match but were the same type of petty criminal who turned violent on those weaker. Tuttle's low-slung brow, the slightly drooping mouth, and the thick jowls hinted at his low intelligence. Was he the type of guy to stalk a woman for months, scout a crime scene, and then lure her to it? Neither man seemed the kind of guy who planned. This breed of assailant reacted on impulse. They didn't plan.

One committed the crime and one watched, maybe even planned. It made sense that Tuttle would have had some kind of handler.

He sent Rachel's sketch out with a BOLO, a Be On the LookOut, and shut off his desk lamp at two in the morning, no closer to an answer.

Now, Tracker settled on his bed by the desk and Rick glanced at his desk to find another stack of files. They were cases of more missing kids. These files had come from the Tennessee Bureau of Investigation. The time span of the twenty-plus files covered the last thirty years.

Bishop arrived minutes after he did, a cup of coffee in his hand. As he took a liberal sip, his gaze landed with weary resignation on the files. "Where did those come from?"

"TBI."

"Since when do they offer up case files without a request?"

"Remember that good ol' boy network you hate so much? My brother Alex is TBI. I'd bet money he sent them."

Bishop studied the stack. "Even a bad system works from time to time."

Deke might have asked or Alex might have heard about the case. Either way, Rick knew Alex had sent the files. He didn't want to be grateful. But he was.

Rick shrugged off his jacket and hung it on the back of his chair. "Will take time to compare Jenna's picture to the files. If we don't get a hit with this batch, then I'll go to Martinez."

"It's a plan."

After arming himself with a strong cup of coffee, Rick

cut the stack in two. Half went to Bishop and half to himself. The reading wasn't easy. Little kids ranging from ages three to ten had vanished without a trace. The detectives of record in at least half the cases reported that the primary suspect had been a non-custodial parent involved in a nasty custody battle. Some of the kids just vanished. No arrests or bodies had been found in any of the cases. The kids had been little innocents who'd seen far too much darkness.

An hour after reading and comparing file photos to the sketch, Rick had come up with nothing. No matches. Hell, not even a maybe. He reached for his coffee, found only dregs, and rose slowly, wincing as his hip muscles pinched. "You got anything?"

"Nothing." Bishop leaned back in his chair and pinched the bridge of his nose. "Not a damn thing."

"Time to make a deal with the devil."

"Your good buddy, the reporter?"

"Yeah. Looks like I've got to have a chat with Martinez."

"She said she'd help, so why the sour face? Boy Scouts don't frown."

"There's always a price to pay and this price is an exclusive on the Diane Smith murder."

"It's an open-and-shut case. Jonas Tuttle stalked her and killed her."

Rick shook his head. "It just doesn't feel right to me. Guy doesn't have the wherewithal to hold down a job for more than a few months but he finds it in himself to stalk an intelligent woman, use sophisticated surveillance equipment, and then pull off a crime that leaves no trace evidence."

"Insanity can be a great motivator." Bishop cracked his knuckles. "But I hear you. It's doesn't smell exactly right."

"The prostitute said he held a gun to her head almost as if he were practicing."

"And how quickly did he screw that up? She got away

from him in a matter of minutes. He's lucky she didn't call the cops."

Bishop leaned back in his chair, clicking a pen he'd picked up from his desk. "So what're you saying?"

"He could've been working with someone. Maybe Jonas couldn't keep his mouth shut and the other guy decided to clean up a loose end."

"Not out of the realm of reality but we've talked to her sister and coworkers. The only guy who had a beef with her was that dude in the association. Hacked over a tree. And his story about the Italian restaurant checked out."

"It wasn't him. The tree came down weeks ago. Jonas, or somebody, had been stalking Diane for months."

Rick shook his head and turned from the files of lost children. "Maybe it's easier to raise questions about Jonas than to think about these files."

Bishop glanced at the files with a deflated, almost sad look in his eyes. "Fuckin' eh."

Rick grabbed his jacket dangling from the back of his chair. Tracker looked up. "I'm going to see Martinez. Her broadcast will get us some exposure and maybe a hit."

"Want me to come along?"

"Is that an offer to help?"

"No. I just want away from these cases."

"Naw, this devil dance is all mine. But I did put out a BOLO last night. See if we've got any hits."

"What's the case?"

He explained the story behind the sketch Jenna had done last night and his theory about two perps working together.

"That's one hell of a tall tale, Boy Scout." Bishop shook his head as he leaned back in his chair and folded his arms over his chest. "Tall tale."

"Fine, I'll check on it later."

Bishop held up his hands. "I'll ask about your BOLO. Do my heart good to bust a rapist."

"Cop therapy."

Bishop flexed his fingers. "The only kind I subscribe to."

The drive to the television station took less than fifteen minutes and he'd intentionally timed his visit so it didn't conflict with the noonday broadcast. One word to the receptionist and she made a quick call that summoned Martinez from the back of the studio. The doors whisked open and she appeared, dressed in a formfitting royal-blue dress. As always, she looked perfect. Each piece of her jewelry coordinated and he imagined she was the type to plan out every detail of her week in advance, including her clothes.

After a few pleasantries, she escorted Rick and Tracker to a back conference room. As she closed the door with a soft *click*, she turned and asked, "So what do you have for me?"

Rick laid a manila folder on the table and opened it. Inside lay copies of the two sketches Jenna had drawn of the Lost Girl. "This is the likeness of the child I mentioned."

Martinez picked up the smiling face and stared at it with an assessing gaze. "Your artist works fast and is very talented."

"We were lucky to find her."

Martinez studied the image without a smile and then she placed the two side by side. "Very talented. Someone will recognize this image. It's a matter of getting it on the air."

"I agree. I think we're going to find that a grandmother or a neighbor remembers that she was there one day and gone the next."

Martinez laid her palm on her chest as if easing the beat of her heart. "Such a pretty girl. And the eyes. The artist really brought her to life with the eyes."

Jenna had said she'd struggled with the eyes as if she knew nailing them was the key.

Martinez tapped a manicured finger on a set of small

initials scrawled on the bottom-right corner of the picture. *JT*. "I still want to meet the artist and profile her."

Rick tamped down a rush of protective energy. Jenna hadn't asked for his protection nor did he imagine she needed it but, like it or not, she had it. "Is that necessary?"

"As I said the last time, the artist will add a living dimension to the story. Some people will look at the face of the child and we might get a hit but if I can profile the artist, then suddenly I have two stories rolled into one. I have a living, breathing person who took time and energy to bring this child to life, so to speak. There aren't more than thirty artists in the country and I know the few in Tennessee. *JT* doesn't match their names."

"She's not with any Tennessee agency. She's from out of state."

Dark eyes sparked with interest. "Is she still in the area?"

His jaw tensed. "Yes."

She sat back and looked at him, relaxed and at ease. He suspected she'd ask the Devil for iced water if she found herself in hell. "Interviewing JT will turn a quick flash of an image into a human interest story. I would like to meet the person behind the face."

"I told her you might want an interview. She's agreed."

"When?"

Rick reached for his cell, not sure why all this bothered him. "I'll call." He found her number in his phone and hit CALL. The phone rang once. Twice. A part of him hoped she didn't answer. Press exposure never led to good things.

Jenna answered on the third ring. "Hello?"

"This is Rick Morgan. I'm here at the news station." He tightened his jaw, released it. "The reporter I mentioned does want to interview you."

A beat of silence and in the background he heard the whisper of wind. She was no doubt sitting on the back deck. Open spaces. "When?"

"Tomorrow morning."

"Where?" He imagined an easel positioned in front of her. Was she working on that bride picture?

"Let me ask?" He cradled the phone against his chest. "Where do you want to meet?"

Susan's eyes sparkled with victory. "How about her studio? Far more interesting than here or the police station."

Nodding, Rick raised the phone to his ear. "Your place."

More silence, as if she weighed and measured more pros and cons. She had chosen a cabin in the woods that had been the scene of a murder. These were the choices of someone who didn't want to be noticed or visited. More *whys* swirled around Jenna.

"Fine," Jenna said. "Nine o'clock?"

"I'm sure she'll make that work."

"No exterior shots of my house. Just the studio."

Still thinking like a cop. "Understood. Her name is Susan Martinez."

"Right." She hung up without a good-bye.

Martinez's shining eyes had the look of a woman who liked to win. "So we're set?"

He relayed Jenna's request, her address, and the time. "I want to be there. This is a Nashville homicide case."

"Sure. We might even be able to use you in the story." She sat back. "You said her name is?"

"Jenna Thompson"

She hesitated. "She's from . . . ?"

"Baltimore."

"Why'd she leave Baltimore?"

"She didn't. She's on sabbatical."

"Why?"

"You'll have to ask her."

"Anything else you can tell me about her?"

"No," he said honestly. "Nothing."

"Okay." Nodding, she rubbed her hands together. "Looks like I have some homework to do tonight."

As the wind blew in through her open car window, Jenna ended the call with Rick and stared out at the small, worn house in East Nashville. The yard had turned to dust and the house's siding, once white, had muddied to a dirty gray. Two old tires lay under a half-dead tree with browning foliage that offered little shade. A broken bicycle leaned against the house.

Jenna got out of her car and moved with purpose toward the front door. Inside, she heard the blare of a television. She rang the bell but it didn't work. She banged on the door once and, when she heard no sound, banged again. Finally, the faint sound of shuffling footsteps drifted out from under the front door. After several chains scraped free of locks, the door opened a crack. An older woman stared up at her, hair graying but eyes sharp as if she were always on the lookout for trouble.

"What do you want?"

"Mrs. Dupree?"

The dark eyes thinned to near slits. "Who wants to know?"

"I'm Jenna Thompson."

"I don't know you. What're you selling?"

Jenna tightened her hold on her purse strap. "My parents called me Jennifer. My older sister was Sara."

Mrs. Dupree shook her head. "This some kind of joke? Because if it is, it's not funny."

"You remember me?"

She clutched the fabric at the base of her throat as if she suddenly felt a flush of heat. "I remember all the trouble that my boy caused that family. And all the trouble the cops and reporters caused me."

Trouble. Okay, if that's what she wanted to call it. "I was hoping I could talk to you about your son."

"Why?"

"I'm trying to understand."

"I'm not talking." She moved to close the door.

Jenna blocked it. "Ma'am, I don't want to cause you trouble. But I've come a long way. I'd like to understand Ronnie better."

"Why?"

For several beats her thoughts slowed and she heard only the birds chirping and the wind rustling. "I don't know."

A sigh shuddered through the old woman. "You have any idea what a nightmare my life was after all that?"

Old bitterness melted away her good intentions. "Have any idea what my life was like?"

Mrs. Dupree raised a defiant chin. "I didn't know what he was planning to do. He never told me."

"He gave you no hint of his plans for my family?"

"No. I told that to the cops over and over. I didn't know."

Didn't know or didn't want to know. She knew from her research that he'd lived in this house. Surely a house so small couldn't hide secrets well. "Did he ever mention my sister, Sara?"

The dark eyes sharpened. "I ain't giving my information for free."

"You want money?"

She folded thin, withered arms over her chest. "I ain't got much."

Jenna dug in her pocket and pulled out five rumpled twenties. "One hundred bucks. That's all I have."

The woman took the money, counted it, and stuck it in the pocket of a housecoat. "He talked about your sister a lot. He said he loved her. Said they were going to get married." She smoothed a well-lined hand over gray hair. "You look a lot like her."

"I've heard that." She glanced past the woman to the den styled with a recliner, a box television, and a coffee table piled high with magazines and papers. "How did Ronnie meet my sister?"

"You mean how did white trash end up at such a nice high school?"

"That's not what I meant."

"It is. But I ain't going to deny who I am or what my boy was. Ronnie could play football. Wasn't so smart but he could tackle better than anyone. He played on that fancy football team in exchange for the education. Then, he got his leg broke and couldn't play anymore. The school gave him a janitor's job, which he took 'cause that's all there was to get. He'd been working at the school a few years when your sister came along."

Sara had been a cheerleader, Ronnie a maintenance man, and they'd have crossed paths. Memories of her sister and father fighting reached out from the shadows. *I'll date him if I want to!* Doors slamming. Her mother crying. Was it Ronnie who Sara had been fighting to date?

"Did they ever date?"

"He said they did. Ronnie stole one of my rings and sold it so he could pay for the tux and the rental car so he could take her to prom. He came home that night and was angry. Said Sara had ditched him for another boy."

That would have been in the spring. By late August her family was dead. "Do you know where he got the gun?"

"No. We never had guns in this house."

"Did he have friends who might have given it to him?"

"Ronnie didn't have any friends. Billy was his best and only friend."

She reached for a pad of paper and pencil in her purse. "Billy got a last name?"

"I never knew it." A loud cheer of applause rose up from

the television and Mrs. Dupree turned. "I'm missing my show."

"I just have a few more questions."

"Well, I ain't got no more answers. I told you what I know. That's all I'm saying." She stepped back and closed the front door hard. Chains scraped back in place over the door.

Threading her fingers through her hair Jenna turned and walked back to her car. From her passenger seat she picked up her sketchpad.

The eyes glowed from the shadows of her memory and she began to draw again. She drew quickly, without thinking and this time, when she finished, she had eyes, a long, angled face, and thin, unsmiling lips on the page.

"Who are you?"

She'd done a search of Ronnie Dupree. Ronald James Dupree. As his mother had said he'd played ball. She'd found his photo in an old newspaper article on microfilm. Big, beefy, and smiling, he'd not fit the profile of an organized killer.

Had Sara broken off their relationship? Had her father been behind the breakup? That's what the cops had theorized. That Ronnie had killed the parents and Sara in revenge. Taking her had been the piece of the puzzle no one had understood.

Her aunt had changed her name from Jennifer to Jenna on the drive from Nashville to Baltimore. Jenna had a bright future, she'd said. What she hadn't said was that Jennifer Thompson, taken by Ronnie, stripped of her family and life, and locked in a closet for nine days, had been broken. And so her aunt had created a new persona out of the pieces.

She looked back at the Duprees' old house. The curtains in a downstairs window fluttered.

"It didn't happen to Jenna. It happened to Jennifer."

The Thompson family murder had been extensively covered in the news and her abduction had overtaken all news for more than two weeks. Out of the shadows vague memories of reporters emerged. Her aunt had been pushing her wheelchair to their car. Camera lights had flashed and popped. She'd ducked her head, not into the pink blanket, but into a new, pristine white one a nurse at the hospital had given her.

Jenna studied the incomplete face on her pad. She raised her pencil to finish it but no images came to mind. She fell back to the techniques she utilized with victims. Don't worry about what he looked like. What did you smell? How warm was the room? Was there music playing?

She allowed her mind to drift and suddenly the subtle scent of aftershave or perfume filled her senses. The scent grew stronger and stronger and in a blink the image of a pacing figure appeared. She'd been looking through the cracks of the closet door. The scent had been strong. And there had been the *click, click* of heels on a wooden floor. Ronnie hadn't worn aftershave. Of that she was certain. But the other figure, Shadow Eyes, had worn a heavy dose of it.

Jenna opened her eyes and erased the outline of the face. She redrew it only this time it was shorter, wider. This person had a wide forehead and a sharp-angled chin.

Her heart raced as her mind reached into the shadows to pull out another memory.

A car roared past her and she jumped, nearly dropping her sketchpad. Panicked, she glanced at the clock and realized it was late. Her bride would be at the house tomorrow to pick up her portrait. She had work to do.

Running her hands through her hair she practiced a bright smile. Brides didn't want a sour artist. Brides wanted happy. And Jenna needed the work. Rent would be due on the Baltimore apartment in a couple of days and it would be nice not to dip into her meager savings to pay for it.

Unpaid leave might have given her time, but it dug into her finances.

Like it or not, she was staying in Nashville for a few more weeks.

The wineglass dangled from Susan Martinez's manicured fingertips as she stared at the messages on her phone. She scrolled through the list, frowning when she didn't see the name she'd been searching.

She took a deep, healthy sip that fell just short of a gulp. The cabernet was smooth and rolled down her throat, almost immediately softening the tension. This was her third glass and, with luck, would finally dull the sharp edges of irritation. She reached for the bottle of prescription pills on the counter, studied the label, and then opted not to take her nightly dose. The pills made her groggy and she wanted to be sharp.

Susan padded across the polished floors of her town house. She'd slipped off her high heels but still wore the tailored skirt and white silk blouse she'd worn on the six o'clock news.

Down the center hallway, she passed a collection of awards, certificates, and photos that she'd hung on the wall. They chronicled a career she'd sacrificed a personal life for. No husband, no children, only work for Susan. Go. Go. Go. And now, her career was careening toward the end and about to combust.

In the last thirty years, there were few times she regretted her choices. She was a big girl after all, with the ability to change course at any time. But the truth was, she loved her work, loved knowing the ins and outs of Music City.

But there were a handful of moments, like now, that challenged some of the choices she'd made. They were few and far between, but they did crop up once in a while.

Draining the last of the wine in her glass, she moved into her office. Like the rest of her house, it was neat and organized. Everything in its place.

She walked toward a bookcase, filled with awards, pictures, and some books. At the end was a simple black box. She'd kept the box in the same place since she'd moved here fifteen years ago. Most of that time it sat untouched, but there were a handful of times that the past summoned and she'd removed the box from its resting place.

Susan stood on tiptoe, grabbed the small, black cardboard box, and carried it into her kitchen. Marble countertops and stainless-steel appliances glistened under three vintage pendant lights that cast a warm glow on hard surfaces.

She smoothed her hands over the top of the box and then carefully wiped the dust off with her palm. A finger tapped on the top as she summoned the courage to look into a past she'd worked hard to forget. Finally, blowing out another breath she opened the lid.

Inside was a small, black-velvet jewelry box resting on a collection of pictures. She opened the box and studied the small, gold heart charm. Carefully she laced the chain between her fingertips and held the charm up to the light. On the back were two letters. *JT.*

Susan clasped the heart in her hand and then carefully replaced the charm necklace back in the box and closed it.

Her attention shifted to the pictures. The pictures weren't professional. They'd been snapped with her thirty-five millimeter camera that she'd bought in college. It wasn't hard to date the images. One glance at the large, curly hairstyles, high-waist jeans, and open vests telegraphed the early nineties.

"No accounting for taste," she murmured.

Carefully, she flipped through the stack of pictures that had never warranted a place in a real album. There were pictures of Susan and her brother at the football game. It had been a high school game and she'd gone not for the sports or the job but to see a man.

Susan had gone through this stack enough to know which picture followed the next and knew in three more images she'd see a picture of him. However, she didn't quicken her pace as she studied one picture and moved it carefully to the bottom of the stack. What was the rush?

Another picture of her brother, sullen and unsmiling. Never smiling. Still to this day, he didn't smile unless it suited him or promised profit.

Another picture of her. Slightly out of focus because her brother had taken the image. She'd had to coax and prod him to take it. "Jerk."

Another picture . . . this one was just of the man she'd loved. This image was crystal clear because she'd planned to frame it and keep it at her bedside. She'd had such plans for them. And then, it had all gone sideways. He'd been shot and killed and she'd been unable to look at his picture for nearly a year. And when she'd been able to look at his face without crying, she couldn't bring herself to frame the picture.

Susan traced the outline of her lover's smiling face. The pain of his death no longer stabbed. It had softened to regrets and a few whispered *what ifs* . . .

The next image coaxed a smile and more regrets than she'd anticipated. This image was of a young girl, just days after her fifth birthday. She had a wide grin that showed a full mouth of even, white baby teeth.

She'd loved that little girl. Loved seeing her, loved hearing about her days at kindergarten, loved buying her ice cream.

If there were any regret in her life, it was that she had not been able to love this child or shower her with the mothering she deserved. Even after all this time, tears filled her eyes, stinging as she struggled not to let them spill.

She retraced the pictures in their original order and carefully tucked them back in the box. As she replaced the box, she locked away her memories and regrets.

Shifting focus from what she couldn't control, she focused on what she could control. Her job. Her work. She clicked on a light, moved directly toward her desk, and flipped on her computer.

If Susan was good at anything, it was unearthing the hardest-to-find facts. She opened a file and studied the sketch of the child Rick Morgan had given her today.

She stared at the initials, JT. Jenna Thompson. Detective Morgan had made mention that she'd come from Baltimore. Thompson. She searched Officer Jenna Thompson and found a few references to some of her forensic art.

Susan sat back in her home-office desk chair, her reflection catching in the computer screen. She touched feathers of deepening crow's-feet around her eyes. Some would call her distinguished. Some might value her experience. But in the age-obsessed world of television she was in the process of doing the unthinkable. She was aging.

She took another sip of wine and scrolled through any reference containing Jenna Thompson. Other than scattered images of her work and a few passing mentions there was little on the officer.

Thompson.

Who did she know in Baltimore, Maryland? Almost all of her contacts were in Tennessee. And then she remembered the new reporter from the Washington, D.C., area. Carolyn March. The reporter was young and looking to move up the chain at the station. She'd hopped around a couple of television markets and, no doubt Nashville would be just one stop of many. Blond, ambitious, there was much to admire about the young reporter who, for some reason, irritated the hell out of Susan.

She dialed Carolyn's number.

"Hello?"

"Carolyn, this is Susan Martinez in Nashville. We met last year at the conference in Las Vegas." She smiled, hoping it reverberated in her voice.

"Hey, Susan. How are you?"

Susan picked up a pen and began to draw boxes on a scratch pad. "I have an East Coast question for you."

"Sure." Carolyn didn't sound as bubbly and helpful as she was when the station brass lurked around at the conference, but she also wasn't rude. Susan might not have many years left in front of the camera but she still had enough pull to do damage to an ambitious reporter.

"I'm looking for a contact in the Baltimore Police Department. I have questions about an officer. Know anyone?"

The rustle of papers sounded through the phone. "Try Derrick Preston. He works robbery. I doubt he remembers me but I interviewed him last year for a story."

Susan scribbled down the number as Carolyn read it off. "Thanks."

"So what's the allure of Baltimore?"

Always looking for an angle on a story. Smart. Irritating. "Just a hunch. Thanks."

Susan rang off and called Baltimore. A few more calls and she had located Derrick. Susan relied on the truth as much as possible. It was the best cover she'd ever found when she needed information. Susan gave Derrick the rundown on Jenna Thompson's volunteer efforts to catch a child killer. That softened him enough and soon she knew what she needed to know about Jenna Thompson.

Back in the day, she'd been careful to hide her personal

connection to the story, but now, she was considering playing it.

Rick Morgan approached the records department of the Nashville Police Department, knowing the guy working the night shift had been a friend of Buddy's. The air was dank and thick in the basement offices, but the fluorescent light humming above was bright, leaving no shadow in any corner.

Rick knocked on the half-open door to Records and poked his head in. Sitting behind the desk was a tall, lean kid who looked fresh out of the academy. He wore blond hair short and his uniform was well starched and fit his trim body well.

"Where's Ben?" Rick asked.

The officer stood, leaving an open magazine and a half-eaten roast beef sandwich on his desk. "He called in sick. I'm filling in. Officer Morgan, right?"

Rick smiled. "Right."

"Can I help you, sir?"

"How's it going down here?"

"Can't complain."

He'd have attempted small talk with Ben but the kid, well, he didn't have a thing in common. Better to just cut to the chase. "I'm looking for an old file."

"Sure, what do you want me to search?"

"Jenna Thompson. She's about thirty and was born in the Nashville area. Your search would go back about twenty-five years because I know she left the area when she was about five."

The kid scribbled down the name. "Anything else?"

"Just keep it to yourself. I don't know what you'll find, but I'd like to play the cards close until I know more."

"Consider it done."
"Thanks."

The music in the bar pulsed loud. The bass of a guitar
thumped. The honky-tonk was off the beaten path from
Broadway and the tourists. This place was reserved only for
locals who after a long day in a trivial job needed a place
to have a few beers and blow off steam. The place teemed
with frustrated men and women who took shit from bosses
all day long. There was so much rage simmering in so many
half-lidded gazes. So much frustration. So much desire to
exact a little revenge against a world that had treated them
so unfairly.

A man by the pool table cradled a bottle of beer close to
his rounded belly. He wore a clean T-shirt but his jeans, held
up by a large buckle that read CSA, were grungy and covered
with construction dust. Dark hair slicked back into a low
ponytail and thick steel-toed construction boots covered
big feet.

The man's name was Ford Wheeler. He wasn't more than
thirty, single, came to this bar almost nightly, and he always
allowed his gaze to settle on a blond woman. No blonde in
particular at first but in the last few weeks he'd fixated on a
waitress.

The waitress was pretty enough. Not more than twenty,
she had yet to earn the world-weary gaze of her older
counterparts and smiled easily at her customers. Ford ignored the waitress. His thoughts were only for another
woman.

Ford had confessed his desires after far too many beers.
Over and over, he talked about dreams of tying a woman to
a bed and standing over her, a gun pointed to her head.

Rising, it took only a few quick steps forward to gain Ford's attention. "Good evening."

"What're you doing here?"

"Just checking in."

Ford dug his fingernail into the label of his beer bottle, scraping the paper away from the glass. He teemed with frustration, a volcano ready to explode. "I ain't so good."

"Why?"

He dropped his voice a notch and ducked his head a fraction. "I want to play and you won't let me. I don't understand why you're making me wait."

It wouldn't take much to coax Ford into a play. Just a light push. Barely a nudge.

Reason shouted from the shadows, "This is a bad idea."

Madness sipped beer, ignoring Reason and savoring the cold bitter taste as it washed down a dry throat. Normally, alcohol was out of the question but, tonight, the needs cut so sharply through bone and sinew, it took drink to dull them.

"You could have the waitress," Madness said.

Ford looked up, startled, surprised his thoughts had been so transparent. "She's not the one I really want. You know that. I like the fancy one you picked out."

"I think it's wise you stay away from that one."

A scold deepened his forehead. "You don't think I can handle her."

Madness loved winding up the toys and watching them dance. "No, I don't. Not now anyway."

Ford frowned. "I can handle her. I'm ready."

"But the waitress is well within possibilities."

It would be so easy to create a scene with Ford and the waitress. So easy.

"I don't want her."

"She's all we have right now."

Ford glowered at the waitress. "I want the other one."

"It's my way or no way at all."

"Okay."

"Tomorrow?"

Ford hesitated. "Sure."

Reason squirmed under the weight of Madness. "You wind him up and you can't predict what he'll do."

Madness's reckless spirit rejected Reason's counsel.

Chapter Nine

Jenna rose with the rising sun. Too anxious to sleep or paint, she opted to take a long walk in the woods. Brush and leaves crunched under her booted feet as she made her way down the old path that the rental agent suggested had been an old Indian path.

The trail ended at a small river that twisted and cut through the woods. It had been a wet spring and summer and the water was high and fast. A couple of times, she'd been tempted to swim in the stream but had opted against it because of the water's speed.

She sat for a long time on the river's edge and allowed her eyes to close as she concentrated on the sound of the woods. But thoughts of Ronnie Dupree and his mother scattered whatever serenity she'd gathered. She just couldn't believe a guy like Ronnie had shattered her life. His type crossed paths with the cops all the time. They were always stirring trouble and landing in jail. But to just walk into a home and kill everyone?

She'd bought the line that Ronnie had killed because of jealousy and insanity all her life. "Sometimes, bad things happen," her aunt had once said. And she might have kept believing all that she'd been told, if not for the growing sense that Shadow Eyes was real.

The crack of a twig underfoot and the rustle of branches had her turning and automatically reaching for a sidearm that she no longer carried. Rick Morgan stood on the path.

He appeared relieved to have found her. "I thought I might find you down here."

She rested hands on her hips. "How would you even know to look?"

He glanced around staring at the woods. "You know the history of your house?"

She nodded, remembering. "The homicide. Did you work it?"

"No. Deke did, but Tracker and I walked the land with him. We needed the exercise and we acted as a second set of eyes for him."

"Did he solve the crime?"

His hair was damp as if he'd stepped from the shower and he smelled faintly of soap. "He did. The woman that lived here was killed because she had information the killer wanted."

According to what she'd read, he'd omitted a world of details. "That information must have been something important."

"It was."

Twigs crunched under her feet as she stepped toward him. "Where's Tracker?"

"I left him at the edge of the woods. Terrain's a little rough on his hip."

She moved toward him, negotiating the uneven rocks easily. "What about yours?"

The careless smile flashed. "Getting better every day. You come out here every day?"

"When I can. Clears my head. And I love open spaces."

"I hear ya." He slid his hand into his pocket. "Ready for Susan Martinez?"

"Ready as I'll ever be. I've given a couple of interviews before. Most of the questions are standard. Should be straightforward."

"Good." He checked his watch. "Speaking of which, she'll be here in ten minutes."

She liked standing here in the woods alone with him. None of the outside world existed and, for just a few minutes, all the puzzle pieces fit where they should. As tempting as it was to keep hiding, it was no longer feasible. Time to go public.

They arrived back at her house minutes later and she immediately moved to the coffee machine to brew a fresh pot. It occurred to her that she should run a brush through her hair and maybe dig up some lipstick but the doorbell rang before she had a chance.

"Showtime," she said.

Rick smiled, hanging back. "I'm here if you need support."

"Thanks." She opened the door to a very stylish woman wearing a turquoise suit. Dark hair skimmed narrow shoulders and gold loops dangled. Her makeup was perfect and the smell of an expensive perfume wafted.

The woman smiled as if cameras had started rolling. "I'm Susan Martinez."

Jenna looked past her to the news van and the cameraman moving up the sidewalk with a camera in hand. "I'm Jenna Thompson. Please come in."

Susan held her hand for a beat, closely studying her face. "I appreciate you seeing us on such short notice. Your sketch was amazing and I had to meet you." The reporter's gaze skimmed over the room assessing every detail. She studied the portrait covered with an oilcloth before shifting to Rick.

"Detective. Good to see you again. I'll be interviewing you as well?"

The earlier ease the detective had enjoyed moments ago had vanished. "If that suits."

"It does. This is my cameraman, Gabe Richards," Martinez said as the tall, burly man with a plaid shirt and full beard entered the house.

Introductions made, Martinez's curious gaze slid back to the covered painting. "You're doing commission work?"

"I am."

"I'd love to see the work."

A knot tightened in Jenna's belly. It was always the way when she showed a picture for the first time. "I'm afraid the client gets the first peek."

A brow arched. "That's fair, I suppose. Do you have a portfolio?"

"Not much of one. I left what I'd had in Baltimore. I'm giving this client a substantial discount because I'm building my portfolio."

"If it's anything like the sketch you did of the child then I'm sure it's stunning."

"Thank you." She learned long ago nothing was off the record with reporters. Still, when she glanced toward Tracker and caught his steady gaze, something inside her relaxed. "Where would you like to conduct the interview?"

"Whatever suits you?"

"How about by the fireplace? As lovely as the view is out the back, the glare from the sun could be a problem."

The cameraman nudged a club chair closer to the hearth. "Have a seat and I'll mic you up."

"Sure."

Tracker's ears perked as Jenna moved to the chairs in front of the cold fireplace and arranged them so that they faced each other. She sat and accepted the mic pack, which she fed up under her shirt. The cameraman had large hands but clipped the tiny microphone with nimble movements.

He stepped back and checked to make sure the mic wasn't too obvious. "Mind saying something so I can do a sound check?"

She sat a little straighter. "Jenna Thompson. One, two, three."

Gabe adjusted the second chair by Jenna's and indicated for Rick to sit. The detective's frown deepened as if he faced the lion's den, but he did as asked and soon was wired for sound. Tracker rose and sat between the chairs.

When Rick looked as if he'd order the dog offscreen Jenna said, "Let him stay."

"Okay," Rick said.

As Jenna settled, Susan slid on her microphone and took a seat across from the two of them. The cameraman moved behind Susan. "He'll start the interview behind my shoulder but may move behind you to get a couple of shots of me, which we'll edit later."

"Fine," Jenna said.

"Sure," Rick said.

Martinez began her questions with Rick, getting background on where the bones were found, the age of the child, and how long the bones had been buried. He gave clear concise answers, his deep, rich voice carrying confidence and authority. Trusting him would be easy. He was the kind of guy who took care of things. He was the kind of guy who kept all the balls in the air. The kind of guy she never dated.

The reporter then shifted through her notes and switched her questions to Jenna. She asked about Jenna's background as a forensic artist and how she went about drawing the face of the girl.

Jenna answered easily and when the reporter dropped her gaze to her notebook she imagined the interview was wrapping up. There were only so many ways she could describe what she'd done.

Martinez smiled, but the action wasn't joyful. In fact, it reminded Jenna of a cat that had cornered a mouse. "I'm a curious reporter by nature and I did a bit of digging."

Jenna said nothing, but felt her spine stiffening.

"You're from Nashville, correct?"

Invisible fingers prickled up her spine, but she brushed them aside. Martinez had found something. "I am."

Martinez leaned forward a fraction. "I dug into your past."

Rick sat forward in his chair as if ready to fight. Tracker, sensing his tension, also sat straighter but neither made a sound.

Martinez anchored her gaze on Jenna. "You were born Jennifer Elliot Thompson, correct?"

Jenna held her breath a beat. And so here it was. Her past laid out. "Yes. That's correct."

"Your family was murdered when you were five. Father, mother, older sister shot to death. The killer's name was Ronnie Dupree."

"Correct."

"Ronnie spared you but took you to his hideout and kept you there for nine days locked in a closet."

"Yes." Jenna saw Rick shift in her side vision but didn't dare look at him.

Martinez maintained a cool, concerned expression but her eyes snapped with a treasure hunter's glee. "Ronnie died of an overdose and you were found hours later by the cops."

"So I've been told." Hearing the story spoken by someone else made it sound all the more tragic, molded into something solid and real, if that were possible. She'd always done a good job of keeping the story at arm's length and pretending it belonged to another. But it didn't belong to someone else. It was her story.

Armor clinked and clanged into place. "All correct."

Martinez smelled blood. "You know the anniversary of the murders is days away."

"Yes. I know."

"Why have you come back now?"

"Maybe it was fate. Maybe my returning to make sense of my past will help solve the case of another little girl that wasn't so lucky." She ended the sentence knowing Martinez had a good interview with a solid stopping point. She pulled the mic off. "Thank you for the interview."

Susan indicated for the cameraman to cut the film, but Jenna was smart enough to know the audio could well be running.

Rick shifted in his seat toward Jenna. He looked so disappointed and shocked. Was he wondering what other secrets she held? Had he expected her to open up this vein of sorrow for him?

A clock ticked. No one spoke. She rose.

Susan rose. "I'd like to do another story on you. A full in-depth look into your family and their murder."

"I'm old news. The case was solved. It's closed."

"I think it would be a powerful human interest story."

Rick rose. No doubt wondering how he could have missed this about her. He moved away from the fireplace to the large window that faced the woods.

Susan, ever the salesman, continued, "The Thompson murders and your kidnapping were huge stories at the time and one of the first I covered in the city. I think the world would like to know how you're doing."

"I'm doing fine."

Martinez cocked her head. "All these years and you've never been back to Nashville?"

"No."

"Why now?"

"Time just seemed right."

"Did it have anything to do with that last case in Baltimore? The girl locked in the closet?"

Jenna released the breath she was holding. "Let's say it was time for me to visit my birthplace."

Rick continued to watch her. She was a cop and knew how cops thought. He was wondering what other secrets she had.

Martinez leaned in a little. "I know a lot about your case. I could share with you what I have if you'll sit down for an interview. Maybe let me follow you while you visit your old home."

Make a wish and it will be granted along with all the unintended consequences. "What's in it for you?"

Martinez's eyes sparked. "A great story."

"If I say no, would you still run the story of the Lost Girl?"

"Yes."

"Good. I'd hate to see her penalized."

"One story isn't conditional on the other."

Her movements were wooden and stiff, like a marionette whose metal joints had not been oiled in years. "Let me think about it."

Rick shook his head, clearly not happy. But he kept his opinion silent.

Martinez smiled and softened her voice as if they were old friends. "I want to tell your story."

"I'll let you know soon." She'd driven to Nashville searching for something and now was her chance to pry open the past and shine a light on it. If this is what she wanted, then why hesitate?

The lines bracketing Rick's mouth deepened. He pulled off his mic pack and carefully wound the cord around the receiver before handing it to the cameraman. "If you've got what you need, it might be best if you leave, Ms. Martinez."

Jenna glanced at Rick, annoyed that he would try to defend her. "I can handle this."

He worked his jaw as if chewing up and swallowing an oath. "Sure."

"Talk to you soon, Jenna." Martinez nodded as if understanding now was the time to retreat so that she could return to fight another day. She and her cameraman left with Rick following behind. She heard him close the front door and she wished keeping the past contained was as easy as closing a door.

Rick watched the van drive off and then faced her. "Why didn't you tell me?"

Defenses slammed tighter in place. "Not something I advertise, Detective."

A brow arched. "Martinez isn't your friend. She's in this for the story. She couldn't care less about you."

"Sounds like experience talking."

"It is."

She folded her arms over her chest. "I can handle her."

His jaw tightened, as if swallowing words too angry to speak. "If I'd known, I'd have never agreed to the interview."

Anger denied just moments ago now bubbled. "You asked and I said yes. I'm a big girl and can handle a couple of softball questions from a reporter."

"You consider that softball?"

The question had tipped her off balance, but she'd not admit that to him or Martinez. "Nothing I can't handle."

"Then why did you look like you'd been punched in the gut? Every ounce of color drained from your face."

She battled the urge to touch her fingers to her cheeks. "Shocked by her question, yes. Very few people know about what happened to me in Nashville, so it never comes up. But, I'm fine. Now, if you'll also leave I have lots of work to do."

His jaw tensed and his lips flattened.

"You don't need to take care of me."

"You're making a mistake."

"Won't be my first."

"Jenna."

"Please. I'm fine. Just go."

With the shake of his head he left, Tracker on his heels, each moving down the front steps with more stiffness in their gait. Rick didn't look back but when he opened the door for the dog, Tracker glanced in Jenna's direction before getting into the car.

She quietly closed the door. No door-slamming dramatics for her. But as soon as the door clicked closed, she turned and slid to the floor. Tears streamed down her face. She should not be this upset about the past. Days, even weeks, went by without her thinking of it and she wasn't sure if the images she had of her family were real memories. Everything she had of her family was secondhand or from a few yellowed photos.

Grabbing her phone, she dialed Mike's number. He answered on the second ring.

"Jenna."

"A Nashville reporter called Baltimore and asked questions about me."

A pause and then a door closing. "It wasn't me."

She ran fingers through her hair. "I know. I know."

"What happened?"

A sigh shuddered through her. Even seven hundred miles wasn't barrier enough for her to open up with Mike. "She put two and two together about my family's past pretty fast."

"I'm your friend." His voice dropped a notch. "Your lover."

The intimacy coating the word had her chest tightening, making it impossible for her to speak. Why had she called him? Why hadn't she just talked to Rick?

"You don't belong in Nashville, Jenna. You belong here. Come home and let me take care of you."

In all honesty, she didn't know where she belonged.

Baltimore had been her home for as long as she remembered but the night she'd found that girl in the closet, the ties to Baltimore had begun to fray. "No. I can't. Not now. I'll call later." She hung up the phone.

Immediately, it rang again and Mike's number popped up on the display. She turned from the phone, folding her arms over her chest. "Damn it."

As the phone buzzed, she pressed her fingertips into her eyes and allowed the tears to flow. A shrink would have had a field day with the motivations driving so many of her decisions lately.

She wanted to prove once and for all that Shadow Eyes wasn't real. She glanced at the display on her phone, now silent. Mike didn't like to lose. Didn't like to hear no. She'd not heard the last from him.

She found the number for Susan Martinez, dialed, and heard it go to voice mail. "It's Jenna Thompson. Let's set up a meeting at my old home."

Rick returned to the station, angry and frustrated. Bishop glanced up from a file on his desk. "I heard it didn't go well."

"How?"

"Martinez called me for a quote. I had no comment."

Rick loosened his tie. "I don't know how I could have missed it."

Bishop closed the old file in front of him and handed it to Rick. "You didn't. I did."

He glanced at the tab on the file. It read: THOMPSON, J. E. He opened the file and saw the picture of a smiling little five-year-old girl. The dark hair, the eyes, no missing now that she was Jenna.

"It was in the stack your brother sent over. And in the pile

I reviewed. I saw *recovered* on the front and didn't read any further."

Rick flipped a page that showed a mug shot of Ronnie Dupree along with pictures of her family's murder. "I wouldn't have read further either."

"I remember seeing *recovered* and thinking happy ending. Fuck."

"I'd have done the same. She wasn't the girl in the pink blanket."

"No." He read notes detailing the murder and recognized his father's dark, bold block lettering. Jenna's entire past had been laid out right in front of them. And no one had connected the dots.

The evening news hummed quietly in the background as Reason stared at the chessboard. Reason liked chess. The rules, the strategy, and a definitive winner and loser at the end all fed into the world order.

Knight had just taken another pawn, an index finger on the piece allowed a change of mind. Finally, satisfied and the finger removed, it was a matter of typing the play into a computer and hitting send.

The chess opponent lived in California and would take time before the next move. The evening news droned and, reaching for the remote, Reason turned to see the face of a woman. Dark hair framed a too-familiar expression. Gray eyes, far more direct than before, stared back at the camera. She didn't demure but seemed to challenge.

The PAUSE button froze the frame as she spoke, allowing Reason time to move toward the screen and trace the outline of her jaw.

Madness awoke from its slumber and looked at the woman's face. *"It's Sara!"*

"No. Not Sara. It's her sister, Jenna."

Madness howled, clawed toward the edge of the shadows. *"Jenna? You mean Jennifer? The little girl?"*

"Yes."

"How?"

"We knew she lived. And now she's back in town."

Madness shook off the grogginess. *"You shouldn't have drugged me."*

"I told you, it's the only way we can survive."

Madness screeched, panicked. *"She knows who we are."*

"I don't think so. She's searching. Wants to find out what happened."

"Ronnie killed her family. Not us."

"But we manipulated Ronnie. He was our puppet."

"No, no, no! It's Sara!"

Mind buzzing and heart rate kicking faster and faster, Reason felt Madness's pull. She did look so much like Sara. God. Sara. Sweet Sara. "She's not Sara. She's Jennifer . . . Jenna Thompson."

"Her name isn't Jenna. It's Sara. Sara Thompson!" Madness screamed.

"Sara is dead." A chill shivered over tight skin leaving waves of gooseflesh. For a moment panic gripped. Chest muscles tightened. Lungs refused air.

Reason rose quickly, trying to get away from the screams of Madness. It wanted control. "We need to think. *I* need to think."

Pacing back and forth, Reason and Madness were chained together. Each wished for the impossible: to be free of the other.

Jennifer was the little sister they'd barely noticed. Sara had had her little sister with her many, many times and had often joked that the two were twins separated by a decade.

"Could she have seen us when we killed Ronnie?" Madness wailed. *"She might remember us."*

"She was so young." When the girl had been found alive,

they'd been so fearful. That fear had been the chip Reason had used to subdue Madness.

"What does she remember? What did she see? Did Ronnie talk about us?"

And then little Jennifer had vanished from the radar for twenty-five years. No one had known where she'd gone. No one had come for them. And life had gone on.

"We should have pressed Ronnie harder before we killed him. We should have made him show me the girl's body."

"You're right."

Youth and inexperience had led to that mistake. Control over Ronnie had not been as complete as they first thought.

"We need to fix this mistake."

"I know."

Time to clean up the loose end of little Jennifer Thompson.

Chapter Ten

Friday, August 18, 6 P.M.

When Rick pulled into the driveway of the Big House, he spotted the black SUV immediately. Alex. Tension creeping up his back, he parked behind the SUV and helped Tracker to the ground. The dog moved toward a patch of woods and hiked his leg. Marking his turf. "I hear ya, buddy."

He climbed the steps and found the front door open. All these months of living here and he'd never changed the locks. Alex remembered his mother had always hidden a key in the side shed.

Through the front door, Rick shrugged off his jacket and draped it over the banister as he tossed his keys in a dish he kept on a small table by the front door. After the interview with Jenna today, he was loaded for bear and looking for a fight. Maybe it was time he and Alex cleared the air once and for all.

Alex sat in the kitchen at the new counter Rick had built. He'd loosened his tie and rolled up his sleeves to his elbows. His hair stood on end as if he'd run his fingers through several times and he held a long-neck beer in his hand.

"Beer is in the refrigerator," Alex said.

Biting back a what-the-fuck-are-you-doing-here, he moved to the refrigerator and grabbed a beer. He twisted off the top and took a long pull. "Change your mind about the land?"

"No."

Anger he'd jealously clung to for over a year twisted in his gut, straining for release. Even the files Alex had sent over didn't soften the sharp emotions. "Then why're you here?"

"You get the files?"

Rick drew in a breath. "Yeah. No matches."

Alex shrugged. "Worth a try. Killers don't always stay in the same jurisdiction."

"Why're you here?"

Alex set his beer bottle down with deliberate precision. "To set the record straight about Melissa."

Rick rested his hands on his hips. "What's there to say?"

Alex's gaze sharpened to a knife's point. "There's a shit ton to say, and I'm hoping this time you'll listen instead of taking a swing."

When Rick had found out about Alex and Melissa, he'd been out of the hospital just days. He'd been on pain meds and deep in the grip of grief for his father, his dog, and the job he thought he'd lost. Alex had come to him, trying to explain, but he'd pulled himself up and landed a punch that had connected with Alex's jaw. Alex had shouted obscenities but had not struck back. Instead, he'd left and the cold war between brothers had been born. Later, Rick had learned through Georgia that he had broken Alex's jaw.

"So, say it."

Alex's gaze locked onto Rick's like a laser. "Melissa lied. She and I were never, ever, an item. Not for a second."

Rick didn't blink as he raised the bottle to his lips and paused as a memory socked him like a one-two punch.

"I can't marry you." Melissa had stood at his hospital bed. Her gray eyes were clear, no traces of crying, and her short, blond hair as perfect as her makeup. She twisted off the ring he'd given her weeks earlier. "I'm in love with Alex. And he loves me."

"My brother! Is this some kind of bad joke?"

"No. I owed it to tell you, face-to-face."

The memory twisted in his gut. "She said she was in love with you and that you loved her."

"She lied. Or was living in such a fantasy world she didn't know up from down. Maybe she just wanted to break up with you and knew this was one of the few things she could say that would really piss you off."

"She said my brother was in love with her." He ground the words out as if they were cut glass.

"Did you stop to think for just one fucking second?" Alex said, his tone low and his jaw clenched. "I'm your brother. I'm your flesh and blood who has known you for over thirty years. I've always had your back. And you took her word over mine. I'm still fucking pissed off about that."

Rick scraped at the beer bottle label with his thumbnail. "Why would she tell me she was sleeping with you?"

"Who the hell knows? She's a nut job. Maybe she was afraid of dealing with a man who might be paralyzed or crippled. Maybe she just wanted to hurt you because she knew you really didn't want to marry her."

"I gave her a goddammed ring! I asked her to marry me. She said yes."

"And Georgia, from the moment she met Melissa, knew it wouldn't last. Melissa was one of your lost souls. Another broken person to fix. Georgia knew you weren't really in love with Melissa."

He slammed his beer bottle on the counter, sloshing beer on his hand. "What the hell does that mean? I never talked to our sister about shit."

"Georgia said it was written all over your face and your body language when you two were together. And if Georgia could see it coming so could Melissa. Melissa might have been crazy, but she wasn't stupid. And that bit about throwing me under the bus was Melissa's final twisted way of getting back at you."

The truth was, he'd had major doubts about the engagement. But before he could process what he was thinking, his father had died and he'd been shot. What had Georgia seen in him? What had tipped Melissa off? The facts danced in front of him but he clung to his fury. "Melissa had no reason to lie."

Alex set his beer down hard on the granite countertop. "I didn't come here to debate whether she's a liar or not. I know she is. I came here to tell you I'm pissed at you."

He shook his head, incredulous. "You're pissed at me?"

"I sure as shit am mad. You should have trusted my word. I've never lied to you. Ever."

Rick stared into the depths of his bottle. The flare of anger dimmed in the spray of logic. Alex had tried to talk to him and he'd not listened. Alex had written him a letter and he'd torn it up. Suddenly, he imagined the universe setting a big plate of crow before him.

Unwilling to release the anger just yet, he asked, "When is the last time you saw her?"

Alex shook his head. "At Dad's funeral. When she was with you. Days before you were shot."

He remembered that cold, rainy day they'd buried their father. They'd stood huddled around the gravesite and he and his siblings had watched as their father's casket had been lowered into the ground. Melissa had clung to him. Too tight from what he'd remembered. He'd had to wrestle his arm free to toss his handful of dirt onto the casket.

Rick rubbed the back of his neck. "Saying that I did overreact."

"Shit. You overreacted!" Of the three Morgan brothers, Alex had the worst temper. It might be covered in layers of ice, but the temper was there. A slight to his integrity would have set him off.

"Saying, I did." Rick blew out a breath. "Then I'd have been wrong."

A heavy silence settled in the room and, for a moment, neither brother spoke.

"Dad had died. You'd just been shot," Alex said. "It was a bad time."

"I was angry." Digging into the muck of emotion was a bit like putting his hand into a pit of snakes. "Easier to be mad at you than everything else." He rolled his shoulders. "I'm sorry."

Alex released a breath as if he'd been holding it for a year and a half. "Accepted."

Rick swallowed emotion too sharp to voice.

Alex took a long sip of beer. "I like what you've done with the house."

The conversation shift was as sudden as it was welcome. "Thanks. And thanks for the files. Especially after all that I said."

"Only missing persons files could be considered a peace offering in this cop family."

"Did you know Jenna Thompson's missing persons file was in the stack you sent? We didn't look past *recovered* on the front flap."

"She's the artist that got blindsided by Martinez in the interview."

"Yeah. Sometimes the answer is right in front of you."

"Jenna Thompson handled it well and her sketch was amazing. You should get a hit soon."

He rubbed the back of his neck. The sound of Jenna's name calmed his blood pressure. "The station is going to run the picture for several more days." Alex had always been his confidant growing up. He'd missed that connection. "Pisses me off I didn't see it coming."

"No one saw it," Alex said.

Rick took another pull on the beer. "Jenna is considering doing an extensive interview with Martinez."

"Why?"

"She's trying to dig into her past. Trying to make sense of it."

"Dad and KC must have handled that case."

"You're right. Dad's handwriting was all over J. E. Thompson's missing persons file."

"No shit." Alex sighed.

"Every time I see his handwriting in a file, I half-expect to see him walk into the room."

"I miss the old bastard."

"Yeah."

Alex straightened his shoulders. "Jenna's got to be carrying some emotional baggage. Shit, no kid can go through what she did and not be scarred."

He remembered her stern, cold expression when she'd closed the door in his face. "She's not crazy, if that's what you're getting at."

"You sure she's not another Melissa?"

Rick shook his head. "She's not."

"Sure?"

Jenna wasn't Melissa. He'd known that from the instant he'd met her. Independent and strong, she'd not even hinted that she needed him or anyone else. Melissa had been the opposite. Always clinging. Worrying. "Jenna might be searching, but she's not crazy."

Alex arched a brow as he raised his beer to his lips. "Defending?"

"No."

Alex shook his head. "Fuck."

"What?"

"You got a thing for her."

No. Yes. Maybe. "I don't know. I sure as hell am not getting into another relationship. Too much work."

A heavy sigh escaped. "Find yourself a nice normal girl with no baggage, Rick. One that doesn't need her life fixed."

"I'm not in the market for broken people."

"You think you can fix everything like you fixed the Big House. You don't need a woman with issues. Find another."

It had been so long since they'd spoken so openly and easily and it struck him how quickly they'd fallen back into old habits. "It's not like I found this one. Our relationship is professional."

Alex laughed. "Then why're we having this conversation?"

"You brought it up."

"Because you defended her. If you were thinking like a cop when it came to Jenna Thompson, we'd not be having this conversation."

Rick entered the forensics lab to find Georgia leaning over a light table gazing through a magnifying lens, the pink blanket for the Lost Girl case spread out. She held a pair of tweezers in one hand and an evidence bag in the other.

"Did you find something?"

Georgia didn't answer but gently tweezed up what looked like a small hair and then dropped it in her evidence bag. She straightened and stretched the kinks from her back. "I don't know. But I thought I'd tell you what I have so far."

"Great."

She reached for a tablet where she scrolled until she found her notes. "This is the blanket recovered at the scene with our victim. It's a baby blanket that can be found in most high-end stores. It's one hundred percent wool and is very well made. I made some calls and twenty-five years ago it would have cost thirty dollars, which is one hundred dollars in today's market."

That could mean any number of things about their victim. Yes, she could have been from a more affluent home, but that wasn't a given. The blanket may have been stolen or bought secondhand. Any number of scenarios could have fit. "What's the brown stain in the upper right-hand corner?"

"That's human blood. I've pulled a sample and sent it off to the lab. If the sample isn't too degraded to test, the lab won't send results back for a couple of weeks."

"Did the blanket tell you anything else?"

"I've pulled a couple of dark hair fibers and bagged them." She pointed to another faint stain. "I've also tested them for DNA. I don't know if it's spit-up or semen or what. Tests will tell."

Rick stood back. "The killer stripped the child of clothes. We don't have a clear reason for that. And then takes the time to wrap her in a blanket. Why?"

"You said it before. Remorse."

"The kid died of a head trauma. I'm seeing a scene where she's crying. Maybe she's taking a bath or getting ready for bed. The parent tells her to be quiet. She doesn't. And the person snaps and hits the kid or shoves her into a wall and wham, she's dead. Panic. Wrap the kid up and get rid of her."

"Damn."

"Yeah. Sometimes this job really sucks."

"You'll let me know about the DNA."

"Bro, you'll be the first."

"Good."

"Tell me we're gonna catch this guy."

He met his sister's lost gaze. She didn't want to hear about the long odds. "You're damn right, we're going to find the killer."

She smiled. "Thanks, I needed to hear that, even if you don't really believe it."

Ford was breaking the rules. But temptation had been so strong and he ached to prove that he was worthy of carrying out the plan they'd discussed so many times.

He stood in the back of the packaging store holding his letter. He had less than fifteen minutes to mail it and return to work or his boss was going to dock his pay. The boss had been riding him for weeks over missed hours and half days. *Be late again and I'll can your ass.*

If he didn't need the money, he'd have quit that loser job. He hated bussing the tables, picking up after sloppy customers who treated him like he was no more than trailer trash. He hated the waitresses who he knew were laughing at him. He hated . . . he hated almost everything.

A glance toward the front of the line and he saw her. She was standing there with a large package, like she did every month. Sending off a care package to her brother who was stationed overseas. She never missed a deadline.

Shoulder-length, curly hair framed her round face and made her round, green eyes all the more vivid and bright. She wore jeans, with rhinestones on the back pockets, and a blouse that she'd unbuttoned to just above the curve of her breasts. Like a tease, she must have known that leaving just enough skin exposed would make any man look twice. He imagined her standing in front of the mirror, fastening and unfastening the button, trying to decide just how much was too much.

Sweat dampened the back of his neck as he shifted his gaze to the box tucked under her arm and hugged close to her narrow waist. He didn't need to see in the box to know what was in it. From the small camera planted in her house, he'd watched as she carefully placed socks, gum, coffee, magazines, and photos. She took great care and pride.

He tapped his finger on the edge of his letter. His assignment today had been simple. Make contact with her. Nothing too big or splashy so that, when the time came, she could look into his eyes and know he'd been in her life not just for hours but days and weeks. He'd tried to approach her before she'd entered the package-delivery office but had lost his nerve. He'd watched her get in line and the people pile in behind her. He'd paced outside, nervous and angry that he'd been such a wimp.

Ford counted the number of people in line. Ten. And the number of clerks behind the counter. One. The clock ticked. He couldn't lose his shit job but his assignment had been clear. Make contact. Show her you're in control. She is the pawn. Not you.

Tightening his grip on his package, he skirted around the line and moved right in front of her. Fear and excitement buzzed in his nerves as he waited for her to respond. She would have to notice him now.

"Excuse me," she said. "I'm next in line. You just can't butt in line."

"I'm in a rush," he said. "I got to get back to work."

He could feel her gaze on him, seething. He'd busted into her regular day and taken control. "We all have to get back to work, pal. Get to the back of the line."

A guy behind her swore. "Do what the lady says, pal. Get to the back of the line."

"I'm in a rush." Mentally, he braced. This wasn't going to be easy for him but she wasn't going to be having any fun either.

He expected the next assault to come from the angry man in line but it came from her.

"Get out of line, pal! I'm not putting up with your bull-shit." She shoved his arm. "Move!"

Inwardly, he cringed. Her words chipped at his fragile confidence. "I'm not moving. I need to mail this package."

She looked past him as if he didn't matter to the postal clerk. "Are you going to allow this!" Others in line grumbled as the clerk waved to someone out of sight.

Shit. He'd meant to upset her. He'd thought she'd crumble at the dominance and let him have his way. But she'd come out swinging. He did not want this kind of trouble.

Clutching his letter close, he leaned toward her. "You're a bitch."

Those wide, green eyes narrowed. "Asshole."

He balled fingers into a fist and if he thought he could risk it, he'd have punched her. Knocked her flat. But he didn't have the time for trouble. He had to get back to work and bus tables.

Ford allowed a hint of pleasure as he thought about the cameras in her house and how he really was the one with control and soon would prove it to her.

Chapter Eleven

Monday, August 21, 8 A.M.

Jenna was poised to paint the last brushstroke on the bride's portrait when the phone rang. She closed her eyes, her fingers tightening on the brush. Since the Susan Martinez report had aired on the Lost Girl Friday at noon, six, and eleven, her phone had not stopped ringing. She'd turned off the phone and spent the weekend hiding out.

The first phone calls had appeared to be legitimate portrait clients. But the conversation had quickly degraded. She'd gotten questions about her past. Did she remember Ronnie? How had it felt to be held hostage? Had she been sexually assaulted?

She'd hung up and put the phone on silence. She'd finished the bride's portrait, not wholly satisfied by the eyes, which conveyed a bit too much confidence to reflect the woman.

Whatever life she'd cobbled together in the last twenty-five years was unraveling because she'd pulled the first thread when she'd moved back to Nashville.

This morning, she'd turned her phone back on expecting

a call from her bride. It had started ringing an hour ago. By her count, she'd had seven calls.

Jenna glanced at the phone and when she saw *Unknown Caller* she rose and moved outside to her deck. She breathed in a lungful of fresh air. Though business could end up booming as a result of the television news piece, she would never allow a profit to be made off a child's death.

The phone stopped ringing and she released a deep breath. "Leave me alone. I don't need this."

Her front bell rang and she cursed, deciding she would not answer. When the bell rang again she got annoyed. "Jenna, it's Detective Morgan."

She hesitated. She couldn't blame him for this mess. She'd made the choice to go public. She moved to the door and opened it. He stood there dressed in a dark suit, a white shirt, and a red tie. No sign of his dog. "Detective. You're rather dapper. Headed to court this morning?"

He straightened. "How'd you know?"

"Every cop has their going-to-court suit. Since that's the nicest I've seen you dressed, I'm guessing court."

"You would be right." He frowned. "Are you saying my other suits aren't as nice?"

She cocked her head, pleased that her teasing had gotten under his skin. "I wouldn't wear my best to a murder scene. Most scenes aren't clean and pretty."

"No, they aren't. But maybe I could step up my game a little."

"Why?"

"I have an image."

That made her laugh. "Really?"

"It's the Morgan family legend."

"Ah, that's right. The homicide legacy or something like that."

"Exactly."

The phone vibrated, humming against a tabletop, and she cringed. "Another admirer."

The good humor softening his gaze vanished. Cold steel replaced it. "Anyone giving you a hard time?"

Ignoring the phone, she nodded for him to come inside. "Nothing I can't handle. A news report like that always brings the nuts out of the trees." The phone went silent. "So what brings you to my neck of the woods?"

"Just checking on you. I didn't like the way that newscast went down. And I'm surprised you didn't say something to me before the interview."

"Like what? Not the kind of thing that comes up easily in a conversation, is it? Besides, my aunt taught me early on to keep that note from my past secret. She said no good would come of talking about it."

"Didn't you need professional help when you were a kid?"

"It probably wouldn't have hurt but my aunt wasn't the most trusting soul when it came to shrinks. She decided the best therapy was a pad and pencil and told me to draw my troubles. When I did, we'd burn them in the backyard and she'd tell me they were gone. We did that a lot in the beginning but, after a while, the nightmares faded."

"You kept drawing."

"Maybe finding other people's demons was my way of working through it."

"Your missing persons file came across my desk when we were trying to identify the Lost Girl. Bishop didn't realize it was you until after the interview."

"So you see, my case is closed." Her flippant tone didn't quite measure up to her feelings. "I have no boogeyman to worry about."

He studied her a long beat. "But there's something that bothers you about this."

She folded her arms over her chest, forgetting for a

moment that he was a homicide cop and good at digging to the truth below. "What makes you say that?"

He shook his head. "There is something . . . those eyes you draw."

She wagged her finger at him. "I'm not one of your suspects and there is no deeper truth to be found. My story was terrible but, in the end, justice was served."

"You believe that?"

"Sure." No. Not really. The perpetrator might be dead but her family was dead and she was left with an irrational fear of small spaces, insomnia, and a host of other quirks.

He rested his hand on his hip and, for a moment, didn't say much. "I was a grown man when I was shot. I was a cop doing his job who understood the risks. You'd think I could handle trauma but I still have nightmares."

She resisted sharing her laundry list of quirks. "No one gets out of life unscarred."

"Aren't we the pair?" His voice had dropped to almost a whisper and she knew the admission cost him a measure of pride.

She didn't want to like or care about Rick. Soon she'd leave Nashville. "Yeah."

Silence settled between them. "Jenna, if you need anything, call me. You helped me out and I want you to know I'm here."

Her tangled past was her problem. She'd never dumped her burdens on anyone else before and she'd not start now. "Thanks. And thanks for stopping by but I'm fine and can handle a few kooks."

A slight cock of his head telegraphed disbelief. "You sure?"

She coupled a grin with an exaggerated shrug. "Please. I'll be fine."

He slid his hand into his pocket and rattled change. "Okay. But promise you'll call if you have trouble."

"Sure. I'll call."

But she wouldn't. She never called for help.

Ford left work early because he'd been so angry. His boss had threatened to fire him but Ford had cut the conversation short when he'd quit. He'd had it with the bullshit and couldn't take the talk, talk, talk knowing that *she'd* humiliated him at the package-delivery office.

His phone rang as he moved toward his car, a beat-up Ford wagon that rattled when he drove. "Yeah."

"You sound upset."

The familiar voice calmed him instantly. "I am. Everything is a mess."

Silence. "Tell me."

Ford hated screwing things up. He'd messed everything up in his life and now here he was again with another screwup. "I went to see her."

Silence. "Not the waitress."

"No."

"You went to see her."

"I couldn't help myself. I just want to do this so bad."

More silence. "What happened?"

He recounted what happened. "It was a mess. I can't do this without you."

Through the line he heard the faint jingle of bells. "This isn't good."

"I know. I'm sorry I screwed up. What do I do?"

A door closed. "Do you remember the place we discussed?"

"Yes."

"Meet me there in fifteen minutes."

"Why?"

"We're going to do it tonight."

Relief and excitement rushed over him. He thought he'd totally screwed up his chances. "Why?"

"Because I want it as well. Don't be late." The line went dead.

Ford got in his truck and drove through Nashville, crossing the Cumberland River until he reached a small, deserted gas station. He got out of his truck in time to see the nondescript, green four-door pull up.

Ford waited in his truck as instructed until his mentor slid into the passenger seat.

In the dim light, he felt the sharp eyes staring as if trying to read his mind.

"I feel like a fool," Ford said.

"No reason to feel like a fool, Ford. In the long run, this might be a good thing."

Ford gently pounded his fist on the steering wheel as if the action would tamp out the memory. "She made fun of me in public."

Even, white teeth flashed. "Don't worry about that. It's easy for her to be brave when there're people around. She wouldn't be so brave if it were just the two of you."

Simple words soothed his wounded soul. "Thank you."

The lights from the dash sharpened the angles of the beautiful face. "I'm your mentor, aren't I?"

His lip curled into a childish pout, childish but he'd felt alone these last few weeks and couldn't stop himself. "Yes. You're in charge. I'll never question you again!"

"Good."

Tears choked his throat. Ford was damned grateful to have his mentor back, that he didn't dare push his good fortune. "What do I do?"

Dark eyes narrowed with approval. "You know where she lives."

"Yes. I followed her all those nights just like you told me."

"Go to her house and wait for her. When she arrives home, do as we discussed."

Excitement simmered in his veins. He'd felt lost these last days without his mentor. "I'll go there now."

"Try not to be obvious."

"And I take her to the house we looked at?" He pictured the rancher in the 12 South neighborhood. It had been vacant for weeks.

"Be very quiet. She can't make a sound."

"She won't."

"Half the fun is killing amidst many unsuspecting people."

"I'll get her now."

"Don't be too anxious."

He drummed his fingers, already halfway to her house in his mind. "I won't."

"Remember how we rehearsed it?"

"Yes."

"You're sure? We can run through it again. Everything has to be perfect."

"I've imagined it a thousand times in my head."

"Good. I'll see you there." His mentor slid out of the car. Ford put his truck in gear and slowly and carefully drove across town. He arrived just after three in the Germantown neighborhood. He'd have to wait for her. Normally she didn't get home until six.

He considered where he should wait. Even he knew not to park a van in front of her house. As he considered his options, he saw a flicker of movement in the front window. Excitement surged as his anxiety rose. She was already home. This was not what he was expecting.

He considered his options. Wait. Call his mentor. Grab her now.

He needed to show some initiative. Show his mentor he was a man to be respected. If he grabbed her now, then he could spend hours with her before his mentor arrived. Private time. Away from prying eyes.

He moved his vehicle down the street and parked in a retail parking lot. He reached for a general repairman's ball cap on his front seat and got out. A few hours alone with her. Yeah. That would be real nice.

Jenna could no longer ignore the urge to see her family's old home, the spot where her life had been shattered and forever changed. Several times, she'd almost gotten in her Jeep and made the twenty-mile drive but each time, she'd lost her courage. Now, with the greater Nashville area knowing she was back in town, it seemed foolish to fear driving by the old place.

She had found the address a couple of years ago when she'd been closing up her aunt's apartment. There'd been a very old letter from her mother to her aunt and printed on the top left corner of each envelope had been her old home address.

The letter had been simple and to the point. *Aunt Lois, sorry to hear about Uncle Henry's death. Know that you're in our thoughts and prayers.*

Love, Carol.

Jenna had been uninspired by the letter that had offered little in the way of her old family. If only her mother had taken just a moment to write something about her daughters or her husband. A few scrawled words . . .

But there'd been nothing but the address.

Now, following the GPS directions she turned into the tree-lined neighborhood located in an upscale community outside of Franklin.

The neighborhood was older and filled with brick homes and large oak trees with large, wide canopies of leaves.

Curb and gutter trimmed the streets and lined green rolling lawns.

A long way from the small apartment she'd shared with her aunt.

The directions ended in a cul-de-sac and she parked at an angle from the home. She shut off the engine of her car and got out. Slowly, she moved to the edge of the yard and stared at the big home made of brick with large windows flanked by hunter-green shutters. A crepe myrtle drooped full and heavy with pink blossoms beside a graveled driveway lined with square stones.

The house, she'd learned, had turned over ownership several times in the last twenty-five years. It was in a prime location and she supposed buyers were willing to overlook its history. To look at the house it would be easy to assume she'd come from money, but her aunt had said the house was mortgaged, and that by the time the house had finally sold a year after the murders, there'd been no money.

She drew in a breath as she stared at the house. A memory flashed. She was running across the lawn. Laughing. She'd been wearing a blue dress and she'd been holding a balloon. Another girl, older, her sister, had chased her. She was also laughing. She closed her eyes, hoping to draw more from the moment but it faded like smoke in the wind.

Jenna looked up at the second-floor window. Her memory shifted and she was back in time. A woman stood in the window. Her mother. She was weeping.

"Why were you crying, Mom?" Jenna's own throat now tightened with emotions that threatened to pry the armor from her heart. She didn't want to feel this. She didn't want to remember. Hers was a good life, and she didn't need the past poisoning what she had.

On reflex, she shifted to cop mode. "Then why're you here? If this was such a happy place and life was perfect, then why're you here? Why're you remembering the image of your mother crying?"

Why did perfect feel broken?

Jenna didn't have an answer.

A dark Lexus pulled up behind Jenna and after a moment, Susan Martinez got out. She walked with purpose up to Jenna. "Thank you for agreeing to the meeting."

She slid her hands into her pockets not sure what to say. "Sure."

Susan held up keys. "Want to see the inside of the house?"

"How did you get those keys?"

"The house is for sale."

"There's no sign."

"In this neighborhood, there often aren't signs. No one likes to see turnover."

"Who gave you the keys?"

"From my realtor friend. He said the owner wouldn't be home for a few hours. We'll have the place all to ourselves."

She cleared her throat. "Why is he selling?"

"Money trouble from what I hear. He's been in the house for twelve years but for whatever reason ran into problems. Who knows? Ready?"

"As I'll ever be."

She followed Susan up the brick sidewalk, concentrating on the *click* of the reporter's heels instead of the *thump, thump* of her own heart. Susan inserted the key into a lock-box by the front door and then removed the house key. A flip of the wrist and the door opened.

For a moment, Jenna hovered on the front porch, bracing as if past ghosts rushed through like an arctic wind.

"You okay?" Susan asked.

She hesitated as she searched for her voice. "Yes. I'm fine."

"Emotions can be overwhelming."

Memories of laughter elbowed to the front of her mind first as she moved to a large, bull-nosed banister that led to the second-floor landing. She'd remembered running down those stairs, excited and happy. It had been her first day of school. She'd been wearing new shoes and had a bow in her hair.

Jenna moved toward the darkened hallway as Susan flipped on the light. She glanced to her left into a parlor that felt similar to her parents' front room. A picture on the wall, a landscape, also triggered a moment of déjà vu. "It doesn't look like it's changed much."

"I was never in the house while I was covering the case. The cops had it closed up for almost a year and by the time it reopened, life had moved on to the next story."

The next story. The Thompsons had been forgotten.

"What do you remember?" Susan asked.

"Very little." A glance toward the kitchen at the end of the hall quickened her heart rate. That was where the police had found her slain family. Father at the back door, likely first shot. Mother by the stove and Sara just inside the kitchen from this hall. Police theorized he'd killed her parents and waited for Sara.

She grazed her fingertips along the polished dark wood of the banister. She drew in a breath knowing smell was a key trigger but her memories, huddled in the shadows, would not be coaxed out. "My room was the third on the right, upstairs. It was next to my sister's."

"Let's go look."

Jenna glanced up the stairs, feeling the interloper and intruder. But this was the chance she'd driven so far to grab. Slowly, she moved up the stairs, hoping each step took her closer to memories that could not be articulated. She peered in the first bedroom. Four-poster bed, neatly made with a blue comforter as smooth as still waters, a gilded mirror above the headboard, and a dresser with brushes neatly cleaned and lined up in a row. She moved down the hallway to the next room. A teen girl's room decorated with posters of rock stars and dominated by a bed made up in purple and covered with dozens of different pillows. Bead strands hung over the windows. In a different decade it could have been Sara's room.

She drew in a breath and stepped toward the room that had been hers. Her mouth grew dry and her hands clammy. She pushed open the door to find the room of a little girl. Pinks and whites dressed a brass daybed. Dolls lined up on the bed's pillow, sheer curtains covered the windows that looked out over the front lawn, and a large teddy bear sat slumped in a corner.

"It's not decorated like it was, but the room layouts are the same."

"Stands to reason, largest to smallest."

She touched the soft coverlet. "Yes."

"Do you remember that night at all?"

"Not much. I fell asleep and when I awoke, Ronnie's dirty hand was on my mouth." *"Shh, be very, very quiet. There are bad guys outside that want to kill you."* She touched her lips with her fingertips. "My next memory is the closet."

Susan shifted her stance, gripping the leather strap of her purse so tightly that her knuckles whitened. "There's no easy way to say it but to just say it."

Jenna frowned. "What're you talking about?"

"I knew your father."

Jenna sat straighter. "Excuse me?"

"He and I knew each other. I met him while I was covering the courthouse."

"Okay."

She dropped her voice and adjusted a gold watch on her wrist. "I cared for him."

Jenna stepped back from the bed. Memories of her

mother standing in the window, crying, flashed. "You had an affair with him?"

A frown stained the edges of an otherwise smooth forehead. "You make it sound cheap."

"No. But let's call it what it was."

"I loved your father. And I know he loved me. I met you once when you were about four."

"Really?" She should have been shocked or angered by this revelation, but the curiosity for her past overwhelmed all other emotions. "Where?"

"You were at the high school football game. Your older sister was cheering and your father took you to the game."

"My mother wasn't there."

"I never saw her." She shifted and managed a smile. "You were a cute little thing. Looked like a mini version of your sister."

"My aunt said that once."

"You've not seen pictures?"

"I just have one. It was taken of the four of us. My aunt said they were all destroyed."

Susan reached in her designer leather purse and pulled out a picture. "I've been thinking about giving this to you since I first saw you."

"You didn't dig into my past. You recognized me."

"I saw your sister and your father in you. And I knew your name was Jennifer, of course. Jenna, Jennifer, not a huge leap."

Jenna struggled to assimilate what she was hearing. "Why didn't you say anything to me before the interview? Why tell the world who I was?"

"I'm desperate for a story so I can keep my job. I didn't stop to think until later. I should have talked to you first."

"Why not expose your own connection?"

"I'm a coward."

Jenna studied her a beat. Her father's affair explained

why her own mother had been crying. Maybe even why Sara had been fighting with her father.

Susan held out the picture. "Take it. It's the least I can give you."

She accepted the picture and stared down at the face of a man, her father, standing with two girls. The older girl, Sara, appeared to be about fifteen and the younger one, Jennifer, four. Sara wore a cheering outfit and she did as well.

As if in explanation, Susan said, "You loved the idea of cheering like your sister. I believe it was your mother who made the outfit for you."

Staring into these faces triggered a surge of sadness and joy and longing. "You took the picture?"

"Yes. That day at the game."

Jenna traced the face of her sister. Her parents' marriage, the affair, even their connection should have been on top of her list of questions. Instead, all she could ask was, "Why did he do it? Why did Ronnie kill my family and take me?"

Susan raised a manicured finger and brushed a single strand of hair back in place. "I don't know. I wish to hell I did, but I don't know. Have you read the police records?"

"Not yet."

"Ronnie worked at the high school around the time your sister arrived there as a freshman. By all accounts, no one ever saw the two together. No one understood the depth of his obsession with your sister. She was out of his league and he knew it."

"He did all this to punish her?"

"That was the theory."

Jenna's emotions swirled around her and she had to struggle to keep them silent. She had no idea if Susan was telling her the truth or lying to get her story. The picture she held in her hand might be precious but it could have been taken by anyone. Her defenses rose.

"Can I keep this?" Jenna asked.

"Of course. I brought it for you."

"Thanks." She glanced down again at the picture. More emotions of loss and longing swirled.

"Sure. Sure. I'm here for you." Susan lifted her hand as if to touch Jenna's hand.

Jenna drew back, straightening. They weren't friends or comrades. All she knew was that she might have a shared connection to her family. "Thanks."

Jenna's phone buzzed. It was her bride. Ready to see her picture. "I've got to go. Thank you."

Susan laid her hand on Jenna's arm stopping her. "You can trust me. I'm your friend."

Jenna hesitated, searched the older woman's eyes, full of sadness. Was she a talented liar or telling the truth? Jenna pulled her arm away and hurried out of the house not sure if Susan had reached out a helping hand or pulled the strings like a puppeteer.

When Rick walked into KC's bar, it was close to midnight and the place was still crammed full of customers. There were two female singers on the small stage. One of the women, a redhead dressed in jeans and a tank top, played a guitar and the other, a blonde, played the violin. The customers crowded around the stage, swaying time to the music.

He glanced toward the bar and didn't see KC but his backup bartender instead. Rick made his way through the crowds toward the back office, where KC no doubt was getting a head start on the night's receipts.

Down a narrow hallway, he spotted the light coming from the door that was ajar. He knocked.

"Go away," KC grumbled.

Rick smiled and pushed open the door to see KC hunched over a state-of-the art computer. He sported half-glasses and a blue Hawaiian shirt that accentuated his balding head and broad shoulders. "KC."

The older man turned and his frown softened when he saw Rick. After all the years KC and Buddy had been partners, KC was like family. He snatched off his glasses and rose, crossing the small office in one step. He extended his hand to Rick. "What the hell brings you out? Tell me you're chasing a woman."

"Nope, not a woman."

KC shook his head. "You're a monk. You need to live a little."

"I could say the same for you." He glanced around the office and the wall of cubbies filled with neatly stacked papers. "I hear from Georgia that you work all the time."

"Don't feel like work," KC said. "I like slinging drinks and not chasing bad guys." He studied Rick with a paternal glare that reminded Rick of his own father. "So what brings you to my neck of the woods?"

"A question about an old case."

He nodded. "Don't tell me, Jenna Thompson."

"You saw the news report."

"Who hasn't?"

"When she showed up here, did you have any hint about her past?"

"Nope. Not a one. The last time I saw Jennifer Elliot Thompson was almost twenty-five years ago. She was just five. When Jenna showed up here, she never once mentioned her past."

"You worked her case with Buddy?"

A scowl deepened the lines of his face. "Everyone worked her case. An entire family was killed and a little girl missing. We were all scrambling to find her. No one figured we'd find her alive."

"What can you tell me about the case?"

"Open and shut. We found the killer. Dead of an overdose. End of story. We were all glad she was alive."

"Why'd he do it? Ronnie. Why'd he kill the family?"

"Best we could figure was that he had a thing for Jenna's
older sister. I've spent the better part of the last couple of
days trying to remember the case but can't seem to jog too
much loose. Have you pulled my case files?"

"I've requested them."

"The files will tell you more than this old memory of
mine. Buddy, being Buddy, kept great notes." KC cocked
his head. "So why the interest in the case?"

"I didn't like being blindsided by the reporter's question."

"That happens. Not a call to dig into twenty-five-year-
old case files."

"I'm curious."

"Maybe you like Jenna. She's a looker and if I were
forty, no, thirty years younger, I'd make a play for her."

Rick laughed, but felt no cheer at the idea of anyone else
dating Jenna. "She likes working here."

KC ran his hand over his graying hair. "They do say
snow on the roof doesn't mean there ain't fire in the stove."

"Right."

KC shrugged. "Might be for the best you stay clear of
her."

"Why?"

"She's a loner and, if I haven't lost my touch, I'd say she's
not going to stick around Nashville long. She'll get what
answers she can and move back to Baltimore soon."

"Why do you say that?" His tone carried more annoyance than he'd intended.

"She only took a leave of absence. And an attractive gal
like her, there's got to be someone waiting for her back
home."

Rick tightened his jaw. He wasn't in the market for a

woman so he shouldn't care one way or the other. But he did.

KC laughed. "You got the same poker face as your old man."

"What's that mean?"

"Means you go all stony and silent when something is bothering you."

"Nothing is bothering me."

"Bullshit."

Rick shook his head. "You're pissing me off."

KC laid his hand on Rick's shoulder, a move he'd not have tolerated from many. "If you like her, then tell her."

"You make it sound easy."

"Closed up and alone isn't the best life plan, kid. I'm living it and it sucks."

When she slowly awoke, she was tied to a bed. Hands fastened to the headboard and feet to the baseboard. As the haze cleared from her body she was aware of two things: her body hurt and the room carried with it the heavy scent of diesel.

"She's awake!" No missing the excitement, even the childlike glee in the voice. Her mouth was as dry as cotton and her head pounded.

Memories trickled back. Horrible images and feelings rushed over her as her stomach turned. Bile rose in her throat and she thought she'd throw up until she realized her mouth had been duct-taped closed.

She forced back the illness rising in her throat and tried focusing on the room. Twisting her head, she looked around the room. Small, it was furnished only with a bed.

"Good, you're awake."

The man's voice had her turning her head sharply to the

left. She couldn't speak to beg but she was ready to do whatever it took to save her life.

But the moment she gazed into the man's eyes, soulless, dark, and delighted, she realized even if she could speak, her words would have fallen on deaf ears.

He moved slowly toward the bed and she recognized him instantly. The man outside her house. The man who'd done vicious things to her body. The man from the post office.

"Recognize me now, don't you?" Glee resonated from each word.

She nodded, hoping to keep him calm. Perhaps she could find a way to reason with him and find a way out of this terrible nightmare.

He puffed out his chest. "I'm in charge now." When she didn't respond, his gaze darkened. "Acknowledge me. I'm in charge."

She nodded.

"You have what you wanted. It's time." This second voice came from the shadows.

The package-delivery-office man shook his head. "I'm not ready to let her go. I want to hear her beg again."

"You've had your chance. Do what you have to now."

"I don't want to." He managed a pout and lost a good bit of his menace as he regressed to the maturity level of a small child.

She glanced toward the shadows. Do what? She'd thought Package Delivery Man was in charge but now she realized he was just as much a pawn as she.

The man from the delivery store reached into his pocket and pulled out a gun. He leveled it toward her head. She knew in this moment that no matter what she did, she was gone . . . leaving this earth. And in these last seconds, they wanted her fear.

In these last seconds, she could die crying and begging or she could cling to what little dignity she had left. She had control over how it would end. She had the power not to show them the tears they wanted.

She stared at Package Delivery Man directly, unblinking, hoping her hate and resentment reached out to him like a hard slap. For a moment his grin held but then as he stared into her gaze, he blinked and then drew back a fraction as if he were afraid. The gun trembled in his hand.

"Stop looking at me like that." Package Delivery Man jabbed the gun at her like a man trying to chase away a snake or a bear.

She narrowed her gaze, doubling down on her hate and resentment.

"You don't have control." The voice came from the shadows.

When she glanced toward the voice she saw only a silhouetted outline and the red glow of a camcorder light.

Package Delivery Man moistened wet lips. His hand trembled harder. "Bitch, be afraid!"

He struck her with the butt of the gun. The pain cracked through her skull sending her thoughts skittering and teetering. It took a moment for her to recover and push away from the pain. She blinked and then slowly looked up at him. Her vision was blurred now but her resentment sharper and brighter than before.

Package Delivery Man shook his head, angry and disappointed like a small child.

And then he fired.

Chapter Twelve

Tuesday, August 22, 8 A.M.

Jenna's bride had been thrilled with her portrait when she'd picked it up yesterday. She'd paid Jenna plus a twenty percent tip and had promised to spread the word about her. Jenna had pocketed the money and thanked her.

"My friends all bet you'd not finish it."

"Why?"

"We all saw the news."

"Ah. I suppose that isn't what you expected when you hired me."

The woman laughed. "No. Are you staying in the area?"

"The reasons to stay are dwindling. You were one of my last ties."

"If you decide to stay, let me know. I can send work your way."

"Thanks."

After the bride left, Jenna had one more item to check off her list. She'd not wanted to do it, even knowing it had to be done.

She downshifted her car and pulled into the cemetery where her family was buried. She drove past a white brick building on her left, the caretaker/sales center, and drove up the hill past the lake. The land had a serene quality that would have been pleasant if not for the reason for her visit.

Past the still waters of the lake, she followed the directions she'd mapped out on her computer. The map had sat in her glove box, waiting for her to find the courage.

She parked at the top of the hill next to a large oak tree just as the caretaker had told her when she'd called two weeks ago. "Can't miss 'em. They're right by the tree and there's a real nice bench at their spot. Top quality."

Out of her car, she smoothed damp hands over her jeans and made her way toward the bench. In front of it was a large headstone that read THOMPSON. The urn in front of the headstone was turned up, empty but cleaned and ready as if expecting flowers. Jenna smoothed her hands over her jeans, sorry now she'd not brought flowers.

Drawing in a slow, steady breath, she sat on the bench. Under THOMPSON were the names of her father, mother, and sister. Her entire family was here, gone forever.

She'd have been at their side if not for Ronnie.

She sat down cross-legged in front of the plot and glanced at her empty hands, wondering why she'd not brought flowers. "Sorry about that."

Closing her eyes, she allowed her mind to return to that terrible night when her world changed forever. For a moment, her mind pinged between the events of the last few days: the Lost Girl's sketch; the call from Mike she'd not answered; the visit to her house with Susan and, of course, Rick. Her heart raced and she wanted to leave this place.

But she kept her eyes closed and held steady. Slowly, her mind stilled.

Memories did not rush back. There was no great flash of insight. Pieces did not tumble into place. But there were whispers. She remembered going to bed early because she'd not been well. She had been annoyed and sick of being treated like a baby. That brought a smile. What five-year-old hadn't protested bedtime? That had been a normal reaction, maybe the last normal emotion. She'd fallen into a deep sleep.

Another memory crashed into her thoughts and her smile faded. She'd awoken to a hand on her mouth. The smell of booze and cigarettes. Foul-smelling.

Her memories faded and facts, supplied by old articles on the Internet, filled in gaps. Ronnie put her in his truck, tape on her mouth, her hands and feet bound.

Newspaper reports filled in the other details. He'd returned to her family's home and shot her father. Then he'd shot her mother. And then, he'd waited until her sister had come home and when she'd entered the kitchen and likely seen the bodies of her dead parents, he'd shot her.

What had Ronnie said to Sara in those last horrible minutes? Had he taunted her with the death of her parents? Had he told her he'd taken Jennifer? Or had he shot her immediately?

Later, when Ronnie pulled Jennifer from the trunk and put her in a closet, he'd said saving her was an act of kindness. He loved her.

"Love. You sick son of a bitch. You took my family and left me all alone." Tears welled in her eyes and one spilled down her cheek. She didn't bother to swipe it away, figuring after all these years she was due a few.

Despite the theories, she realized no one would ever say why Ronnie had chosen her family. Life had dealt her a shitty hand and that was that.

Rick got the call just after lunch. A fire in the Germantown neighborhood. Framed, one-level home, burned to the ground. Neighbors had reported the flames just after ten and had called the fire department but the fire had been too hot and too fast and the home had turned to cinders in a matter of an hour.

He arrived at the scene to the fresh scent of cinder and ash. Yellow crime-scene tape roped off the house and yard and corralled a large group of onlookers. The media van was parking, but instead of waiting for a barrage of questions, he strode under the tape as he pulled on a set of rubber gloves.

Jake Bishop moved toward him, a dark scowl on his face. "We've another body."

Rick rubbed the back of his neck, hoping to soften the tension. "Any evidence to help us identify the victim?"

"No, but the body was found in the area of the house that would have been the bedroom."

"Anything to connect this death to Diane Smith?"

"Don't even know if the victim is female at this point. There's not much left."

But that in itself was a connection. Fire had obliterated the last crime scene. "Jonas Tuttle could not have killed this woman."

"No." He reached for his notebook.

Inspector Murphy strode toward them, his thick fireman's jacket open. His Nashville Fire T-shirt was soaked in sweat. His head cocked a bit to the right as if it too were barely hanging on.

Rick stuck out his hand. "Inspector Murphy."

Murphy clasped his hand and Bishop's. He nodded toward the charred remains behind him. "I thought you two found the guy who set the last blaze."

"We thought we did too," Rick said. "Lots of evidence linking him to the murder." And yet, here they stood inhaling cinder and smoke, waiting for timbers to cool so another body burned beyond recognition could be removed.

Murphy's radio on his jacket squawked a request and he silenced it with the flick of a button. "Looks like arson."

"The house burned fast like the other one?" Rick asked.

Murphy glanced back at the burned remains, staring as if in a silent communication. "It did. It went up very quickly."

"Same accelerant?" Rick asked.

"As a matter of fact, I just got word back on the accelerant used in the first fire. Tests confirmed it was a mixture of diesel and a product called Thermite, a pyrotechnic mixture. Burns fast and hot. If I had to guess on this fire, I'd say the same cocktail."

Bishop rested his hands on his hips. "Whoever set this fire wanted to make sure there wasn't much left behind."

Murphy nodded his gaze appreciatively. "Whoever set the blaze knew what the hell he was doing. This isn't this firebug's first rodeo. And seeing as we've ruled out your dead suspect, I'd say look for a guy with a history of arson. His earlier fires might not be as big or as successful as this one but, somewhere along the way, he got a taste for fire."

The haystack of suspects might have shrunk but they were still searching for a needle. They thanked Inspector Murphy and he moved back toward the ruins.

"House is owned by Nancy Jones, age thirty-four," Bishop said.

"Anyone seen Nancy lately?"

Bishop shrugged. "The rumblings I heard from the crowd say no, but I've not had time to ask."

Rick glanced at the collection of neighbors, many dressed in sweats or casual clothes. Time to start searching for the needle. "I'll tackle the neighbors."

"You take the left side and I'll take the right," Bishop offered. "Maybe we'll get lucky and our firebug stuck around to see the show."

Arsonists often lingered, hoping to get a glimpse of the mayhem their fires created. The aftermath was often as thrilling as the flames. "Let's hope."

Rick scanned the faces of the crowd. No one stuck out but that didn't mean much. He moved to the crowd of on-lookers, wondering if the killer had mingled among them.

He unhooked his badge from his belt. "Who lives around this house? Who knows the occupant?"

A murmur rolled over the crowd before two people, a man and a woman, spoke up. The woman had short, sandy-brown hair, and wore thick Elvis Costello glasses and a yoga hoodie and tights. Beside her stood a man with dark hair and a square jaw covered with salt-and-pepper stubble. Rick waved both down past the crowd. He ducked under the tape and led them a few more paces down the sidewalk.

He looked at the man first. "Your name?"

"Randy Kincaid. "I live in the house behind Nancy Jones's house."

"You know Nancy Jones?"

He rubbed the stubble with long fingers. "Well enough. We've been neighbors for a couple of years."

"What can you tell me about her?"

"Nice. Kept her lawn in good shape and had done some good renovation projects in the last year that increased the value of her house."

Another renovation project. "Know much about the woman?"

"Not much."

"Issues, problems?"

"None that I knew of. Why're you asking these ques-tions? It was just a fire."

Rick ignored the question. In a neighborhood filled with young, working professionals, most were too busy to notice the day-to-day stuff. "What did she do for a living?"

"She works in real estate, I think. She's coming and going all the time. But like I said, I don't see her much. Today is my day off. Normally, I'm never home."

"You have much interaction with Nancy?"

"Just to wave and smile on the rare times we saw each other." The medical examiner's car pulled up and the man's frown deepened.

"Do you think Nancy was in the house?" The question came from the woman, who folded her arms over her chest and hunched forward slightly.

"I don't know much at this point." He tossed her a smile meant to be friendly but he suspected it fell short. "What's your name?"

The woman shoved her fingers through her hair. "My name is Linda Nelson. I live on the other side of Nancy. And she wasn't dating anyone as far as I knew. She worked hard. It was all about the job."

"How well did you know Nancy?"

"Nancy and I were good friends. We just went out for drinks last week."

"Tell me about her."

"She had a boyfriend but they broke up last year. In fact, he broke up with her. She works as a manager in a real estate firm. She liked her job and her boss liked her." She glanced back toward the ruins. "I smell fuel. That fire wasn't an accident, was it?"

"I don't know. Nancy have anyone bothering her lately?"

"No. Not really. I mean she did text me yesterday about a guy at the corner package-delivery office. Said the guy cut in front of her and was a real jerk. She couldn't believe it. Nancy, being Nancy, told him where to get off."

"Did she ever see this guy before?"

"She didn't give me the impression she had. She'd have told me if someone was hanging around or stalking her."

"What delivery office does she use?"

"Normally, she goes to the one on Church Street. It has later hours and she's often racing to make it there before it closes. She sends packages to her brother. He's in the military."

"You saw no unusual people around here last night?"

"No, Nancy would have said something if she thought she had a problem."

Diane Smith had not been killed in her own home so it was possible that whoever had died here was not Nancy. "Do you have contact information for Nancy?"

"Yeah, sure." She dug a cell from her back pocket. "Want me to call her?"

"Yeah."

She hit SEND, put the phone on speaker so they both could hear it ring. On the fifth ring it went to voice mail. Nancy had a soft, pleasant voice.

Rick scribbled down her number. "Did Nancy ever mention a woman named Diane Smith?"

"Not that I remember."

Doubtful he'd find a connection this easily to the other victim, but it was worth a shot. "How long has she been in the neighborhood?"

"Six years," Nelson said. "She'd talked about moving but decided against it because it's too expensive right now. She'd just sold her mother's house and moved her into an old folks' home. The process took it out of her and her mother died just a few months ago. That's why she opted to do the renovation work instead. Redid the bathrooms."

"Who did the work?"

"I've no idea but she liked the work he'd done." Linda stared at the ruined house. "It was all normal twelve hours ago. All the work and love she'd put into the house was really showing and now it's destroyed."

Whoever had done this had planned carefully. It would take planning to buy the diesel and if Thermite had also been used, it would take more time to get that. Rick handed his card to the neighbor. "Call me if you think of anything."

Rick returned to his office to find the Thompson murder case files on his desk. Dusty and faded with age, the cases took up five file boxes that the clerk had stacked around his desk. Curious, he moved to the top box, flipped off the lid, and opened the first file. Investigating officers were Buddy Morgan and KC Kelly. He shook his head, staring at his father's bold handwriting. Buddy Morgan, the legend. Closed more murder cases than anyone else in the history of Nashville homicide.

Whereas his older brother, Deke, had tried to live up to the legend, Rick had never suffered under such pressure. He wanted to close cases, be the best cop he could be, but he'd had no desire to chase Buddy's legend.

He glanced at the black-and-white forensic photos of the Thompson house. A brick Tudor-style home, it was ringed with manicured shrubs and adorned with meticulous beds. One glance told him it was pure, old Tennessee money. He read Buddy's detailed description of the father, Ralph Thompson. A judge in family court, Judge Thompson had a reputation for toughness and fairness. He'd made a fair amount of enemies during his ten years on the bench and when the cops realized the five-year-old daughter, Jennifer, was missing they'd assumed the killing and kidnapping were connected to the job. But initial searches didn't land them any solid suspects. A friend of the family had mentioned Ronnie's name to the police. He'd done some handiwork for them months earlier and had spoken about little Jennifer. She'd reminded him of his sister.

Judging by the press-clipping file Buddy had saved, the media attention had been huge. Susan Martinez was quoted in quite a few articles and cited as the leading television journalist on the story. That explained her connecting the dots in the case so quickly. He reached a section with family photos. The picture of Jenna or Jennifer was that of a dark-haired little girl with a round face, bright green eyes, and a wide smile. Just like the one in the missing persons file.

A smile tugged the edges of his lips. She'd been a cute little thing and the idea of Ronnie killing her family, and grabbing and locking her in a closet for nine days set a cauldron of anger simmering in his belly. He turned the picture over and shifted his gaze to Jenna's older sister, Sara.

If Rick could have imagined Jenna at age sixteen she would have looked like Sara. Same hair, same smile, same dimple in the chin. If Sara had lived, he imagined she'd have looked a great deal like Jenna today.

More reading and he discovered that the medical examiner had reported that Sara had had intercourse within an hour of her death. The doctor had been unable to determine if it was forcible or consensual. The cops had found Ronnie in his apartment, dead from an overdose. Another overdose.

As he read about the reports of finding Jenna in the closet, his anger fired. He sat back in his chair, rolling his head from side to side and channeling distance and objectivity. "Get a grip."

Another glance at the images tightened his belly. He closed the file. He'd read through dozens of missing children's files in the last few days and managed to stomach the carnage. But Jenna's case cut deep.

He wanted to quit reading.

But he didn't.

The elaborate chess set revealed a game in play. Madness flexed stiff fingers and moved a bishop to knock out another pawn. Another worthless player gone, off the board for good. The bishop was now within striking distance of the white queen.

The white queen stood tall and straight, taunting all who saw her. "So much like Sara."

Sara had been a selfish girl, tossing back another's love as if it were garbage. The decision to kill her had come easily, but the planning of the deed had taken time. And so Ronnie had been recruited. That simple boy who'd worked in the school and had always had a thing for sweet Sara. Ronnie was the windup doll easily set on a path of destruction.

But Ronnie had not been as predictable as anticipated. Don't take your finger off the player until you are very certain of the next move. Ronnie had gone against orders. He'd not only failed to set fire to the house but he also had not killed the entire family. He'd taken Jennifer and kept her for himself.

Ronnie had sworn he'd killed the girl and he'd been so convincing that believing him had been easy. Shoving the needle in Ronnie's arm had been effortless. The fool had welcomed the promised relief. Ronnie's temporary reprieve from stress had been permanent and he'd taken to the grave a terrible secret: the girl lived.

Long fingers wrapped around the queen and squeezed. Today's scene had nearly gone sideways. Ford had approached Nancy early at the delivery office and caused a scene. The little puppet had taken matters into his own hands and grabbed her early. He'd said they'd not made a sound in the hours he held her in her own home but there was no way of telling. Not good. Not good at all.

A measure of control had returned by the end of the scene but then it had been shattered by the woman's defiance. Her eyes blazed until the very last moment life had left her body.

Tracing the face of the queen, he turned his thoughts back to Jenna. Diane's death had brought short-lived pleasure. Nancy's had brought even less pleasure. Already the thrill of that kill was fading, leaving Madness frustrated. Why couldn't this hunger be satisfied?

"Jenna, like Sara, will satisfy me."

"You've said that before. You're out of control. You don't know how to stop anymore. Soon the cops are going to be here."

"I can stop. After Jenna." Madness raised a trembling glass to parted lips. The idea of prison, capture, ruin, deeply unsettled Madness. *"Yes, give me Jenna and I will be happy."*

"You swear?"

"Yes."

"How can I believe you? You always want more."

"You can believe me. I'm telling the truth. Just give me Jenna."

"If we keep on, we'll be caught." Reason grew increasingly nervous. They danced on the razor's edge but Madness didn't seem to care.

"I will be satisfied with Jenna. I swear."

"What if she isn't afraid? What if she's like Nancy?"

"We'll make her afraid. We're good at that."

Chapter Thirteen

Tuesday, August 22, 10 P.M.

Jenna shifted the gears of her Jeep and drove off the exit ramp that took her into the rolling hills and toward home. She was tired. Instead of going by KC's tonight she'd set up her easel on the Cumberland River at the park. There was an old-car show in town and the streets teemed with tourists. It hadn't been too hot, so folks were happy to sit and have their picture done. She'd made a few hundred bucks, enough to pay another month's rent if she wanted to stay in Nashville longer.

She glanced in the rearview mirror, spotted the set of headlights, and gave little thought to the second car as she punched in a different radio station and turned up the radio. She liked music. It pulled her out of dark places quickly and she'd used it often in her life. She never went anywhere without her music.

She took a corner and then a quick turn down a smaller road. Just four miles from her house, she longed to strip off her jeans and sweater, slip into a hot bath and then into her pajamas. She'd made a pot roast the other night and knew it would warm up well. A good night just to cocoon and forget about killers, loss, and sadness. She turned the radio up another notch.

This time when she looked, she realized the lights had drawn closer. Tightening her hands on the wheel, she sped up. The second car not only matched her speed but also increased until it was inches from her bumper.

"No way. No way." She pressed her foot on the accelerator but her old Jeep wouldn't move much faster. Cursing, she shoved her foot almost to the floor.

The second car could have hit her bumper but instead cut hard to the left and came along beside her. She glanced into the other car but only saw a dark hoodie. The driver held up a gloved middle finger and then cut his car hard to the right and smacked into the side of her vehicle.

Old training kicked into play. She kept her gaze ahead as she swerved into the other lane. Praying for no traffic, she hit the brakes and watched as the other car zoomed ahead. She quickly got back into the right lane and kept driving as she watched the car up ahead. Damn.

For a moment, the car lights grew distant and the brake lights tapped on. She immediately slowed and cursed the two-lane road that gave her nowhere to go. The brake lights clicked off and then reverse lights appeared. The driver was backing up and heading straight toward her.

Heart pounding in her chest, she spotted an easement on the side of the road that led toward a field. Gunning her engine, she drove toward the patch of dirt and whisked off the road seconds before the other car barrelled past her.

The Jeep's undercarriage bumped and scraped against the field's rocks and ruts, jostling her against the side door. Her shoulder hit hard. She gripped the steering wheel and jammed on the breaks. When it came to a stop, her thoughts jumbled into a mix of anger, adrenaline, and fear.

Jenna reached for her glove box where she kept her Glock. She unholstered it as she glanced back toward the road to see if the driver had returned. Heart beating in her throat, she searched for the car. Only when she was certain it was gone did she fumble for her phone and dial 9-1-1. Backup. She needed backup.

"Nine-one-one operator."

Again old training came into play. Once a cop always a cop. She gave her location and a description of what just happened as she searched in her rearview mirror for signs of the second car. In the distance, the glow of headlights appeared.

"I'll have someone out there immediately."

The dispatcher's even, measured tone fueled rather than calmed her jazzed nerves. "Have them hurry. I think he's turned around and headed back for more."

"Can you provide a description of the car?"

She focused on facts not fear. Shutting off the engine, she killed her headlights. In the dim moonlight she could make out the car's silhouette. "Appears to be a four-door sedan. Dark color. Too much in the shadows to make it out."

"License plate?"

She tightened her grip on her gun as she waited for a sign the driver was getting out of the car. "Can't see it."

"We've a car on the way."

"Good."

The car paused for a long, tense second, its lights blaring in her direction and its engine humming. He had to see her. Her phone rang, making her jump. A glance at the screen told her it was a local number.

The car then backed up, turned around and sped off, kicking up gravel. The large engine rumbled down the deserted road. Hands trembling, she reached for the phone. "Hello?"

"Ms. Thompson, what's your status?"

She dropped her head back against the seat and held her semi-automatic close. Adrenaline snapped and bit and then just as quickly faded as it evaporated. "The driver has left. He just drove off."

"I'll stay on the line with you."

"Okay."

"Is your car damaged? Is there any gasoline leaking?"

She sat up for a moment, sniffing for any signs of leaking gasoline. When she didn't smell anything, she dropped her head back against the seat and closed her eyes. "No. No gas leaks."

"Good."

Damn it. Damn it.

"I'm getting out of the Jeep."

"You feel strong enough to walk?"

"We'll see."

Talking calmed her thoughts. Gun in hand, she opened the door and stepped out. She climbed up the small embankment to the road and stared down the winding road. One hundred yards ahead, the road hooked to the right and vanished.

She didn't have to wait long before she heard the police sirens and then saw the flash of blue lights. "I see the lights of the police car. Thanks."

"Yes, ma'am."

She closed her phone and tucked it and her gun in her waistband at the base of her spine and held up her hands. The cops on duty knew they were headed into trouble. They could just as easily see the gun in her hand and figure she was the problem. Hoping to avoid more problems, she waited until they stopped and shone lights on her. The deputies got out of their vehicle.

"I'm Jenna Thompson. I called the accident in." She explained she was carrying a legally registered weapon.

The officers took the gun from her and once they had control of the situation, asked, "That's your vehicle at the bottom of the hill?"

"It is. I left my purse inside. It's on the floor. It has my identification."

"We'll get that for you." The officer was midsized, had a flat belly, and sported a thick mustache and a Tennessee drawl.

"Would you mind notifying Detective Rick Morgan of the accident? I just consulted with him on a case."

Dark eyes narrowed and his frown deepened. "You're that artist."

"That would be me."

"Yeah, I'll get him on the horn. Have a seat in my car. It'll be a few minutes before a tow truck arrives."

"Thanks."

"You need an ambulance?"

She'd be sore tomorrow but nothing was broken or really banged up. "No. Nerves are shot but I'm fine otherwise."

As the tow truck pulled her Jeep out of the hollow and onto the main road a set of headlights appeared on the road and the car pulled off to the shoulder. Rick got out of his car, the badge fastened to his belt buckle. His expression was tight and drawn as he moved along the side of the road toward her.

She unfolded her arms and did her best to look relaxed as if they'd just run into each other on Broadway. "Funny meeting you here."

Rick's gaze traveled over her as if assessing and cataloging injuries. When he didn't find anything he nodded toward the car. "What the hell happened?"

"A car ran me off the road." Her training shifted into play, pushing aside the emotion and forcing her to focus on the facts. Later, she might melt into a pool of nerves, but not now.

"And you aren't hurt?"

"I'm fine."

The winch of the tow truck groaned as the Jeep settled

at the top of the hill. Surprisingly, other than a few clumps of grass and dirt in the front fender, it didn't look too much worse for wear.

"Any idea why?"

"I honestly don't know. If the guy was tailing me, then I missed it. I was playing the radio and just trying to get my head in a good place when the headlights appeared."

"See anything?"

"Gave what I have to the officer. Four-door, American car, dark color. That's all I have."

"It's the news report about the Lost Girl," he said. "It's shaken a couple of nuts loose from the tree."

The theory made sense. "I gave a face to a set of bones that might not ever have been identified."

"You've made someone nervous."

The cops had found the bones. She'd simply been the messenger. But messengers got shot all the time. "I'm handy to blame. Everyone saw my face on television." Deep satisfaction teased a smile to the edges of her lips. "This is a good thing."

His frown deepened. "I'd hate to see your idea of a bad thing."

She pulled a clump of dirt from her front fender. "This means the killer of that little girl was paying attention to the news the other night."

The frown held steady. "It does?"

"Oh, yeah. I've rattled someone's cage but good."

He rested his hands on his hips. "That's all fine and good, but how did this person get a bead on you, Jenna?"

"Martinez's news report released just enough information to the public. If a motivated person wanted to find me, then they could. I'm not exactly in hiding."

"You should be more careful."

She studied his face in the moonlight. "Why're you

frowning? I got into a little fender bender but I'm fine. And honestly, I saw worse on the job in Baltimore."

He didn't respond right away. "What if it doesn't have anything to do with the Lost Girl but more to do with your past?"

She rejected the uncomfortable theory quickly. "My family's killer was found dead from an overdose. The case was closed twenty-five years ago." She shook her head. "I have no family in Nashville and anyone I would have known dates back to kindergarten." An amused brow lifted. "A playground squabble is hardly worth all this trouble."

Her attempt at humor fell flat. "I pulled the records on your family's case."

Curiosity mingled with annoyance as she slid her hands in her back pockets. "Funny. I considered asking you to do that."

"Why?"

"My aunt never talked about it growing up. I asked a few times but she dodged the questions."

"KC and my father dug deep into Ronnie's life. Best they could come up with was that he worked at the school your sister attended."

She stuffed down her disappointment. "Random killings are frustrating but they do happen."

"Ronnie didn't have the brains to kill your family alone. He barely graduated high school and had a habit of shooting his mouth off after every crime he committed. Did you know he tried to burn your parents' house down after the murders?"

"No. I didn't."

"The fire didn't take. Burned around the kitchen but the fire went out."

"By then, I was in the trunk of his car, bound and gagged."

His hand slid into his pocket and he rattled change. "He died of a drug overdose nine days later."

"And I was found."

He leaned toward her a fraction. "I've had two murder victims in the last week and a half. Both were shot and both of the crime scenes were burned to the ground."

"Sounds like a pattern."

"You'd think, but we found the first killer dead of an overdose before the second victim died."

"So it's not the same guy."

"No. In fact, we've film from a delivery-store surveillance camera just an hour ago. It showed a man cutting in front of a woman named Nancy Jones, who we think is our second victim. The two got into an argument. We're looking for him now."

"You think he was working with the first guy?"

"I don't know."

"So why're you telling me this?"

"I don't know. The whole setup reminds me of your family. Stalking. Shooting. Fire."

Hope flickered, but she tamped it out. "A bit of a stretch."

"There're lots of similarities between these two cases and your family's."

There'd been a time when she'd have laughed off his theory. Her case was closed. End of story. But in the last few weeks, with the appearance of Shadow Eyes, she didn't feel much like laughing or calling him a nut. "The anniversary of my family's death is coming up."

"Four days."

The tow-truck driver called Jenna over and she went immediately, suddenly wanting to be home and away from all this death and violence.

The driver was tall, lean, and wore a red T-shirt covered in grease smudges. "The Jeep appears to be drivable," he said. "You didn't do any damage to it. Just got it stuck."

Escape. As long as her wheels were functional she could

deal. "That's the best news I've heard all day. What do I owe you?"

The tow-truck driver named a price and she went to the Jeep, got her purse, and dug cash out of her wallet. The cash had come from the bride portrait. She paid him one hundred dollars.

She tossed her purse back on the passenger-side seat of her Jeep. "I'm not sure what to say now, Detective Morgan."

"Where are you headed?" Rick asked.

"Home. I need a cold glass of wine and a hot bath."

"Is that smart? Going home alone?"

"I'll be fine."

The deputy returned and gave her back her gun. She tucked it in her purse.

"I don't like you going to that cabin alone."

"Don't worry, Detective. I managed to survive working on the streets of Baltimore for nine years. I think I can get myself home. Besides, this guy has got to be long gone if he has even half a brain."

"You don't have to be smart to be mean and determined."

"Well, I'm smart. And I'm a good shot. And going forward, I'll have my antenna up."

"I could leave Tracker with you. He's not fast but he's got a mean bite."

The offer touched her deeply. She understood the depth of the gesture. "Thanks. I know he's a tough dog. But he's better to stay with you. I'll be fine."

Jenna stopped at the hardware store on the way home long enough to ask a clerk where she could find nails and a hammer. Following instructions, she strode to aisle six, walked down the row until she came across a wall of nails. She selected a heavy gauge and then tracked down a hammer.

After checking out and looking twice before she crossed

the parking lot, she slid behind the wheel of her Jeep, wincing only a little as her bruised shoulder reminded her that two hours ago, she'd been tumbling down a hill.

In that moment, the weight of the accident caught up to her. She sat there, key in ignition, wondering again why she'd returned to Nashville. Ronnie's motive had been as simple as insanity. He was dead. She had justice. She should have peace and a sense of well-being.

Maybe Shadow Eyes was just a figment of her imagination, a representation of her doubts or delayed post-traumatic stress. Maybe, as a therapist had once suggested, the past might one day catch up to her. Now that she had dealt with Ronnie, maybe Shadow Eyes would go away.

Maybe, maybe, maybe.

She fired up the engine and drove back to her house. Soon, her leave would end and she'd leave Nashville behind. There'd been a time when it conjured only bad memories but going forward, many of the new memories would be good. Georgia, KC, and Rick.

Jenna liked Rick. Liked his swagger, his deep, rough voice and the way he looked at her as if she were the only person on the planet. His gray eyes reflected loss and worry that she knew mirrored her own. He understood facing death. Understood having your life ripped out from under you. Understood that on a cellular level it could all go sideways in a beat.

Rick or no, it didn't make sense for her to stay here much longer. She had a job, friends, an apartment, and a life waiting for her. Nashville wasn't real life for her. And sooner rather than later, she'd have to get back to real life.

Rubbing her tense neck with her hand, she exercised the stiffness now creeping in after the accident. She needed a hot shower, as she'd originally planned, and a good glass of wine. But first, she'd pound a nail in each window frame on the first floor so that no one opened her window without her knowing it.

Rick and Bishop got the call an hour later: unidentified male, dead of an overdose in a downtown alley. The lights of Broadway winked against his windshield as he drove past the tourists toward the river. A right on First Street and he spotted the collection of cop cars.

He and Bishop got out of the car and made their way to the uniformed officer standing at the edge of the yellow crime-scene tape. Rick shook his hand as did Bishop.

"What do we have?" Bishop asked.

"The victim's name, according to the driver's license in his pocket, is Ford Wheeler. He's thirty-six years old and works as a busboy in a chain restaurant. Lots of scrapes with the law."

Rick scribbled down the details in a notebook. "How did he die?"

"He's got the look of a drug addict. Old needle marks on his arms. Medical examiner will have to make the final call. But if I had to guess, he overdosed."

"Thanks." As the officer looked away, Rick said, "Another overdose on the heels of a murder and fire."

"Fits the pattern."

"I know." Again his thoughts circled back to the Thompson murder, and the fire and death of their killer. Was that a part of this pattern or a strange coincidence?

The detectives ducked under the tape and, donning rubber gloves, moved toward the body covered with a blue tarp. Rick knelt down and lifted the edge to find the body faceup. "Have a look."

Bishop studied the man's face. "He's the dude from the package-delivery-office video. The one that cut in front of Nancy Jones."

"He sure is." Rick studied the guy's arm and noted the track marks.

Bishop searched the man's pockets and pulled out a hardware store receipt. "He bought gasoline two days ago."

"Another successful woman and another loser guy who kills her. What do you think we'll find when we see his home?"

"Pictures of Nancy."

"It would be my guess." Rick searched his pockets but only found a gum wrapper and a few pennies. "What the hell is this? Some kind of murder club?"

"I don't know what it is. But Tuttle and Wheeler are connected in some way. These two cases are just too damn much alike."

"Wheeler could have read about the first murder in the paper."

"He got too many details right that weren't released."

"Let's have a talk with his boss."

The drive to the brightly colored restaurant took twenty minutes and when they arrived, the parking lot was full. They found the hostess who, seeing their badges, took them to the manager. He was squirreled away in a small office, counting receipts.

The manager was a tall, heavyset man with dark hair parted deeply on the right side. His white shirt was crisp, his name badge polished and level straight. The badge read BOWER. "I'm Seth Bower and I'm the manager."

Rick noted the extra emphasis on the tail end of the sentence before making introductions. "We're here about an employee. Ford Wheeler."

"Ex-employee as of one o'clock yesterday. He said he had to go to the package-delivery office and would be here for the afternoon rush. He never showed, so I left him a phone message and told him not to come back."

"How long did he work here?"

"A year, give or take. He was good at first. Seemed to try hard and did well with the customers. Then about four months ago he started to get belligerent. Started acting like he was the boss. I couldn't have that."

"What do you think caused the change?"

"That's about the time he started dating his girlfriend."

"What's her name?"

"Nancy, I think."

Rick reached in his coat pocket and pulled out the DMV photo of Nancy Smith. "She look like this?"

The manager studied the image and nodded. "Yeah. That's her. Maybe she can tell you what ideas she was putting in his head."

Bishop scratched behind his ear as if annoyed. "She never came by the restaurant?"

"Not once. I saw other photos of her and I never would have put a gal like her with a guy like him. He was nice enough but he didn't attract an A-list kind of woman, if you know what I mean."

"Did he have any other friends here at work?" Rick asked.

The manager glanced toward a waitress who held up a bill, her gaze questioning. He held up a finger as if asking her to wait. "Friendly, but he never went out drinking with the other waiters when they did go. Kind of a loner until Nancy." The manager studied the two detectives. "So, what's this about? This some kind of domestic problem?"

"Ford Wheeler was found dead in an alley a few hours ago. Drug overdose."

"No shit." He rested his hands on his hips. "I knew he'd had problems with drugs a couple of years ago. He told me straight up when I interviewed him. I told him I appreciated his honesty and he seemed relieved, as if my approval mattered. He appeared clean until a few months ago. Maybe this Nancy chick got him into drugs."

"We don't believe he was dating Nancy," Rick said. "We believe he was stalking her. Do you know where he lived?"

The manager blinked and shook his head. "This is the kind of crap that happens on television."

"It happens everywhere," Bishop said. "You got that address for Wheeler?"

"Yeah." The manager ran tense fingers through his hair. "I got one on file."

"I'll need that," Rick said.

The manager shook his head. "To think the guys were a little jealous of him. All his talk about how wonderful his girlfriend was and all the fun they were having was psycho crap."

"We think so."

The manager snorted. "Did she file a complaint against him? Did she catch him looking in a window or something?"

"No," Rick said. "She was murdered."

"What the hell. Did Wheeler do that?"

"That's what we need to figure out."

The detectives arrived at Ford's small apartment a half hour later. Rick drew in a breath as he pulled on a fresh set of gloves. Keys in hand from Ford's coat pocket they opened the door and flipped on the lights. The living room was barren, and there was not a stick of furniture except for a recliner and a television balanced on a couple of crates. However, the room's lack of furnishings was lost immediately in the shadow of four walls covered with thousands of images. They all featured Nancy. Hundreds and hundreds of images of Nancy. Smiling. Talking. Rushing. Jogging.

"Holy crap," Bishop said.

Rick walked into the center of the room as his gaze

scanned. "He's been following her for a while. Several seasons."

"Tuttle started stalking Diane last fall."

Rick shook his head. "No way this is coincidence."

"Medical examiner has still not identified Nancy. It's taking time to track down dental records."

Rick moved to the wall filled with endless images of Nancy Jones. "Really think our victim isn't Nancy Jones?"

"No."

Rick studied the photographic collection. "Think it might have been some kind of pact between the two men?"

"Neither had the brains for this kind of organization."

"I agree. But maybe together they figured it out?"

Bishop looked around the dirty room filled with pizza boxes, trash heaps, and too many empty beer cans to count. "I don't see this guy planning much of anything."

"So someone got ahold of these two men and set them on this path."

"That would be my guess."

Rick turned from the images. "We'll search everything in both men's backgrounds and compare. Maybe we'll get a hit."

"Maybe."

Rick studied Nancy's pictures and his thoughts returned to the Thompson case as he reached for his phone to call a forensics team. He called in their discovery to the team and then slowly slid the phone in his coat pocket.

He watched as Bishop took pictures of the room with his cell. He'd been careful about opening up too much to his partner, knowing the guy wasn't crazy about his appointment. Though wiser not to say a word, he heard himself saying, "I read through the Thompson murder files."

"Jenna Thompson's family."

"Yeah."

Bishop turned his gaze, teetering on amused. "So is that

your idea of a good time? Reading up on old murder cases?"

"Just struck me as odd, her being in town so close to the anniversary of her family's death and her hooking up with KC and Georgia."

"I'll admit there're too many coincidences for my taste, but why dig into the murder? You feel guilty about Martinez sharing Jenna's history?"

Bracing, he said, "I wasn't happy about it. Irritated me that she found something I missed."

"Jenna Thompson is a big girl. She knew what she was risking by talking to the media. Hell, she might have agreed to it knowing she might be exposed."

"The point is," Rick said, "reading the files set off alarm bells."

Bishop didn't speak, but his attention didn't waver.

"I see similarities between the Thompson case and these two."

Bishop laughed. "Boy Scout, you're really reaching. The Thompson case is twenty-five years old."

"I know. It sounds nuts."

Bishop folded his arms. "But—"

"First," Rick said, holding up his index finger, "the victims were shot in the head. Second, there was accelerant in the house and scorch marks. The fire didn't take. Sara Thompson was sexually assaulted. And the killer was found dead of a drug overdose."

Bishop's smile faded a fraction. "No kids involved in any of these new cases."

"August twenty-six is the twenty-fifth anniversary. Might have triggered something in someone."

"Triggered something? Like in Jenna?"

"No."

"Don't be too quick to dismiss the idea, Boy Scout. She

could be pulling the strings of these men. She has the brains and know-how to kill someone."

"Shit, no! That's not where I'm going at all."

"You should be. Think about it. She returns out of the blue, sets up her easel in front of KC's bar, befriends Georgia, and volunteers to help on a case. Well isn't she the model citizen." He shook his head. "Perfect setup. Maybe what happened twenty-five years ago damaged the hell out of her and the anniversary is some kind of trigger."

The logic fit. But he couldn't swallow it. "No."

"Dude, make sure the big head is thinking right now."

Rick shoved out a breath. "The big head is doing the thinking."

"If it's not Jenna, then who? This mystery manipulator has been off the radar for years."

"Hell if I know. But it wouldn't hurt to check into old homicides involving fires."

Bishop rested his hands on his hips and shook his head. "Old homicides involving fires. You got any idea how long that will take?"

"A lot of time."

"Time neither of us has."

Rick imagined the number of dusty files that would have to be read. "Then let's narrow the connection. Who was in the Thompsons' life who had an influence on Tuttle and Wheeler?"

"It's a needle in the haystack."

"Those parameters narrow the haystack."

"Not by much."

Rick pinched the bridge of his nose and thought about his two victims. Successful. Female. Mid thirties. And then, he remembered something Linda Nelson, Nancy's neighbor, had said. He flipped through his notebook until he found her contact information, a personal cell. He called and she answered on the third ring, "Linda Nelson."

"Ms. Nelson, this is Detective Rick Morgan. You said Nancy's mother was moved into a nursing home."

"That's right."

"What happened to her house?"

"Nancy sold it."

He pictured the trampled FOR SALE sign in Diane's yard. "Do you know which realtor she used?"

"No, sorry. All the records would have been in her house."

"If you think of it, call me."

"Sure. Have you found Nancy yet?"

"No. Not yet."

"Call me when you do."

"Sure."

He hung up. "Nancy sold her mother's house and Diane was selling her house."

Bishop snapped his fingers. "Now that's a connection that makes sense."

Rick flipped through his notebook again. "The sign in Diane Smith's yard read 'Nashville South Realty.'"

Bishop shrugged. "It wouldn't hurt to talk to this group."

He plugged the name of the agency into his phone and after a few seconds a website appeared. "I've got an address."

"Unless they have an all-night realty service, it's going to have to wait."

Rick checked his watch. It was well after midnight. "Right."

"We'll be there bright and early, Boy Scout."

Rick scratched the back of his head. Forty-eight hours until the anniversary. Made no sense that these two cases would be connected to the Thompson murder, but he couldn't shake the sense that they were and the clock was ticking down fast.

Chapter Fourteen

Wednesday, August 23, 7:55 A.M.

Rick and Bishop arrived at Nashville South Realty located in a storefront office of a strip mall. They crossed an empty parking lot and arrived at the front door to find an OPEN sign.

Checking his watch, Rick realized they were early. "Nice to see some folks still get to work early."

Bishop rubbed his eye. "So you ain't the only eager beaver in Nashville?"

"Maybe we should start a club." They walked up to the empty receptionist desk and rapped his knuckles hard. "Hello."

"Just a moment." The clear voice emanated from down the long hallway filled with doors leading into dark offices.

Seconds later, steady footsteps sounded on the tiled hallway and a midsize man appeared. He wore dark suit pants, a crisp white shirt, and a red tie. His dark hair was slicked back and gold cuff links winked at his wrists. He extended his hand. "I'm William Spires. Can I help you?"

"I hope so." Rick pulled his badge from his breast

pocket. "I'm Detective Rick Morgan and I'm with the Nashville Police Department. I'm checking into a couple of listings, one was handled by your company."

"I can look them up for you." Spires moved to the receptionist desk and sat down in front of the computer. "What's the addresses?"

"The first is in the 12 South neighborhood." He read off the address.

Spires typed on computer keys. Seconds later his smile faded to a frown as he stared at the screen. "That house burned eight days ago."

"There was a house sold by a Nancy Jones six months ago. It's located near Germantown."

Spires typed into the computer and then waited a beat as the information popped up. "That house sold for a nice profit."

"Did the same agent handle these properties?"

Spires studied the computer screen. "No, different agents. But both houses were multiple listings. Any number of agents could have been in either house." He sat back. "What's this all about?"

"We're investigating two homicides. Both women had been involved in a real estate transaction in the last year."

"Like I said, a few agents would have had access to the properties. And, of course, each house had a key box, which meant as long as a realtor had access to the box they could get in the house. It's all very common. In this day and age, houses can be a tough sell and realtors are willing to share the commission for a sale."

"Who had the listings on these homes?" Rick asked.

Spires checked the computer. "The Jones house was listed by Larry Martin and the Smith house was listed by Janet Douglas." He scribbled down information on a piece of scratch paper. "Here's their contact information."

Rick glanced at the numbers and scribbled them down in

his notebook before handing the paper off to Bishop. "Know anything about her realtor?"

"I know them both. I trained them both in a sales seminar last summer. They have solid reputations and have been in the business for years. Each does have their own website and they will feature properties daily. If it's on the web there is no telling who could have seen the homes for sale." He leaned down and typed in a web address and turned the screen toward the policemen. The screen featured a good-looking guy, sporting a leather jacket. "This is Larry. Like I said, great guy."

"Thanks."

Spires reached into his pocket and pulled out a business-card holder. "Take my card. If I can be of any help, let me know."

Rick glanced at the card. NASHVILLE SOUTH REALTY, A SUBSIDIARY OF TEMPERANCE REAL ESTATE. "How long have you been with Temperance?"

"About a year. They acquired us."

"Why?"

"It happens all the time."

"But it always happens for a reason."

Spires shrugged. "We had the contacts that were valuable to them and they had capital that the company needed. It was a win-win for everyone."

"So this means Temperance had access to your records?"

"Sure. That was part of the deal."

Rick flicked his finger on the edge of the business card. "Thanks for your help."

"Like I said, call me any time."

Jenna arrived at KC's at four to set up her easel and stool. Within ten minutes, she was drawing the face of a young woman out partying with a group of her friends. The woman had a quick smile and a relaxed manner that Jenna could only fake on her best day.

As she sketched the woman's jawline in charcoal, she wondered if there'd ever be a day when the weight of her past was lifted and she could breathe without feeling a pressure on her chest.

An hour and a half past and she drew three portraits. No one wanted the forty-dollar pictures. Twenty dollars seemed to be the afternoon's limit. But she'd pocketed one hundred and sixty dollars, enough to keep gas in her Jeep for a few weeks.

Three men, dressed in jeans and dark T-shirts, stopped to look at her art. They had short haircuts, tight on the sides and high on the top. No doubt military men on leave. She sighed, knowing they'd not want a picture. She started to pack up.

"Hey, you finishing up?" one of the guys asked.

A tart response danced on the tip of her tongue but she swallowed it. "That's about right."

"How about you have a drink with us?" another offered. The men exchanged glances that didn't set well with her.

Before she could answer, she felt a presence and glanced up to see Rick Morgan standing behind her. He didn't physically touch her, but the energy radiating from his body electrified her body.

"She's having a drink with me," Rick said.

She'd have argued with him, if not for the guys who looked as if they didn't take no for an answer easily.

"Thanks, but not tonight, guys," she said.

"What if we want a picture?" the tall one asked.

Rick, silent, shifted his stance and, as one guy strolled away, he said, "She's done for the night."

She collapsed the legs of the easel and then the stool.

Both fit into her large satchel along with her box of pastels and pad of paper. "You heard the man."

The trio frowned as if they were itching for a fight as much as a drink or a woman. As if reading their thoughts, Rick put his hand on his hip sliding his jacket back a fraction so that his badge and gun showed. "Move on."

Their expression softened. Each was smart enough to know a tangle with the law would not bode well. They turned and ducked into the bar next to Rudy's.

Jenna watched them leave, not ready to turn her back until they were out of sight. "Thanks for the backup. How'd you know I was here?"

Rick's gaze lingered past her in the direction of the men a beat longer. "KC called. Said that art kid was on his doorstep."

"Kid. I haven't heard that in a while."

"To KC, anyone under sixty is a kid." He nodded toward Rudy's. "Want to grab a coffee?"

"Or a beer."

He smiled. "Sure."

They followed the music into the bar and found a back corner that could pass for quiet. KC appeared at their table before they could get totally settled. He glanced between the two as if searching. For what, Jenna didn't know, but she was too tired to worry about it.

"So what can I get you?" KC asked.

Rick turned to Jenna. "What'll it be?"

She'd eaten here enough that she knew the menu by heart. "A beer and a small pizza."

"I'll take a burger and soda," Rick said. "Still got a bit of work to do tonight."

KC nodded. "Will do."

Jenna sat back in her seat. "You checking up on me?"

"Yeah. Wanted to make sure you haven't had any more road problems."

"Not a one. A very peaceful night and day."

Rick loosened his tie and sat back in the booth. A blues song crooned in the background. "I thought you had portrait work."

"Finished. She loved it."

"Why do the street drawings? Seems a waste of talent."

"Street drawing keeps my sketching skills sharp until I return to the real world and my old job. And it pays the rent. I'm on unpaid leave and have bills to pay in two cities."

Rick didn't comment even as a tension rippled over his expression. "When will you go back?"

"Who knows? A week or two."

He sat back in the booth. "What's holding you here?"

She arched a brow. "You in a rush to see me go?"

"Not at all."

"So what do you do when you're back in Baltimore?"

She glanced up, a half smile tugging the edge of her lips. "Nice conversation shifter."

"I like to think I'm smooth. What do you do?"

"Before my aunt died, I hung out with her. I have friends. We drive to the harbor or hang out. Regular stuff."

KC arrived with their drinks and set them on the table. He looked as if he wanted to stay and talk but a glance from Rick sent him back to the bar.

Jenna laughed. "That look sent poor KC scurrying away. You must be one scary dude." She sipped her beer savoring the flavor as it cooled her dried throat.

His smile did little to soften the intensity that she guessed grew exponentially the deeper it went. "KC is a good guy. But he'll stand here for an hour talking."

She traced the rim of her cup. "Any leads on the Lost Girl?"

"Not yet." Rick sighed. "There was no report filed on a

child of her description during a twenty-five-year time frame." He shrugged off his jacket and rolled up his sleeves. "You and the Lost Girl are about the same age."

"I thought about that."

"We've dates when the pond was drained and the burial site accessible. But no hits."

"Ever thought the killer worked for the parks system? Hell of a long shot to just stumble onto the drained lake."

"I checked with the head of maintenance. Each time they drain the pond, it's announced in the media. But you're right about a possible job connection. We've got the parks system compiling a list of employee names."

"And the blanket?"

"Georgia went over every square inch of it. Found a couple of hairs, a bloodstain, and two other stains. DNA on the hair and blood and she thinks the other stains were food."

"High- or low-end blanket?"

"High. But not so special that it would only have been exclusive. Dozens of stores could have sold it."

"It just might come down to my sketch."

"That's what I'm thinking."

KC was grateful to focus on food rather than emotions. The pizza crust was crisp and the sauce and cheese blended perfectly. She savored every bite. Rick, like her, also concentrated on his food. He was a cop, after all, and ate when he could. Cops never knew when they'd be called into the field or for how long. Eat when you can. When their meal was done, Jenna pushed her plate away and dug two rumpled twenties from her pocket. "This one's on me."

He balled his napkin and held it in his fist. "You get the next one. I got this one."

She crushed the bills in her fist, ready to toss them on the table. "A next time? Who's to say there'll be another time?"

He placed the crumpled napkin by his plate. "You're on Georgia's radar. She's yet to land her first cold case for this team she's assembling in her mind and I suspect she won't let you go so easily."

Jenna laughed. "I liked helping her. But my paying job is in Baltimore."

He ignored the Baltimore mention. "She'll have more cases for you. She's a woman on a mission."

"Georgia wants to find all the missing. Wants to bring them home." Jenna traced the rim of her cup. "That's not always possible."

"Don't tell her."

"I did a lot of reading on Nashville. Dug through the newspaper on microfilm for the last twenty-five years."

"So you know about Georgia?"

"Yeah. I can relate to her. We've both lost mothers." She stopped short of saying they'd both been murdered.

His jaw tightened. "She doesn't talk about it. She's pretending it never happened."

A sad smile tipped the edge of her lips. "She hasn't forgotten. It's still there. She just can't deal. Yet. It took me twenty-five years until I ran into a trigger that set me off."

He picked up the paper that had covered the straw and folded it over and over until it was a small box. "The girl in the closet."

"Yes."

"So what's your plan?"

A shrug. "I go back to my life in Baltimore and live happily ever after." That had been the tentative plan when she left Baltimore but, now, going back didn't feel exactly right, as if somehow this journey had already changed her.

Smiling, she gathered up her supplies. "I better get home. It's been a long day."

He moved to slide out of the booth. "Let me walk you to your Jeep."

"I'm fine. Parked out back. KC is always nice enough to let me use his extra reserved spot."

Rick glanced toward the former cop who stood behind the bar and laughed with customers. "Good."

"Take care, Detective."

"Until next time."

She laughed, not sure if she was glad to be leaving or glad this wasn't the end of the road for them.

Rick was finishing one of KC's strong coffees when his cell rang. A glance at the number told him it was the main desk at police headquarters. He answered on the third ring. "Morgan."

"Detective, we've a call from a woman who says she recognizes the sketch of the Lost Girl you showed on television."

He was still, skeptical, and hopeful. The false leads had been frustrating, but it only took one good one to close a case.

"Who is she?"

"Says her name is Ester Higgins and she lives in the Hillsboro area. She says the girl looks like her grand-daughter."

He pulled a pen and notebook from his breast pocket. "Did she leave a number?"

She supplied the number. "I've also notified Detective Jake Bishop and he's en route."

Rick checked his watch. "I can be there in fifteen."

"He said sooner, rather than later."

Annoyance snapped. "Sure."

He downed the last of his coffee in one swallow, tossed money on the table to cover the tab, and headed to his car. As a patrol officer, he'd learned the streets of Nashville well. Seems he'd traveled just about every dark alley and back street in the area.

He arrived in the Hillsboro area twelve minutes after the call and easily found the one-story cinder-block home. Its white paint had faded to gray and large sections were peeling. The path to the front steps was cracked and infested with weeds and the shutter to the right of the front door was broken and dangling from a hinge. The house wasn't bad but needed a hell of a lot of work. Most of the houses on the block had been refurbished with new paint, siding, and landscaping. But this house remained a holdout.

The neighborhood might be up and coming, but whoever owned this house was one of the holdouts from the old guard. They could have sold, but were just too old or poor to move.

Bishop's car pulled up behind his and it gave him a measure of satisfaction to know the cop trailed him. He got out, his face sullen. He studied the house as he locked his car and absently checked his gun on his belt.

Rick waited until his partner joined him and the two made the short walk to the front door. "You get any more details from dispatch?"

"No." He angled his neck from side to side as if fingers of tension had tightened around the tendons. "Just a name and she claims to be the grandmother."

"Let's see." Rick knocked.

At first, the only sound from the house was the hum of the television and, then, as Rick raised his hand to knock again, he heard the slow shuffle of footsteps followed by the scraps of a chain lock.

The door opened a fraction and then wider. An old

woman with graying hair tied in a bun peered out at them with dark gray eyes. "What do you want?"

"I'm Detective Rick Morgan and this is my partner, Jake Bishop. You called about a sketch on television."

The eyes sharpened. The scent of mothballs and some kind of microwaved dish swirled around her. "I just called an hour ago."

"We're following up on all leads."

She lingered a moment longer and then opened the screened door. "Come on inside."

Both officers glanced at each other. Neither was sure if this would be the lead that cracked the case or was just another wild-goose chase. The house was dimly lit and the strong scent of mothballs lingered in the air. The walls were jammed full of pictures, most of which appeared to be of a young girl. Judging by the age and time, that girl would have been in her late forties or fifties now.

Ester guided them into a small living room where a large television blared the latest Kardashian reality show. She sat in an easy chair, well worn and flanked by a table piled high with magazines and dishes. She nodded toward a long sofa covered in plastic and indicated the two sit as she reached for a remote and muted the sound.

Rick glanced at the pictures on the wall looking for an image of the Lost Girl, but saw none.

"Can I get you boys a soda?" the woman offered.

"No, ma'am," Rick said. "You said you recognized the image on the television."

The lines around her mouth deepened as she smoothed deeply veined hands over her brittle hips. "I watch TV a lot now that I'm retired. I'd still be working at the plant but I'm too old and not fast enough anymore."

"Yes, ma'am." Impatience nipped, but he resolved to take this slow.

She stared sightlessly at the television as one of the sisters drank and another painted her nails. "Back in the day they'd never have allowed this kind of show on the air. And now here they are and I'm grumbling about them even though I don't miss a show."

The detectives nodded, neither speaking.

Mrs. Higgins reached for a small scrapbook on the side table and opened it. She studied the images. "I dug this out when I saw the news the other day. I've been looking at the pictures over and over ever since. Wasn't sure if my mind was playing tricks and, at first, I didn't think I should call the police. Then I realized I had to call, even if I was wrong." She looked at Rick with a watery gaze. "It's been twenty-six years since I saw my baby girl Heather. The last time I held her hand, her fingers were sticky from a candy cane."

"May I see the pictures?" Rick asked.

Arthritic hands held the scrapbook another moment and then handed it to Rick. His gaze and Bishop's dropped to the picture of the smiling infant.

The infant was no more than three months and it was hard to tell if this was their Jane Doe. He turned a page and saw a picture of a slightly older baby. Still not easy to tell. He feared Mrs. Higgins's images of her granddaughter were not going to help until he turned the next page and saw a picture of a four-year-old. She was standing on a stoop and smiling into the camera. She wore a pink dress.

Bishop hissed in a breath as if he'd just sunk the eight ball in the side pocket.

The same rush of a win washed over Rick. This was their Lost Girl. "You said her name was Heather. What was her last name?"

"Briggs. Her mamma, my daughter, married a guy; at

least they said they was married. I never liked him but she couldn't say no to him."

"When was the last time you saw Heather?" She'd already told him but he wanted her to repeat the information.

"Twenty-six years ago. She spent the night with me and then her mamma came to pick her up and I never saw her again."

"Her mother's name?"

"Loyola. Loyola Briggs."

He kept his voice even and as relaxed as he could manage. "We didn't have a missing persons report for a Heather Briggs."

She shook her head. "When I hadn't seen her for a few weeks I asked Loyola. She said she gave the girl away. An adoption. Said it was best for everyone."

"And you didn't question her?" Bishop asked, his tone as rough as sandpaper.

"I was sorry I'd never see the child again, but I was glad for Heather. Loyola and Danny weren't no kind of parents. And Heather deserved better."

Rick scribbled down the name Danny. "Danny Briggs?"

"Yeah."

Rick jotted the name down as well. "Did your daughter tell you about the family who adopted the child?"

The old woman shook her head slowly, as if over-whelmed by old memories roaring to life. "I asked. And she just said they was real nice and that Heather was better off."

But Rick strongly suspected that Heather had not been adopted. No doubt by the time Loyola had spun her story the child was dead. "Where is Loyola now?"

"Works at a gas station off of I-40. I ain't seen her in years, though I hear she still lives in East Nashville." She rattled off an address. "Without Heather there wasn't much reason for me to see her. I didn't like her much."

"And Danny?"

"Danny Briggs was in prison last I heard."

Rick pulled out his phone and snapped pictures of the little girl.

The old woman clutched the light blue fabric of her well-worn housecoat with knotted fingers. "Do you think that girl on the TV is really Heather? They look alike but that don't mean they're the same." Under the words was a silent plea. *Please tell me I'm wrong.*

Rick shook his head. "Ma'am, we won't know for sure until we run a DNA test."

"So, there's a chance?" She released the fabric, taking care to smooth out the wrinkles.

Rick couldn't confirm what his gut was telling him— they'd found their Jane Doe. "Ma'am, your Heather looks a lot like our sketch."

She leaned forward as if her worst fears poked her in the back. "But you don't know for sure?"

As he stared at the blue eyes that looked so much like the ones Jenna had fashioned he knew they had their child. Now he needed to track down Loyola and Danny and find out what happened to Heather. "Ma'am, it'll take DNA tests to prove one way or another. Would you be willing to give a DNA sample?"

"Sure. I'll give you whatever you need."

"Good, that will help."

"What about Loyola? You going to test her?"

"Yes, ma'am. And Danny Briggs, when we find him."

Tears glistened in old eyes. Frown lines around her mouth deepened. "So you'll know for sure?"

"Yes, ma'am."

"When?"

"I promise to call as soon as the DNA tests are run."

She slumped back in her chair, as all the hope leaked

from her body in one breath. "So right now you don't know nothing for sure and my baby Heather might have found a new home."

Feeling the tension snapping through Bishop's body, Rick refused to let anger derail him. "Anything is possible."

She looked at him, her old, watery gaze desperate for hope.

"Ma'am, is there anyone that can stay with you?" Rick asked.

"There's a neighbor."

"Let me call the neighbor for you." He couldn't leave her alone now. "I need a number."

She finally rattled off a number and Rick called a neighbor. Once he explained the situation, the neighbor agreed to come sit with Mrs. Higgins.

Both Rick and Bishop were anxious to talk to Loyola Briggs after leaving Ester's house. Back in his car Rick did a computer search of Loyola Briggs and quickly found a list of minor arrests for drugs and prostitution. Age forty-two, she listed her home address as an apartment on the east side. While Bishop stood by his car, he searched Danny Briggs. "Danny-boy was released from prison two months ago."

"Why was he in prison?"

"Drugs. Assault. Five to ten years for possession."

Bishop fingered the pinky ring on his right hand. "Hope he doesn't get too used to being a free man."

"We'll do the DNA but I'd bet my last paycheck we've found the Lost Girl."

"No way it could be anyone else. No freaking way."

Rick and Bishop drove to the East Nashville apartment building about an hour before midnight. The parking lot was full of cars and a dozen-plus people milled around. The building's white siding had faded to gray, the few patches of grass had dried to a light brittle brown and the sidewalk leading to the building entrance was cracked and covered in graffiti.

"I did my share of drug busts here," Bishop said as he got out of his car.

"Me too. Last assignment I had here was a prostitution ring. We made twelve arrests that night. Looks like most are back here working again."

"Same shit, different day."

"Yeah." Rick glanced at his screen to double-check the apartment number. "She's in number six."

"I can't wait to meet Loyola." There was an anger bubbling inside him as he imagined the tiny skull that Jenna had given a smiling face.

A hard knock on the door got him no response. "Let's find out where she is."

It took another fifteen minutes to track down the manager, who supplied the detectives with a work address. Sure enough, they found her at a truck stop off I-40.

The parking lot of the truck stop was full with big rigs and a few pickup trucks. A large neon sign above the building flashed WHITES.

Bells jangled overhead as they moved through the front door to a cashier stand where a tall redhead stood. The noise of conversation mingled with plates clattering and a country-western song blaring on the jukebox.

The redhead eyed the two detectives with suspicion as if she knew they were cops and cops meant trouble. She snapped her gum. "Who do you want?"

"Loyola Briggs."

She chewed, her gum snapped again. "She's in trouble again?"

"Not right now. We got a few questions for her."

"Always starts with a few questions." The woman arched a brow. "Right. Kitchen. Through those doors."

The detectives passed by tables full of haggard, bearded drivers, hunched over greasy food and thick, black coffee. Through double doors they were greeted by the smells of frying chicken and biscuits.

When the doors whooshed closed behind them the cooks, dressed in greasy white uniforms, glanced over. One tall man covered in tattoos narrowed his gaze and tightened the grip on his carving knife. Another stiffened and looked toward an exit.

Rick held up his badge. "Looking for Loyola Briggs."

Several of the men relaxed. One nodded toward the back just as an unseen door in the rear of the kitchen slammed open and shut. Both officers hurried through the kitchen and drew their guns as they pushed through the back door. Once outside, they found themselves facing the back parking lot and a row of dumpsters. A lightbulb spit out light, casting a weak halo around the door. For a moment, there was no sign of anyone and both stopped and listened.

"She can't be far," Rick said.

Bishop nodded toward the second green dumpster. "There."

They split up and moved toward it. As Rick came around the left side, he spotted the woman's outline in the shadows. He leveled his gun. "Police. Come out where I can see you with your hands up."

The shadowed figure whirled around, but he still couldn't see her face. She hesitated. He tensed, aiming his gun, not knowing if she was armed.

"Out now!" Bishop said. He'd come around the other side of the dumpster. "Move toward the other officer."

The shadow shifted and then slowly moved toward Rick. She stepped into a ring of light. Dirty-blond hair in a layered cut framed a thin, pale face. A drug addict's wild eyes, as sunken as a hollowed-out skull, stared out at him.

Bishop came up behind her and as he holstered his gun he took her right hand in his and clamped a handcuff on it. He locked the other hand in the cuff.

"I ain't done nothing wrong!" she wailed. "I ain't done nothing."

"Are you Loyola Briggs?" Rick asked.

"Yeah. But I ain't done nothing wrong. Ask my parole officer. I make my meetings."

Rick reached for his phone and pulled up the picture of Heather Briggs. "Is this your daughter?"

Loyola didn't look at the photo. She sniffed and shook her head. "I ain't got no children."

"Your mother says you have a daughter named Heather."

Loyola met his gaze. "I don't have no kids."

Chapter Fifteen

Wednesday, August 23, 11:30 P.M.

Rick's grip on the phone tightened. "According to your mother, Ester Higgins, you do have a child. Her name is Heather."

Loyola stopped her struggles and for a moment stared at him as if he were a ghost from the past. "What?"

"Heather," Bishop said. "Your daughter was Heather."

The woman shook her head and dropped her gaze. "No."

Rick gripped his temper. "Where's Heather?"

She sniffed and kept her gaze on the ground. For a moment her gaze turned vacant as if she traveled backward in time. "I gave her away."

"Gave her away?" Rick asked.

"Yeah." She shrugged her shoulders. "To a good family. That was a long time ago. Is she looking for me? I've seen stories on the television, you know, where kids come and find their real families."

He wondered how many times she'd told herself this story over the years. "You think she's looking for you?"

"Sure. That's what adopted kids do. Like I said, I seen it on those movie channels before."

Bishop muttered a curse. "You didn't give Heather away."

"Yes, I did." She raised her gaze staring at him with vacant eyes. "I did. To a good family."

"Who did you give her to?" Rick asked.

"A good family. A really good family."

"I need a name," Rick insisted.

She shook her head. "I don't remember the name."

Bishop sighed. "You gave your child to a family and you don't have a name?"

"That happens with adoptions. I think they're called closed adoptions."

Bishop growled. "This is a waste of time. Tell her."

Rick shook his head. "Loyola, we've found the body of a child. A girl. And we think it's Heather." He scrolled through his phone and found Jenna's sketch. "We think this is Heather."

Loyola didn't look at the image. "No. That's not Heather."

"You haven't looked at it," Rick said.

She folded her arms, as if donning armor. "I don't need to."

"Do me the favor of looking at the picture." No missing the order behind the soft tone.

Loyola's gaze flickered to the image, but didn't focus on it. "That's not her."

With deliberate slowness, Rick turned off the image and tucked the phone in his breast pocket. "Know how we came up with this picture?"

Loyola sniffed and glanced toward her feet. "I don't care."

Bishop twisted his pinky ring. "You aren't the least bit curious?"

"I've got to get back to work. Please take these handcuffs

off." She moved as if to leave but Rick stepped in her path, blocking her escape.

"We found a skull, Loyola. In the Centennial Park." He didn't say exactly where in the park because he wanted to hear that from her. "Skull was wrapped in a plastic bag. Didn't take the medical examiner long to tell us the skull belonged to a five-year-old girl." The desire to back this woman up against a wall and demand a confession was powerful. But he kept it in check. The medical examiner had pulled DNA from the skull's teeth. "We'll match that DNA to yours, which is on file."

Loyola chewed her bottom lip. "I gave her away. She's living a good life now. And I ain't giving my DNA to nobody."

Rick's grip on his pen tightened as he clicked the end over and over. *Click. Click. Click.* "She was your daughter. And you can't tell me who has her now?"

"They wouldn't tell me who was gonna get her."

"They? Who are they, Loyola?"

"I don't remember."

A smile tipped the edge of his mouth. *Click. Click. Click.* "No more stories. Let's talk about the truth. Did you kill your daughter, Loyola?"

"I didn't . . ." She hesitated. "I'd never hurt Heather. I loved her."

"She's dead. Someone killed this child. We found her body."

She squeezed her eyes closed. "I wouldn't . . . couldn't. You've made a mistake. You didn't find my Heather."

"If you didn't . . ." He leaned a fraction closer as if they were conspirators. "Then you know who did. Who did you give her to?" She might have given the child away or sold her to people who enjoyed hurting children. He'd seen it before and it never failed to sicken him.

"I don't know."

"That's not going to cut it, Loyola." Again, Rick kept his voice nonthreatening. He didn't like this woman but he needed her to talk. Not for himself. But for Heather.

"Let's haul her ass to jail." Bishop's anger rumbled like a growl that all but radiated from his body.

Loyola shook her head. "I ain't going to jail. One more strike and I go to prison."

"Too damn bad," Bishop said. "Nothing would make my day better than watching them slam the door on your pathetic face."

Rick stepped in front of Bishop as if to protect Loyola. "I need you to talk, Loyola. I just need the truth. I don't want to see you go to prison."

Tears welled in her eyes as she shook her head. "I loved Heather."

"I know you did," he said softly. "Tell me what happened. When was the last time you saw her?"

The tears flowed as she seemed to claw through the years to dark memories.

"What was she doing the last time you saw her?" Rick asked.

Loyola swiped away a tear. "She was crying."

"Why was she crying?" he asked softly.

Bishop paced behind Rick as if he were a caged animal. Loyola's gaze flickered to him and then quickly settled on Rick as if she'd fled to a safe harbor. "I don't remember."

"Was she hurt?"

She chewed her bottom lip. "She must've been sad. She loved me and didn't want to go to the new family."

"Was she hurt?" he repeated, as he laid a gentle hand on her shoulder.

"I don't remember."

"I think you do."

"Danny was there," she whispered.

Bishop stopped pacing but glared at Loyola as if to tell her the threat of jail remained.

"Danny was Heather's father," Rick said.

"Yes."

"What happened?" Rick had to be careful here. He didn't want to put ideas in her head about what had happened. He wanted all the facts to come from her.

She picked at her sleeve. "Nothing happened. Danny loved Heather."

Rick's anger simmered under the surface even as he kept his hand on her shoulder. He was careful to keep his fingers relaxed. He wanted her to think of him as a friend. Getting a pound of flesh right now wouldn't help Heather. "What happened?"

She squeezed her eyes closed as if the scene played right before her. "Nothing happened."

Bishop hissed in a breath, his anger as thick as the humidity soaking the night air. Both cops knew Danny Briggs's rap sheet went back thirty years and was littered with violence and drugs.

Loyola kept her gaze on Rick as if he had become her sole lifeline.

"Where'd you see Heather crying?"

"In her bed. Danny said we needed to find her a new home. And I knew he was right. He took her to the new home."

"He took her?"

She shrugged. "He took her away. I never knew where. He took her away and I never saw her again." She looked up at him, her gaze pleading for forgiveness he could never give.

"Did he hurt her?" Rick asked.

She glanced up, her gaze wild, bloodshot and watery. "No. He loved her. He just took her away."

The likes of Danny Briggs trampled children in their wake.

Rick nodded to Bishop, who quickly grabbed hold of Loyola's handcuffed arms.

But Rick shook his head. Until he had a confession or a solid witness statement, he didn't want to lose the fragile trust Loyola had given him. "Loyola, we need to go downtown."

"Why do we need to go anywhere? And I'll be good without the handcuffs, I promise." She looked at Bishop and then Rick, pleading.

Rage roiled in Bishop's gaze and, for a moment, he looked as if he would respond with a harsh comment. But he caught Rick's warning glare and fell silent. Rick didn't question his partner. They all had those moments, those cases that struck deep nerves that could paralyze with pain and anger.

"We need to talk more," Rick said. Until he squeezed every bit of information he could out of Loyola, he'd play nice. *Sometimes you have to dance with the devil to solve a case.* How many times had he heard his father say that? "Bishop, remove the handcuffs."

Bishop's glare darkened, but he fished the keys from his pocket and unlocked the cuffs.

Rubbing her wrists, Loyola looked up at him, her gaze bewildered and confused. "I told you what I know."

Rick shook his head. He wanted to know how a woman could allow a goon like Briggs around her child let alone allow the man to take her away. "My guess is there're a few more details."

After Rick and Bishop found drugs on Loyola Briggs, a violation of her parole, they booked her in the jail. The charge wouldn't hold her long, but at least that had her location nailed down for no less than twenty-four hours.

Danny's parole officer got a wake-up call at four in the morning. He'd been groggy, his voice deep with sleep, but he'd promised to head into the office and pull Danny's file.

Two hours later when Rick got a call from the parole officer, he had had a chance to swing by his house for a quick shower and to pick up Tracker. Armed with a last-known address for Briggs from the parole officer, Rick and Tracker swung by the office and picked up Bishop.

Tracker sat alert in the backseat when they parked in front of the one-story clapboard house covered in a blend of old paint and mold.

Bishop glanced at the house and the pile of garbage by the front door. "Delightful."

Tracker's gaze looked at the house and he barked again.

"What's with the dog?" Bishop asked.

Rick and Tracker shared a strong connection and he'd learned long ago if the dog was barking he needed to pay attention. "I don't know."

Rick got out and opened Tracker's door. The dog barked.

Bishop slid out of his seat. "Why you bringing the dog?"

"He's restless. Don't worry, he'll behave."

Bishop slammed his door.

When Rick and Bishop banged on Briggs's house door, Tracker sat at the bottom of the stairs, his ears perked and his gaze bright. It was seven in the morning.

No one answered. Rick banged again.

Bishop stood back, flexing his fingers. "I'm looking forward to meeting this guy."

Rick shook his head slowly. "Let me do the talking. You're angry and that's not good."

"Aren't you angry?" Bishop asked.

"Yeah. But I'm better at locking the anger away until I'm ready to pull it out."

Bishop's jaw tensed. "I'll be fine."

Rick met his gaze. "I do the talking."

"Understood."

Rick hammered his fist on the door. "Police. Open the door."

A light clicked on inside and the shuffle of feet moved toward the door seconds before it opened to a woman. In her late thirties, she had light brown hair, bloodshot eyes ringed with day old mascara, and pockmarked skin. "What do you want?"

"We're looking for Danny Briggs," Rick said.

She coughed. "He left yesterday. Took off like a bat out of hell."

"What's your name?"

"I'm Cindy Gavin. I'm his girlfriend for lack of a better word."

"Mind if we search the place?"

She wore a silk robe that gapped slightly at her breasts. Smiling, she opened the door wider and stepped back. "Help yourself. He ain't here."

The two officers moved into the small house. It was decorated in a cat theme from the black carpet to the leopard drapes to the striped wallpaper. Pictures of lions and tigers hung on the wall. Mugs on the kitchen counter were striped like a tiger. While Bishop stood in the living room with Cindy, Rick searched the house. There was no sign of Danny Briggs.

Rick emerged from the bedroom. "Did he say where he was going?"

"Nope. Just packed a bag and took off."

"Why'd he leave?"

She shrugged. "We were watching television, the news came on, and he got real sick-looking."

"What was on the news?"

"I don't know. I was reading a magazine. He was waiting for a sports score update and then there was some news story about an artist and he was gone."

The story about Jenna and the Lost Girl had spooked Danny. "Any idea where he might go?"

"He's been staying with me since he got out of prison. He's got a few friends from before he went up. I guess he's with one of them."

"You have names?" Rick asked.

"Yeah, sure." She rattled off several names as she reached in the pocket of her robe and pulled out a pack of cigarettes. She lit one. "What's he done now? Guy's got a hot head and isn't afraid to use his fists."

"He ever mention anything about a kid or a wife?" Rick noticed the faint yellowing of a fading bruise on Cindy's wrists as if they'd been gripped hard.

"No. You telling me he's got a wife or a kid looking for him?"

"Not exactly," Rick pulled a card from his pocket and handed it to her. "We'll track down his friends, but if you see Danny, call me."

She flicked the edge of the card as she raised the cigarette to her mouth with the other. "He's really screwed up this time, hasn't he?"

"He sure did," Bishop growled.

Rick smiled, no hint of anger. "Let's just say we got a few questions for him. And you'd be wise to call if you see him."

"Yeah, sure. Why not? He's a pain in the ass and it would be great to get him out of my life."

The detectives turned and started for the car when

Tracker glanced past Rick to the side of the house. The dog began barking loud.

Bishop glared at the dog but Rick immediately reached for his weapon and whirled around. Following Tracker's gaze toward the side of the house, he instantly saw the flash of a gun muzzle as a tall man stepped out of the shadows.

"Drop your weapon!" Rick shouted.

Bishop reached for his gun just as the man in the shadows raised his gun.

With Tracker barking angry and loud, Rick pointed his weapon. "Drop your gun now!"

Bishop leveled his gun. "Drop it! Now!"

The man hesitated and then, seeing he was outgunned, lowered his gun to the ground. He raised his hands.

Bishop raced toward the man, gun drawn. "On your belly now!"

The man held up his hands over his head and dropped to his knees as Bishop kicked the gun away. Rick reached for his cuffs and secured the man's hands behind his back. Rick rolled him to his back.

No missing the man's identity. He matched the picture the parole officer had on file.

"Danny Briggs," Rick said. "Thought you were out of town."

He reeked with the stench of whiskey and cigarettes. "What the fuck do you want with me?"

"The gun alone is enough to send you back to prison, Danny." Adrenaline surged in his veins.

"The gun's just the start," Bishop said.

"Fuck," Briggs said. "I ain't done nothing wrong."

Bishop grabbed the man by the collar and twisted the fabric in his fist. "Then tell me where we can find your daughter Heather."

The sound of the girl's name had his gaze narrowing. "I want a lawyer."

"I bet you do."

Twenty minutes later Briggs and his girlfriend were in the back of a squad car. As Bishop spoke to a uniformed officer, Rick leaned against the car and looked down at Tracker who now played with his rubber chew toy—his reward for his work.

"Did real good, T. Real good. We still got the moves."

After Bishop spoke to the uniformed officer, he moved toward Rick and Tracker. He paused, rested his hands on his hips, and studied the dog. He worked his jaw as if chewing on nails. "I owe you two both."

"Thanks goes to Tracker. He's the one that sounded the alarm."

"Yeah." He met Rick's gaze, a mixture of relief churning with humility. "And you listened to him. Thanks."

Rick nodded. "Anytime."

Rachel Wainwright arrived at the justice center just after seven A.M. She glanced over at Detective Deke Morgan who sat behind the wheel of the SUV. He stared ahead, his dark glasses hiding his eyes. "You're sure you want to do this?"

"No, but someone has to do it." She'd gotten a call early this morning from the public defender's office regarding a case. A woman, believed to be the Lost Girl's mother, had been arrested. Her name was Loyola Briggs and police believed she'd killed the child or knew who did. Cops had yet to prove a biological connection between Briggs and the child, but mitochondrial DNA, DNA passed from mother to child, would determine if the cops had arrested the right woman. Right now, Loyola Briggs was being held on a parole violation.

"Rick believes she's guilty." The scents of soap and after-shave wafted around Deke.

Rachel liked the mornings best when the day was fresh

and hope had been renewed. This morning had started off nice but had soured with the public defender's office. "Test results have yet to confirm a connection to the woman. And Rick told you last night that he and Bishop arrested Danny Briggs."

"That doesn't mean Loyola Briggs is innocent."

"Maybe."

He turned toward her. "You're an idealist."

She shrugged. "It's a dirty job but someone has to do it."

A smile tweaked the edges of his lips. He leaned over and kissed her. "I love you."

She touched the side of his face, savoring the strong set of his jaw. "I love you."

"Try not to piss off too many people today."

She laughed, feeling stronger knowing he might not like what she did, but could accept it. "Honey, that's what I do best. See you tonight."

"Can't wait to hear about your day."

Out of the car, Rachel showed her ID and the guard glanced up at her. Defense attorneys, even one dating a homicide cop, didn't win any popularity contests in this system. "Morning, Lee."

He arched a brow as he sent her purse through the scanner. "So what fine citizen brings you here today, Ms. Wainwright?"

She could play coy, but there was little point. They'd all know before she left. "Loyola Briggs."

"The baby killer."

She cringed, knowing a moniker like that, especially if picked up by the media, would have her client convicted before they got to trial. "She's not been charged with murder. From what I understand, she's being held on a minor drug charge and parole violation."

"That's temporary."

She walked through the scanner, and picked up her

briefcase and purse. She'd learned not to argue with the guards. No point. When it came time to argue this case, she'd try it in court, not in the hallways or by the water cooler.

She made her way to the visiting room and took a seat at a metal table and bench that were bolted to the floor. This early in the morning, few families visited. This was the time of day for defense attorneys like her to call on a client before court.

She pulled a legal pad and a pen from her briefcase as the deputy opened the door and escorted in a petite, paper-thin brunette with hollow cheeks. Smudges darkened the skin under her eyes and her hands trembled.

Rachel attributed the shakes not to fear but to alcohol or drug withdrawal. She wasn't so naïve that she thought her client was innocent, but she believed in the right to a valid defense. Everyone deserved her day in court.

The female deputy walked the woman up to the table. "Are you Ms. Briggs's attorney?"

"I am."

A dark brow arched. "I see you a lot down here."

Rachel had slept little last night and her patience had thinned to breaking. "I get around."

What she didn't add was that the city had tossed her several tough cases since her very controversial handling of the Jeb Jones case last year. Though DNA had definitively cleared her client of a thirty-year-old murder conviction, many didn't like the fact that she'd bucked the system and won.

The deputy was too professional to speak her mind, but the hardness in her gaze told Rachel she was in for another uphill battle. "You have thirty minutes."

Loyola sat, but her gaze remained on her nails, which had been chewed to the quick.

"Loyola Briggs, my name is Rachel Wainwright. I'm your court-appointed attorney."

"They said they was holding me on a parole violation and drugs. Don't seem like I need an attorney for that."

"You've been in trouble for drugs before. If you're convicted this time then it means prison."

She managed a small shrug. "Okay."

"You're willing to go to prison?"

"I can tough out a year. Won't be much more than that for what the cops found on me."

"You do understand the cops are trying to link you to the Jane Doe child they found in the park. They believe you're her mother."

"Like I told the cops, my baby daddy gave our girl away to a loving family. I didn't hurt her. They're gonna figure out that the bag of bones they found ain't my kid."

Either the woman was a practiced liar or so deep in denial she'd lost touch with reality. "Loyola, Danny Briggs was arrested an hour ago."

"Danny?"

"Yes. Danny. He's been arrested. And it's a matter of time before he implicates you."

Loyola looked at her shorn, uneven fingers. "I didn't kill my baby. I didn't kill my baby."

Rachel had dealt with many accomplished liars in the few years she'd been a public defender. Most were guilty but it was the stray innocent who kept her going. As easy as it was to try to convict Loyola in her mind, she'd put her emotions aside and do what she did best—make her case in court. "All right. Let's see if I can get you out on bond. They're holding you right now on a minor parole violation. They can't argue for murder until you've been charged and that's going to take DNA."

Loyola leaned forward, her dark eyes searching. "You're

going to get me out? I shouldn't be here because someone found a bag of bones."

"That bag of bones was someone's child."

She sat back and folded her arms over her chest. "Wasn't mine."

If not for her commitment to the law and the justice system, she couldn't do this work. "For the short term, yes, I'll get you out."

Chapter Sixteen

Thursday, August 24, 10 A.M.

Jenna woke before the sun, but the fatigue had been overwhelming. She allowed herself the luxury of dozing until ten in the morning. She'd slept little last night, her conversation with Rick Morgan buzzing in her head like a swarm of bees. The constant replay of words had made little sense until it struck her that last night had been the first time she'd ever talked about her past. Her aunt had always brushed the bad events aside and, without words, taught Jenna to do the same. The only time the past had come up in Baltimore had been at her interview for the academy and she'd done what her aunt had always done . . . she'd brushed it aside. *I don't remember.*

But she was remembering now. More and more each day, a new detail slipping through another crack in the wall.

First, it had been Shadow Eyes. Then details of the closet. Her sister angry with her father. Ronnie arguing with someone up until the end. And then . . .

More details danced on the edges of her memory and if they took one small step forward into the light, she could reach out and grab them. But they hovered in the darkness, elusive and out of reach. That's why she'd gotten up and started to draw.

She sat up in bed and swung her legs over the side and shoved her hands through her hair. Barefooted, she padded into the living room, glanced at the covered portrait she'd begun last night. This image didn't feature a bride or a smiling face. This was the portrait of Shadow Eyes who had broken into her thoughts three weeks ago, the night she'd found the little girl in the closet. But as she stared at the face, recognition did not flicker. For all she knew, the image might have been an amalgam of suspect faces she'd drawn over the years.

Shaking off a shudder, she moved into the kitchen, needing a cup of coffee to chase away the heaviness of fatigue. Minutes later, coffee gurgled from the machine and she was leaning toward it, counting the seconds until it finished brewing. Finally, it was finished and she took coffee in hand and moved toward the back door, anxious to be in the fresh air.

The morning dew had long burned off the back deck that overlooked the small, green backyard and the ring of woods behind the house. Outside, she was more connected to the world. She could breathe. She wasn't sure how long she stood there but when she turned, she spotted something in the corner of her eye. Setting her mug down, she moved toward the white bit of plastic resting on the back rail by her house. As she got closer, she realized what was in the bag. A head.

For an instant, she recoiled as her heart raced and her chest tightened. She inhaled deeply and steeled herself. She peered in the bag. It was a doll's head and scrawled across the forehead was the word BITCH.

The eyes staring up at her were blue, bright, and lifeless. White hair stood straight up, spiking as if the electricity had raced through the doll, or what remained of her.

In a snap, her brain shifted to cop mode. Who had sent her this? Her work with the Nashville Police Department came to mind. She'd created the sketch of a child's face. Instead of being afraid as she was of Shadow Eyes, she knew this doll's head was tangible and she understood tangible. "I've struck a nerve."

Mindful not to touch the doll, she retrieved her phone from the house, took pictures of the doll's head, and then called Rick Morgan.

He answered on the third ring and his voice was gruff and deep. A dog barked in the background. "Jenna."

"I'm texting you a picture. It's of a doll's head left on my back patio."

"A what?"

"A doll's head. I think my drawing has gotten someone's attention."

Silence crackled on the line. "The child's grandmother saw the picture you drew on television last night and called us. We questioned a woman last night who we believe might be the child's mother. We're running a DNA sample of the mother and the child. We also arrested a man who we believe was the child's father."

"You arrested him?"

"He drew on us."

The understated words hinted at what must have been a heart-stopping scene. She'd had a gun drawn on her once, when she'd patrolled in Baltimore. She remembered holding her gun steady and shouting for the man to put his gun down. She'd been lucky. He'd listened and laid his gun down before kneeling with his hands behind his head. She'd shaken for two days after. "So you have them both in custody?"

"We had to release Loyola Briggs, the alleged mother, early this morning. We can't charge her until we prove the child is hers. Danny Briggs, the father, was just arrested and won't be getting out anytime soon."

The thrill of success hummed in her body. Another sketch. Another arrest. "You think they're the parents?"

"Your picture looked exactly like photos the grandmother had in a scrapbook. And Danny Briggs had scratches on the side of his car. Looked like he might have sideswiped someone."

"He ran me off the road?"

"Looks like it."

She ran her fingers through her hair, grim satisfaction giving her little pleasure. "Good. You have a lead."

"It's a hell of a lead. How long do you think the doll's head has been on your porch?"

"I don't know. I wasn't out on the porch yesterday."

"Danny Briggs wasn't arrested until a couple of hours ago. He could have left it."

She turned from the bag and the doll's head. Moments like this made being a cop so satisfying. "You'll tell me what the DNA reveals?"

"Of course. Without you, we wouldn't be here now."

"Want me to bag the doll's head?" she teased.

"No." His voice radiated with force. "I'll send an officer."

Disappointment snapped. "I can do it."

"I've no doubt, but we don't want any defense attorney saying you tampered with the evidence."

He'd all but called her an outsider. "Okay. But I'm watching when they do their thing."

He chuckled. "Why doesn't that surprise me?"

She laughed.

"Jenna, be careful."

"Always."

Seconds after she ended the call, her phone rang. She glanced at the display on her phone and saw the Baltimore area code. Mike. Straightening, she considered ignoring him but at the last, hit ACCEPT. "This is Jenna."

"You're sounding fairly formal." His deep voice rumbled with fatigue.

Two weeks ago she'd have been glad to hear Mike's familiar voice. Now, well, his calls triggered a jolt of tension. "I wasn't sure who it was."

Her lie didn't exactly ring true but he didn't bite. "Wouldn't want you talking dirty to the wrong guy."

Mike could always break the ice even if it were thick, but not today. "No. That would not go over well."

Mike cleared his throat. "Remember the kid you found in that closet?"

She stilled. "Yes."

"I checked in on her. She's in a good foster home and she's doing well."

Well. Jenna couldn't remember what it had been like after her rescue. But her aunt had said she'd been quiet and withdrawn for months. "How is she physically?"

"Malnourished. But the docs and the foster parents are working on that."

All her good humor trickled away. "Do they know how long she was in the closet?"

"Months at least."

Months. Tear welled in her eyes. One tear escaped. She swiped it away.

"Jenna?"

"I was just processing."

"You can see her if you want."

Her heart clenched. "Why would I want to see her?"

"I saw the Nashville news report. You understand where she is mentally."

She pressed her fingertips to her forehead. "Who else in Baltimore knows?"

"Not too many."

"Translation: everyone."

He dropped his voice a notch. "It'll be fine. We all understand it happened a long time ago. It's a part of you and you're a good cop."

"Maybe."

"We miss you, Jenna. You're a hell of an asset. When are you going to get tired of country music and come back to the real world?"

A tentative laugh stuttered across her lips. "Nashville isn't real?"

"Nope. It's all about Baltimore as far as I'm concerned." He sighed into the phone as if hurt. "Come back to Baltimore, Jenna. Your old job is yours for the taking."

She cradled the phone close to her ear. He was again coaxing her back into the group on the other side of the blue line. And right now, she wanted back in; she wanted to take down lowlifes that killed children and raped women. But did she want Baltimore? "I don't know, Mike."

A breath seeped free. "Not knowing is better than a flat-out no."

"I do miss the work. I'd be lying if I said I didn't."

"Damn straight you miss it. You miss us. You miss me."

She frowned. "Don't get carried away."

"You do. You miss me, Jenna. I sure as hell miss you."

She moistened her lips and rotated her head from side to side. "Mike, we're not talking about us. We were never an us."

"Not in my mind. Leaving was your idea, not mine. I thought we were finally headed in the right direction."

"I told you the sex didn't change anything." It never changed anything.

"Your body sure responded to me."

She closed her eyes, not sure what to say to that. She cared deeply for him, always would, but she'd never sleep with him again. Whatever they had, wasn't enough. She'd never been able to tell him about the loss of her family. She'd been more candid with Rick Morgan over one meal than she'd been with Mike all the years they'd worked together. That wasn't Mike's fault. So many times he wanted her to open up to him.

He cleared his throat to break the silence. "Look, I don't want to throw us into the mix. That wasn't why I called. I just wanted to pat you on the back and tell you the kid is doing well."

She didn't quite believe him but she was willing to pretend. "What's her name? The little girl, what's her name?"

"Sarah."

Sarah? She dragged a ragged hand through her hair. Shit. "You okay?"

"Yeah." She straightened. "Thanks, Mike."

"Does that mean you'll think about returning? Your leave is almost up."

The clock ticked. Soon, she'd have to make some decision. She couldn't afford the two apartments and she owed it to her friends back home and the Baltimore Police Department to make a decision. "Yeah, I'll think about it."

When the doorbell rang, Jenna expected to see the uniformed officer that Rick had sent. She'd not glanced in the peephole or peeked out the window. It wasn't like her to be distracted.

She opened the door to Susan Martinez. The reporter was dressed in a black pencil skirt, a white tailored shirt, red four-inch heels, and large, dark glasses. Pearls hung from her neck and a gold watch winked on her wrist. "Jenna."

Jenna's hand gripped the edge of the door and straightened as if someone had taken an unexpected swipe at her. She needed formality with this woman. "Ms. Martinez."

"I was hoping we could talk."

"About what?"

"We received quite a few calls and e-mails on that piece. People were touched you survived and thrived. If you would let me interview you, I think quite a few people would be inspired by you."

"I don't think so, Ms. Martinez. I'm not interested in re-hashing my family's tragedy for everyone to see. But feel free to tell your own story and how you were tangled up with my family."

A wrinkle formed between the reporter's eyes. "No one cares about me. They care about you. You'd be going full circle if we spoke again on television."

"I don't need to go full circle."

"The cops, hell, even the reporters, worked nonstop for weeks until you were found. Believe it or not, there were seasoned cops crying when you were found alive. I think you owe it to them all to show that you're doing well."

She understood what those cops had gone through emotionally. She'd been in their shoes before. She'd wept tears for children like Sarah.

"The case was solved and closed. Leave it alone."

Jenna thought about the uniformed officer whom Rick was sending. She did not need Susan Martinez here now. One thing to dig up the past but it was quite another to talk about an active case with the media. "Now's not the best time. I have a client coming by to talk about a portrait."

A spark in Susan's eyes suggested a shift in tactics. "KC Kelly was one of the cops on your case. I could interview you together. It really would be a great story."

The woman didn't know when to let go. "KC's not a fan of interviews."

"He had his share of troubles last year but I won't bring them up. I promise."

The sincerity underscoring the last word rang false. "No. Not now."

The reporter didn't blink or budge. "How is it that you came to draw in front of KC's bar? Was that a one in a million?"

"It happens."

"I don't think so."

"What's that mean?"

"You came back to Nashville for a reason. You found that girl in the closet and started to remember. You're still remembering more and more each day."

"I needed to make sense of a terrible thing. That's all."

"And you're at peace with what happened to your family?"

"I have to be. Look, Ms. Martinez, I don't want to have this conversation. I don't want to do an interview. I need you to leave."

Susan stood her ground. "Is it because of what I told you about your father and me?"

"You're too close to the story."

"I'm not, I'm a reporter first."

Jenna shook her head. "No, Susan. I can't do this now."

"Every day on the anniversary, I put flowers on your family's grave." She whispered the words as if in confession.

"Why?"

"Because they were good people. They should be remembered. Helps me to remember them."

"I do remember them. I don't need to relive the past in public."

Susan's eyes danced with desperation. "I'll be at the gravesite tomorrow. Maybe I'll see you there too."

"Good-bye, Ms. Martinez." She closed the door. For a few long, tense minutes, the woman stood on the doorstep and didn't move. Then finally, she turned and left.

Jenna watched her leave but sensed she'd not seen the last of her.

* * *

Rick got out of his car and studied the high-end dress shop Pamela's. The one-story building was painted in blues and grays and a gilded *P* decorated the glass front door. He didn't know much about the place but had been willing to visit when the uniformed officer had called him an hour ago. "Lady says she's got a stalker. A guy that's always just there. Seeing as you've had two murders thought you'd want to know."

Rick had searched the woman's name, Pamela Grayson, and discovered she'd had no priors and had not filed any stalking claims before. When he did an Internet search on her and saw the picture of her standing in front of her store, he realized she fit the profile of Diane and Nancy.

Jangling his keys, he moved into the shop immediately assailed by the scent of expensive perfume and bright colors.

A tall woman with dark hair glanced up at him. She stepped around the counter, a pink dress hugging her slim figure. Clearly, she realized he didn't belong in a place like this. "May I help you?"

He removed his badge. "Detective Rick Morgan. Nashville Police Department. I'm looking for Pamela Grayson." A dress here would cost more than most cops made in a month. "I understand you filed a report yesterday."

Relief softened dark eyes. "Yes, but I wasn't sure anyone was really listening."

"I'm listening. What's going on?"

Pamela sighed. "A few months ago, I got the feeling that someone was watching me. At first, I just dismissed it. My mother always said I could make a production out of nothing." Absently, her right hand went to the gold watch on her left arm. "So I just kind of blew off my worries. But my skin kept tingling."

"Tingling?"

"Yeah, I know. Sounds dumb. But there you have it. Tingling skin. Anyway, I really started to pay attention to my surroundings. I read that book on fear. I know you're not supposed to dismiss it."

"Okay."

"Anyway, I was driving to work a few weeks ago and I see this red truck. It's old and beat-up. Before I can really worry about it, it's gone. No big deal. Then two weeks ago, I saw the same kind of truck parked across the street. It was just there for a few minutes but it was there. So, I'm at the mall, scoping out the competition when I see a guy. Grungy. Kinda weird. Again he's there and then he's not."

So far, nothing much Rick could use, but he let her keep talking. "Two days ago, I'm buying coffee in Nashville, twenty minutes from here. Same truck. And same guy. When I came out of the shop I look up and he's staring at me. I know that was no accident."

"I understand you snapped a picture of the truck with your phone camera."

"I did." She turned to the counter and picked up a phone in a bejeweled case. She punched in the security code and scrolled to the image. "I caught him as he was getting into his car. I don't think he saw me take the picture."

Rick studied the picture. A man faced away from the camera so there was no clear image of his face. He was dressed in jeans and getting into a pickup truck. He was a classic Nashville character. "Can you describe him?"

"Not really. I just got a glance at him. I mean I remember thinking he wasn't nice-looking, but that's all I can remember."

His thoughts turned to Jenna and her talent for giving a face to images trapped in the subconscious. "What if I hooked you up with a forensic artist? She might be able to help you create a picture."

"I don't know if I got that good a look at him."

"Would you try?" He had two dead women and now a third woman, who fit the profile, being stalked.

"Sure. I'll try." She shook her head. "So I'm not losing my mind?"

He shook his head. "You were smart to listen to your instincts. I'll be in touch."

Jenna sat in her car cradling a hot cup of coffee she'd bought at the drive-through. Despite the day's rising heat, a deep chill iced over her bones. The officer had come by and taken the doll's head away, but its arrival coupled with Susan's visit had unsettled her more than she was willing to admit.

Her phone rang and she tensed, ready to ignore it, and then she saw Rick Morgan's name. Despite herself she smiled. "Detective."

"Did my officer come by?"

"He did. Took care of business." She considered telling him about Susan but decided there was no point. She was a big girl who could handle a reporter.

"Can I call in a favor?"

She closed her eyes and savored the heat of the sun. "I thought you already did that?"

"Okay, you got me. But I was hoping I could call in a second favor?"

A smile tipped the edges of her lips. "I think this will be the third."

"Rachel asked for the other favor. Technically, this is my second."

"By the way, did anything come of the sketch I did for Rachel and her client?"

"No. Not yet."

A DUI case from a nobody wasn't at the top of anyone's list. Nice if every case got the same priority treatment but the reality was that time was precious and cops had to pick and choose. "So what do you need?"

"Another sketch." He explained what was happening.

Jenna rested her head against the headrest. Just the idea of a job calmed her racing nerves. "Give me the address."

It took Jenna thirty minutes and a few wrong turns before she found the dress shop in Franklin. It was a cute place, though she decided that wasn't her style. It had the look of money, and she'd be willing to bet the dresses cost more than she'd ever be able to afford. She grabbed her sketchpad and slid out of the car. Rick Morgan emerged from the front door, looking much like a fish out of water. She had to smile.

"I thought your tastes weren't pastel."

He laughed. "Don't underestimate me."

The smile again transformed his face from stern and severe to almost handsome. She cleared her throat. "You need a sketch?"

"I do. I'd like you to meet Pamela Grayson." He shifted his gaze to the woman who emerged from behind the counter.

Pamela extended a manicured hand as if this was some kind of new business presentation. "You're Jenna Thompson. I saw your sketch on the news. I remember your story when you were little. It was all over the news."

She accepted Pamela's hand. "I seem to be the news of the day."

The woman's hand was soft but her handshake strong. "You were brave to go on television. It must be hard having the past dug up?"

"All for a good cause."

"Have you gotten any leads yet on that poor missing girl?"

Jenna glanced toward Rick, unwilling to blow any leads he might have in the Lost Girl case. "You'll have to ask the detective. I was simply the artist."

Rick cleared his throat. "Let's say we've made substantial progress since the picture aired. You'd be surprised how accurate Ms. Thompson can be."

Pamela shook her head. "I don't see how you can help me. I barely saw the guy."

"I'm a regular magician when it comes to pulling memories to the surface. I'm assuming now is a good time to work?"

Pamela nodded. "I'll close the shop for the afternoon. We can take as long as you need. I want to figure out if this guy is for real or if I'm just being foolish."

Jenna set her sketchpad on the table. "Never ignore your instincts. They pick up more than you realize."

Pamela's face relaxed a fraction as if she needed to hear the validation. "Thanks. That's good to hear."

Jenna turned to Detective Morgan. "I always work alone. I don't allow anyone else in the room while I work, even other cops."

Rick arched a brow as if he couldn't quite believe she was kicking him out of this party.

"Why?"

"Just like I told Rachel, you'll skew the results or shut down memories. You wouldn't mean to, but you would. It's just Pamela and me for this job. Ask Rachel. I kicked her out when I did her sketch."

Hands on hips, Detective Morgan looked as if he'd argue.

When he didn't move, she arched a brow. "My way or the highway, Detective."

"So, I'm supposed to sit in my car and wait?"

"I suggest you get back to work. This could take a couple of hours."

"Hours."

"At least."

"Rachel said you were bossy."

Jenna winked. "It's a gift."

"Fine. But lock the door behind you. I've got a bad feeling about this."

"We'll lock the door. And I know how to take care of myself."

"Are you armed?" he asked.

"Yes."

Shaking his head, he finally nodded. "I'll check with you in a few hours."

"How about I call you when we're done? I don't like to be rushed or think there's a clock ticking over my head."

"I want to see that sketch sooner rather than later."

"Sooner will come when you leave."

His annoyance palatable, he glanced toward Pamela. "She's bossy, but she's good."

Pamela folded her arms and nodded. "I got that sense."

Rick left and waited by his car as Pamela crossed the store and locked the front door. When the dead bolt clicked, he slid behind the wheel and left.

"You've annoyed him," Pamela said.

"I'm fairly good at annoying cops." She nearly described herself as a cop and then stopped. She was a cop and she wasn't. "I know how to get under their skin."

Pamela smiled as she looked out the front window and watched as he drove off. "I don't think Detective Morgan is used to not getting his way."

"He'll survive." Jenna smiled. "Ready to get started?"

Pamela nodded. "We can sit in my office. Can I make you a coffee?"

"I'm fine. But make yourself a cup if you think it will relax you."

They moved behind the counter into a midsize office. Unlike the front of the store, this space struck her as chaotic. Dress samples hung from a hook on one wall, the chairs in front of the desk where piled high with catalogues, and magazines cluttered a chunky desk with carved, round legs. On the walls hung images of models though Jenna, judging by the fashions, guessed the pictures had been up for a few years.

Pamela cleared a chair in front of the desk. "I'm sorry this place is a wreck. I spend all my time up front with the customers and it seems there's never time to clean the office."

"No worries." Jenna settled in the chair and as she unfolded her sketchpad, Pamela cleared and settled into the chair opposite her.

"I still feel kind of silly. There's been no crime."

"That doesn't mean there won't be one if we don't catch this guy. You were smart to call the police."

And so they began, Jenna asking Pamela questions about face shapes, hairlines, eyes, mouths, and ears. She would listen as Pamela described and then sketch the image. Pamela, as it turned out, had a great eye for detail and once she saw a bit of the sketch would make changes. This process went on for nearly two hours and by the time they'd finished, Jenna had a sketch that could easily be matched to a suspect or even a mug shot. As she stared at the picture, she hesitated. She'd seen this guy before.

She turned the picture around so that Pamela could get a full view of the work. "Look familiar?"

Pamela looked at the picture and nodded as recognition flared in her eyes. "That's him. I don't know how you did it, but that's him."

"It's what I do." She stared at the image. There were slight differences but then two different women had described him. She'd drawn this face before. She reached for her cell, snapped a picture of the sketch, and texted it to Rick.

Within fifteen seconds her phone rang. "That's the guy?"

"Pamela confirmed it. Would you like me to drop the sketch off at your office on my way home?"

"That would be great. I'm going to send this out now."

"Rick, I've drawn this guy before."

"What do you mean?"

"For Rachel. This is the guy who attacked her client a couple of months ago."

Silence crackled over the line. "Are you sure?"

"Compare this sketch to the one I did the other night. It's the same guy."

By the time Rick had collected Jenna's sketch from reception, he'd used her digital image to issue a BOLO, Be On the LookOut, for the man believed to be a stalker and a rapist. He called Rachel and informed her of the connection Jenna had made.

"So what do you know, I was right," Rachel said.

Rick liked Rachel and respected the hell out of her after the help she'd given Georgia last year, but that didn't soften his annoyance over her defending Loyola Briggs. "You get one right from time to time. But you're wrong about Loyola Briggs."

Silence snapped. "I protect the integrity of the law, Rick."

"Did I mention Jenna found a doll's head by her front door this morning? The word *bitch* was scrawled on its face. Smacks of Loyola."

She lowered her voice as if she sensed she was losing him. "Rick, I don't think Loyola has the wherewithal to pull a stunt like that. She could barely walk this morning."

"That's assuming she's not faking."

Rachel sighed. "We'll sort this out as soon at we get DNA."

He moved his head from side to side to release the tension. "Right."

"Keep me posted."

"Always, Counselor."

He studied the image that featured dark, glaring eyes, a thick jaw covered in a blanket of stubble, and the receding hairline. The beat and patrol officers knew their neighborhoods and often knew the characters they dealt with on a regular basis. The cops might not have given the sketch much of a look when Rachel had passed it around, but they'd listen to him. This guy was just distinctive enough to get himself noticed and, if he were stalking Pamela, there was a chance someone had pointed him out to a cop along the way.

Rick's cell buzzed. "Morgan."

"This is Officer Brandt. I got your BOLO. I know this guy."

"Really?" Rick stood up and snapped his fingers to get Bishop's attention.

"Cyrus Mitchell. I've arrested him for indecent exposure. The guy flashed himself to a group of women about a year ago. Stalking would be his style."

"What about rape?"

"It would fit."

Rachel's client had said there'd been a second man in the room. Jenna had not drawn that face yet and he was thinking now more than ever it was important.

Rick typed Mitchell's name into his computer and a mug shot appeared. It was a perfect match to Jenna's drawing. "Well, I'll be damned. I think we've a match."

The officer chuckled. Everyone enjoyed the rush when they fingered a bad guy. "Glad to help."

Rick hung up and mentally gave a point to Jenna. Another of her sketches had a hit.

Bishop strode into the room, a cup of hot coffee in hand. "What do you have?" Bishop asked.

"The guy that might have been stalking Pamela. Jenna did a sketch and a uniform just identified him. And remember when Jenna did the favor for Rachel and drew a sketch of the rapist?"

"The one we all thought was make-believe?"

"The sketches she did with Pamela and the rape victim match."

Bishop studied the computer screen picture, his gaze narrowing. "He's like Tuttle and Wheeler, not the type to plan."

"No, but he looks like he could be easily manipulated. And remember our alleged rape victim. She said there was a second guy in the room."

"I think we should pay Cyrus Mitchell a visit."

"Agreed."

Twenty minutes later, blue lights flashing from the marked backup cars, Rick and Bishop stood on either side of Cyrus's East Nashville front door. The house was one level, made of cinder block and covered in a gray peeling paint. Rick pounded on the door, his hand on his weapon, his body clear of the door and the potential line of fire.

Memories of last year's I-40 traffic stop flashed in his mind. The *pop, pop, pop* of gunfire ricocheted in his head.

Shit.

Shaking off the memory, he banged on the door again with his fist.

Finally, footsteps sounded in the house and the door snapped open. Standing before them was a midsize man wearing a T-shirt and jeans. "What do you want?"

Again, Rick was struck by how much the man looked like the sketch. "Cyrus Mitchell."

Seasoned eyes narrowed. "Yeah, who wants to know?"

Rick and Bishop held up their badges and identified themselves. "Ever met a woman named Pamela Grayson?"

Even as he shrugged, his eyes widened just a fraction. "Am I supposed to?"

"She thinks you two have met."

Narrowing eyes reflected pleasure. "What's she saying about me?"

Rick shook his head, declaring he ran this Q and A. "Do you know her?"

He shrugged. "Does she run a fancy dress shop in Franklin?"

"She does. Have you ever been to her shop?"

He scratched his chest. "Yeah, sure, I made deliveries. But I never went into the shop."

"That so?"

He smiled, revealing yellowed teeth. "Do I look like the kind of guy who visits dress shops?"

"You'd be surprised."

Mitchell shifted his stance as tension rippled over his features. "Did she say something about me?"

"She did. She says you've been following her."

He flexed the fingers on his left hand. "Why the hell would I follow her?"

Rick slid his hand to the handle of his gun. "You tell me. She says you've been following her around for weeks."

"She's wrong. I might have made a delivery to her store, but I don't know the woman. And I sure as shit wouldn't care enough to follow her." He shook his head. "A store like that means she's got money and money means time to stir trouble. Rich women are a pain in the ass."

Bishop adjusted his pinky ring. "Why would a woman like her stir trouble?"

"Bored. Or maybe she's a vindictive cunt who likes to put the screws to a guy."

Anger leaked through the words. "Why're you mad?"

"I ain't mad. I just hate it when a woman thinks she's all that and goes out of her way to ruin a man."

It didn't take much to stir this guy's temper. Another push or two and he'd say something he hadn't intended to say. "Is that what she's doing, ruining you?"

"You're here, ain't you?"

Rick held up pictures of Tuttle and Wheeler. "Ever met these guys?"

His gaze barely skimmed the pictures. "What, do they think I'm stalking them, too?"

"No, but they did their share of following women around. A lot like you."

"Hey, just because they do that kind of stuff don't mean I do." He rubbed a calloused, beefy hand over an unshaven jaw. "I got my hands full looking for a job."

"Your job." Bishop wagged his finger as if he'd just remembered something. "You get fired from your last job?"

The play was all bravado. They'd not tracked down his former employer yet.

Mitchell's scowl deepened. "Got downsized. That wasn't my fault."

Bishop rubbed his square chin as if he were a poker player assessing a winning hand. "According to your ex-boss you were hassling a female employee."

"Well, he's a damn liar. And my ex-boss is worried about being PC and not getting sued so he took her side over mine."

Rick picked up the threads of Bishop's bluff. "Lots of liars in the world. And they're all ganging up on you."

"All I know is that I ain't been bothering nobody."

The man's nerves oozed tension and worry. Rick kept his expression relaxed. "Mind if we take a look around your house?"

Mitchell shifted and raised his hand to the doorjamb.

"Matter of fact, I do mind. You can't just bust in here like a bunch of Nazis."

Bishop dialed his phone and seconds later said, "Magistrate's office. I need a search warrant."

Mitchell huffed. "That supposed to scare me?"

"Nope." Bishop sounded bored. "Once we get the search warrant, we'll see what you have to say."

Mitchell's agitation grew. "You can't just come into my house. This is my property. My land."

"No, but we can arrest you on suspicion of stalking and rape." Rick reached for his cuffs.

Mitchell tensed. "I ain't raped nobody."

"Got a witness that says otherwise."

"Fuck. She's a liar."

Rick rested his hands on his hips. "I say we don't search his place or bother with the rape charges. I say we leave him for the other man to kill."

Bishop chuckled. "That's not a bad idea."

"What the hell are you talking about?" Mitchell shouted.

"Whoever is pulling your strings, did the same with a couple of other guys," Rick said. "Both those guys ended up dead in an alley. Drug overdose."

Bishop checked his watch. "They were dead within twenty-four hours of the crime. My guess Mitchell is next on the list."

"This is bullshit," Mitchell said.

Bishop glanced at his nails as if he was already bored. "I say leave him to his boss. Let him do his thing."

Neither had any way of knowing what would happen but if they were right about a master manipulator, Cyrus knew it as well.

"We got another errand to run, so you be careful, Mr. Mitchell," Bishop said.

Rick paused before he turned. "And in case you're

wondering, Pamela's got around-the-clock surveillance. So does that gal you raped."

Mitchell's face flushed red. "I ain't like those other guys. I ain't done nothing wrong."

Rick tucked the cuffs back on his belt. "Then you don't have anything to worry about."

They left Mitchell shouting obscenities. Neither was in a rush as they moved toward Rick's car. As they slid into the front seat Rick's cell phone rang. "Morgan."

"This is Dr. Heller."

"Doc, what do you have for me?"

"That second murder victim from the fire is Nancy Jones. I just confirmed with dental records."

"Thanks." As he fired up the engine he relayed the information to Bishop.

"Two successful women. In real estate. Both with dark hair. Attractive." He leaned back in his seat. "Now we need to figure out who knew both these women."

Georgia glanced up from her computer screen when she heard the tap of knuckles on her door frame. Rick stood with his feet braced, as if ready for a fight.

"You're always in battle stance," she said. "Like you're always expecting a fight. Waiting for a challenge."

He shrugged and didn't bother to deny it. "We all have our crosses to bear."

"Not me," she teased. "I have no issues."

He laughed but was smart enough not to detail her quirks. "Right."

She cocked a brow. "What, you don't agree?"

He held up his hands in surrender. "I'm not here to judge or comment. You said you had information on my case."

"Right, I do." She shuffled through file folders. "We had a look at the handwriting you found scrawled at the first fire. The word was *faithless*. I got the bright idea to cross-check the handwriting against the word *bitch* written on the doll's head left at Jenna's house."

He moved into the room, his interest humming. "And?"

"The two words have three letters in common. The *I, T* and *H*." She fished through the file and found samples of both words that she'd snapped with her digital camera. "Note both words are written in block letters. Not upper and lower case but all upper case. Almost as if the word is being shouted. And note the top of each *I*. There's a slight gap between the top slash and the middle line. Not noticeable at first glance, but look at it long enough and you see stuff like that. Also look at the last letter of each word. The end of the *S* and the *H* both curve in slightly."

Rick drew in a steadying breath. "The guy who was a party to Diane's death also left this doll on Jenna's porch."

She leaned back in her chair, rolling her neck from side to side, grimacing when she seemed to touch on stiffness. "It's not out of the realm of possibility."

"Did you pull any prints from the head?"

"Wiped clean. Not one print. The guy pulling the strings is very careful. We knew that. Would be a rookie mistake if he did leave prints."

"Criminals make mistakes. This guy has been careful. We've nothing to link him to the first two kills but he's picking up steam, which, to me, translates into a mind growing more and more out of control. A matter of time before he slips up."

"If this mastermind recruited Cyrus, then he's made a mistake. Cyrus is sloppy."

"You got someone watching Cyrus?"

"Yeah. Sooner or later, he's going to reach out to his boss."

Georgia picked up a pencil marred with chew marks and rolled it between her fingers. "Jenna does fit the profile of the two dead women and Pamela. Dark-haired. Assertive. And this guy left a memento on her doorstep. She's on his radar."

"The other women were stalked for almost a year. Jenna has only been here a few weeks."

"Her family is from the area." Georgia bit the end of the pencil. "And what if your crazy theory about this case being linked to the Thompson case is right. Jenna looks like Sara."

Rick loosened his tie as if it were a noose around his neck. "The Thompson family were all shot point blank in the head and the shooter tried to set the house on fire."

Georgia pointed a finger as if aiming for a bull's-eye. "But the arsonist used gasoline. It ignited too quickly and didn't burn as planned. The scene was not destroyed and the bodies were found." When he raised a brow, she shrugged. "I saw the files on your desk and read a few."

Rick didn't want to be right. Right meant Jenna was in real danger. "All those men, Tuttle, Wheeler, Dupree, and even Mitchell weren't great thinkers or planners."

Georgia scraped her thumbnail against a spot on the arm of her chair. The spot was well worn, a divot created by endless hours of pondering.

Rick's neutral tone didn't hint at the emotions swirling in his gut. "So do we have a new puppet master or is the old one back in the game?"

"The killings started about the time Jenna arrived."

"Weeks before the twenty-fifth anniversary of the original killings."

Madness saw the cop car parked in front of Cyrus's house. Instead of being afraid, Madness welcomed the cops. Let them follow Cyrus around for a day or two. That would be just enough time to finish it all.

A ringing phone forced a glance from the scene to the phone's display. Cyrus Mitchell. The phone was a burner, untraceable by the cops. Cyrus was a nervous sort and would keep calling and calling. Fine, let him. The longer Cyrus kept the cops distracted, the better. Soon it would all be over.

"The cops are smart. They're going to figure out our connection to Cyrus," Reason said.

Madness savored the surge of adrenaline that heralded excitement. *"Stop whining. Just let me take care of this."*

"When you take over, we always end up in trouble."

"Stop worrying."

"Wait until it all goes sideways. You'll come crawling back. And I only hope I can fix the mess this time."

"Worrier."

They'd been careful never to use their real name with Cyrus and never gave him any identifying information. A wig, glasses, and baggy clothes had altered their physical appearance so whatever description Cyrus gave to the cops would be inaccurate.

"You swear Jenna will be the last."

"Of course."

"You've lied before." Reason's wail sounded childlike.

"I always lie. But not this time."

Reason went silent. This game with Madness was never going to end. Madness would destroy them both.

Chapter Seventeen

Thursday, August 24, 6 P.M.

Rick and Bishop pulled up in front of the East Nashville home. The white on the siding had faded to a muddy brown and the cracked sidewalk was a hazard even in daylight.

As they approached the front door, Bishop tugged his coat in place. "I can't believe you talked me into this."

"It won't take long." Rick knocked on the door. Inside a television blared. Footsteps sounded and the front door opened to an old woman with stooped shoulders. He held up his badge. "Mrs. Dupree."

Old eyes narrowed. "Yeah."

"We'd like to ask you a few questions about your late son, Ronnie."

"Ronnie again? I knew when that woman showed up trouble wouldn't be far behind."

"Woman?" Rick asked.

"That Thompson girl. Wanted to know why Ronnie did what he did."

Jenna had been here. Rick's irritation coated his next words. "And what did you tell her?"

"I told her I didn't know. Ronnie was a good boy. He loved me. But I didn't know him as well as I thought."

"You never had any idea why he killed that family."

She shook her head. "No."

"Did he have any friends that he hung out with? A friend that might have been smart or a fast talker."

"The only friend Ronnie had was Billy."

"Billy," Rick said. "Where did they meet?"

"At the school. I don't know exactly where."

"Do you have a last name?"

"Whenever I asked, Ronnie always got huffy about answering questions about his friend. So I dropped it. I was grateful the kid had somebody."

"Do you have any pictures from that time?"

"I burned 'em."

"Burned them?"

"Seemed fitting. Ronnie and his friend liked fires."

Sitting at the edge of the bar, a small woman with dirty-blond hair lifted a glass to her mouth with a trembling hand. She stared into the mahogany depths as if willing the liquid to transform into courage and give her strength. She sniffed, set the glass down hard. She ordered another drink.

Silently, Madness rose and took the seat beside her, allowing her to order another drink. Impatience nipped at Madness, but lessons from Reason kept a tight hold on the reins of action.

The woman downed the drink in one shot and then watched as the bartender poured her a fourth drink.

Madness had moments like this. Ones that were so charged with energy or loss or anger that the only thing that could dull the throbbing sensations had been booze.

The bartender, a woman in her mid fifties with blond

hair and dark eyebrows, frowned as she reached for the drink. "Go easy or I'll have to cut you off."

The woman sniffed and snatched up the drink. "I ain't drunk. Not by a long shot."

"I can't afford to have you stumbling out of here."

"I don't stumble, asshole."

Madness loved chaos. "Looks like you've had quite a day."

She didn't raise her gaze as she downed the next drink and then set the glass down hard on the bar. "One for the record books."

"I've had my share of those. Somebody must have really dumped on you hard."

"You don't know the half of it. Do something nice for someone a long time ago and then everyone is trying to pin a murder on me."

The report was old news now. The Lost Girl's identity had been made and a woman, Loyola Briggs, was suspected to be her mother. She'd been brought in for questioning last night. There'd not been enough evidence to hold her, so she'd been released. However, those in the know said this gal was on borrowed time. Weeks separated her from hard time in prison.

"Got to feel kinda helpless." A raised glass got the bartender's attention. When the glass arrived, Madness slid it toward Loyola. "Looks like you could use this more than me."

"What do you want for it?"

"Nothing. Just thought I'd be nice."

Her gaze settled on a crack in the bar as she shook her head. "No one is nice unless they want something."

"I don't want anything from you." The fishing line dangled in front of her, the whiskey was the bait. She'd not be able to resist the glass, and soon she'd not be able to resist what came next.

"I can help."

She downed the glass. "How?"

"I know the woman who got you into trouble. The one that drew the sketch of that girl."

The woman raised her gaze, filled with anger and confusion. Ah, here was another kindred soul whose reason battled with madness. By the looks, her madness won regularly. "That picture ain't of my kid. My kid is living a happy life in California."

"Of course she is. Shame though someone would tell such horrible lies about you."

"She's a bitch." Another glass of whiskey was ordered and quickly tossed back.

"Want to get even?" Madness could have a sweet and kind voice when it suited. "I can help."

Loyola stared into the empty depths of her glass as if lost. "I don't know where she lives."

"I do."

"Why would you care?"

"Maybe I don't like her either."

She swiped the back of her hand over her mouth. "What did she do to you?" She had the eyes of a dead woman.

"Doesn't matter. You in or not?"

Loyola held up her empty glass and smiled as he refilled it. "I'm in."

"Excellent."

Twenty minutes later they stood in front of Jenna's house. Loyola swayed, so drunk she could barely stand.

"What're we doing here?"

"This is the house of the woman who drew that picture of the Lost Girl. She's the one that started all your trouble."

Squinting, Loyola glared up at the cabin. "She lives here?"

"She does. I hear she's the type of woman who likes to stir up trouble for the sake of it."

"Some secrets need to stay buried," Loyola said.

"They surely do. No good comes from dredging up the past."

"No good."

Loyola shifted her stance and flexed her fingers. "Bitch."

In a voice low and sharp, Madness asked, "How about we give her a little payback for all the trouble she's caused?"

"I don't need no more trouble."

"You wouldn't get into trouble if you were careful."

"I ain't careful. I mess up everything I touch."

"I know how to be careful. Very, very careful."

She shook her head and rubbed her eyes as if swatting away a memory. "I screw up everything. Everything. My father kicked me out when I was seventeen and my husband was pissed when I got pregnant and kept saying I was no good for him. I tried and tried, but it never seemed to matter. I always screwed up."

If not for her sins, one might almost feel sorry for her. She was like everyone else, rich or poor, famous or unknown. She wanted to be loved. "Would you like to do something right? I can show you how."

"I can't."

What had Sister said once? *You could sell ice to Eskimos.* "You can. With my help."

She looked up into eyes filled with worry, fear, and loss. "Why would you help me? We just met."

"I see a lot of myself in you. Someone who is lost and wants to connect but just can't seem to say or do the right thing. If I'd had a mentor my life would have been different."

"What's a mentor?"

"Someone who guides you. Helps you. A friend."

She raised two clenched fists to her temples and pressed them hard against her skin. "What does all that mean?"

"It means, I show you how to get a little revenge. It

means, we could do something fun. Like burn down Jenna's house."

She moistened her lips as if she savored a delicious flavor. "Why?"

"Why not?"

She stared at the house, her gaze burning with a white-hot desire. "If she'd not drawn that picture everything would be fine."

"That's right. If not for her, it would all be fine." He settled his hands gently on her shoulders.

"Is she in the house?"

"Yes."

Tension rippled through her shoulders. "I shouldn't be here."

He held her steady. "In for a penny, in for a pound."

"What's that mean?"

"The cops are coming after you."

"How do you know?"

"I know. They're going to make sure you rot in jail. At least know that Jenna isn't laughing when they take you to jail."

"She laughs at me?"

"All the time."

Loyola grit her teeth. "Is it hard to burn a house down?"

"No, it's fairly easy."

Normal people slept at night. They closed their eyes and let the day's events sort themselves out. They decompressed. Shut down.

For Jenna, nights could be painfully long if she didn't sleep. She rolled on her side and punched her pillow. When she'd been in Baltimore there'd been friends she could call at night. Always someplace open that would welcome her;

she could pretend it was a case bothering her and not some insane quirk she couldn't shed.

She rolled on her back and stared at the play of shadows on the ceiling. Counting the now too familiar cracks in the ceiling, her thoughts turned to Sara. Her sister was arguing. Her voice had crackled with anger as she'd stood toe-to-toe with their father. *I hate you!*

The echoes of slamming doors rattled in her memory. Her father was yelling. Her mother crying. She huddled under her blanket, crying, wishing someone would take her away.

Her wish had been granted. The shouting had stopped. And she'd been taken away.

"Be careful what you wish for." She glanced at the clock. How many hours would have to pass before sleep returned? Too many.

Frustrated, she tossed her blankets aside. As much as her mind ached for the release of art, her bones needed a break. In Baltimore, nights like this were spent watching television. She had an intimate relationship with the top infomercial presenters on television, and she'd caught just about every movie made in the 1960s. Here, though, she had no television and relied on a downloaded movie.

"Maybe Cary Grant and Audrey Hepburn will keep me company tonight," she said.

With daylight just a couple of hours away she dressed in jeans and a pullover sweater. Running a brush through her hair, she tied it up in a ponytail. She might not be able to control when she slept, but she would control what she could.

She was nearly in the den when she smelled the first traces of smoke. Smoke? Her thoughts went first to an electrical fire. She thought about her coffeemaker and wondered if she'd left it on or if the automatic shutoff hadn't worked. And where was her cell? Most nights she charged it by her bed but hadn't tonight.

The scent of smoke grew heavier and heavier and when she reached the living room, a wall of flames rose up. Her entire back deck was on fire and it had eaten into her living room. Thick, black smoke billowed and whipped up the wall and over the ceiling. Fire had slithered across the floor closer and closer to her art supplies. Not her art!

How had the fire started? The question rattled in her head for only a moment before she realized that right now the answer didn't matter. Her art didn't matter. Nothing mattered. What mattered was getting out of the house. She coughed and hurried toward the front door, grabbed her purse, and ran outside.

She drew in a breath of fresh air, coughing and sputtering. She fished her cell out of her purse and dialed 9-1-1.

Chapter Eighteen

Friday, August 25, 12:20 A.M.

Flashing lights of three fire trucks and a rescue vehicle greeted Rick when he pulled up at Jenna's house. Leaving Tracker in his car, he strode toward the rescue truck, doing his best not to run or give in to fears. God, what the fire could have done to her.

He found her sitting on the back tailgate of the rescue vehicle, an oxygen mask on her face. She glanced up at him, removed her mask, and said, "Insomnia rocks."

Relief washed over him, extinguishing the worry in a loud hiss. "What the hell happened?"

"I can't sleep. I prowl a lot at night. I got up, went into my living room, and my entire back deck was on fire as was the back of my house."

"It started on the deck? Do you have a grill?"

"As I told Inspector Murphy, no grill. No candles, no lanterns, no funky wiring issues, no stored fuel. Plain old deck."

He rested his hand on his hip. "I suppose the firebugs have put you through a lot of questions and answers."

"As they should. My place did just burn down for no

reason. And I know about the other fires. They should be grilling me."

She was a cop, logical in the face of turmoil. Later, when the adrenaline deserted her, she'd be left with a lot of unanswered questions and maybe some fears that would let loose. He turned back toward the house, now a charred stick structure. It was a complete loss. "Damn."

"You're telling me." She put the oxygen mask aside and moved beside him.

"Aren't you supposed to be wearing that?"

"I'm fine. If I breathe any more oxygen, I'll float away. Don't suppose you can give me a ride into town? My Jeep is blocked in by the fire trucks. I'm not even sure if it escaped the flames."

"Where're you going to go?"

"Hotel. I've also got to call my landlord." She held up her purse. "I did manage to grab this, so I can at least function." Adrenaline coursed through her veins and her body all but vibrated with it.

A slow shake of his head told her he understood what was happening to her physically now. "You can stay with me."

"No, thanks." With this kind of emotion surging through her, it wouldn't take much for her to seek a sexual release with the good detective. And right now, the last complication she needed was a relationship.

A quirk of his lips suggested the same idea had also crossed his mind. "If it will make you feel better, Georgia lives at the house from time to time. She said she'd be bunking with me tonight so you'll have company."

"I thought she lived in town."

"She's kept her apartment in town and stays there when she works a long shift, but off times she's at my place."

"I didn't know that."

"She doesn't like to publicize the fact that she basically moved home. She wants everyone to believe she's fine but last year was tough for her and she needs home base to catch her breath from time to time. You can do the same. There is a guest apartment on the property above the garage. It's clean, though I've not had a chance to renovate it yet."

An apartment over the garage meant doors and real estate separating her from Rick. She glanced toward the rubble that had been her home. Money saved on a hotel could go toward art supplies. Or a car rental that would take her back to Baltimore. "Thanks. That sounds great."

"I'll call Georgia and have her come get you. I'll be here for a while."

"Yeah, sure. That's perfect."

As the sun rose, Georgia handed Jenna a hot cup of tea. Jenna had showered the smoke and cinder from her skin and hair and changed into some of Georgia's clothes. Jenna was a good three inches taller than Georgia so the sweats hit her midcalf. Top of her list today was to get wheels, and buy clothes and art supplies.

Jenna sipped. "My life just went up in flames."

"Well, the stuff went up in flames." Georgia sat across from her on the large couch and crossed her legs as she cradled a cup of coffee. Tracker lay on the floor at Georgia's feet but his gaze went from the door to Jenna and back to the door. He was waiting for Rick.

"Stuff can be replaced."

"I know. I know. And I'm grateful to be whole and in one piece. Thank God my first client picked up her portrait yesterday. All the other pieces I have, well, I haven't lost too much time. And the bulk of my stuff is in my Baltimore apartment."

Frowning, Georgia sipped her coffee. "I keep forgetting you really live there."

Jenna cradled her warm mug close as she sipped. "My

life and job awaits. And whatever reason brought me here to Nashville, doesn't make sense now."

"Why did you come?"

"To find out why my family was murdered. I keep thinking there must have been a reason. But there was no reason. Just an insane man driven by unknown reasons."

Georgia glanced into the depths of her coffee. "Finding reason isn't always easy. That's hard to accept."

Jenna raised her mug. "Here's to reason."

"I'll toast to that." She clicked her mug against Jenna's. She sipped and grew pensive. "I was hoping we'd grow on you and you'd stay."

"Baltimore used to feel like home and then, suddenly, it didn't. Then I came here. I thought maybe I'd find something but I might have jumped from the frying pan into the fire. And I do miss police work."

Georgia raised a brow. "I bet I can give you more sketches. If we get a conviction on the Lost Girl case, my brother Deke might be willing to give me and a few of my friends a cold case to work on. I'm sure we could use your skills."

"Tempting. But I'll still have to pay the light bill."

"Keep painting. I bet you could pick up commissions easily. Painter by day, crime fighter by night."

She laughed. "Who have you enlisted in your merry band so far?"

"Well, you for now, but there're others I have in mind. Rachel would be game. KC. The three of us would be a start."

"I give you credit for trying to get something going."

"If you build it, they will come."

"Ah, a fan of *Field of Dreams*. Also a fan of all baseball movies?"

"All movies."

The front door opened and Tracker rose up from the floor

and, tail wagging, barked as he made his way to the foyer. Rick's deep voice was filled with genuine affection as he greeted the dog.

As he moved toward the den, Jenna could hear the slight misstep of his pace. Most wouldn't have noticed it but she realized when he was tired, his gait wasn't even.

He appeared in the den, Tracker at his side. He'd loosened his tie, had removed his jacket and rolled up his sleeves. He smelled of smoke and cinder. "Good, you've made yourself at home."

Jenna sat a little straighter. "Thanks to Georgia."

"I'm trying to convince her to stay in Nashville and work with me on my cold cases."

He frowned and Jenna wasn't sure which part of the statement bothered him. "Georgia rarely takes no for an answer."

"So what did you find at the crime scene?" Jenna asked.

Georgia rose. "Rick, sit. You want a cup of coffee? And I made muffins."

He relaxed back into a chair as if he'd just released the weight of the world. "Coffee would be great. Instead of a muffin, could I get a sandwich?"

Georgia arched a brow as she studied him. If he'd not been bone tired, she'd likely have told him to get it himself, but she took pity. "Be right back." She scurried into the kitchen.

In a low voice, he asked, "She didn't try to give you any of her baking, did she?"

Jenna dropped her voice. "Yes. It was good."

He shook his head as if he smelled a lie. "You're a guest, so I understand that you have to be kind."

"I tasted lots of love." And clumps of flour. "I never say no to home cooking. My aunt wasn't much of a cook. She tried, but most of our dinners were takeout." She glanced toward the long farmhouse dinner table. "I imagine you shared quite a few dinners at that table."

"We did."

"Nice."

"Sometimes. And sometimes it was World War Three."

"Who was the troublemaker?"

"Deke is the oldest and he challenged Dad the most. Alex always had his eye on where he was going after dinner. Georgia was the baby, so she got what she wanted."

"And you?"

He loosened his tie. "I was stirring trouble but just not as overtly as Deke. There were a few times when Dad called me down at the table. Not pretty."

Despite his description, she pictured a scene right out of a Norman Rockwell painting. "And I bet you all laughed a lot at the table."

"We did."

"Nice. And very lucky." She cradled her mug close, savoring the comforting heat. "I have only vague memories of my older sister teasing me."

"Tell me about your sister."

"Until recently, I'd have told you she was perfect. Cheerleader, good grades, boys loved her. But lately, I'm remembering that it wasn't all as perfect as I'd like to remember. She and Dad fought a lot."

"What did they fight about?"

"She was staying out past her curfew. I'd hear the front door open real quiet and then I'd see the hall light flip on as Dad headed her off before she could sneak into bed. He called her a drunk a couple of times. Said she was throwing her life away."

"She was dating someone."

"I think so. I think it was someone Dad didn't like. Amazing how much parents say in front of the little kid and don't realize what they're doing."

"What else did you hear?"

"My parents fought a lot. Over the years, I've built it up to be a happy home, but it wasn't. It wasn't happy at all." She pulled at a loose thread on the hem of her shirt. "Susan Martinez said she knew my father."

That one-two punch caught him off guard. "Say again."

"She gave me a picture of my sister, Dad, and me at a football game. She said she took the picture."

"When you met at your old family home." The frown furrowing his brow deepened. "Where's the picture?"

"Thankfully, in my purse." She leaned forward, rummaged through, and retrieved it.

Georgia appeared with a sandwich plate and a cup of coffee. "Here ya go, Rick. I also made extra for Jenna. You must be hungry. All you ate was half a muffin. And as much as I'd like to sit here with you two and chat, I have the afternoon shift and need a couple of hours' sleep."

Rick rose and kissed her on the cheek. With a wave to Jenna, she was gone, leaving the two alone. Rick lowered back into the chair.

"How much does your hip bother you?"

He didn't answer right away. "Long days it can ache. Nothing I can't manage."

"You like to pretend it doesn't hurt, don't you?"

He held up the sandwich plate and when she shook her head no, he selected a ham and cheese. "It doesn't."

She leaned back, a smile curling her lips. "And my past doesn't bother me. I don't have sleepless nights and I don't imagine Shadow Eyes following me around."

He paused, the sandwich inches from his lips. "Shadow Eyes?"

She shrugged. "Makes no sense."

"I'm all ears." He bit into the sandwich, his gaze on her.

"The guy who took me and killed my family is dead. I know that. But in my dreams, there is the other man."

"What other man?"

Frustration snapped quick and sharp. "That's the thing, there is no other man. Ronnie Dupree acted alone."

"But you believe he didn't?"

"I've no proof. No hard and fast memories. Just a gut feeling, which I think is way off base."

He finished his sandwich and as he wiped his mouth with a napkin, reached for his coffee. "What if there were two men?"

"Wouldn't they have found him?"

"Not necessarily." He sipped his coffee. "I spoke to Ronnie Dupree's mother. As I understand you did too?"

A shrug. "She was a piece of the puzzle."

"She said Ronnie had a friend. Billy."

"I remember."

"Name ring a bell?"

"No. I wish it did. But I was just a kid. So much floated right over my head."

"Saying Ronnie didn't act alone. Saying there was another person there. He or she would have left evidence behind that should have been destroyed by the fire that didn't take."

"I'm assuming there was quite a bit of forensic data collected. Maybe Billy or this mystery person left something behind."

"I've thought about that. It all boils down to time and sifting and retesting what was collected."

She nodded. "Time and money. Seems it always comes to that."

"Yeah." He took another sip of coffee. "You've got to be tired."

Since he'd entered the room, she'd wanted to touch him. That desire now sent energy snapping through her body. "Par for the course when you have insomnia."

"Let me show you to your room."

"Thanks."

He rose and led her through a door off the kitchen that connected to a staircase up to a small room. He flipped on the light. The room was small and furnished with a brass bed that looked as if it was a century old. A worn, well-made quilt warmed the top along with several extra blankets. On the wall were paintings of the countryside.

"Who was the artist?"

"My grandmother. My mother was her only child and she had time to paint. Mom always said she'd have painted if she had less chaos in her life."

"Sounds like you kept her fairly busy."

"More than anyone has a right to."

She set her purse beside the bed, not wanting the smoky scent to spread. "It's a nice room. I don't see why you'd renovate."

"The bathroom doesn't have a shower. Be nice if it did so guests wouldn't have to go to the main house to bathe."

"Makes sense."

"Stay as long as you want. Like I said, the place is huge and its just Georgia and me."

"Thanks."

She looked at him and something inside of her released, as if she'd had an iron grip on her life for as long as she could remember.

She moved toward him, closing the gap in seconds. Inches separated them. Her heat mingled with his as she waited for him to step back or give her some sign that he didn't want this kind of attention. He didn't move.

She wrapped her arms around his neck and kissed him gently on the lips. For a moment he didn't move, as if giving her the chance to back out. She deepened the kiss and this time his arm banded around her waist. Though he still made no move to kiss her, as he watched as she moistened her lips and savored his salty taste. She kissed him again. A brush of her body against his told her he wanted her.

None of this would change anything, she told herself as she pressed her breasts against his chest. She needed to feel human contact. To feel alive. She would not get attached and she would not care.

She slid her hand up under his shirt, against his flat belly. Energy thrummed in her veins as she kissed him harder. He backed her up to the bed until her knees touched the mattress and then slowly he lowered her to a mattress that sagged under their weight.

His hand slid up her sweatshirt to her breast. When calloused fingers rubbed against her bare breast she hissed in a breath.

Neither spoke as each tugged free of their clothes, which landed in scattered piles beside the bed. She traced her hand over his broad back and over his buttocks seconds before he pushed into her. She savored the sensation of being full and alive, as all the nerve endings in her body danced. Slowly, he moved inside her, building into a fever pitch until both found their release.

He collapsed beside her, his breathing labored and fast. Her heart thrummed. He pulled a blanket over them and spooned his body next to hers, tucking her bare butt next to him.

There was probably a lot they had to talk about. She wasn't sure what she'd say exactly but, at this moment, she wasn't worried about words. Her eyes drifted closed and in his arms she fell into a deep, fitful, dreamless sleep.

Susan was preparing for the midmorning newsbreak when Andy approached her. She glanced up, wondering if today was going to be her last day. She rose, deciding she'd face her executioner.

"Did you hear? Jenna Thompson's house burned last night."

Her heart jumped a beat but she kept her voice even and steady. "Is she all right?"

"She escaped. House is a loss."

Her mind started spinning, not with worry but stories. "Do they have a suspect?"

"Word is they think it might be the mother of that girl that was found dead."

"Loyola Briggs."

He arched a brow. "You're on your game."

"Pays to know. Want me to cover the story?"

"Already sent Brandy."

"Brandy?"

"Like I said before, she polls better than you."

Anger didn't bubble but simmered. This day had been coming for a long time. Still, she couldn't resist mentioning, "I started this story."

"And Brandy is going to finish it."

Susan glanced at the clock. Ten minutes to airtime. As she opened her desk drawer and removed her purse, she realized in thirty years she'd never missed a cue or broadcast. Today would be a day of firsts. "Andy, I quit."

He cocked a brow. "You have a broadcast."

When Jenna had refused her story idea, she'd known her time on the job was dwindling. She'd cleaned out her desk yesterday, knowing when the time came, she'd walk out with her head held high. "I'm sure you've got some nice young thing waiting in the wings."

When Jenna woke the afternoon sun shone through lace curtains and sunlight slashed across the bed. For a moment she didn't know where she was and then she remembered the fire and . . . Rick. They'd made love twice, the first time heated and quick, each surrendering to an animal need. When the storm had passed, Rick had traced his hand up her belly and circled his calloused finger against the hollow of her neck. She'd sucked in a breath, heat and fire reigniting. She'd arched her back. Her lips had parted and his name had escaped on the wings of a soft moan.

Jenna smiled at the memory. She'd liked making love to Rick Morgan. Liked it a lot. Twenty-four hours ago, the threads holding her to Nashville had been fraying, but now . . . well, she still had three weeks. She couldn't make promises beyond that, but there was now.

As she sat up in bed, she searched for a feeling inside her that might be akin to belonging. She'd never had that feeling in Baltimore and not in Nashville either.

The moments in Rick's arms, there'd been no worries about past, present, or future. No dreams of Shadow Eyes. No insomnia. Simply safe.

She glanced around at the empty, rumpled bedsheets. The impression of his head in the pillow remained a hollow reminder of what they'd shared.

She looked around the room, listening for any indication that he might be in the adjoining bathroom or nearby. When there was no sign of him, she dressed, and moved into the kitchen. She found no note from Rick.

She'd gone out of her way to remind him that she was leaving soon. That Nashville was not her home. Made sense he'd not leave a note. Why did it tweak her that he'd not?

In the kitchen, it took her time to find the coffee and to figure out the coffee machine. The process, which should have been automatic, was a time-consuming reminder that, despite great sex, she was an outsider. Normally, she accepted that status with grace, but this time, regret burned. For the first time she wanted to belong.

Rick arrived at his desk with Tracker, and a strong cup of coffee in hand. Tracker eased down on a pad by his desk. It was three in the afternoon and there was no sign of Bishop. Jenna had mentioned that her sister had had a boyfriend and that her teen years had been troubled. He'd made a few calls very early this morning to a friend who worked in juvenile records, hoping to get more information on Jenna's sister, Sara.

Sipping the coffee, he opened the file. Sara's trouble with the law had begun when she was fourteen. She'd been arrested for shoplifting, a charge that was dismissed thanks to her father's intervention. Sara didn't stay out of trouble long. Three months later, she shoplifted again. And two months after that, she was in the car when her boyfriend was arrested for driving one hundred miles an hour on I-40. The social worker on the case wrote several notes. *"Problems began when Sara started dating her new boyfriend, Billy Martinez. Sara defends boyfriend. Sara expresses a desire to leave home."* Comments like this continued throughout the file.

The boyfriend's name was Billy Martinez. Billy. Ronnie's best friend. Susan Martinez. A brother perhaps? He studied the picture featuring a kid with long, blond hair and with blotchy skin; Billy appeared to be about eighteen or nineteen. Rick searched the kid and got a hit. A few phone calls and he had the kid's record.

Billy had met Sara at the high school football game. According to his record, he had come from a low-income family but had a charming personality that could convince anyone to do just about anything. Classic bad guy meets and corrupts good girl? Billy's record started with a theft charge and within six months had progressed to arson. Arson. The fires had been small but most arsonists started with small fires. And as their need for excitement and thrill grew, so did the fires.

There'd been a small fire at the Thompson house the day the family had been slaughtered. But that fire had burned itself out far too fast. Had Billy set the fire? Had he been the shooter or working with the shooter? And if Billy had been involved, what had set him off? Often, the motives were simple. Love or money. Maybe it was as simple as Billy and Sara had suffered a falling out.

Billy's police file ended right before the Thompsons' murders. He'd avoided jail time but had been remanded to the custody of his sister, Susan. He dug deeper in the files searching for Susan's last name. A flip of a few pages and he found the name. Susan Martinez. Half sister. The two shared the same mother.

Rick sat straighter. Susan Martinez had said she was having an affair with Jenna's father. They'd all walked in the same circles. He called Susan's cell but the call went to voice mail. He called the station and learned she'd quit.

Rick snapped a picture of Billy's mug shot and on a hunch texted it to Jenna.

Can you do an age progression?

Seconds passed.

Must buy supplies.

Short, clipped, pissed. "Shit, Rick. Try a little harder." He texted her again.

I'm not just thinking about work right now.

More seconds passed.

Tell me.

Later. In private.

We'll see.

He smiled at the response. If he wanted Jenna Thompson in his life, he was gonna have to work for it.

Rick got the call around five P.M. that Loyola Briggs had been spotted at a hotel that rented by the hour. He'd driven directly to the motel. The manager had taken him to her room and when they had entered, they'd found her splayed on the motel-room bed, unconscious. Rick checked for a pulse and found it very weak and thready.

Rick hung up and relayed the information to his partner. "Is she dead?" Bishop asked.

"Damn near close. She's on her way to the hospital. Seems she's got such a high tolerance for the stuff she didn't overdose like a normal person."

"Shit. I don't want to lose her. I want Heather's story told."

"What about Danny? Has he said what happened to Heather?"

"No."

Rick rubbed the back of his neck. "Loyola is gonna live and Danny will talk."

"You can't bulldoze your way through everything, Boy Scout."

"Watch me."

* * *

When Rick and Bishop arrived at Loyola's hospital, a news crew greeted them. He glanced around expecting to see Susan Martinez, but found a blond reporter in her early twenties headed his way.

"Detective Morgan," the woman shouted. "I'm Brandy Corker with Channel Five. Can you tell me if you've found the mother of the Lost Girl?"

"Where's Martinez?" Rick mumbled to Bishop, waving Brandy away, as if swatting away a fly. He and Bishop turned and hurried into the hospital.

"Flew away on her broom."

"I suppose."

Bishop glanced back at Brandy. "She's a looker."

Rick shook his head. "Don't be fooled. She'll eat you up and spit you out for a story."

Bishop glanced back toward the reporter. "I might risk it."

The detectives found Dr. Bramley, Loyola's doctor, on the second floor at the nurses' station.

He was a young guy, not much more than thirty, with thick brown hair and a young face weighted down by fatigue.

Opening the chart, Dr. Bramley read over his notes. "You got her here just in time. Five more minutes and she'd have died."

"So she'll live and stand trial." Bishop flexed the fingers of his right hand. "Good. When will she be awake?"

Dr. Bramley closed the chart and tucked it under his arm. "She's making some sounds now."

"Can you give her something to wake her up?" Rick asked.

"Her system has been through a real trauma."

Rick dug deep for an ounce of pity but couldn't find any. "She's a suspect in a missing child case and, most recently, an arson case. I need to know why she set the fire and if she had help."

"I can't stimulate her with drugs, but if you make noise, talk to her as loud as you can, you might reach her. It's clear she's used before and is burning this stuff off faster than most."

"Thanks."

Rick and Bishop pushed into her hospital room, the doctor on their heels. Rick approached the bed, staring at the pale, thin figure.

"Loyola!" Rick spoke sharply, hoping his tone would reach through the haze.

She stirred but didn't open her eyes.

"Loyola!" He clapped his hands and this time she did stir.

"Go away," she mumbled. She turned her head to the side and tried to bury it in her pillow.

Rick clapped his hands again. "I'm not going anywhere. Why did you set the fire?"

She flinched and moaned. "I didn't . . ."

"You did. We found accelerant in your motel room and pictures of Jenna. When did you decide to burn her house down?"

"I didn't . . ."

"You did. You tested positive for accelerant. You set that fire."

She tried to lift groggy lids. "No."

If Rachel Wainwright remained her attorney, all this would get thrown out of court. But he wasn't worried about an arson conviction right now. He wanted whoever put her up to the fire and then he'd nail her on murder charges.

Rick leaned close enough to get a whiff of a sick, sweet smell emanating from her body. "Loyola, who told you to set the fire?"

She shook her head. "I set it."

Rick patted her face with his hand over and over until she

opened her eyes and looked at him. "No way. You couldn't have found Jenna's address that fast."

She stared at him, eyes part vacant and part defiant.

"Tell me who showed you how to set the fire. Let me help you."

Her brow wrinkled. "You don't want to help me."

Bishop nudged Rick aside. He drew in a calming breath, sat at her bedside, and laid a gentle hand on her arm. "I do. I do. But you've got to work with me." He smiled.

Touch was a powerful tool and Rick knew Loyola craved approval. He knew this, but was too angry to give it to her.

She swallowed as if her throat hurt. Her gaze locked on Bishop. "I don't have a name."

Bishop took Loyola's hand in his. "No name?"

"I didn't ask. I didn't care." Her voice drifted and Rick sensed he was losing her.

"How about a description?" Even Bishop's normally abrupt accent had softened.

She closed her eyes. "Not tall. Not thin or fat. Just regular. Wore a bulky hoodie."

"Hair color. Eyes?"

"Brown and brown." Her breathing grew deep and though he repeated more questions, she was drifting back into unconsciousness.

Bishop rested his hands on his hips. "That description narrows it down to about a million people."

Rick resisted the urge to shake the woman.

The sun hung low in the sky as Jenna returned to the Big House, her arms loaded with art supplies and a few bags of clothes she and Georgia had found at the consignment store. She'd bought a couple of pairs of jeans, a few sweaters, and a pair of sneakers and a killer pair of black boots. She'd also picked up a phone charger as well as a few toiletry items. They'd driven by her house, not pausing to dwell on the charred remains, so that she could pick up her Jeep, which had survived the inferno. Other than a few lost sketchbooks and clothes, she'd come through fairly unscathed. She was out only a couple of hundred bucks that she'd spent on clothes and new art supplies.

In the Big House, she dropped her bags and flipped on a light. Georgia had left for work, leaving her alone to glance around at the framed family pictures on the walls. Rick might have gutted the kitchen, but he'd saved and framed the pictures of his family. One image had been taken in this very spot. Buddy Morgan and his wife stood front and center and their children were gathered around them. Buddy wasn't smiling but there was pride gleaming in his eyes. His wife grinned as if privy to a joke. The four children clustered around: fifteen-year-old Deke, twelve-year-old Rick, eleven-year-old Alex, and five-year-old Georgia who stood in front of her brothers, her hands on her hips.

"You're a lucky guy, Rick Morgan."

She'd not heard from him for hours but refused to fret. If he wanted to see her again, he could dial her number.

Flipping on more lights, she curled up on the couch tucked in the alcove by the kitchen. She pulled up the picture on her phone and studied the image of the boy who had dated her sister over two and a half decades ago. She had no memory of Billy Martinez, which seemed odd. If he'd dated her sister, surely he'd come by their house at some point. But there were no memories.

She stared into his eyes in the photograph and then flipped open her sketchbook. She opened a new pack of pencils and began with the eyes just as they appeared on the picture. When she'd drawn the eyes, she sat back. Her heart skipped a beat.

Shadow Eyes.

Jenna glanced at the boyfriend's face. How could he be Shadow Eyes? He had just been a kid—nineteen or twenty—when her family had been killed. This could not be right.

She began with the age progression. She had no access to his genetics or habits in the last twenty-five years, which played a huge part in how a person aged. So, she guessed and generalized.

After an hour, she had a sketch. She stared at the face. It was a closed-lipped expression. She'd given him slightly darker hair and had thinned it a fraction. But as she stared at him, there was no flicker of recognition. "I have no idea who you are. None."

She snapped a photograph of the picture and texted it to Rick. All she typed was *age progression complete.*

Her cell rang and she was disappointed to see that the number wasn't Rick's. She considered ignoring the call after all the prank calls the television interview triggered, but, thinking it might be Rick from a different phone, she took the call. "Jenna Thompson."

"Ms. Thompson, this is Officer Woods with the Nashville Police Department. Detective Rick Morgan asked me to give you a call."

"Okay." He couldn't call her directly. The idea burrowed under her skin. "What does he want?"

"He has a question about a sketch."

"What question?"

"I don't know, ma'am. A question about a sketch. He said to call and I'm calling."

"So am I supposed to call him?"

"He'd like you at the station."

"Really?" Why was she annoyed with Rick? He'd made no promises. She'd wanted no promises. But he was treating her like another cop. Which is essentially what she was, but . . . "Fine."

"We're sending a car for you."

"When?"

"Any minute."

"Fine."

She grabbed her purse and phone and headed out the front door expecting to see a marked car driving down the long drive any moment. She'd taken one step off the porch when she heard the crunch of gravel and the very sharp sting of electricity shooting through her body. She jolted, faintly remembered being tased at the academy, and then passed out.

Rick read Jenna's text about a half hour after she sent it. The instant he opened the image he rocked back on his heels. He recognized the face instantly.

Rick dialed Jenna's number a second time and a second time got no answer. Georgia had said she was back at the house and drawing. "Where the hell are you?"

Bishop looked up. "What's eating you?"

"Look at the picture of Sara Thompson's boyfriend."

One glance and Bishop cursed. "Fucker was right there all along."

Rick called Jenna again. No answer. "Jenna isn't answering her phone." He made a second call to Georgia. She picked up on the third ring.

"What's up, Bro?"

"Where's Jenna?"

Through the phone, he heard the rustle of papers as if she'd put aside what she was working on and shifted all her attention to him. "I left her at the Big House. She was doing your sketch."

"She's not answering."

"Why the red alert?"

"The age-progression sketch she did of her sister's

boyfriend, Billy Martinez, looks like William Spires, a realtor that we interviewed."

"Shit. Do you think Susan Martinez knows?"

"I don't know." Rick's nerves tightened like a bowstring. "I do know all the murder scenes were for sale."

"William Spires had access to all the locations."

He drummed his fingers. "Where the hell is Jenna?"

"She could be taking a walk."

"She keeps her phone with her." And her face and family history had been all over the news thanks to Susan Martinez. If she knew what her brother was doing then she'd served Jenna up to him with that interview. "Where is she?"

A chair squeaked as if she leaned forward. "Her old family home is for sale. She mentioned it earlier while we were shopping."

"Shit." Worry pounded in his chest, reverberating through muscle and bone. "Thanks."

"Call me when you have something."

"Yeah." His mind already raced ahead. He turned to Bishop who watched him closely, and relayed what Georgia had told him.

"Saying she is missing and in trouble, a fact we've not confirmed. Would it be so simple as him snatching her and taking her to her old home?"

"He's not strayed far from his comfort zone. He picks a home he's seen and toured. He picks surrogates to take the women."

"Tuttle, Wheeler, and Mitchell."

"And Ronnie. Ronnie killed Jenna's family. But Ronnie fucked up the fire and he didn't keep to the script. He took Jenna."

"Spires/Martinez gets smarter and the next go around, he's on scene during the killing and then kills the surrogate almost immediately. You think he turned Loyola loose on Jenna?"

Tumblers clicked into place as a lock opened. "I do. We need to go to the Thompson house." He flipped through one of the Thompson murder files on his desk and found the address.

Chapter Nineteen

Friday, August 25, 9 P.M.

When Jenna awoke, she realized she was on a bed. Her hands were tied to the headboard and her feet to the baseboard. The strong scent of diesel hung in the air.

Quelling a surge of panic, she forced her mind to clear as she looked around the room and tried to figure out who had taken her. She moistened dry lips and did her best to ignore the ache and stiffness radiating through her limbs. She swallowed. "I know you're out there. You wouldn't set this little event up and just walk away."

Silence. And then the shuffle of footsteps and the sound of breathing.

Jenna twisted her wrists in metal cuffs that chafed her skin. She looked around the room, doing her best to get her bearings. Her gaze darted from a dresser to an overstuffed chair and ottoman and to an area rug. She'd been here before. Days ago with Susan Martinez. This was the home she'd lived in until she was five. This was the house where her family had died.

Sadness and panic welled inside her as she closed her eyes for a moment and struggled to get control. *Keep it together, Jenna. He wants to see you afraid. He wants to taste your fear.* She dug deep for steel and wrapped herself in it. "Kind of trite bringing me to the place where it all began. Couldn't you have come up with a better spot?" She laughed. "I could've done a better job."

A shadow appeared at the door's entrance. She couldn't see a face, but knew she'd gained his attention.

"What, you can't speak?" she taunted.

A strike of a match and then the flicker of a flame. The flame hovered in the air. She thought about the diesel soaking the carpet and bed and wondered how fast it would all ignite. Did he mean to burn her alive?

"I didn't think this was part of the scenario. I thought your surrogate shot your victims first?"

The shadow tossed the match on the floor in the hallway. It flickered, just out of reach of the fuel, and then went out.

Her pounding heart rammed her rib cage. If he was trying to ignite fear, he was doing a good job. She drew in a slow, steady breath. "Okay, that was quite the show. What next?"

Another match struck. Unseen lips blew it out before it fell to the floor, inches from the other match. "You're doing a good job of sounding brave, but I know you're afraid."

The sound of the graveled voice took her by surprise. She wasn't sure what she'd expected him to sound like, but hearing his voice stirred another jolt of panic. "I drew an age progression of your high-school mug shot and sent it to Rick Morgan, Billy. Rick's going to figure this out."

"I'm not really worried." For the first time he stepped from the shadows and stood at the door's threshold. He was a tall, lean man, dressed in khakis and a white shirt. His face was pleasant and the slight smile tweaking the edge of his lips was almost charming.

"Why not?"

"No one gets off this planet alive," he said. "We all have

to die sometime. And the way I see it, all the killing ends tonight."

She jerked at the bindings holding her arms. "What's that mean?"

"Madness has been chasing me for years. He's the one who brought you here. He's the one who's been screaming for your death for days. But I'm in control now."

"Who are you?"

"I'm Reason, the part of us that has kept us employed and out of jail."

"You're Reason?"

"And he's Madness. I'm Jekyll and he's Hyde."

Her heart slowed as she processed what he was saying. "Did Madness kill those other women?"

"Yes. I didn't want him to, but Madness threatened to ruin me if I didn't let him out to play. He threatened to destroy our sister."

"Sister?"

"Susan Martinez. You've met her."

"She's your sister?" Puzzle pieces scrambled into place. "You met my sister because of her."

"Rather, she met your father because of me. Their shared troubles of two unruly teens pulled them together."

Fear threatened to overwhelm her. "How did you get control now?"

He pulled a bottle of pills from his pocket. "He wasn't paying attention after he tied you to the bed so I took these. They keep Madness calm."

She moistened dry lips. "If you're in charge now, you can let me go. I can be gone before Madness knows."

"I want to, but I can't. Madness will never give me peace until he has you. He's sworn he'll go back to sleep if I give you to him."

Panic thrummed in her head. "You don't have to do this. You don't."

He dragged long fingers through his hair. "I'm tired of being held hostage. Madness is tired of being denied. If you die today then all the chaos will end."

"How will you control Madness after I'm gone?"

"I have a foolproof way."

"What?"

He leaned forward and whispered, "I'm going to kill us all."

A killer who wanted to die was much harder to negotiate with. She had everything to lose and he had nothing to lose. "Why did you and Madness kill Sara and my parents?"

"Ours was an old story. Romeo and Juliet. Young lovers who wanted to be together but denied by controlling parents. For a long time, she didn't listen to her father and then, one day, she broke up with me . . . just like that. She tossed me aside. Said she needed to get on with her life."

"That's why you killed her?"

"The urge to kill her was strong. But I was afraid. I was young and didn't know much. And I didn't have the courage to pull the trigger. Madness came up with an idea."

"Ronnie."

"Poor, dumb Ronnie. Was more than happy to help."

"You're Billy?"

"Yes. His only friend. He couldn't set the fire correctly and he couldn't kill you. He was supposed to shoot you in your bed but he couldn't. And so he took you."

"It was you I heard in his apartment when I was locked in the closet. It was you who gave him the overdose."

"It was Madness." He moved toward the bed and sat on the edge. The mattress sagged under his weight as he laid a gentle hand on her leg, absently stroking the soft fabric of her jeans.

"I remember you opened the closet door."

"But Ronnie hid you well. Madness didn't see you. Madness is bold, but scattered. He feared the cops would show any moment. It was a matter of time before they tracked down the hiding place. We left, never realizing you were there."

"Did your sister know?"

"She never asked. But she suspected. After the Thompsons died, she forced us into the hospital. She got Madness under control."

Downstairs, she heard the slam of one car door and then another. Her heart jumped but she kept her gaze on him, hoping he didn't hear it.

He smiled. "Looks like Rick might have figured it out. I knew he would. He's clever." From his pocket he pulled the box of matches and quickly lit one. He stared at her over the flame and then dropped it to the fuel-soaked carpet.

Jenna screamed. "Rick, I'm up here! Rick! He's burning the house."

Flames licked on the floor around the bed teasing the edges of the four-poster frame and then slinking up the wood toward the mattress.

Jenna twisted the cuffs as Billy moved to a corner and pressed his back to a wall. He lit another match and dropped it to him feet. Fire immediately exploded around him.

White smoke rose from the flames, quickly darkening to an inky gray. The smoke would kill her before the flames. Rick might find her, but he'd never get her free of the bed in time.

Gun drawn, Rick raced up the stairs to the sound of screams and Bishop's footsteps behind him. Halfway up the stairs ink-black smoke rolled down to greet them. This killer's fires moved fast and Rick knew he had seconds to find Jenna.

He entered the back bedroom. The room was ablaze.

Through the smoke and flames he saw Jenna handcuffed to the bed. She was screaming.

In the corner stood William, flames licking up his body as he raised a gun to his head. "You're too late to save her. Now you get to see the flames eat at her before they drive you from the room."

William pulled the trigger and the bullet cut through his skull, killing him instantly.

Rick coughed, pushed through the smoke and the heat of the flames. He saw that Jenna's hands were handcuffed to the bed. Shit. He reached for the handcuff key on his belt and tried them in the lock. The lock was jammed.

She looked up at him and then to the flames slithering up the comforter. "Get out of here."

"I'm not leaving you."

"Get him out of here!" she yelled to his partner.

"Fuck that." Bishop grabbed a chair and hammered it against the post at the end of the bed. The post, weakened by fire, snapped. He wrestled free the wood, loosening it from the cuffs.

Now the hands.

In the black smoke taking a deep breath was impossible and only seconds remained before the fire took them all.

Rick got up on the bed and positioned himself by Jenna. As flames seared up the bed, he kicked his booted feet hard into the bedpost, missing her hand by inches. The wood bowed but didn't give. He kicked hard, shoving all his anger and frustration behind the kick. The wood cracked. Another kick. And another. The bedpost broke.

Jenna coughed, rolling to her side as Rick kicked the second post. A dead-on strike splintered it. Rick and Bishop picked her up, one at the head and the other at the feet, and raced out of the room as the flames jumped onto the bed. Dark, billowing smoke rose up the walls, traveling to the ceiling, creating a dark hollow as it sucked the last of the oxygen out of the room.

Outside, the wail of sirens pierced her shock as she sucked in fresh air. She was aware of Rick removing the restraints from her ankles. His touch was gentle. Steady.

When she opened her eyes, he was staring at her. In his eyes she saw a mixture of relief, love, and longing.

"Jenna," he said, his voice hoarse from the smoke.

"I'm okay." She managed a smile, tried to sit up, but when her head spun, she collapsed back against the cool grass.

"The medics will be here soon."

"Okay."

"You scared the hell out of me." He brushed the hair from her eyes with calloused fingertips.

It wasn't like her to lean on anyone or depend on anyone. But for this one moment, just this one moment, she allowed a smile as she squeezed his hand. He cupped both her hands in his. She couldn't see beyond now, but she could admit she liked having this guy around.

Epilogue

Seven weeks later

Amazed that her entire life fit in the back of a fifteen-foot rental truck, Jenna followed the exit-ramp signs on I-40 toward the small farm north of Nashville. With her Jeep hitched to the back she'd made the seven-hundred-mile trip in thirteen hours, opting to stop only for gas and a sub sandwich she ate on the road.

And as the sun hung low on the horizon she took a series of now familiar exits until she wound off the main road up into the Tennessee rolling hillside.

The last six weeks had been a whirlwind. The fire. Her being treated in the hospital for burns on her legs and feet. Rick wanting to stay at her side but being forced away by doctors who treated the burns on his hands.

After she'd been discharged from the hospital, Rick had been waiting, taking her back to the Big House as if he'd been doing it for a lifetime. They'd spent the next three weeks together but in the end, the pull of Baltimore and unfinished business grew too strong. She'd kissed him and promised to return. He'd stood stone-faced. He'd kissed her but had not asked her to stay. He'd let her go.

She gripped the wheel of the rental truck, wondering if he wanted her now. They'd never talked about the future, which had been her choice. And they'd not spoken in the last month.

Jenna blew out a breath. "It's been a month since you saw him. So much can change."

It had taken time to resign from the Force and sublet her apartment. There had been a few parties in her honor and Mike had done his best to get her to stay. But through it all, her thoughts returned to the place of her birth. Yes, it was marred with violence and loss but it had something Baltimore never would have. Hope.

She pulled in the driveway. "I should have called. It's not smart to surprise people." She hated being surprised.

And still she drove down the graveled length until she saw the white house, backed by rolling hills.

There was a construction dumpster outside. Rick. He'd talked about more projects when they'd been here but hadn't seemed the least bit motivated to tackle one.

She parked and got out of the truck. A dog barked in the distance. Tracker. If Tracker was running around barking, it meant Rick was close. She smoothed damp palms over her jeans.

As she moved up the front steps, her stomach knotted. Never in her life had she put herself out there like she was now. She rang the bell. And waited.

William Spires, Billy, had been Susan Martinez's younger brother. The families had intersected when Billy and Sara had met at school. The judge and Susan had begun an affair and lost track of Billy's growing mental instability.

Before she'd left town, she'd met with Susan Martinez and challenged her about William. Susan had denied all knowledge of her family's murder. She'd known her brother was ill but had no idea that he could be linked to the killings. Susan had hospitalized her brother but had argued he'd been suffering with depression for years and she'd only been responding to his dark moods. As much as Jenna wanted to see Susan punished in some way, there was no proof, other than a madman's ranting, that she'd known he was a killer. In the end, no charges had been filed and the reporter had gotten her blockbuster story, which she'd sold to Channel Five's competition.

William had worked successfully in real estate for the last twenty years. He'd made a good fortune and was considered a success. What most didn't realize was that he'd made large bets in the last year on a couple of properties that had gone sour. He'd lost a fortune. Had it been the pending anniversary of her family's death that sent him on a downward spiral, the loss of his money, or both?

In a back bedroom of William's small house, Rick had found scrapbook after scrapbook of old articles featuring little Jennifer Thompson, the kidnapping, and her vanishing from Nashville all those years ago. There'd also been many pictures of Sara. And Diane, Nancy, and Pamela, who looked much like Sara might have if she'd lived. Clearly, seeing them all had triggered something in William.

There were also files on Tuttle, Wheeler, Mitchell, and Dupree. He'd chosen disaffected men, who'd been easy to manipulate.

Jenna glanced at the closed door in front of her. She raised her fist and knocked hard. She'd made it this far. She'd at least see Rick face-to-face. At first, there was no answer. She knocked again.

Tense seconds passed. And when she thought she couldn't wait another second before trying the door, she heard the thud of footsteps in the front hallway. The door snapped open.

Rick stood there, his face tight with annoyance, his T-shirt and jeans covered in a white powder. His gaze settled on her and, for a beat, he said nothing. Tracker's bark echoed in the

house and he appeared at Rick's side. The dog barked at
Jenna, wagged his tail, and moved toward her. She knelt
down and scratched the dog between the ears.

Her stomach churned as she looked up at Rick. "Hoping
you can help me find a place to live. I gave up my apartment
in Baltimore."

Rick stood silent.

So he was going to make her work for this. Fair enough.
She stood. "I'm moving to Nashville. Going to put down
some roots. Maybe I can even land a job as a sketch artist.
I don't know if you've heard, but I'm pretty good."

He arched a brow. He wanted more.

"I missed you." God, she hated baring her soul. "This is
the one place I'm whole. You're the one person that seems
to get to me."

"You make it sound like a bad thing."

"It is. And it isn't. But I know I don't want to spend any
more time without you." She smoothed her hands on her
jeans, her bravado waning. "That's if you still want me."

Finally, a slow smile curled the edges of his lips and he
took a step toward her and pulled her into his embrace. For
a long moment, they just stood there holding each other.
"What the hell took you so long?" he breathed into her hair.

"I'm slow. But I do figure things out eventually."

Please turn the page for an exciting sneak peek of

Mary Burton's next romantic-suspense thriller,

I'LL NEVER LET YOU GO,

coming in November 2015!

January 25, Midnight
Four Years Ago
Nashville, Tennessee

Leah never slept deeply. Her brain, always on alert, skimmed just below consciousness, waiting for him to return. Not a matter of if he'd strike. A matter of when.

When floorboards creaked and a cold wind whispered in the shifting shadows of her first-floor apartment, Leah bolted up in bed. Gripping the sheets, heart slamming, she reached for her phone on the nightstand and waited, her thumb poised over the emergency 9-1-1 speed dial. Seconds passed. Was this another false alarm? Another nightmare? Or had her estranged husband finally come to kill her as he'd promised?

Adrenaline surged and rushed through sinew and bone, pricking the underside of her skin as she listened and waited.

The temptation to call the cops pulled, beckoned, screamed. But she'd cried wolf too often. Too many false alarms had been sounded. The last annoyed officer, his voice rough with frustration, had told her to count to ten before she dialed again.

"One. Two. Three." Her breathing quick and shallow, she listened, expecting footsteps, but hearing only silence and the *thud, thud, thud* of her heart.

God, she was so tired. She needed sleep. Freedom. Peace. She needed her life back.

During the day, Philip was always there, standing and watching. He sent her flowers. Called her cell at all hours. Left scrawled messages under her windshield wipers. *You can't escape. I own you.* Months of his relentless pursuit had stretched frayed nerves to breaking. During the day she jumped at every creak, bump, and footfall and at night, terrors jerked her from sleep, leaving her fully awake, tension fisting in her chest and shallow breathing chasing a racing heart.

Holding her breath, she listened as she stared at her locked bedroom door. Again, she heard nothing save for the hum of the heater.

"Four. Five. Six."

She scrambled for a logical reason to explain this latest scare. It was Tuesday. That meant her roommate, Greta, was working the late shift at the bar. Greta closed on Tuesdays. How many times had Leah awoken, screaming on a Tuesday night when Greta had returned home late? Poor normal Greta, grad student and bartender, now moved slowly and quietly on Tuesday nights, fearful that innocent moves would send her roommate into hysterics.

Leah glanced at the clock. Midnight. Too early for Greta. She listened, heartbeat still racing. No more sounds. Had this been another dream? Another false alarm? Yes. Maybe. "Seven. Eight. Nine."

Slowly, she lowered back down to her pillow, clutching the phone to her chest, eyes wide open, staring at the swath of shadows slicing across the ceiling. Breathe in. Breathe out.

The day she'd finally fled her marriage had begun as it always did. Fights, a barrage of questions, her promising to come home as soon as she got off work. But that morning, she'd been at her desk when a coworker had asked her about the bruise on her arm. She'd lied, of course, but this time, the words hadn't tumbled freely, but had soured on her tongue. Sickened, she'd asked for the afternoon off. No matter how much she'd hoped, his contrition always faded and his temper flared, quick and hot, scorching *I'm sorry* to ash.

She had no plan when she'd returned to their apartment and begun cramming clothes into three green trash bags. *Take what you need. The basics.* The words had hummed in her head as her hands trembled.

When she'd twisted off her wedding band and laid it on the kitchen counter, it was exactly three o'clock in the afternoon, just thirty minutes before his shift ended. She'd dragged the bags into the hallway and when the apartment door slammed behind her, she'd actually felt free. *It's over. It's over.*

But it wasn't over.

Philip had called her cell seconds after five that same day. Guilt had prompted her to take that first call as she'd sat in the shabby motel room, surrounded by her life in trash bags. He'd begged her to return. *I love you. I love you. It will never happen again.*

Of course, he was sorry. He was always sorry.

He'd sent flowers. Called. Waited outside her office. No matter where she looked, he was there. *Come back to me. God, I love you so much.*

Floorboards creaked in her closet, and she bolted back up, clutching her hand to her throat, the pulse drumming under her fingertips. This time, logic couldn't silence the alarm bells, which clanged louder and louder until reason scurried away like a frightened mouse. The last time she'd seen Philip, he'd been clutching the restraining order, furious. *No piece of paper will separate us!*

Her fingers poised over the 9-1-1 direct-dial button, her gaze scanned the darkness. At first glance, nothing was out of place. Her door was closed. Locked.

And then, the faint flutter of movement in the shadows inside her closet. Another cold breeze from a half-open window brushed her skin like a wraith.

"Hello, Leah." Philip's deep voice sounded amused as he stepped out of her closet.

Philip! How had he gotten into her room? Mentally, she ran from lock to lock in the apartment, checking.

He clicked on the overhead light, making her wince at the burst of brightness. He was tall, wearing a dark turtleneck, jeans, and boots, and his broad shoulders ate up the tiny space of her room. He stared at her, his long fingers clenching and unclenching at his side. Attached to his waistband was the brown leather holster that cradled a six-inch knife blade. The blade was inches from his right hand.

"Philip."

"Leah." His voice lacked concern or fear as it always did when he came to a decision.

Without taking her gaze from him, she hit 9-1-1. A distant, "Nine-one-one, what's your emergency?" echoed out from the phone.

"My husband's going to kill me," Leah said. "I live at 112 Main Street, Apartment Two. Treemont Apartments." How many times had she practiced this line, imagining this moment over and over?

"Ma'am, repeat what you just said." The operator's voice was clean, crisp, and so blissfully free of fear.

Leah's hand trembled so badly she thought she'd drop the phone. "He's found me. He's in my room."

"Who's found you, ma'am?"

Philip arched a brow, unconcerned, as he rested his hand on the hilt of the knife.

"My husband. Philip Latimer. He's going to kill me." How long would it take for the cops to arrive? Five minutes? Ten? And how long would it take for him to cross the room and stab her? Seconds.

"How do you know he'll kill you?" The operator's voice was flat, emotionless.

"He's in my bedroom. He has a knife."

Philip knew exactly how long it took the cops to respond. He was a cop. Saving people like her was his job.

"What's your name?"

"Leah Carson. Leah Latimer." She rattled off her address again, fearing she'd be dead before they arrived.

"I'll send a car," the operator said. "Stay on the line."

The words were cold comfort. Philip had broken the protective order. He didn't care about an arrest. He'd crossed an invisible line, knowing his was a one-way trip. His only goal now was to kill her.

Tears filled Leah's eyes as he slid the knife from its holster, the cold metal catching and glinting in the moonlight.

He moved toward the bed, slowly and unhurried. He'd slicked back his thick, blond hair away from his angled face, now hardened with purpose. Once, she'd considered his face handsome. Once, she'd looked into those vivid blue eyes and seen love. Once, he'd made her feel protected.

"You're so beautiful." His deep voice was smooth, silky as if they'd bumped into each other on a street corner on a sunny afternoon. He smelled of fresh, cold night air and whiskey.

During their marriage, she'd learned to fear him most

when he wasn't ranting or raving, but when he was cool and controlled. "Philip, what do you want?"

"I've been telling you for weeks. But you won't listen. I want you back home with me."

With deliberate slowness, she pulled her covers over her T-shirt that strained the outline of her breasts. "Philip. How'd you get in here?"

Keep him talking. Buy time. How much time did she need? She'd timed the route once or twice. Without traffic, it took ten minutes.

Those long, calloused fingers slid up the blade to the tip. "I've missed you."

"Philip, you shouldn't be here." The evenness in her voice belied her fingers tightening into a white-knuckle grip on the comforter.

His thumb circled the knife's hilt. "Why not? You're my wife. And this is our wedding anniversary."

Twelve months ago today, they'd exchanged vows. "You need to leave."

"And if I don't? What're you going to do?"

"The cops are coming."

He traced the knife blade's tip over the comforter, snagging ice-blue fabric. "I don't care."

"Philip. Just go. Get away while you can."

He raised the blade to his thumb and pricked the edge. Crimson blood bloomed, dripped before he raised his thumb to his mouth and sucked the blood dry. "You were so pretty on our wedding day. Such a beautiful white dress. You carried those pretty purple flowers. What were they called? Irises?"

"Just leave me alone, Philip. Go away. I don't want to see you arrested. It will ruin your career." Her pulse thrummed against the soft skin of her neck.

"Until death do us part, Leah. I promised. You promised."

Keep talking. "You love your job. You're a good cop. Respected."

"Without you, it doesn't mean much. You're mine, Leah. We're two halves of a whole. Restraining orders and cops can't keep us apart."

Chin raised, tears pooled, spilled. Buy time. *Buy time!* False promises of love and devotion danced on her tongue and readied for declaration when the truth stubbornly elbowed past. "We're over, Philip. I'm not coming back to you."

He traced his hand over her leg, rough callouses on smooth white skin. Skin prickled, she flinched and rolled her leg away. Gaze darkening, he clenched the blankets in his large hand. An onyx pinky ring marked with the letter *L* winked in the moonlight before he yanked the covering off the bed. She was left half naked, wearing gym shorts and a T-shirt. Cold air skimmed her naked legs. Gooseflesh puckered.

"Philip, please—"

For a moment, he sat as still as a statue, his terrible beauty etched in calm repose. And then, like a rattler riled, he struck, moving with lightning speed. He climbed on top of her, the rough fabric of his jeans scraping against her bare waist. He pressed the knife blade to her throat.

Their gazes locked, as he smoothed the steel tip over her chest to her flat belly. She flinched. Braced.

"Philip, don't. Please."

This close, his eyes red-rimmed as if he'd been crying, bore into her. "I'll never let you go. You belong to me. I love you." His body hummed with need. Need to own her. Need to possess her. Need to hear her words of love.

More tears spilled down the sides of her face. He controlled so much in this moment. Life or death rested in his palms. All she controlled were her words. The truth. If she died tonight, Philip would know her heart. "I don't love you."

He flinched as if he'd been slapped. "You've been brainwashed. Your mother and your friends filled you with lies. Poisoned you against me."

"I don't love you." Defiance pricked as sharp as the knife's tip. "You don't own me."

Pain deepened the lines of his face, even as his teeth bared into a snarl. He lowered his lips to her ear. Warm breath against her skin raked over her nerves.

"I love you," he whispered. "I love you. Why can't you understand that?"

Out of habit, not love, she raised her hand to his muscled arm, her touch gentle as if soothing a beast. "Philip, this isn't love."

He burrowed his face in the crook of her neck. Hot breath brushed the nape of her neck as his hand fisted her blond hair in his hand. "It's love. It is."

"No, Philip." A lie crept from the shadows. "You deserve better."

A fist pounded on the apartment's front door. "Ms. Carson! Ms. Carson! This is the police!"

The officer's voice cut through the door and relief collided with tension. The cops!

He flinched. "Shh. It's just us, the way it's supposed to be."

Her fingers hardened into a grip. "Help me! Please save me."

Philip rose up, eyed her, disappointment mingling with anger. "Carson. You told the operator your name was Carson. You took your maiden name back."

The anger-coated words stoked a flicker of guilt. His temper, his abuse was not her fault but even after all the pain, he could so easily press the button that triggered guilt. Her weakness shamed her. "The cops are here. Go! Run while you can, Philip. Leave through the window. Just go! You don't want to go to jail."

He pressed the knife's tip to the hollow of her neck. "That would suit you just fine."

"I don't want to see you in jail." She prayed the directness in her gaze covered the lie. "You don't deserve jail. You need a doctor."

"I don't need a doctor. I need you!"

"Ms. Carson!" the officer shouted. "Are you in there?"

Nothing would sway Philip. Nothing. "Yes!" she screamed.

Philip winced and pressed the tip of the knife to her neck. The tip scraped skin and drew blood.

How much longer before the cop got into her apartment? How long to slice skin? Seconds?

Blood flickered along the narrow column of her neck and dripped on her hair. "Please."

"We're meant to be together." Desperation tinged the anger.

"Just leave. While you can."

He dragged the tip of the knife over her belly, etching a red scratch along her pale midline.

Fear contorted her gut as keys rattled in the front door. Had the cops gotten the apartment manager's master key? *Hurry!* A door opened and caught on the security chain. The balance of her life depended on seconds.

Philip mopped up the blood trickling from her neck with his forefinger and smeared it across his forehead. "We live and die together."

He raised the knife and plunged it into her gut. At first, shock and then agony sliced and burned through her insides as she stared into blue eyes that danced with satisfaction. He pulled the knife back and drove it down toward her neck. It skidded over her collarbone, before he sliced her cheek and her arms.

Cops pounded on the door. "Ms. Carson!"

Screaming, she grabbed the blade. The edge cut her palms. Blood gushed from her hands as he pulled the blade free and raised it again. She lost count of how many times he stabbed her before he rose breathless and stood over her. He stared a long moment at the blood blooming on the bed-sheets. His eyes filled with fresh tears. "What have I done? God, I'm sorry."

In the next instant, he vanished through the window, leaving her alone and bleeding. Stunned by pain, she lay still, feeling the warm blood pool around her body.

A scream caught in her throat as her hands went to her belly, now crimson and wet. The front door banged open and then the bedroom door. The silhouette of the cop appeared in the doorframe. "Leah Carson?"

The cop's gaze settled on the blood pooling around Leah and then swept the room for threats. When he determined the room was clear, he holstered his gun and pushed a button attached to the mike on his vest. "I need an ambulance . . ."

His deep voice drifted away as her insides burned and her heart pumped hard. She lay as still as possible, fearing Philip had severed an artery.

Her mind drifted to a sandy beach where the breeze was gentle, the sky a bright blue, and the sun warm.

"Ms. Carson, can you hear me?" Desperation edged the words. "Open your eyes."

She looked up and saw the blurred face of an officer with dark, graying hair. Kind, worried eyes.

"Can you hear me?"

"Yes."

"Who did this to you?"

Air hissed from a slice in her chest as she gasped in a breath. "My husband. Philip Latimer."

The room chilled quickly. A shiver passed through her

body, and she imagined her spirit leaving, drifting above, looking down at the pale lifeless body that had been her.

Her eyes closing, her mind traveled to a warm beach, where the sky winked crystal clear and the waves lapped against fine sand. A seagull squawked. A gentle breeze. So far away from the pain, Philip, and Death.